PRAISE FOR DEANNA KING

This story is intense, timely, and terrifyingly real throughout, with confident narration that elevates the work above the average cop thriller.

~K.C. Finn-Readers' Favorite

It's a fantastic police procedural novel, running at breakneck speed for a rainy day read, which won't be easily put down because you'll never know what character to trust.

~KT Bowes, Readers' Favorites

High Tension and long buried secrets. Faded Blue by Deanna King is a fast moving detective story.

~Lucinda Clark, Readers' Favorite

Driven by a fast-paced narrative and creative storytelling, Faded Blue is a smart and stylish police thriller that will keep you turning the pages!

~Robert E. Kearns, Author of Unto Dust and The Factory

ISBN: 979-8-9856982-7-5

Edited by: David Eskridge

Covers by Chandra Fry – https:stainedglaspublis.wixsite.com/bookpublisher/ppromoting

Formatted by: Atticus

Published by Deanna King Writing

Deannakingwriting.com

To All the "True " Blue Bloods

Faded Blue
A Jack West Novel
Deanna King

Deanna King Writing

1

THE CATASTROPHE AT THE courthouse broke the proverbial camel's back. As the entire courtroom looked on, someone shot the defendant, killing him. It happened so fast; it took everyone by surprise. By the end, many who'd been involved met horrific fates—some blown apart, others slaughtered or locked away in dark prison cells. Even individuals of the highest integrity compromised their principles for several reasons.

The Cartel struck terror into the hearts of countless people—synonymous with drugs, torture, corruption, money, treachery, and savage homicides. There were only two options: join them or fight. Jack chose to fight.

His stocking feet propped on the coffee table, Jack sat in his two-bedroom studio in Deer Park. He lofted the icy Bud Light, took a long swig, and snagged a handful of corn chips, thinking back. After the courthouse debacle, he and DEA Agent Medina had spent time together, sharing laughter and companionship.

She was an incredible lover, though he'd never expected things to reach that level. Given their shared trauma, it was inevitable they'd find solace in each other. Their relationship was not based on love, but on a mutual need for temporary companionship.

Jack still mourned Gretchen; day by day, his heart continued to ease. He closed his eyes, lost in recent memories.

HER BRUNETTE TRESSES SPLAYED against the pale blue sheets. Her chocolate-hued eyes, languid after their lovemaking, peered at him.

"You've been the highlight of this assignment, Jack."

He brushed strands of hair from her flushed cheek. "Yeah. Unexpected, huh? Guess it happens."

"Jackson West," she said with a grin, teasing his scowl at her using his full name. "I'll only call you that when we're alone, I swear." She crossed her arms over her chest.

Jack's hand covered her bare breast as he leaned in for a kiss.

Her expression darkened. "I never sleep with co-workers. You're the first. I keep my life private—"

Jack pressed a finger to her lips. "I'm not a kiss-and-tell guy. No locker-room bragging in high school, or at the station. I promise."

"Thanks, Jack." She grew thoughtful, forehead furrowed, eyes distant, and he watched her thoughts ripple across her face.

"Spit it out."

"I'm leaving in two days."

"Oh, new assignment?" She might not have clearance to discuss it; he understood.

"Yeah. Can't say what, and I won't have contact with anyone for a while. Jack, it's been spectacular, but—"

He shushed her with a finger.

"We're not in love, and we have lives to move on with. No complications, no promises. We agreed. Tonight, we go to Quinn's. Call Kasper; see if he can bring a date. Make a night of it. Talk, laugh. Then we come back and share one last night together. I'll make pancakes before I send you off."

"What a charmer you are, Jack. Sounds like a helluva plan."

It was a splendid night with friends. Afterward, at Jack's place, they made love until dawn.

He made her blueberry pancakes drenched in maple syrup. They drank coffee, chatted, and savored the quiet morning together. At nine, they said adios—but not goodbye forever.

———

BY ELEVEN-THIRTY, CHIPS WERE long gone, three empty beer bottles sat on the table, and Jack finished the fourth. He cleared the bottles, washed the Fritos bowl, checked all the rooms, set the alarm, and headed to bed. His temporary DEA assignment behind him, he was a recharged Jack West, ready to catch criminals and put them away.

2

It was just another day at the Houston Homicide office—detectives buried under a mountain of murder case files, both new and old.

"Roni wants you."

Jack tucked his cell into his rear pocket. "Guess my number came up."

"It pops up a lot these days, doesn't it, Jack?"

"What's stuck in your craw, Dawson?"

Dawson Luck waved overhead toward Justice's office. "Go find out what she wants. Don't screw with me—not today."

Jack patted Dawson's shoulder as he passed. "Skip won't be your partner forever."

Dawson's lips bent downward. "From your mouth to our captain's ears. Man, I can't stand that turd."

Jack felt the same. Both Webb and Nichols were Brooks' butt-kissers, along with other detectives still trailing their ex-captain like dogs in heat. It made no sense that Brooks, a thirty-two-year veteran, hadn't retired. He could receive his full pension and work freelance—or take off fishing.

Why hadn't they pushed the old geezer into retirement? Another big mystery.

With a light knuckle-rap, Jack poked his head into her office.

"Cap, you needed me?"

"Come in and close the door."

Jack took a seat, watching her shuffle papers. He noticed her foot patting the floor—a nervous habit she'd carried since he returned from his sabbatical.

"Sorry," she said, rifling for a form that required her signature. "Give me a—oh, here it is." She pulled it from under a stack of reports, scrawled her signature, and tucked it in the desk drawer.

Now relaxing, she looked at him. "Things good?"

"Yeah, Roni. Everything's perfect."

She held his gaze, and he hers. "Gotta ask you something."

"Fire away."

"Are you going to ask if I'm okay for the rest of my career?"

With a breathy chuckle, she lifted her shoulders. "Guess not. Seems I've made it a habit with you since ... ancient history. And it's not why I called you here."

"Then why am I here?"

"To make Dawson Luck's life happier. First, a favor—but it stays between us." She narrowed her eyes, lips forming a straight line as she studied him.

"Whew. By your expression, I'm not gonna like it too much, but whatever—you're the boss. I can keep a secret."

Jack's thoughts turned to Sophia. Kasper Bergman was the only one privy to their relationship, and he trusted him with his life—including his secrets.

"I want y'all working together again."

"Dawson's going to be so happy he'll pee his pants. What else?"

Veronica Justice drummed her manicured nails, staring at nothing while Jack waited.

She straightened, pulled a drawer open, and extracted a manila envelope, placing it on top of her desk.

"Jack," she began—but stopped.

"Roni, whatever it is, you can trust me."

"I do, but it's sensitive—and you've got a rotten history with this person."

"Oh, for Pete's sake, just say it." Her hemming and hawing irritated him; he had work to do.

"Jack, I'd like for you to poke around into some stuff IA is investigating concerning Brody Brooks."

Jack nearly fell out of his chair.

"Internal Affairs? They think Brooks is involved in ... what?"

She waved her hand to stop him. "Vance said the list is long and won't say everything. A major concern is evidence tampering."

"Robbery evidence?"

"He didn't specify, but it goes deeper than that. They've been watching him—and a few others—for some time, getting nowhere. Jack, who knows what else this could involve, so keep it close to the vest. Vance thinks they need someone inside—but not from Brooks' department—to keep eyes and ears on him. I have no earthly idea why he picked you, since Brooks hates you. Exercise diplomacy. Try not to piss him off. Take these files Vance gave me—personal data, a few case logs. Read them, see what you can dig up. You've got buddies in Robbery—show your face there, put your ear to the ground, and keep me posted."

"When do idiots and a-holes want info?"

Roni's eyes lit up. She loved his nickname for Internal Affairs. "If they press me, I'll press you." She smiled, bright teeth contrasting with her delicate, almond-toned skin. "Now go make Dawson's day. The man could use a pick-me-up."

Jack grinned. "On my way to make Detective Luck's day—and ruin mine."

He could still hear her laughter down the walkway to the Homicide room.

"NO KIDDING? THAT'S FREAKING fantastic, Jack! Woo hoo!" Lucky, exuberant over the news, got a little loud.

"Hey, Luck, why are you woo-hooing?" Jace Severson rolled his chair closer.

"I'm back riding with Jack. I can drop Webb."

"Ah, the diabolical duo is back. Is that it?" Xi smarted off.

" Nope, it's the dynamic, handsome duo, you twits," Lucky spouted.

Severson grimaced. "Nah. Jack's got the looks. Dawson—you've got the hairy unibrow, the nose, and the big feet."

"Hell, he's got a gorgeous wife. Does that count?"

"You mean my next ex-wife, Xi?" Severson slapped his thigh, snickering.

"Hey," Jack said, leaning back, "better to be a diabolical duo than Dumb and Dumber."

Jack listened to the banter, a grin playing on his clean-shaven face.

This was what he'd missed: these goofballs and working in Homicide.

3

Xi GLANCED UP. "Hey, Luck, here comes Webb."

Jack eyed him as he walked behind Dawson's desk, Webb's face twisted with anger.

"Lucky, you asshole. You asked for a new partner, kicked me to the curb. Do you wanna tell me why I'm not suitable?" His body stiffened, his already ugly mug growing uglier.

"Talk to the captain if you want answers, Skip, 'cause this was her call, not mine." Lucky didn't turn around, keeping his nose in a file.

"Webb," Jace addressed him, "who got stuck with you?"

"She paired me with Calvin Hardin, like it's any of your business, Severson."

"Isn't he the new fella who transferred from Jacinto City?"

"Yeah, Xi, a dog catcher turned homicide dick who doesn't recognize his ass from a doughnut hole."

"Stop bitching, Skip, and just work your job."

Skip Webb looked at Jack, who jumped into the conversation.

"Ah, the prodigal famous dick speaks. They all look at you as a hero or Super Cop. Your subterfuge may deceive others, but I ain't fooled."

"'Subterfuge': big word for your pea brain, Webb. Did the letter S from the Encyclopedia Britannica come in the mail?" Xi Chang jested.

"Fuck you, Chang." Webb glowered at West.

Jack stayed seated but shoved his chair back to view Skip fully, giving him the eye from his dull black loafers to the top of his skull. "I ain't fooling anyone, nor hiding behind anything. And nope, I'm not Superman either, just doing my job." He crossed one ankle over the other after stretching his legs out. A contemptuous look cut across his face.

"You punch a superior officer without consequences and get away with murdering that convict, and this makes you feel invincible, but people got their eyes on you, so I'd watch my step if I were you."

Jack's jaw clenched, resisting Skip Webb's goading. It wasn't worth the repercussions.

Severson noted Jack's anger and rejoined, "Webb, trot over to your side of the office and work for an effing change. Better yet, find the new guy. Teach him to be like Jack, not you."

Skip turned on his heels, flipping the middle finger. "Fuck y'all." The door banged shut.

Jace said, "Gosh, I think old Spider Webb still loves ya."

Jack's face brightened. "Me too. Man, I can't wait until the next time he asks me to dance—gonna give him a big fat hug with a knee kiss to his privates."

"I'd like a ticket to that dance," Lucky remarked.

"Now the real news. Did you dudes hear Chang here took the sergeant's exam?"

"Hey, Xi, that's great. When do you expect the results?"

"Uh, well, I didn't take it—"

Jace whipped around. "Why the heck not?"

"If you'd let me finish ... 7. Lord. 'Yet,' I was gonna say 'yet.' I haven't taken it yet. I missed the last test date; had personal business, and it couldn't wait. I'll take it on the next testing date."

"Now damn it, 11, I was hoping to have a colleague with the word 'Boss' stamped across his forehead."

"Sorry I'm such a disappointment to you, 7." Xi sounded perturbed before grinning.

"You'll ace it," Jack said.

"You should take it, Jack. Advance in the department," Xi said.

"Yeah, and I'd never hear the last of Jack's Super Cop stories." Lucky looked up, seeing three sets of eyes staring at him.

"Oops, did I say that out loud? Sorry. Crud, Webb was my freaking partner for over a year, and wherever he goes, Earl Nichols follows like a bitch dog in heat. Every time I defended Jack, they gave me a bunch of crap. Those ding-dongs blabbered nonstop, goading me, and I tried hard to keep my mouth shut. It was an ass whooping."

Jack spoke first. "No worries, pard. We understand." He slipped the file Roni gave him into his top drawer under a pile of other papers. He'd peruse them at home without chancing curious eyes sneaking a peek.

"I'M GLAD WE'RE GETTING to work together, Jack. Feels like old times, don't it?"

"Yeah."

"Hey, that Medina gal, nice lady, isn't she?" Lucky asked across the half partition separating their workspaces. He wanted to find out if they'd crossed a proverbial line as colleagues.

"Yeah, she is, and a helluva DEA agent."

"She's a knockout too."

"Lucky, come on, don't go there." Jack wouldn't satisfy his curiosity.

Dawson shrugged, eyes glued to an old autopsy report on a cold case. "Just saying. If you two get together, nobody cares. It's been a while." Dawson never talked to him about Gretchen. He wanted to, but couldn't. Her murder left Jack in a state of emotional turmoil. Lucky decided not to delve further, concerned about the impact it might have on Jack's mental health. If the man felt like talking, fine. Otherwise, the subject would remain taboo.

"Webb—man, I can only imagine the challenges of dealing with him daily." Jack mentioned, thumbing through a stack of witness reports.

"Skip to my Lou is the biggest narcissist asswipe. I mean right behind Brooks." Lucky couldn't stand Webb. Being partnered with Jack again thrilled him. Ole Spider Webb was dangerous, and Lucky worried the creep would pull him into something unscrupulous—either costing him his job and pension, or getting him killed.

"Yeah, Brooks leads the pack where I'm concerned. Webb, Nichols, and Golan come in a close second, third, and fourth," Jack intoned.

"Oh, I forgot about Golan, who's a douche. He's been sniffing Webb's butt ever since they moved him over from the substation in the Second Ward. Don't like him."

"Another nice thing about working with the DEA—I haven't had to deal with him."

"Yeah, about that. I read the newspapers, but it isn't the complete story, is it?"

"Papers nailed it."

"Ah, Jack, don't be a killjoy."

"Sorry, Luck, but you get how it is. Stuff's need-to-know only."

"Yeah, I don't need to know. I get it," Lucky huffed.

A little chuckle popped out of Jack. "When I can tell ya, I will. For now, let's look at these old files until a fresh one comes in."

"Fine. Hand me a file. And I'm thrilled to be back working with ya."

"Yeah, Luck, me too."

ON HIS WAY HOME, he bought two Antone's Originals and a bag of wavy chips, opting for water because the caffeine jitters had started. Truck parked, he reached under his seat, pulling out the "for his eyes only" manila envelope. It looked like rain. He restarted the engine, tapped the remote, and cussed. His lawn equipment was in the middle of the garage, along with boxes he'd been cleaning out. He hit the remote, grabbing the envelope—not motivated to move everything inside.

Inside, he relocked the front door, dropped the bag of food on the table, and headed to his bedroom to change into comfortable duds. He snagged two bottles of water and headed to his living room, plopping onto the sofa with a relaxed sigh.

He let his head loll back, closing his eyes. No sounds—his ears heard too much silence. One eyelid raised a slit, only to locate the remote. Air burbled from his lips. He got up, snatched the device off the arm of his recliner in the far corner, and dumped himself back onto the sofa. Jack aimed it at the entertainment center, turned on the TV, and brought up classical music. No words required. He limited his music choices to Mozart, Beethoven, Debussy, Chopin, or Bach—pieces of magnificent music that created calm without cluttering his mind.

He unwrapped a sub, biting into the delightful taste of what he considered a perfect sandwich. The envelope on his coffee table glared at him. An imaginary flashing neon sign blinked: *read me—read me.*

Food first, his stomach said, as his brain reeled out another message: Take a break, dope, de-stress. Relaxing wasn't part of Jack's DNA—not since Gretchen.

Oh, he'd gotten better once the DEA assignment and his triple homicide concluded. Sophia had been a breath of fresh air for him.

Debussy's *Clair de Lune* began. Jack closed his eyes, letting his stress ebb away,
flowing out through his pores as the music played. He inhaled, holding it, then
exhaled, releasing every ounce of tension. Each fiber in his frame folded into his
overstuffed couch, eyes shut, listening to the sounds of Debussy.

The next piece was Chopin's *Marche Funèbre*—the Funeral March. A laugh
sputtered as he yanked up the manila packet. Yep, if it goes sideways, it's your
funeral, bud.

Internal Affairs had been surveilling Brooks for ages. The info Captain Justice
supplied him couldn't be all there was. Brooks—on the job two decades—and
these partial files were all he had. Reports of behavior such as (but not limited
to) sexual harassment, excessive force, gender equality misconduct, and abusing
subordinates (including non-uniformed staff). Jack read. Different departments,
singular officers called in; they were cross-examined, or perhaps volunteered information. All speculation at best.

Hearsay only. No witnesses to his abusive actions with fellow officers—including rudeness, non-cooperation with officers in charge, or disrespect of female
officers and administrative staff. Complaints filed by non-aggrieved parties caused
uproar among Brooks' buddies, who said he was the target of baseless attacks,
convinced people were just jealous.

The responsibility of investigating record-keeping should have been with Human Resources or the Union, not IA. None of this pointed toward criminal
acts. Heck, Jack had been on the receiving end of Brooks' sharp-tongued abuse
without complaining. Brooks wasn't worth the air out of his lungs to lodge a
grievance, nor the waste of his precious time.

Irritated, he opened a water bottle, chugged it, finished his second sandwich,
and thought a beer would be a fitting dessert. He went to the fridge. Why did
Roni have him reading this mundane stuff? None of it, he thought, was an IA
issue. He'd agreed to read, but tomorrow they needed to talk.

In his bare feet, he tiptoed to the living room, grabbed the bundle of papers he
had yet to read, flopped onto his recliner, and pulled the lever. The footrest shot
up. He crossed his ankles, straightened the papers. Nothing garnered his interest
until midway through. A name popped: Frank Windom. Jack's first partner.
Dead. Windom died of coronary failure. Almost sixty and ready to retire, his

number got punched too soon. A cop's life had worn him down, but he'd been the best teacher, and Jack missed him.

Anxiety filled his gut as he prayed he wouldn't uncover any negative info about Windom. Brooks, yeah, that he'd believe—but please, not Frank. Windom was the noir, Mike Hammer type: salty, gruff, no-nonsense. Brooks gave off a sketchy vibe.

Jack read insignificant reports. Did it amount to something greater? And if so, what?

4

1980, Houston Police Department

"Get the shop ready and move your ass, Brooks."

"Yes, sir." Brody Brooks glared at Lamont Jones, his FTO (Field Training Officer). He hated the man for the power he held over him as a rookie—a mere stinking boot.

Brody hated his job as a rookie patrol cop. One: he had no control, feeling like a lackey doing what others demanded. Two: his FTO put him down constantly, calling him stupid. Three: his paycheck wasn't worth risking his life for.

"Get used to it, Brooks. No one gives a rat's ass about what you think, least of all me. Just follow my rules, Boot, and stay out of my way. If I say jump, you jump—and don't ask why. You understand me?"

"Sir, yes, sir." Brody wanted to slap the tall, dark man's face.

Two hours into their tour, they got a report about a domestic violence situation at State and Michigan in South Houston. Code blue—lights and sirens off.

"Brooks, we're ten minutes out. Call it in." A swift U-turn and burst of speed got them there in eight.

"Vest up," Jones instructed, pulling up to the end of the rundown mobile home. He parked behind a brand-new '79 Oldsmobile and a faded green '62 Chevy Nova that had seen better days.

Jones' first words to him, day one: "Without argument, follow my orders, 'cuz I'm gonna save your life, you pissant. You can thank me later."

Out of the car, Brooks waited for instructions.

"Eyes on me. Leave your weapon holstered, grab your baton." Jones motioned for him to follow.

Baton in hand, Brooks shadowed his FTO, keeping his eyes on Jones. The commotion intensified: two women, two men, a shitload of screaming—it was three a.m.

AFTER HE SMACKED HER, she fell, grabbing the first object she could find—an old wooden baseball bat. Blood oozed from her nose; he'd busted her lip.

"Beat it before I call the cops, you motherfucker!" she screamed.

The man, wearing a light blue leisure suit, a dark button-down knit shirt, pointy-toe patent leather loafers, with a chewed toothpick between his teeth, snarled, "Put the goddamned bat down, Gina, or I'm gonna hafta smack you around."

"Hafta smack me around? You shithead! See this bloody nose and black eye? Like you ain't already slapped me around enough just 'cause I quit an hour early?"

"No, Gina, it's 'cause you pinched two bills. You ain't nuttin' but a whore and a thief. Boss says teach you a lesson. I gotta do what he says." He spit out the toothpick, hitching at his belted pants, coughing up a loogie.

"Leo, don't hit her no more. I got two hundred I'll give ya, plus hers," Gina's pal Deb whined, stepping in.

"Zip it, you fat, pathetic, worthless pig. Give me the dough and get your ass back in your stinking rotten trailer—or I'm gonna have Paulie use you for target practice."

Deb, weighing 215 pounds, wearing a tight silver spandex miniskirt and a double-X purple tie-dyed T-shirt cinched under her protruding belly, shrank back. Scared, she retreated inside, letting the door slam. She dropped to her knees at the window, heart pounding, lips moving in a silent prayer, hoping Leo didn't bash her friend's brains out.

Leo Goldberg stepped forward. Gina swung the bat, trying to stave him off. He caught the end, jerking her to her knees. His right foot caught her ribs, sending her sliding over the hard, grassless yard. Bat in hand, ready to bust her head wide open, he froze when Jones yelled:

"Drop the bat! Step away from the woman. Now!"

Paulie's gaze fixed on the rookie cop. "You just graduate, pup?" His laugh dripped with disrespect.

Jones' attention never wavered. "I said drop it before I drop you."

Leo complied, holding his hands up. "Okay! Okay! Jesus, calm down. You ain't hurt, are ya, Gina?"

"Brooks, get her up. You asswipes," Jones barked, pointing at them. "Hands on heads. Step back. Slowly. Face the trailer."

Brody helped the girl, and the men followed Jones' orders.

"Boot, over here!" Jones thundered. "Cuff 'em, read them their rights."

Goldberg protested. "Why ya arresting us? We ain't done nuttin'."

"I'm sure the lady wants to file a report," Jones said, pulling out his notepad.

Gina shook her head. "I ain't gonna press charges. Mr. Goldberg was just, uh, doing his job, and I shouldn't've swiped the cash. Deb!" she called out. "I swear I'll pay ya back this time."

Jones shook his head. "Uncuff 'em. She won't press charges. We can't make her, and they'd lawyer up anyway. Back on the streets in hours. Not worth the paperwork."

Brody had the men turn; he uncuffed them. Leo muttered under his breath, "The douche orders you around like a pussy. You ain't no pussy, are you, officer?"

"Shut up," Brooks warned, tone firm.

Paulie chimed in, "You from the old neighborhood, ain't ya?"

"You got me confused with somebody else." Brody slipped the cuffs back into his belt.

"Nah, I know my faces. Ethan Wygant, he's your people, right?"

Brody glanced at Jones. "My cousin. How you know him?"

If this guy knew Ethan, Brody should recognize him—but he didn't.

"We went to the same Catholic school. I dropped out in the ninth. Ask him about me, Paulie Baglio. Back in the day, we hung out."

In the car, Jones fumed. Women letting men treat them that way would end up floating face down in the bayou. He'd seen plenty of rough lives, beat-up women, fatal car crashes—but murder wasn't a daily occurrence.

———————

A MONTH LATER, BRODY, Ethan, Paulie, Leo, and Sam Coolidge—another officer—had dinner at Vino's Bistro, owned by a mafia family. The top three families: the Beruttis, the Castellanos, and the De Lucas. Who owned this eatery? Brooks didn't ask.

"As long as no one gets hurt or killed, I'm in—even if you ain't, Brody. Keep your trap shut, 'cuz I'm your cousin." Ethan gave him a hard stare.

"You can't mention me either. I got lots of pals. I'll hear." Sam glared.

"You threatening me, Coolidge?" Brody's ire rose.

"Calm down, kid. Learn to let shit slide. Keep your feelings in check. Never let 'em see or feel your fear. Got it?" Baglio replied.

"Brody," Ethan said, "if you don't want in, fine. You never hafta commit murder—just a few illegal things. Cops do it all the time. And the money alone ... HPD ain't gonna rack me up serious cash, but don't mess it up for me, understand?"

"Yeah, E. I swear I'd never jam you up."

"Sure, Brody, no worries."

"Get me another scotch, would ya? I gotta hit the can." Brody excused himself. One glance back, and he saw the four of them, heads together. His involvement could lead to one of three things: discharge, jail, or death. Money—was it worth it?

Later that night, the cousins talked.

"Nah, E, I'd rather keep my nose outta stuff for now. Won't say anything to anyone. You got my word."

"Just think about it. The money alone's worth the chance. Build a nest egg, then get the hell outta the country. Be nice to leave this humid place."

"What? Live in Mexico? The other humid place?"

Ethan punched Brody in the arm. "No, dork. Maybe over the pond. Move somewhere without extradition."

Brody's expression darkened. "Uh, Ethan, what you gonna do might make you hafta skip the country?"

"Nuttin'. I swear. Just wanna end up living with no worries, capiche?"

THIS CONVERSATION REPLAYED IN his head. Cousins or brothers, it didn't matter—the bond was strong. Ethan was the only person Brody trusted, protected him, loved him, and would never harm him. If Ethan jumped ship overseas, Brody would follow, no questions asked. If Ethan said it'd be okay, he'd trust him. But why was he hesitating?

5

BRODY STEERED CLEAR OF Ethan's doings, those connected with Baglio, Goldberg, or Coolidge. He looked the other way. He never narc'd on them, didn't know what the hell they were doing most times, and never asked Ethan anything.

"Best you don't tell me, and we don't talk about Ethan. I don't wanna be called up, understand?"

"Yeah, Brody, I got you, and hey, the offer still stands. You want in, say the word."

Brody only nodded. Ethan figured after his dear cousin saw the dough he was saving up, he'd want a piece of the action, but nope—Brody D. Brooks stayed on the straight and narrow. Until he didn't.

Ethan transferred to the Eastside Division in mid-1981 and moved closer to the station and the fellas he hung with.

"Ah, Ethan, you don't need to move. It ain't too far," Brooks droned.

"Fine, you drive it—but I'm moving, B."

Ethan moved out after much deliberation, leaving Brody to stay alone in the apartment, not thrilled at losing his best friend.

"Let me know what days you're off when your duty roster comes up, and I'll request the same days off. We'll go fishing, or whatever, 'kay, pal?"

"Sure, E. Sure." Brody's heart was heavy as he said the words. Work schedules, extra duty, and Ethan's extracurricular doings meant no time for fishing, hiking, clubbing, or any of the fun stuff they used to do. Time passed; Brody saw little of Ethan. His duties kept him busy—and often pissed him off. Six months after Ethan left, Brooks got assigned to district seven—police beat 07C10, the Greater Fifth Ward.

1983, PRECINCT OF DISTRICT Seven

"Sick of taking orders from a woman."

"Ah, Brody, man up. Women make decent officers, too. Barbara Kilgore does okay as the new lieutenant. Give her a break."

"We heard you're pussy-whipped at home, so you fit right in, don'tcha, Emmerson?" Brody Dean Brooks was ending his second year and in three months would turn twenty-five. Raised in a man's world—a world where women were subservient. Brooks had the idea he was Super Cop, and males ruled the earth.

"Thinking you heard wrong there, Brooks. My wife doesn't boss me, and I don't boss her. If you get a female partner who's got seniority, whatcha gonna do about it?"

"Shit! Put her in her place and request a transfer."

Sal Dellucci eavesdropped with a smirk on his face. He liked the guy and gave thought to how Brooks would fit into his clique. After three years as a cop, Sal needed to supplement his pay and used his badge to accomplish this. Nobody was the wiser because nobody got hurt that didn't deserve to be hurt. Brooks—yeah, he'd keep a watchful eye on this fellow.

SAL PICKED UP VARIOUS life lessons while growing up in his neighborhood. Some harder than others. Somehow, he'd found a way out of the troubles he'd gotten into, surprised to have avoided jail or death during his wild youth. He didn't know how, but his mother had fixed every problem he'd encountered. So, unlike Brody Brooks, Sal knew women held a definite power. His father—who the hell knew who he was? He had no male leadership except an uncle or maybe a cousin. Faced with a juvie record and the prospect of her boy heading down a path of criminal activity, his mother pushed him to do right and enroll in the police academy. "Do good," she'd said.

His admittance into the academy was a more biblical miracle than water being turned into wine. It had seemed impossible with his history. Sal questioned the people his mother knew that could make her desires a reality. Dear Mom beamed with pride, despite his low grades, the day he graduated from the police academy. Momma didn't care about the grades—only her pride in seeing her boy, Sal

Dellucci, standing with a group of his peers, reciting the oath of a police officer, wearing his dark blue uniform, his badge pinned to his shirt. Tears filled her eyes.

1983, District Seven, Precinct Parking Lot

Three-thirty in the afternoon. Cars lined up, ready to hit the streets for their shift. Officers readied equipment, doing vehicle checks as they began gearing up for a long twelve-hour tour from four p.m. to two a.m.

Brody leaned against the trunk of his police car, while his stupid partner took a piss before they left, watching the other lackeys working up a sweat in the hot late afternoon sun. In his peripheral vision, he saw Sal approaching.

"Got a sweet deal if you want in, Brody."

Brooks eyed him. He knew Sal had been tailing him, watching him, but didn't know why. What was the man's deal? The fellas who hung with Dellucci were not the sort you wanted as chums. These cops received rips along with suspensions, causing waves in the department. Brody's indifference was obvious. The man didn't care. In fact, he agreed with some things they'd gotten in trouble for, thinking it wasn't fair, but kept his thoughts to himself. He didn't consider himself better than them, just smarter. He knew that the holier-than-thou cops who lacked the wit to stay out of other people's business got ostracized and compelled to transfer to another division or jurisdiction—or sometimes just quit.

Brooks wasn't gonna quit, nor be strong-armed. He dreamed of power in an authoritative position. Of being well-off. If you rose in the ranks, you could achieve power. But the wealth wouldn't happen—not on a cop's pay.

"Sweet deal how?"

"You wanna make five easy bills?"

Brooks' eyes squinted up. "Depends if I gotta sweat or not."

Sal Dellucci nodded. "I gotcha, and nah, ain't no hard labor required. Only gotta keep your lips zipped. Ain't too hard, ya think?"

"No dead bodies, either, capiche?" Brody figured this dill wad was yanking his chain.

"Hey, I'm a cop, not a hit man. Jesus, Brooks!" Sal lifted his service cap, running his hand over his hair, thankful no one was around to overhear. "It's a simple pickup-and-drop-off. We get five C-notes—it's an easy score. Ya don't know what's in the package. Or who's getting it, see? Alls we gotta do is guarantee that no one gets pinched during the handoff, and tomorrow night we go collect our payoff."

Three days later, it began. Brooks was in.

He called Ethan, worried, sweating, and terrified of what he'd gotten himself into. They met at a small bar near the port. Ethan talked him down from the edge.

"Man, E, I had no idea what I was getting myself into. I swear, I didn't know they was gonna mess the guy up! Almost killed the dude, and I was a witness. Jesus Christ!" His hand raked down his face. Picking up his second double scotch, he downed it.

"Slow down on the booze, bud, and listen to me. Same thing happened my second time they asked me to do a drop—I had no idea they were gonna pistol-whip the guy. But man, I was already in, and no way to back out—or I'd be fish food, hear me? Later, I mentioned I'd handle tasks without resorting to violence or harm. Said I'd do my share of looking the other way, and other stuff not costing me my badge—"

Brody's fist hit the top of the old, scarred, dingy wooden countertop. "Cost you your badge. Shit, E, this will have them shoving your badge up your ass and tossing you in a cell so the cons can fuck you six ways to Sunday."

"We won't get caught, B, if we're smart about it. Guys been doing this shit for years. Just listen to me, will ya?"

Brody listened.

―――――――――――

1990, Houston Police Station, Night Shift Roll Call

"Alright, listen up for your assignment!" the lieutenant bellowed.

He got to Windom and Brooks last. Total opposites.

"Brooks, Windom's with you tonight. Sal called in. Coolidge is riding with Yardley, and Johnson's still on administrative duty until the doctor clears him. Make it work or ya both'll get rips. Dismissed."

The room cleared. Windom and Brooks were the last two out.

"I'm driving. You get the gear checked. I'll be there in ten."

"Says you. You aren't the boss, Brooks."

"Just clam your mug and do it. I got seniority over you, you dipshit."

"Piss on you," Windom rejoined and left to get their gear. He didn't give a fat rat's ass if the gear checked out for Brody Brooks, but he did for himself. He'd do it, but he wasn't thrilled about taking orders from the butt-faced pig.

It'd been a slow night. Windom felt ready to eat his gun from having to listen to the blowhard Brooks.

"Got about eleven of 'em. Best fly and deep fishing rods made. Got me several Zebco's, top of the line, and got my eye on a boat, too. Told the fellas we'd go on a jaunt." He stopped to give Frank a side-glance. "Not you, just the guys I like."

"Like I care. I don't fish. It's a stupid hobby," Windom said.

"What's your hobby? Tiddlywinks?"

"Brooks, stop your yammering. Just drive."

The oaf huffed air out of his nose but didn't say another word.

Three hours later, Brooks left their patrol area, driving towards the Gulf Freeway.

Frank gave him the eye.

"Hey, douche, where ya going?"

"Nunya. Why not enjoy the ride for one night, Windom?"

"Look, dildo, I'm not gonna get a rip 'cause you're a jackass. Turn around. Get back to our patrol zone."

Between clenched teeth, Brooks said, "Zip it. I got an errand to run. It ain't gonna hurt for you to sit back and keep your pie hole shut about what I do."

"I ain't that dipshit Gary, or that scaredy-cat Sam Coolidge, so don't act like you can run roughshod over me."

"Nah, you're a pussy, like Johnson. What a nimrod. At least Sam don't question every step I make or breath I take."

"He threw his back out; it doesn't make him a wuss. And Coolidge is a robot follower." Frank's jaw muscles tightened.

"Hell, the dude messes his back up lifting. Not a work comp case, either. What a putz. Listen here, Windom. Sam knows his place. Seeing as I'm senior officer on this ride, you'd best be remembering it." He turned, giving Frank the stink eye.

"What you should care about, Brooks, is how many times Sal calls in sick? Other than Coolidge, he's the only copper in the precinct who wants to ride with you. Everybody else avoids you. Why you think that is?"

"Shit, Frank, I shouldn't dignify that with an answer, but since you asked: those fellas, Dellucci and Coolidge, know a first-rate officer when they see one. Been in the department longer than you. You can't see the big picture, can you, Windom?"

"Oh, for fuck's sake, a whole two months longer. Good for you. We're just looking at two separate pictures. I see the city of Houston; all you see is your ugly mug."

The car stopped. Frank looked around. Nothing but darkness. A closed container yard, no activity—it felt wrong.

"Why're we here?" His hand moved to his holster.

Brooks' resonant voice filled the car. "Take your hand off your piece, Windom. You ain't in danger."

As Brooks opened his door, the inside light illuminated the interior. "Wait here. And, Frank," his tone no-nonsense, "this brief stop ain't to be gabbed about, got me?"

"Are you issuing me a threat?"

"Nah, only a friendly warning. Don't make me get unsociable."

Brooks slammed the door, walking off in the dark, his flashlight creating his path between rows of containers. Frank watched.

Whatever Brooks was involved with, he didn't care as long as the man didn't commit murder. Frank wasn't gonna cross the invisible blue line and have the entire department come down on him. Crossing that line meant all cops—good or crooked—would under no circumstances trust him again. Frank didn't want to ride with him again. He'd speak to his Commanding Officer to make sure. And he never wanted to ride with Gary Yardley or Sal Dellucci, either.

6

In the two years after riding with Brooks, Frank had kept a watchful eye on him. Sal Dellucci and Sam Coolidge as well. All three were disreputable sleazebags. Cops—ha! Calling them cops was as accurate as calling the Pope an American. Frank likened them to wise guys who wore badges; only he had no tangible proof. The exchanges he witnessed weren't proof of wrongdoings—however, his gut screamed that something was off.

Frank took the Detective's exam, aspiring to be miles away from guys like Brooks, Dellucci, and Coolidge—even that douchebag Gary Yardley. He wondered why they never tried to climb the ladder. Yardley—what a nincompoop. The asshat got shot in the knee. The story was laughable. All it took was blowing off his left kneecap to land him on desk duty for the remaining years of his career.

Frank had enough of patrol, fed up with drunk drivers, domestic calls, B and E calls, and cruising the streets for troublemakers. Windom wanted to do investigative work. Homicide seemed like the job best suited for him. After he passed the Detective's exam, Frank left patrol with a box of personal crap and moved to the Homicide table. His desk was an old, marred, wooden piece of furniture. He loved it—a desk with history. His partner was four-year Homicide veteran James Parrish, AKA Jimbo. Windom's learning curve was short. Frank was a natural investigator, passionate about the job. In time, he became the job.

1994

Jack West, fourteen; Cole West, almost nineteen and would be leaving on a full ride to LSU. In these last days of summer, a bunch of kids planned a huge get-together, and Cole Arron West was eager to blow off steam with the fellas. Jack begged to go, but big bro said, "You can't go—not this time, little brother."

Richmond Avenue, not yet a through street, was perfect for kids to hang out. It was a chill place for teens, away from traffic and cops. Cars coasted in, dropping kids off, passengers and drivers checking out who was there and who wasn't. Beater cars, lowriders, and kids using their parents' vehicles cruised for many reasons: drugs, hook-ups, booze, and camaraderie.

Committed to a drug-free lifestyle, Cole steered clear of any trouble. A bunch of older guys from different high schools came—siblings of the new grads. Friends of friends and even gang members were present. The party was in full swing; the place alive with booze, toking, and snorting. Kids canoodling in back seats of cars. Girls in short shorts and halters on truck tailgates. Acts of random wildness. Clean-cut teens mingling with naughty kids amid boisterous laughter and arrogant displays.

While chilling with three other guys, Corey, 23, a Heights High alumnus, observed the others. Why did girls flock around the goody-goody superjocks? Untouchables—and if caught red-handed when cops drove up, no one would hold them accountable. Men who acted superior to him.

A few drinks gave them the guts to hang with the kids who normally snubbed them. Even younger kids considered the four beneath them, much like they did the gang members who traveled the area. The difference was, the crowd feared the gangs—but not the Italian wannabe wise guys.

Gresham, Olsen, Conti, and Carver. Outsiders in this massive group of teens and young people. Four Italian boys from the old neighborhood. Raised traditionally in the old neighborhood. The hoodlum stigma stuck to them.

———

"Yo, Corey, got any nose candy on ya tonight?"

"What makes you think I got blow, Henry?" Corey took his eyes off the pretty girls draped on the arms of the footballers.

"We heard your old man busted up a drug ring. Doesn't he get dibs on the product?"

The other guys laughed.

"You're an ass, Gresham. My dad's a cop." Corey glanced around to see who might be nearby and listening. Sometimes his pals were dangerous to hang with, especially after drinking, 'cause they never knew when to keep their mouths shut.

"Yeah, not what we got wind of. Folks say he's on the take, 'cause you live too high and mighty on a poor flatfoot's salary. It's what my pop says."

What the hell was Henry's problem tonight? Corey resented his pal's attitude and wasn't in the mood to dick around with this usual line of banter.

"What the fuck does your pop know, Gresham? He's a dumb truck driver. We all heard his load got hijacked, and he got tossed around a little and cried like a scared broad," Corey shot back, intending to shut him up.

"Yeah? They broke his damn arm, did you know that? Anyway, your dad showed up at the scene and didn't do diddly. Took my pop's statement and they sent him to the hospital. He's on the hook for the cargo. His boss got pissed."

Henry's anger was genuine, and Corey wanted to de-escalate but had to defend his father. "What's he supposed to do, make your pop's cargo reappear?" he fired back, wanting to silence him.

Henry Gresham looked at Corey's feet. A laugh snorted out. "Seems like he did. His cargo reappeared on your feet, you motherfucker."

Corey's eyes widened. "My shoes? Nah, pop gave 'em to me for my birthday."

"Right. On a cop's salary, you get a hundred-twenty-dollar pair of Air Jordan Xs? Shit, man, your house, and your mom's car. No way a cop pulls down that sorta cash, and your mom don't work either."

Corey huffed, waving him off. "You're just jealous 'cause your old man ain't good with money." His eyes moved toward the pretty girls nearby; he hoped they were hearing every word.

"Right, and you selling nose candy to make quick cash. Where's it coming from? Your dad's stash? The stuff he steals from evidence, 'cause that's what the story is." Henry looked at the other fellas.

It was the coke. That's all Henry wanted. Him causing a scene for some nose candy was agitating the piss out of Carver, but before he could say another word, Andy Olsen jumped in.

"My dad says Corey's pop's a shady cop, in bed with the criminals like the Berutti family. And we heard Carmine is your granddaddy, but your last name ain't the same as his, 'cause you're a bastard just like your dad."

Now shit was getting real. Carver's anger let loose as the alcohol-fueled joking gave way to fiery tempers. The situation grew volatile in a heartbeat. Their usual friendly banter turned to stinging insults.

"You and him," Corey thumbed toward Henry, his eyes moving back to Andy, "you guys think your dads are choir boys? Shit, we've heard stuff goes missing off trucks all the time, and no one reports it, and it ain't cops who are driving those trucks, assholes, it's your dads."

"Yeah, fucker, 'cause they get hijacked by the mob, who your dad works for and who pays him the big bucks. How do you like being related to thieves and murderers, Carver?" Andy stood his ground, sticking his hands in his pockets, his inner fear of retaliation real. Carver was well-connected in the neighborhood. That was no secret. If anyone messed with his pop, Sal, it brought trouble, so messing with Corey, his kid, was double trouble.

"Whatever your dads do ain't none of y'all's business," Lucas Conti piped up for his cousin Corey. "Don't affect you unless your pops go to jail, and besides, they're grown-ass men."

"Shut it, Lucas, you're a pussy. Stop trying to fix shit." Andy Olsen sidestepped him, knocking his shoulder against the boy. "We just wanna get some blow from Carver 'cause we know he has it."

"Huh, your pop goes to jail, then your momma gonna hafta get a job."

Corey took a step toward Henry, his face inches from him, his teeth set on edge. He didn't say a word, but Henry Gresham kept mouthing off. He pulled the gun out of his jacket pocket, not aiming, pointing the barrel just over Henry's head. He shot off a round, then another.

Andy Olsen, who was also carrying, pulled out a small .22 caliber, shooting rounds into the ground, just past Carver and Henry's feet, sending dirt flying.

Between the crowd and the music blasting, it took a second for anyone to realize those pops were gunshots, and not Black Cat firecrackers.

"You jackasses," Lucas ground out. "Stuff the guns! Holy shit, now someone's gonna call the cops."

Stunned at first, Henry laughed. "Jesus Christ, Carver, you're a lunatic! I just wanted some coke, you dickwad."

Carver gestured to his car. "We better bounce, 'cause I got eight ounces on me. I can't go to jail if cops show up."

They piled into Corey's car and no one took notice as the dark green 1986 Oldsmobile Cutlass pulled out, leaving the soon-to-be disrupted crowd of kids behind. Slow-moving cars, booming music, guys hanging out of windows, shouting at girls and other guys. In that moment, vehicles drove by with occupants shouting lewd sayings, making obscene gestures. Corey did a slow weave in between these other cars at the end of the unfinished cul-de-sac on Richmond Avenue, laughing about what just happened. This kinda crap went down regularly with these four. Tough guy shit, they called it, and they moved on with no grudges. Thing was, this incident would haunt them forever.

Back at the hangout spot, all heads turned at the sounds of a screaming girl pointing at a boy lying on the ground, blood oozing from his upper chest. Cole West lay dead. Sirens wailed.

***

Present Day

Still reading, Jack rubbed his tired eyes. It was the first time he learned Frank and Brooks had ridden together. Of course, he'd never asked him about his patrol days, and Frank wasn't the type who told you, either. The man wasn't a spill-your-guts type. Him being dead, Jack couldn't ask him—but Frank, no doubt, would've been a straight shooter.

Brooks' list of colleagues was brief: Training Officer Lamont Jones. A few minor reprimands reported; however, no one incident raised any significant red flags. Just the typical complaints cops handled during their rookie year. Leaning back, fanning the papers, he thought about it. He hadn't been the Rookie of the Year either, making mistakes—yet none too costly. Rookies always acted like hotshots, himself included. Become a cop. Save the world. Brooks was not the type. Was he ever a young, eager guy wanting to change the world? Jack couldn't envision Brooks in that capacity. He continued his read.

After he'd completed his training, they partnered Brooks with Gary Yardley, a six-year street veteran. Officer Yardley remained on patrol, citing that he preferred the range of duties and the excitement the city of Houston lent to the job. After taking a bullet to the kneecap, he worked at a desk to get in his twenty. Nothing too exciting.

Next partner: Joan Whitmire. She got the short stick, Jack figured. They were partners for almost nine months before she requested a transfer to the Harris County Sheriff's Office.

His last patrol partner was Sal Dellucci until Brooks advanced upward in the ranks. Jack scratched his jaw in thought. Were any ancient roster sheets still around? Had they been shredded? It could be nothing, but his curiosity was aroused all the same. Frank Windom came up after Brooks, by a year. Officers rode with different fellas when need be, and Jack knew that's how Windom ended up with Brooks. These two were oil and water. They'd never mesh to make a respectable ongoing team.

Next: Brooks' disciplinary records. Documents no one was privy to but higher command. It was a little treat, giving him ammo to hurl back at Brooks. Jack admonished himself. Nope, that's the Brooks way—not his way.

He skimmed over the pages, scanning the reports. Accusations of theft, evidence mishandling, even witness tampering, going back as far as his days in patrol. Jack read the accounts: no charges, no suspensions, and no dismissal of one Brody Dean Brooks. Given the weight of each individual accusation, it amazed him that Brooks suffered no repercussions.

Accommodations were next, which had Jack puffing a laugh. Brooks wasn't hero material. He did the job without going above or beyond. From Patrol, he advanced to Vice. Jack figured that, being the underbelly of the world, Vice was a perfect fit for the tub of lard.

He thumbed through the pages of Brooks' career that Roni had supplied, which weren't much. A spattering of highlights at best, and he'd bet there was much more. What was Roni hoping he'd find that no one else had?

His feet pushed down on the footrest, causing the recliner to snap back into an upright stance. Fed up with reading about Brooks, Jack grabbed his tennis shoes and keys. Time to hit the road to jog away thoughts of Brody Brooks.

7

"HEY JACK!"

"Gilly, it's been a while. How are things?"

"Aw, hard at work like always, pulling our hair out over several upscale robberies."

"Oh? What's the deal?"

"No prints, no forced entry, and yep, no one's seen a thing."

"When you say upscale, what area?"

"Douche's primary target is River Oaks."

"How many?"

"A dozen plus. Expensive jewelry, high-end watches. Cash, if they found any. Firearms and smaller electronics. You know the drill, resalable stuff. No large-ticket items, like stereos or flat screens."

"He's a picky thief?"

"It's not one person. Gotta be a crew."

Jack sipped his coffee, which'd gone lukewarm. "What makes you think that?"

"Because someone burglarized three homes on the same night, several blocks apart. Got us scratching our heads."

"Hard to believe these homeowners don't have cameras or alarm systems."

"Oh, they do. These thieves covered the cameras during the incidents and bypassed the alarm systems. It's people who know their stuff. Uh, sorry, but I gotta get back. We've got interviews with the victims' neighbors."

"Sure, better run. Good chatting, and, Gilly, tell everyone howdy for me."

HER DOOR WAS ALMOST never closed, but today it was. Jack almost knocked, but recognized a voice inside her office—Brody Brooks.

The last thing he needed was for Brooks to catch him eavesdropping.

While moving backward, he caught his name being said. Now he wanted to listen. By timing it correctly, he could carry out a swift escape through the hallway, deceiving Brooks into believing he had just walked in. It'd worked one other time.

Jack reflected on the night he'd overheard Brooks on a telephone call. Although he'd only caught the fat man's side, it'd sounded fishy—Brooks had no valid reason to be at the station late. Any detectives working a new murder, yeah, a late night seemed reasonable. But Brody Brooks? Never.

With his shoulder against the door, he leaned in, trying to hear. With Brooks' booming tone, it was not a problem. Roni wasn't a lightweight either; her tone resonated with anger. Jack knew Brooks had pissed her off.

"If you ever need Homicide's help, you will, let me repeat, will take whichever detective I believe is fit for the job, Brooks."

"I'll make that call, Justice, not you."

"Don't try to strong-arm me with your seniority horseshit. It ain't gonna fly. This is MY department. Was yours once; you screwed it up. The guys from my division, like Webb, Nichols, or Golan, they like you. Why not ask them to transfer? That way they'll be at hand for whenever you need your ass kissed. Get them to assist you if there comes a time you need homicide investigation skills. Oh, and good effing luck with that."

"Roni, you're a bitch."

"Oh no, my secret is out! Brooks, get the hell outta my office, and stop dictating the boundaries of what I can do with my detectives, you pompous asshole."

At a fast speed, Jack walked along the hallway, turned the corner, and counted to twenty before pretending to have just exited the stairwell, hoping to encounter Brooks. He wasn't scared of the prick one bit.

Red-faced, Brooks muttered some obscenities, slamming Justice's door. He grumped toward the elevator doors and caught sight of Jack.

They arrived in front of the elevators.

Jack faced him. "Commander."

"West." One word, his tone dry, yet hate radiated from that single syllable and his eyes.

Brooks' intense hatred for him was something he never comprehended, even from the beginning. Under his breath, he said, "Don't get it."

"You say something, Detective?" Brooks asked.

"No, sir, just mumbling."

"Mumble alone, not when you are facing a superior."

That was it. Brooks hit the button for five, one floor down.

Jack continued to the boss's office. *My superior, my ass,* he thought. He wished Brooks would choose the stairs. Even one flight would be total exertion for him. Everyone knew if there was a fire, the heavyset man would drop to his knees attempting stairs.

"Hmm, need the crew to send Brooks a box of doughnuts," the evil side of Jack grinned as he tapped on Roni's door.

"Enter," her one-word response.

"You need me?"

"Close the door, Jack. Did you see Brooks out there?"

"Uh, yeah, I did."

"He's a stick up my—oh, never mind," she said, relaxing back. "You read over any of the files I gave you?"

He nodded.

"Well, what do you think?"

"That it was a bunch of useless crap."

Her head bobbed. "Figured you'd say that."

"Okay. Why am I reading this stuff, Cap?"

"Curious if you'd create a mountain out of a molehill; given the fact you detest Brooks."

"Yeah, be a thrill for me, but I'm not that sort of fella. So, Roni, what gives?"

"What if I gave you a bigger mountain to work with?"

This aroused his interest. "Could you elaborate?"

"I'll get back to you. For now, keep your ear to the ground. Go interview Joan Whitmire, Gary Yardley, and Lamont Jones. Sam Coolidge, too, if you can find him. I've cleared it with the brass, so Personnel will have their contact information waiting for you."

"And ask them what?"

"Jack, you're one of my best detectives and you're asking me this. Are you joking?"

Jack sat, facial expression intense, waiting. He would not make assumptions.

"Oh, alright. Ask them about working with Brooks in the past. What sort of cop he was. Any issues, personal or job-related. Try to make them open up. If they ask if he is under investigation, tell them no. You're doing contextual work for me without knowing the reason—just following orders."

"Won't be a lie because I don't have the foggiest what IA is doing."

"Gonna keep it that way. Do this on your off time. Keep a record of hours worked. I'll see you pull the OT on your paycheck."

He rose. "Anything else?"

"Yeah. Hang out in the Robbery Division some."

"I see. Keep my ear to the ground on Brooks' doings, and put my head right in the way of his big fat boot?"

She snorted a chuckle. "That's about it. Can you do it?"

He nodded, eyes focused on the corner of her desk and the short stack of files, wondering if he should admit to thinking this same idea. Nah, best coming as an indirect order, not something he did on his own.

"You got pals you can chat with on five?" She stared at him.

"Sure, a couple. Won't be a problem. Brooks is a prick, but his department has decent people."

"Good. Go to Personnel. Get the addresses. We'll talk later. I need you to investigate an unsolved. Dawson has the files. Bye, Detective West, shut the door behind you."

"THIS IS COMPLETE HORSESHIT. I can't believe how these motherfuckers treat files with information vital to working any incident." Luck stood, swearing, flipping through the book, popping open the binder, yanking out pages.

"Dawson, are you cussing me?"

"Nah, Jack, you're not the reason for my foul attitude."

"Who or what is?" Jack took his chair, tossing the empty Styrofoam cup in the trash.

"Incompetent people who don't know their ass from a crater in the ground as big as the Grand Canyon. These files are a disaster. That's why I'm bitching."

Luck sat with a thud, hands pushing the rolling cart heaped with three-ring binders to the side and the six binders on his desk toward the center, papers crumpling underneath.

"Want me to help?"

"I'd rather do it myself, but yeah, here, take these two. Organize it by report type and date, wouldja?" Dawson handed them over the partition.

Jack grimaced, puffing out a hefty sigh. "Alright, whatda we got?"

He laid them on the desk, clicking one open, removing pages, and fanning them out to view as he began shuffling.

"Old reports we gotta sort through before we can work just one of them, since they've gotten intermingled. How does this even happen?"

Jack peered down to the signatures. "Look at the names on the reports. That'll tell you how."

Dawson let out several expletives. "Skip Webb, Earl Nichols," he flipped a page, "and Leon Golan—the department's version of the Three Stooges. Three assholes!"

Although he bitched, Dawson had one binder emptied, reorganized, and stacked before Jack was halfway through his.

"Wish I was as speedy as you are with organizing this paperwork, Luck. How the hell do you do it?"

"Talent, West, pure talent. In addition, I read fast, too. Matter of fact, got the last file for this binder organized. Give me yours, slowpoke. I'll do it."

"You sure? I mean, you're better at it, cuz I suck." Jack piled the papers in a stack, delivering them over the half-partition.

"Yeah, yeah, West, keep blowing smoke up my butt. It's eleven-thirty. Lunchtime. Why don't you go get me a sandwich?"

"I can't leave you to deal with the rest of the binders on the cart, man. Ain't fair."

"Already did 'em."

"When did you have time?"

Dawson stilled his hands, looking over with a grimace. "While you were farting around doing who knows what. Looky here, Jack, you'd better not keep secrets from me again, cuz I'm damned tired of being blindsided."

"Two Antone's Originals. You want chips?" Food would take his partner off track. He had no intention of hiding anything, but Justice gave him a direct order not to talk to anyone until given the green light. It meant he'd have to sneak around hoping Lucky didn't figure it out. If he did, he'd key the Captain in straightaway.

"Add another sandwich. I'm starved, or I can pocket one for later. Get me a bag of those deli chips, the pickle-flavored kind."

"You mean salt and vinegar?"

"Potato, potahto—same thing."

Jack stood, grabbed his phone and keys. "Be back soon."

Dawson Luck raised his head. "And soon means soon, Jack. No pit stops. Get your cowboy heinie back with my sandwiches. Oh, and I like the Jam Park case."

Jack turned back, chuckling. First, though, he intended to make a quick side trip to Robbery. Lucky would be oblivious.

8

"HI, JACK, WHAT BRINGS you to our humble floor?"

"Hey, Penny. Headed to Antone's for lunch. Stopped to see if anyone needed something."

Penny Salato, nicknamed "One Cent" by her co-workers, narrowed her eyes. "You aren't one to drop by asking about lunch, Jack." Her voice lowered. "What's up?"

A grin creased his face. "Want lunch or not?"

She crossed her arms, tapping her foot. "Umm, uh, tuna for me. Get Gilly turkey and Swiss." She reached into the back pocket of her jeans, pulling out a twenty. "This ought to cover it."

Jack took the money. "Chips?"

"Nah, have a large bag of Fritos at my desk. Just the sandwiches. And Jack," she leaned closer, "you're a nice person, but you've never come down here to ask if anyone wanted lunch before. So?" She gave him her best 'what's up' stare.

"Tell ya later—I mean, if I'm allowed." He saw the Commander approaching in his peripheral vision and backed away from Detective Salato.

Brooks folded his beefy arms over his oversized belly. "West, you lost? Need directions to your office?"

Brooks eyeballed Detective Salato. "Don't you have work to do?"

"Yes, sir, but I asked Detective West if he was going to Antone's today, and if so, could he bring us sandwiches so we could eat and work since we've picked up this fresh robbery."

Craig Gillespie overheard the conversation, ready to bail his partner out of Brooks' crosshairs. "West? Did Penny give you my order of turkey and Swiss?"

"Yeah, Gilly, she did." Jack's eyes never left Brooks' ballooned cheeks.

"Add in an Antone's Original. I'm hungry. Penny, spot him another ten. I'll pay you back. Commander, you wanna sandwich too?" Gilly offered, straight-faced.

Brooks cleared his throat. "I'm running behind. Have a meeting. West, grab the cash, then get out. Drop off the food; don't dick around, cuz my detectives have real work to do."

One Cent pulled a crumpled ten from her pocket, handing it to Jack. "I got this, Craig. You buy lunch tomorrow."

Jack straightened. "See ya later, Detective Salato." He looked at Brooks. "Hope not to see you when I deliver the food."

Brooks opened his mouth, then closed it, realizing every detective there had their eyes averted but their ears in the air, listening to every word. Without a by-your-leave or an adios, Brody Brooks turned, harrumphed, and plodded to his office, invisible steam coming out his ears. Jack West rankled the piss out of him.

Gilly walked to where Sparks and West stood. They witnessed Brooks disappearing into his office and closing the door behind him with force.

Penny spun to gaze at Jack. "Okay, I covered for your butt. Why are you here, Jack?"

"To goad Brooks. I love doing it whenever I can, and wanna make sure he has a stupendous day."

"Well, thanks loads, Jack. We'll catch hell from the old fart now," Gilly snickered. "But it comes with food. We'll get over it."

Craig headed to the whiteboard he was working, with parting words: "Hurry back with our lunch, Jack."

"Thanks for backing me up, Penny."

"Sure, Jack. You're gonna tell me why later, right?"

"Ah, it's nothing. Right now, I gotta run, or Dawson's gonna send the troops to look for me. Better Brooks be mad, not my partner."

ONE LAST STOP BEFORE he took off for Lucky's sandwiches. The HR office was empty except for three people staffing the phones. Yvette Rogers sat filing her long nails. A huge smile covered her face when she saw Jack.

"Oh my, as I live and breathe, Jack Rabbit. You hunky cowboy. How you been?"

"I've been doing well, Yvette, thanks for asking. And you? Things good?"

"Oh, baby, doing super. Caught me a new boyfriend. Ronnie's mighty fine, but not as fine as you is. My goodness, Jack, you looking marvelous." Her face lit up, her pearly whites in contrast to her dark, mocha-chocolate skin, as her snappy peepers looked at him from his head to his boots, inciting his blush.

"Oh, I love it when you blush, such a cutie patootie, mmm-mmm-mmm. If I didn't have a man, I'd be trying my best to hook you."

"You always say that, but," he placed his hands palm side up, "I never get a chance, do I?" He winked. She giggled, covering her mouth with one hand.

"Now we're done flirting. What can old Yvette do ya for?"

"My captain called in for some information for me. Should be in a pouch with my name on it."

"Uh, right here." She handed it to him. The phone jangled. She winked, picking up the line with, "Personnel, Yvette Rogers," her face a huge smile.

With a nod, he stuck the envelope in his back pocket, leaving her cackling on the phone with the caller.

———

Two bags of subs with chips sat in the passenger seat of Jack's truck outside Antone's.

He slit open the envelope and read the names: Gary Yardley, Joan Whitmire, Lamont Jones, Sam Coolidge, and Sal Dellucci.

Yardley lived in Galveston, Joan Whitmire in Nassau Bay. Jones lived in Houston, as did Dellucci. Gary and Joan weren't down the street. Jack preferred not to talk over the phone, but he'd hafta place a call first because he didn't just want to show up. Coolidge had a phone number and PO Box. Terrific. This had to be a phone call. Jack's low groan puffed out as he turned the key. Back at HPD, he dropped off food to Gillespie and Salato, hotfooting it back to Homicide.

"My lord, it took you long enough. Hope my sandwiches haven't wilted." Dawson Luck grabbed the bag from him, dug out his three subs and a bag of salt-and-vinegar chips to go with his lukewarm coffee, and feasted.

"Dawson, stop bitching. I've got a headache, and you aren't helping."

A food-filled mouth garbled something. Jack gestured with his hand. "Yeah, I gotcha. You eat, while I flip through these files."

He received a nod as Lucky stuffed the sub in his mouth to take another ravenous bite.

They'd selected the shooting case in Jam Park and began reading as they ate to familiarize themselves with the incident.

WEST PUSHED HIS CHAIR away to stretch his legs. "Let's get outta here. Drive over to the crime scene. Take the photos. Might as well canvass the area again. Find out if anyone's talking yet."

Luck flipped a page, reading the same stuff again. "Sure, I'll drive."

"In your car or Viv's?"

"Does it matter?"

"Yeah, your jalopy is embarrassing."

"It's a classic. Stop bitching."

"Dawson, it's a Volvo. Cops don't drive Volvos."

They had a solid laugh on their way to grab a department car.

DESPITE THEIR EFFORTS, THEY had failed. No one was talking; the park was void of visitors. After driving to several addresses with no success, they figured it was time to quit for the day and headed back to headquarters.

Lucky's sedan was parked two cars away from Jack's truck.

"Alright, gonna run in and grab my keys. Catch ya in the morning."

"Yep, later," Lucky said, walking to his sedan, frowning. He'd seen Jack pocket his keys when they left. Why was he lying—again? He'd slough it off—for now.

Jack didn't enjoy fibbing to Lucky, only he couldn't discuss this Brooks stuff yet. His other worry was Penny Salato. She was gonna come at him with crap

about Brody Brooks, too. No matter what the deal was, Brooks caused him
unwanted agony from every direction.

9

In the office, Jack straightened his desk, turned off his computer, and set both binders on the floor underneath.

"West, you still here?"

"Hiya, Jace. Yeah, we're working on an unsolved, just got back from an afternoon of finding nada. Why're you here?"

"Hell, 11 texted me. We got a callout. He's on his way to pick me up, but I left my notebook at my cubical."

"You find out the skinny yet?"

"Nah, but you can bet there's a stiff involved." He grinned.

"You're heartless, Jace."

"It is what it is, Jack Benny." Jace's phone sounded. "That'll be Xi, waiting downstairs. See ya." He waved overhead and darted for the stairwell.

Jack, satisfied he'd gotten his area cleaned, took the stairs to the fifth floor, not expecting anybody to be there. He was surprised when he found two detectives in the briefing room.

"I'm guessing Penny's gone for the day?"

"Yeah, you missed her by ten. You West?"

Jack extended his hand. "Yeah. You Dunwell or Glover?"

"Dunwell." He thumbed at the other fella. "He's Glover. Nice to meetcha."

They all shook hands. Jack remarked, "So, you guys think I'm a complete POS?"

Glover smirked. "Oh, in the last year we've been told stories, multiple variations. We especially love the one where Brooks cries like a schoolgirl stomping his feet, ready to go tell his mommy you slapped him."

A smile spread over Jack's face. He liked these two. "Hmmm, hadn't heard that one. Sounds fun. Only don't say I said so. Listen, anybody else here?"

Alex lifted his stained coffee mug, gesturing toward Brooks' office. "Only us lowly peons, but the Commander is in his office."

"Most days he's gone when the whistle blows at five or fifteen minutes after. It's odd he's still here."

Glover looked at his watch. "Oh man, Dunny, I gotta scat or my bride will kill me. If it happens, Jack here will have a fresh murder to investigate. See ya in the morning—eight. Jack, nice to meet you in person."

"Same here, Glenn. Drive safe." Jack waved.

They watched him dart out the door at a sprint, heading downstairs in a rush.

"So, you need to talk to Penny? Want me to give her a message?"

Jack felt a hair of jealous undercurrents and wondered, so he went fishing for the dirt. "Yeah, tell her I dropped by. You know, Penny's a terrific gal, and a hella smart detective, too."

"Yeah, I've heard. Like to get to know her better."

"What, no wife?"

"I've had two. Not looking to repeat."

"Were the two gals your wives or someone else's?" Jack muffled his laughter, mindful of not arousing Brooks' curiosity to avoid a potential outburst.

"Nah, they were mine. I was younger and dumber. How's about grabbing a beer? You seem like a righteous dude, not a stuffed shirt."

"Sounds like a plan, but tonight I just wanna get home. Been a long day," Jack remarked.

"Gotcha. Um, listen, if you and Penny are, well ... I'll step back."

"We're just friends. It's not me you should be asking."

"Oh? Who?"

"Gilly, I imagine."

"Well, if they are, it doesn't show. But it does happen with co-workers some-times," Alex said.

Jack's thoughts turned to Sophia. It happens sometimes, and sometimes it even ends well. "Word of advice, Alex?"

"Of course."

"Move slow. Keep Brooks in the dark about our beer plans. It'll cause you hella misery."

"I hear ya. I'm not worried. Had similar crap at my other job. I'm no stranger to that type of stuff, believe me."

"Why don'tcha tell me your story over some brewskis? I'll call ya. If you aren't knee deep, we can meet up."

"Hell, Jack, we're always gonna be knee-deep investigating something, but let's make time to chat. I don't have many buddies. A drinking buddy would be nice."

"How long you been here in Houston?"

"Transferred from the Newark, New Jersey, police department sixteen months ago."

"Glover from Jersey too?"

"Nah, the li'l shit's from Joplin, Missouri. His wife's mom lives in Katy, and she's got dementia. The spouse wanted to live closer to her and her sister. Plus, he's new to robbery."

"What'd he do up in Joplin?" Jack leaned a hip against the empty desk next to Alex.

"Department lead in Transportation, and the only openings for him to choose from were Vice or Robbery."

"At least there were openings. So, tell me, Dunwell, why'd you transfer, if ya don't mind me asking?"

"Cuz of budget cuts, and I hated Jersey winters."

"Were you in robbery up there?"

"Okay, my policing history goes like this: street patrol for eight, a stint in the Auto Division for two, General Crimes Division, moving over into Robbery four years later. Now here I am, in your big state."

"Be warned, winters here in Texas aren't a picnic. I needta dash. Tell Penny I stopped in. And one night I'll introduce you to my favorite pub. It's called Quinn's."

"Here's my card. Call when you wanna get drunk and chase women."

He watched Jack leave through the stairwell door, and his forehead crinkled. Something felt off. He felt it in his bones. With a heightened sense of perception, a skilled detective could detect the tense atmosphere of an internal investigation, attuned to the silent screams it emitted.

JOAN WHITMIRE: A STARTING point for his investigation into Brooks' history. Jack punched her address into his GPS and headed to Nassau Bay. Once he hit I-45 (the Gulf Freeway), it was a straight shot south to Webster, Texas. After that, head east to Nassau Bay.

He turned on the radio to classical tunes. While he drove with the crazies, classical kept him calm. In another life, he'd listened to country music and classic rock, reliving his teenaged era through the tunes.

Since the death of Gretchen at the hands of a monster, and punching Brooks in his fat, globular nose, sending him to his knees, he'd used classical music as a soothing therapy. With rock 'n' roll, he preferred old tunes: Van Halen, Journey, and the Bee Gees, to name some. He was a Johnny Cash and Garth Brooks fan, too. He had eclectic tastes—he'd even tuned into jazz—but more often, he had Beethoven, Debussy, or Mozart playing.

10

TIME FLEW. BEFORE HE knew it, Jack was at his exit. As he slowed, stopping at the first red light, he noted the area. Nassau Bay appeared to be a pleasant place.

He turned into the Shell Station on the corner, used the facilities, and purchased a stale sandwich to hold him until dinner, thinking he'd grab a burger and fries—or chicken—on his way home.

Back in his truck, he scrolled through the map for his route: a straight shot on E. Nassau Parkway to Bel Harbour Drive, then continue to Sailboat Drive.

Nice boating district, he thought, driving past several homes. Him? Nah. He wasn't a water person. He'd never liked to fish or camp—too much wildlife, which included serpents. His idea of roughing it was a three-day stakeout without a shower or shaving, the men's room a porta john.

Within minutes, he pulled into the driveway of a two-story condominium on Sailboat Drive. Whitmire had agreed to a face-to-face meeting after he mentioned discussing her time in Patrol—and a sensitive matter.

Just as he reached the door, it opened.

"Detective West, come in. I've got fresh coffee and homemade cinnamon rolls waiting in the kitchen." Joan led the way, and he followed.

"Smells delicious."

"The coffee or the cinnamon buns?"

A grin played on his lips. "Both, ma'am."

"Call me Joan."

"Sounds perfect. So does coffee and homemade buns."

Joan poured two large mugs of coffee and set a plate of cinnamon rolls on the table. Jack dug in, savoring each bite. Between bites, he remarked on how marvelous they tasted—he had had none since his parents retired to Florida.

"You get to visit your folks, Jack?"

He shook his head as he swallowed the last bite, wiping his mouth. "Not as much as I'd want. Not big on water activities." He waved his hand. "I'd bet you're a boat person. Sailing, fishing, or both. Me? Not a fan of snakes or any reptiles. My parents live in a place in Florida similar to this. Near the water. My dad loves the lake, ocean, whatever. They both fish, love deep-sea fishing, boating, even going into the marshier areas on airboats. I prefer land. If I'm on the water, it'll be on a cruise ship."

"Fraidy-cat." A laugh bubbled in her throat. "I get ya though. My husband, Miles, is part amphibian. Fishing, diving, skiing—he loves everything. Me? I enjoy sailing, not the other stuff."

"Your husband here?" Jack looked around. The place was lived in, not extraordinary, neat but homey. Photographs of her and her hubby hung on the walls—huge smiles, epic catches, beach trips, sailing, airboat rides, lounging on a dock.

"We own a charter business. He took a charter out early this morning."

"It's a nice place. How long have you been here?"

She rose to take the pot off the burner and warm the coffee. "Over two decades." She sat back across from him. "Now, Jack, tell me the real reason you came by."

"Thirty years ago, you worked with Brody Brooks. Tell me your story."

Her lips turned downward. "It wasn't the best moment of my career."

"How long did you ride with Brooks?"

"It took eight months to be free of the bastard."

Jack, taken aback by her harsh tone, wanted her to know he was an ally. "He's a fat SOB—and several expletives I can think of. I've had some run-ins with the man. I understand your animosity toward him."

"Jack, I almost quit."

"Oh?"

With a sigh, her eyelids blinked shut. She let her thoughts drift back.

"I started my career in Sugar Land. Very different from the streets of Houston proper. I loved the work. It was rewarding—believing I was helping people and the city. After a year, I met a fellow named Neal. We got serious. He started his own skip-trace service and got an offer for an office in East Downtown. Me, dumb, thought I was in love, so I followed him. This took me to the east side of Houston, too far from Sugar Land's streets, so I applied for a position in Houston proper."

"So, they teamed you with Brooks right away?"

"No, Georgie Savata, nice older guy. We rode together for three years until he retired."

"Never heard of him. Lots of cops on the payroll in Houston, though."

"We patrolled Memorial Park. Don't know if routes have changed."

"They've increased police presence and tightened things up. Back to Brooks. He was your next partner?"

"Nah, Michelle Luna. First-rate cop. Rode together more than a year. She came up pregnant and six months later put in for a desk. Stayed there because after having her kid, it scared her she'd catch a bullet, leave her kid motherless."

"It's understandable in our city. Tough place most days for all cops. Brooks?"

"The guy makes me want to hurl. To think he was supposed to protect and serve. Ha!"

"Trust me, Joan, he hates my guts, and I don't know why. This has everyone in Homicide scratching their heads."

"Y'all never had cross words?"

"Nah, didn't even know him until they transferred him to Homicide. After they promoted Davis Yao to Chief of D's, Brooks came in as our new leader. Lots of water under that bridge. Him going back to Robbery as the Commander—gotta tell ya, this overjoyed Homicide."

She sat quietly for a minute, brain clicking on something. A perceptive smile curved her lips. "Jack West, you that Jack?"

"Unless there's two Jack Wests at HPD."

"Aha! I remember you. You're the hotshot who made it to Homicide in two. Was that what, ten years ago?"

"Guilty. Only it's been eighteen years."

"Time flies, huh? Okay, now I understand why Brooks hates you. He hated Windom. It's that simple. They rode together when they had to." She reflected a second. "Did Frank ever discuss Brooks with you?"

"Never."

Joan studied her hands, worry lines on her face. "Brody Brooks is a crook and a liar. Frank could've told you a lot, only I guess he thought it best to keep you out of it. Brooks climbed in bed with the wrong folks. It's only hearsay, but for the ten months I rode with him back in 1998, he had shady goings-on. Told me to keep my trap shut if I knew what was good for me and said I'd better not cross that sacred blue line. One night I saw him taking a package from a known criminal.

Brooks told me they'd threatened him and if he didn't comply we'd both be dead. I didn't believe him, but knowing who the man was, I decided not to take a chance. So I kept my mouth shut."

"Who was it?"

"Man named Angelo Conti. He's dead, Jack, murdered in 1979, so it don't matter. But he was part of Houston's Italian Mafia, close to the top dog."

"You think he paid Brooks to do things?"

With an offhand shrug, she said, "Yeah. Two weeks later, two of his thug pals were out of jail, exonerated. Evidence disappeared, and without that evidence, charges dropped."

"How does this link with Brooks?"

"Two weeks prior I watched them exchange words, and right after Conti gave Brooks a bulky envelope, they shook hands. The timing was too perfect."

"Alright. He carried this package back to the vehicle. You ask what it was?"

"Even if I had, Brooks wasn't gonna say, and he'd warned me to be quiet. Jack, he scared me. Word was he had friends in dark places, individuals who could ruin you—or even disappear you."

"You never reported it?"

Sad guilt lingered in her eyes. "No. Wish I had. One scumbag they freed killed a man three days later, a family man with a wife and three kiddos. Brooks helped him get freed. I know it in my bones, but I've got no tangible proof."

"You confronted Brooks?"

"I did, mad as hell. We got into a screaming match outside of the motor pool. Brooks grabbed my arm, hauled me around to the backside of the building, and told me he wasn't taking bribes, and I needed to shut up. It'd be in my best interest, he said, if I got his drift. Later, a couple of his cop pals threatened me, and I took this at face value. I backed off. Some weeks later, I met Frank. I'd seen him but never talked to him. By this time, he'd moved over to Homicide. Smart cop, job-minded, a bulldog.

"Brooks and Frank began their careers seventeen months apart, only Frank moved ahead faster. Everyone liked Frank. He was popular; Brooks wasn't. Brody was a showoff, raunchy, always trying to be important, and he wasn't. Frank worked that murder case, was one of his early homicide cases, and had his eye on Brooks."

"You tell Frank what you suspected?"

She let out a long puff. "Yeah, I did."

"And?"

"We spent time together while I worked at finding him evidence. I kept logs, watched Brooks, noted who he talked to, met with—and tried to get the jerkoff to tell me something that might incriminate him, or a clue to dig further. It didn't work.

"Frank was easy on the eyes and respectable. People thought we were sleeping together, but we weren't. I was seeing Miles. I think Brooks caught on to what I was trying to do. That's when he tried coming on to me. Brody thought he was hot stuff. One night his advances went too far, scaring me, so I slapped the holy hell outta him. Soon after, he made my life hell. Told me he wouldn't report me for taking a swing at him if I kept my trap closed, and to not discuss his doings on night shift or who he met with."

"Why didn't you report him for his advances?" Jack was confused.

"No proof, and the slap I walloped him with left a mark because my ring scratched his face. His word against mine, and he'd been part of HPD longer. He spouted nasty crap about what he'd make happen. Jack, I didn't want to get involved in an HR nightmare. This might've cost me my relationship, and nothing was worth losing Miles over."

"Did you request a transfer to Harris County Sheriff's Office, then?"

"Yeah. Anyway, it worked out in the end because Miles took a new position three months earlier working for Harris County Fish and Wildlife as a Game Warden. Best move for me, and my career. We got married a year later."

"No association with Brooks after this?"

She was silent and pensive. "IA called me about Brooks," she said, fidgeting. "They grilled me like a hog on a spit."

"This happened after your transfer?"

"Yes. I tossed all the info I'd logged about Brooks in a fire and exited as fast as possible. Look, Jack, I'd rather this not become a problem for me. Understand?"

"I do, Joan, but you haven't told me any news meriting an ass-biting."

"Fine. I never saw this, which means I can't speak of the validity of what I'm fixing to tell you. You need to find the proof yourself. Get my drift?"

He nodded, but stayed silent, letting her control the conversation.

"Focus on the evidence room. Examine logs and records, and go back several decades. Understand?"

He nodded, lifted his coffee, and drained the mug, looking at her.

"You care if I take a couple of these cinnamon rolls for the road?"

With a smile, she wrapped some up for him.

———————

THE CINNAMON ROLLS, COVERED with wax paper, were tucked in a paper bag on the passenger seat. She'd given him a to-go cup of coffee, and it thrilled him to have the caffeine for his drive home.

He felt a surge of excitement with this added piece of his investigation of Brooks' exploits. His shady doings didn't surprise him; it made sense in a weird way. Deep down, on several levels, Jack saw Brooks as crooked—like the cops created for TV shows or movies: corrupt, deceitful cops hiding behind the uniform and badge, carrying weapons and exploiting authority to subjugate others, believing themselves beyond accountability.

11

He and Dawson tackled the Jam Park shooting/Jon Martin murder case in silence.

Several hours in, Dawson stood and looked over the cubicle partition.

"Jack, my neck is killing me. How about lunch? I'll buy."

Jack stretched his arms overhead. "How about you go pick it up?"

"How about we get out of here?"

"Nah, it's calm in here for a change; I'm enjoying it. You got a hankering for specific food?"

"Thai or Mexican." Lucky grabbed his keys and holstered Greta Glock.

"Thai sounds good. Malai's?"

"Yeah, their spicy basil fried rice is tasty."

"Get me the house spicy chicken. You wanna split an order of crispy rolls?" Jack reached for his wallet, took out two tens, and handed them over.

"Sure. You want Diet Coke?"

"Nah, planned on making coffee."

Jack counted to twenty, giving Luck time to reach the stairwell. His plan: visit the fifth floor, find out what he could stir up. Twelve-fifteen. Most of the fellas were at lunch. He'd take a chance.

Jack opened the hall door, poking his face in, glancing everywhere before stepping inside. Robbery was not bustling, so he headed to Penny's and Gilly's desks. Most cubicles were empty. Detectives went right back to work, giving Jack only a brief glance.

"Jack, you lost?"

"Nah, just getting some exercise. Penny around?"

"She's canvassing the vicinity of the last reported break-in."

Jack glanced behind him. "Gilly with her?"

"He's in evidence." Dunwell looked up, squinting. "Something I can do?"

"Nah, just popped in to say, hey."

"I'll tell 'em you dropped by." Dunwell got a gut feeling this wasn't a casual trip to say howdy, and wasn't gonna drill him, so he waited.

"Brooks here?"

"Want me to get him for ya?"

A huffed laugh exited Jack's nose. "Nah, ask Penny to give me a ring when she has time."

"Will do," Alex said, diving back into the report he was typing.

"Hey, can we borrow a dozen coffee filters?"

Alex waved his hand. "You know where the breakroom is." He never looked away from his computer, knowing Jack didn't need coffee filters, just an excuse to walk past the Commander's office. A sly smile played on his lips. Jack wasn't deceiving anyone; he was keeping a watch on Brooks. The question echoing: who asked him to?

JACK'S BOOTS TREAD ON the Berber carpet toward Robbery's breakroom. Although his door was shut, he could still hear Brooks' low, grating voice. He was just beyond the door.

With a backward glance, he saw no one was watching. He leaned closer to hear better.

Unaware of listeners, Brooks spoke in his normal, brusque tone.

"I don't care, it's what I heard, and I ain't happy about it either, or wanna find out why someone's looking into this now." He stopped. No other voices sounded in the room. Brooks was on the horn.

"You think I give a rat's ass? Make certain the paperwork reflects those dates. And, for Christ's sake! Don't get caught—what?"

Jack's interest sparked with that comment: *don't get caught.* Who was he talking to?

"Hell no, I ain't signing off on no transfer, you idiot. You'll stay right where you are, and keep eyes on him since I can't, dummy."

Brooks was silent. Jack strained to listen.

"Who cares if that big-eared, big-nosed dwarf ain't your partner any longer? Just play nice, Webb. Don't mess this up. I gotta go. Don't call me. I'll call you, you twit."

Jack heard the handset hit the base. He turned, hurrying through Robbery. Passing Dunwell's cubicle, he left out the side hall exit, headed for the stairs. Alex shifted his gaze and saw Jack wasn't carrying any coffee filters; he smirked. Jack West had something going on, only it wasn't his concern.

JACK WAS AT HIS workstation for a brief couple of minutes when Lucky walked back in with plastic bags from Malai's. The appetizing smell of Thai food wafted through the air.

"Man, I'm starved. It smells delish. Thanks for going. And, uh, for buying."

Lucky passed Jack his steaming Styrofoam container of spicy chicken fried rice. They dug in, relishing the silence that enveloped them as they savored their meals, grateful for the temporary respite from the chaos of the squad room.

Jack munched a crispy roll, his thoughts on the overheard telephone conversation. Brooks was talking to Webb; Webb would need watching. Another thing on a list of things.

AFTER A SOLID WEEK of running down names of people to reinterview, they got the name of Jon Martin's cohort in crime: Kenny Roberts. Once they got him in the station, as the kids these days say, it got real.

Kenny swore he had nothing to do with Jon's murder. Yes, he'd been in the park, but never came forward, afraid of gang retaliation. He and Jon had landed themselves in what they thought was a scheme to make easy money—and ended up in the middle of a gang dispute they'd started.

They'd intercepted a mess of drugs waiting for pickup from the Dragons and got it into their heads to sell the dope to the highest bidder, setting up a middleman. Terrible idea. When five Dragons showed up to claim their property, eight Brown Cobras showed up to buy. Roberts and Martin claimed to be the rightful owners, citing possession as nine-tenths of the law—and that's when bullets flew.

After grilling Kenny—scaring ten years off the boy's life—a crucial new witness emerged: his sister, Theresa Roberts. She'd followed Kenny to keep watch on him. Their mother had worried her boy was traveling down a path of drugs and gangs, and she'd not been far off.

When shots rang out and pandemonium began, Theresa, afraid to run for fear of being seen, stayed hidden and used her cell to video record everything. Although it wasn't the best quality, HPD's technical division cleaned it up, providing a clear look at the shooter. They sent the Violent Task Force to pick up a Dragon: Darvon Lee Smith, aka Squeaky, who, after six hours in the hot box, confessed to pulling the trigger and grabbing the dope.

They stood in COD's office while he finished a phone call with the Metro Police Commander, who oversaw the Metropolitan Transit Authority of Houston (MTA).

Davis hung up, jotted a note, and turned his attention to his detectives. He listened as Dawson gave him the rundown of the shootings and a copy of the perpetrator's signed confession.

"The kid made a deal with the ADA to plead murder two. Squeaky hadn't planned on shooting anyone. He only wanted his drugs back," Jack said.

"Excellent job, you two," Yao praised them.

"Thanks, Chief," Dawson remarked, his fingers turning the doorknob, Jack on his heels.

"Jack, a word."

From the side of his mouth, Dawson responded, "Guessing your number is up again, partner."

He watched Dawson go out the stairwell exit and slam the door.

"Shit." The word sizzled between his clenched teeth. When would Dawson stop acting like a kid who got chosen last for kickball?

12

"Close the door, have a seat."

They lowered into the chairs, eyes locked. Jack's fingers drummed lightly on the armrest; Yao's brow creased as he weighed the moment.

Jack kicked things off. "You wanna discuss Brooks?"

The Chief's forehead rutted. "Why would I wanna discuss Brooks?"

"Cuz, it seems it's all my superiors wanna talk about when we have a private word. Since I can't discuss it with him, this cloak-and-dagger crap is pissing Lucky off, too."

Yao leaned back, lips pressed, gaze flicking to the window before meeting Jack's again. "Some fellas consider us a brotherhood; and we look after our own. Being a snitch can ruin a colleague. Most cops never cross that blue line unless there's something in it for them, and it has to be something big."

"Yeah, it's just like how they portray it in the movies. You know, you cross the line, you might as well be dead—or leave the country."

Yao's eyes pierced Jack, silent but intense.

Jack shifted, leaning in slightly, cocking his head. "As I see it, there are two blue lines, sir."

"Two?" Yao's brow lifted.

"Yeah. The right—or wrong—side of blue. It ain't a line. You gotta pick one or the other; you can't be both. You can pretend because you wear a badge you're on the right side, and anything you do you can try to justify, using the badge to hide behind."

Yao's chin dipped; his eyes followed an invisible line on the floor as he considered Jack's words.

Jack steered the conversation. "It is a choice, sir. Depends if you straddle the fence or not. Me? I stay off that fence, planting my feet only on the side of right."

"All the time, Detective West?"

Their gazes held. Yao's jaw tightened. The memory of Shelton flickering briefly, then fading. Jack's composed posture betrayed nothing.

West sensed Yao's curiosity simmering beneath the surface. The silence stretched, heavy with unasked questions. Jack let it hang, hands resting lightly on the chair arms, steady, focused. The past was past. Houston was safer now, and that thought steadied him.

Ready to move on, Jack rose, eyes fixed on Yao. "Chief, throughout my entire career I've done nothing I'm ashamed of or regretted."

"Sit down, Jack. I'm not faultfinding."

He sank back, a diminutive frown creasing his face.

Davis Yao exhaled, shoulders relaxing. "Patricia told me to ask you to dinner soon. She and the girls always enjoy a visit from you."

Jack's lips softened into a hint of a smile. "Your wife's a fabulous cook."

"I'll tell her you said so."

"Good."

"You're a bulldog, Jack, and a helluva cop."

"Thanks, Davis."

"Why not take the sergeant's exam, bump your pay up?" Davis leaned forward, curious.

"Nah, I enjoy fieldwork, and suck at paperwork and schedules. Is this why you wanna talk to me, sir?"

"No, not really. But if you could, give me a short list of guys you think would make an acceptable sergeant."

"Chang, Cooper, or Reed. Short enough?" Jack snickered.

"Yep. Damn short." Davis cleared his throat, then leaned back. "Okay, let's discuss Brooks. I know all about IA's ... let's call it exploratory review of Brooks. Roni and I've discussed it, and I just wanted you to know you can say no—I mean, if you'd prefer to stay away from Brooks."

Jack's lips pressed into a line. "I can handle it, Davis."

"It's your history with Brooks. I'm worried—"

Jack cut in, leaning forward slightly. "Think about it, Chief. This history would've never existed if brass hadn't moved him to Homicide. Thing is, he came in hating my guts, but no one knows why. Do you?"

"No, I don't."

"What difference does our past make, then? Brooks hates me now, and if this presumed inquiry doesn't settle in his favor, well, I'd say he'll have a valid excuse to hate me."

"You could end up in someone's crosshairs, and you—" Davis began.

"Aw, Davis, come on. Cut the bullshit. I'm fine as far as Brooks is concerned. Roni isn't trying to handle me anymore. When are you gonna stop?"

Locked in a dead stare, Yao studied Jack's face, noting the determination and grit etched there. He'd treated Jack with kid gloves after Gretchen's murder. He remembered the coldcocking of Brooks then Jack's walking away from his career to drown in the bottle.

The worry he'd carried then lingered now, tightening in his chest. He didn't want his detective heading down another gloomy trail—and he feared Brody Brooks was the gateway to that dark path.

Locked in a dead stare, Yao studied Jack's set jaw and steady gaze. Few men could hold that kind of focus; determination and grit radiated from him.

"Detective, you shouldn't have anyone trying to handle you, including me. Just watch your step and do thorough work, because I know Brooks, and he won't play fair."

"Understood. You ever miss it, Chief?"

"In the field?"

"Yeah."

"Sometimes. Other days I wanna retire before I am an old geezer. You gonna call it quits after thirty?"

"Are you, Davis?"

"Unlike you boys, my job doesn't put me in harm's way, so I plan on doing thirty, maybe even forty. You?"

"Maybe thirty. Might even open a PI service. I enjoy working and solving things."

"Jack, you'd make a spectacular PI."

Jack rose, hand reaching for the door. "Just don't tell Dawson."

Yao leaned his forearms on the desk, frowning. "Why not?"

"He might want to work for me." Jack left the COD laughing behind the closed door.

Dawson. Oh crap. He was gonna ask what Yao wanted—what was he gonna tell him?

13

His boots tramped down the concrete steps of the stairwell. He entered the sixth floor and strode to the breakroom. Just as he pushed the door open, he found himself face–to-face with Veronica Justice. His mind had been on other things; her sudden appearance startled him, and they almost collided nose to nose.

"Lord, Cap!"

Roni jumped, sloshing her coffee. "Crap."

"Sorry." He stepped aside and grabbed a napkin for her.

"S'okay, no harm. Get your coffee. Then a word in my office."

Another private word. Terrific.

———

Seated, sipping the deep brown sludge they called coffee, he waited. Roni was always pleasant; however, today her mood seemed worried.

She took a sip and placed the chipped ceramic HPD mug on a cork coaster. "Coffee's bitter. Thought we could replace our Mr. Coffee with a Keurig. Pods are pricey though, and regular Folgers are sold in three-pound cans, also in unique blends. Was a dumb idea, cuz we don't require special—we just need caffeine."

Jack swallowed, cutting his eyes up at her. "You brought me in here to discuss coffee?"

"Just commenting."

"You asked Elijah Vance about Dawson?"

"He's out of town. Chat with anyone on the list yet?"

"Whitmire. Planned to meet with Yardley; can't find Coolidge."

"And?"

"Still working on it, Cap."

Her frowning face tilted; her eyes narrowed. "Part of the procedure, Detective, is keeping me updated."

He studied her face. "I realize I'm supposed to keep you updated, so when I have something significant to report, you'll be the first to know."

A stale moment passed. Roni relaxed her upper body, propping her right forearm on the desk. "Don't leave me hanging for long, Detective West, because Eli Vance is going to be breathing down my neck. Got it?"

"Yes, ma'am, and uh, I didn't mean to sound disrespectful. It's just ... well, got nothing of real importance to report."

"No apology needed, Jack. I realize you're doing all you can with what little you've got. Just keep at it."

"I will." He stood, taking a step toward the door. He turned back. "Oh, I'll say this though: Joan Whitmire can't stand Brooks."

"Ah, the list grows. Our little heated fracas bumped me right up there under your name." A smile appeared on her face. "Alright, get to work."

He glanced back. "Closed, or open?"

"Closed. Thanks."

In the corridor, Jack twisted on his heels, walking to the other end, making his way back to his desk. He was ready to face Dawson Luck, his personal Spanish Inquisition.

"PERFECT TIMING, JACK. LET'S go."

Jack's forehead puckered. "Where're we going?"

"Crime scene, idiot. It's a component of our job."

"Yeah, Lucky, you donkey's ass, but where?" Jack grabbed his suit jacket, following him through the hallway.

"River Oaks, burglary case."

"We're not Robbery."

"Don't matter, we've been called to the scene. Don't know what's up," he huffed.

"Maybe they want our help cuz we're so good." Jack's eyes bugged.

"Or how about this: it's because I worked robbery in Arizona. They need my help, and not yours, for a change."

Jack's shoulders quivered as he held back a chuckle. "That would be a change."

Dawson Luck turned and mouthed the words *Fuck off*, with a smile.

Jack knew about the burglary cases. Gilly had mentioned it, and this was his chance to work with Robbery—which meant he'd be in Brooks' department, closer to his other investigation: Brooks. He scowled. Brooks could put the kibosh on him being there, couldn't he? Nah, he couldn't. He'd overheard Roni telling Brooks he couldn't dictate which detective worked within her division. This was her squad, not his. Perfect.

An evil smile played on Jack's lips as Lucky trotted ahead into the parking garage. Brooks would blow a gasket, and he'd be powerless to act. Jack loved it, knowing he could hold his stare longer. Brody Brooks always blinked first, never realizing what hit him.

DAWSON WAITED UNTIL THEY were three blocks from the station before speaking.

"I'm going to ask even if you say you can't tell me. What'd Yao want?" He blinkered, turning as the light changed.

"Wondered when I planned on trying to make sergeant. I told him I hated paperwork, and creating work schedules."

"Hmm. What else?"

"Asked me if I could give him a list of dicks who'd make suitable sergeants." Jack, thankful he wasn't lying, thought this might satisfy Lucky.

"I'm gonna leave it for now, but it ain't everything, is it?"

"No, it's not. Before you get your big honker so far out of joint you've got it sitting in your left ear—just listen." He stared at Luck's profile.

Dawson gave him a sharp side-glance; his lips bowed in a ghoulish way.

"I talked to Roni. She promised to see what she could do, since it's not my call. Crap, Dawson, I trust you with my life, and would take a freaking bullet for you, but damn, I'm not the boss."

"Like I don't?" Luck rushed his next sentence. "Forget it, cuz I know you know I do, and I should stop bitching." His face softened a smidge, gaze steady ahead. Traffic on Allen Parkway bottled up. They hadn't even made it to Shepherd Drive.

He stared at Jack when they stopped at the next red light. "Jack, yeah, I realize you trust me, and I could help. I ain't a dummy."

"No, you aren't. Let's just see what happens next. Deal? Hey, gonna be fun working with Robbery again," he said, trying to lighten the atmosphere.

"Not if Brooks is gonna be hollering your name, pretending to be a bullhorn every second of the day."

"Yep, that'd be a drag. No, wait. We have firsthand knowledge Brooks never helps his detectives."

"That's a valid point," Lucky said, focusing on traffic.

THE HOUSE WAS ON Inwood Drive, where large homes backed up to the River Oaks Country Club. The club featured a golf course and multiple tennis courts; River Oaks National Tennis Tournaments had been held since 1931 on their famous red clay courts. Old money abounded in this locality. Jack never aspired to be a country club member. With his simple style and being a regular Joe, he'd never fit into this snobbish atmosphere.

Not all people with wealth were snobs, he reasoned. Memories of Shayla Stegwig Burnett and the double homicide they'd solved floated up. Shayla, not one ounce of snobbery in her demeanor, took everything, and her brother received life in prison. Funny, she'd not cared about the money. She'd have given it back to have her mother alive.

Dawson noted Jack's sudden melancholy. "Thinking about Shayla Burnett, Jack?"

"Yeah, a first-rate woman. Money or not. Hope we're not headed to homes with haughty people peering down their long, rich noses at us."

"Well, fear not, my friend. I got a nose to out-nose all of 'em." Dawson jerked his face upward to bring up his huge schnozzola, sniffing with an evil, twisted laugh. Jack shook his head, rolling his eyes.

Lucky slow-drove past a marked blue-and-white Ford Taurus Interceptor, the department's new ride. Behind it, on the front walk, sat an older black Chevy Caprice. Jack was familiar with its grill mounting and knew the blue and red flashing lights were an aftermarket addition. He motioned to the older auto. "Looks like what the jokers from Robbery drive."

Dawson glanced sideways. "Can't tell who's driving what these days. Could be anybody. I hope it's Salato and Gilly."

"Me too."

Up the driveway sat a Chevy Tahoe, marked "Crime Scene Unit." Luck pulled past it, parking at the curve of the horseshoe-shaped, tree-lined driveway and cutting the engine.

Out of the car, Jack slipped on his dark sports jacket, checked his weapon, patted his pocket for his notebook and pen, and looked at his badge clipped to his belt. Dawson Luck followed a similar routine, checking his hair in the side mirror. Jack smiled.

Walking up to the steps of the exaggerated front porch, Jack took in the showy flower vases, noting the flowers stood upright, their petals unfurled, scents filling the air. The hedges were all pruned with perfect symmetry; the lawn cut to a height suggesting heavenly plushness. It would look like a blanket of vibrant green once the colors darkened. Daily watering, he thought, was a must—but when you were affluent, others turned a blind eye.

Deep in thought, he couldn't shake the realization that some members of the police department leveraged their authority just like the rich leveraged financial status. This was how they escaped accountability—by exploiting the badge, just as the wealthy exploited their money.

14

"NAME, BADGE NUMBER?" THE uniform at the front recorded the info on the incident log.

Jack glanced at his badge. "Officer Stanley, who's here from Robbery?"

"Gillespie and Salato, sir."

Penny Salato strolled down the long foyer, her badge on a lanyard around her neck, her game face on. She greeted them. "Thanks for coming."

"Detective Salato." Jack shook her hand.

Dawson stuck his hand out next. "Gillespie in the back?"

"Yeah, taking information from the housekeeper."

"Got a dead body," Jack peered at Dawson, "or y'all need Luck's robbery experience from hotter-than-Texas Arizona?"

Penny smirked. "Well, Dawson, if the dicks in Arizona have better ideas how to solve a robbery, we're willing to listen. Come on, follow me."

They followed, neither protesting about the view. Not the view of the luxurious home, but the sumptuous swish of Penny's shapely hips in snug jeans belted with a thick brown belt. Her forest green t-shirt was tucked in, her dark hair up in a ponytail, and she wore a ball cap touting the HPD Robbery Division. Her Nike running shoes made a soft, padded sound on the expensive Calacatta Gold marble tile of the capacious front foyer. She led them through an enormous living area to a rear doorway opening onto a small garden veranda.

Craig Gillespie handed his card to the terrified housekeeper after pocketing his notebook, stepping up to the group. "Hey fellas, nice of y'all to join us."

"Gilly." Jack outstretched his hand. "Nice to see ya."

Luck stepped in, shook his hand, and continued right to it. "Why we here?"

"Man, Dawson, you dive right in, don'tcha?" Craig reacted.

"Yeah. That's what we get paid for. So?"

A sigh left Craig, and he beckoned them to follow. "Over here." He led them out into the private garden area. One table and four chairs sat under a retractable awning. The metal table was positioned on a dark gray-and-black ribbed rug, and an overturned chair and shattered glass fragments were scattered around. Gilly strode around the mess and pointed. "Blood."

Jack stepped around, careful not to touch anything or get his feet near what could be a homicide scene. "No corpse, weapon, or shell casings. We know for certain this is blood?"

"CSU did an onsite test; it's blood alright. And yeah, no weapon or casings," Craig supplied.

"How long has that been there? Can we find out?" Dawson leaned in, taking a gander.

"Suzy Wong said CSU has a test called, uh, Raman Spectroscopy. And no, not Ramen noodles, Dawson, in case you're gonna make a joke." Gilly gave him the eye.

"Wasn't gonna say a word, I swear, but now you mention it," Dawson groused.

"Anyhow," Craig went on, "it can date two-year-old bloodstains."

Jack looked back at Penny. "Okay, so we assume it's one of the owners' blood on the rug?"

She shrugged. "Don't know. The housekeeper said her employers are divorcing; they fight a lot."

"So let me get this straight. You guys are called because of a bloodstain, and Homicide didn't receive the call?"

"No, Jack, for gosh sakes. The housekeeper, Mrs. Valdez, called about a break-in. The rear entrance was ajar when she arrived. She thought someone hadn't pulled it closed, but no one was home. It didn't worry her, since the employers have a fortified fence enclosing the entire back area, and you need a code to enter. The front door was still double-bolted from the inside, and even with a key, you can't unlock it. Gotta go through the back gate, use a code, then another code for the back door."

Jack's eyes widened. "Sounds like Fort Knox, for crying out loud. So again, why did she call you?"

Penny's hands moved to her hips. "Lady said she ran around checking. Noticed some stuff out of place, and missing items."

"What went missing? I see a television and stereo system still in the far corner." Lucky focused on the most profitable looted items.

"No big-ticket items. Diminutive items, yet valuable. Ming vases, solid silver flatware, high-end jewelry, and—"

Jack cut her off. "How does she know what's disappeared?"

"Mrs. Valdez's been here for years. The lady of the house leaves her jewelry lying around upstairs in her dressing area, doesn't bother with the safe. The couple has separate dressing rooms; the mister leaves his expensive cufflinks and watches out too. They have an alarm system; seems the thieves bypassed it."

"So, this blood minus a body, or anything, and you call us because you think someone—like the owners—set up burglary to cover a homicide?" Jack eyed the place.

"Hey, weirder things have happened. We can't locate the missus or the mister. No one's answering their cells, neither is at work, and no one's seen them for ten days." Penny, hands still on her hips, surveyed the small, well-kept garden.

Jack's detective brain went into gear. "We'll put out an APB for the owners. Gill, can you contact family members and employers? We'll help with the calls. Let's get some answers, then decide if it's a homicide or missing persons." He scratched at his chin. "Penny, contact CSU to verify if the blood is human."

An incredulous expression crossed her face. "Ask if it's human? You think it isn't?"

"There's a dog bed." He pointed to the far corner. "Too large for a small breed, unless the pooch has claustrophobia. I'm betting it's the size of a small horse. Maybe their pet got injured. Not enough blood for a lifeless body. Only someone got hurt, no doubt. Several scenarios fit this scene."

The others turned to look. Indeed, the dog bed was massive. Penny moved over to see.

"Whatever the breed is, it sheds, and no dogs barked. None have been underfoot since we got here. So yeah, where's the dog?"

"Anyone else here other than the housekeeper?" Dawson went to the front door.

"No. They have grown kids who don't live here. Ms. Valdez said she, the cook, and the gardener had seven days off with pay. Mrs. Jessup texted her, asked if she could shampoo the upstairs carpets since no one would be home for the next seven or eight days, and she'd get a bonus," Craig supplied.

Lucky leaned against the interior doorjamb leading into the foyer. "If they're fighting all the time, maybe they're headed for a divorce. Did Mrs. Valdez mention they were selling the house?"

Penny paused a second before saying, "No, and we didn't ask, but could be. If they're planning to sell, best to get dog smell out of the carpets. I'll call her, ask about a dog."

"What we can tell you," Craig interjected, "is the area has become a target. Several unsolved burglaries. If this is a homicide with robbery, suspects have upped their game."

"Yeah. We gotta find these guys before someone's killed. Lucky and I will dig into the couple. Keep us updated." Saying goodbye, Jack waved to the two Robbery detectives, Salato and Gillespie, who waved back with a "See ya."

THE SEATBELT WARNING BLEEPED as Luck reached the first stop sign. He glanced at Jack. "Buckle your seatbelt, dude."

"Sorry." Jack clicked it; the dinging stopped.

"Yeah. I'm gonna order a couple pizzas to be delivered."

"Lucky, no need. We aren't staying too late."

Dawson again cut his eyes over to Jack. "It's four-thirty, close to dinnertime, so I'm ordering an extra-large pizza. You don't hafta eat any. I'll keep the rest in the fridge, warm it later. Why you in a rush? Hot date?"

If Jack said yes, he'd be ecstatic. Lucky thought, ever since Gretchen, Jack acted like a celibate hermit, never bringing up dating or anything along those lines.

"No, don't have a date. Can't do too much at this hour, and I wanna relax. Maybe have a couple of beers." He paused, then added, "Considered getting a dog. What do you think?"

"A dog? You're kidding, right? You can't have a dog, West." Lucky listed the reasons Jack should forgo a pup: never home while working a case, no time to play with it, housebreaking takes effort, and a companion dog would double the work.

"Nah, a pup wouldn't match my lifestyle," Jack commented as they pulled into the underground parking at HQ. "Since we can't speak with the owners, let's do background checks and criminal history checks on the owners-slash-victims. Whattaya say, pard?"

"Right behind you, Jack, just like always."

After the pizza arrived, Jack relented, eating three pieces. Dawson, starving, ate the rest as they pressed on.

15

After the pizza arrived, Jack, looking through their orders, Dawson at the ... no, they passed on—

"MY NECK IS ACHING. Think I'll call it a night. I need a hot shower, eat, and—"

Jack cut him short. "Dawson Luck, you ate over half a large pizza, buddy, and you're hungry?"

"I will be once I'm home. The pizza sucked—not enough meat, thin crust. I have to have real food and some solid hours of sleep. We've got leftover stew and cornbread. I'll see you in the morning, say sevenish?"

"Sounds like a plan."

Dawson logged off, piled his reports on his desk, locked it (as did Jack), and stood. "You coming, bud?"

"You go on ahead. I'm printing copies of these forms. Our printer's on the fritz, so I'll send them to five, go get 'em, and head out."

"Yep," Dawson said, holstering his weapon as he headed to the exit.

If Jack could've seen his partner's face, he would've noticed the scowl lines and suspicious look in his eyes. What in the hell is Jack pulling? The printer was fine—he'd used it that morning. Why go to five? Unless...? His glower softened a fraction. Was it Penny? Did they have an intimate tête-à-tête? Penny Salato and Jack—nah, Dawson didn't see it, but that didn't mean it wasn't happening. It didn't involve him, though. Jack dating someone at work? Not a smart plan. Gossip said she and Craig Gilly were an item, albeit both denied it. Smokescreen, a diversionary maneuver—this was the word for the week. Could this be a smokescreen? Dawson intended to find out.

In the parking structure, he pulled out and drove to the upper level, parking next to a cargo van, five spots from where Jack was. He cut the engine, took out his cell, and dialed Viv's number.

"Hey baby," her tinkling voice sounded.

"Hiya Viv, you still at work?"

"I have more to do. Another hour. Why, you headed home? I thought you guys caught a fresh case?"

"We've started investigating the victims, poked into all the usual stuff. Not much we can do until tomorrow."

"So, are you on your way home?"

"Uh, about that ... no, I'm on a secret mission."

Vivian laughed, but when Dawson didn't, her tone changed. "You're serious, aren't you, babe? What's going on?"

With a brief explanation, he gave her little detail, only what she needed to know. Dawson was worried about Jack; keeping secrets between partners was a no-no.

"If he doesn't want you involved, Dawson, and he finds you lurking around, invading his personal space, do you think he'll be okay with this?"

"Viv, there are tons of what-if scenarios. One I can't ignore: what if Jack gets into hot water and needs backup? What happens next—him getting hurt or worse?"

He could hear her exhale before responding. "Dawson Luck, be careful you don't get yourself into a jam, you know—"

"Vivian Marie Luck," he interjected, "Jack would never do something dishonest or immoral. As his partner—no, scratch that, his friend first, colleague second—I'll have his six no matter what."

He could hear her smile over the phone after a pregnant pause.

"Are you smiling, Viv? Did you just set me up?"

"I did, and you took the line and ran, my sweet, big-nosed, big-footed man. Dawson Daniel Luck, it's why I love you—your big heart, your loyalties ... oh, and because of your enormous feet."

A robust laugh popped out, and he said goodnight, adding that he loved her. Vivian replied with "be careful" and "see you when I see you." They ended the call just in time—Jack opened his truck door, got in, and cranked it. Dawson waited until Jack reached the lower level, then followed.

QUINN'S CROWD OF MIXED patrons was booming. By blending in with a diverse group—men and women, professionals and laborers—he could watch Jack without arousing suspicion. Dawson opted for a table toward the back, under subdued lighting, giving him a view of Jack and an unknown man.

As people milled around—from the darts to the bar—it kept him hidden from Jack's direct line of sight. The spot gave him a visual advantage, though he couldn't hear them. Too bad he never learned to read lips. Alright, Plan B. He turned on his mobile camera, flash off, and snapped a series of pictures of Jack and his companion.

Ten minutes later, he caught a break. Jack went to the men's room. His companion rose, ordered two more beers, and walked past. Dawson got a full-face shot: perfect.

After buying a short beer to avoid looking odd, Dawson noted that Jack and the older gentleman had ordered full meals. Once the server set their meals on the table, they dug in, giving Dawson the opportunity to slip out unnoticed.

In his car, he switched on the ignition, letting it idle in park. He stared through the windshield into the darkness, mind whirling.

An older gent, maybe in his sixties. Jack mentioned no older male friends. Lucky had never met all of Jack's friends, and why should he? But they'd been riding together long enough now, and Jack was usually open—so why the secrecy now?

Okay, Jack had a thing. He wasn't prone to discussing women in his life, but this was a man. Could it be a relative? But Jack only spoke of his mom and dad, never any other kin. Scratch the family idea.

What niggled at him most was Jack's behavior two years back, working under the radar on the triple homicide. Could this be another case? Another secret assignment? Again, sworn to secrecy?

16

"First time here. Decent food." Gary Yardley had another taste of his Reuben and, after, a healthy swig of beer.

Jack nodded, chewing, glancing around Quinn's, but he hadn't seen Grady in the vast crowd. Maybe he wasn't here tonight, but knowing the cagey fart he was, Quinn was most likely blending in.

"Yeah, started coming here a while back." Jack didn't elaborate—the place he'd come after Gretchen's death had become a sanctuary, and Grady Quinn a new friend.

"So, you retired and moved to Galveston?" Jack took another bite of his Swiss mushroom burger, wiping off the juices that dribbled onto his chin.

"Retirement wasn't for me. Drove me stir crazy in a week. I'm doing freelance security for an international cruise line and work some with the Port Authorities."

"Huh, free travel. Nice perk."

"When I travel it's never for relaxation." Gary swallowed the last bite of his sandwich. "But it can be fun at the various stops if I've got time."

"Eastern and Western Caribbean tours?"

"Meh, visiting the same places becomes boring. I work for international cruise ships—Greece, Japan, Europe. Headed to China next."

"And you live in Galveston?" Jack asked, puzzled. He knew none of these voyages departed from there.

"I can fly to the ships, so no biggie."

"Still married, Gary?" Jack's question was more intrusive, but it didn't phase the other man.

"Widower. Wife passed fifteen years ago. Never remarried. My two sons live in Galveston with their families, another reason to home base here. Jack, why did you call me? Can't be about my personal life."

Yardley's eyes opened wider as he raised his mug and sipped.

"Brody Brooks." Jack watched Gary closely, searching for a reaction.

Gary set the mug down with purpose, wiped his mouth with a napkin, shoved his plate to the center, and propped himself on his elbows.

"West, I'm no rat. Back in our day, no one—no one—crossed that blue line. But..." His palm lifted, signaling Jack to hold back. "...times have changed. A corrupt cop was a problem even back then. We got away with stuff we shouldn't have, and it wasn't right."

"How long did you ride together?" Jack steered the conversation back to Brooks.

"Two years. I can only tell you what I know. Everything else is hearsay."

"Why stop riding with him?"

"Got capped in the knee and assigned to a desk afterward."

"Take a bullet on the job?"

Yardley snickered. "Yeah, of all things, my partner shot me."

"Brooks shot you?"

"Accident. They cleared Brooks of wrongdoing. Still working?"

Jack rubbed the back of his neck. "Yeah."

"Thought the old fart retired."

Jack didn't expound on Brooks' move from Robbery to Homicide and back. "Gary, you willing to tell me what you can about Brooks?"

"After the knee, I worked at a desk to put my twenty in, so never rode with him again. Not sure what I can tell you."

Jack drained the last of his second beer. "You familiar with Joan Whitmire, Sam Coolidge, or Sal Dellucci?"

Gary's head bobbed. "Sam, odd fella, okay cop. One day he quit. Kid had aptitude, but nobody knows why."

"Whitmire or Dellucci?"

"The woman, nah, didn't know her. Never had to ride with a female."

That phrase—*had to*—caught Jack's attention. Yardley sounded misogynistic.

"Sal Dellucci and Brooks; we called them the Siamese twins in blue." He snickered.

"Best buds, huh?" Jack thought anyone who liked Brooks was a sucker; Brooks having friends was unfathomable.

"What're you looking for, Jack?"

"Not sure, Yardley."

"Sounds like an investigation."

"Nah, it ain't," Jack lied. "Just gathering info. Wasn't told why. Sometimes people get vetted for advancement. Maybe that's it."

Yardley's eyes dropped. He picked up a small bit of french fry, squished it, and wiped it into a napkin. "Brooks was like us—working for a paycheck. Era of money and power."

"Why does that matter?" Jack crossed his arms.

Yardley snorted. "Money motivates people. Some fall into traps they can't untangle."

"Like?" Jack's eyes narrowed. No matter the amount offered, decent cops didn't get swayed. Was Gary implying Brooks might've been corrupt?

"Look, Jack. Power or money can drive men into darkness or an early grave." He stopped at Jack's look of horror. "In those days, coppers turned blind eyes to small stuff to earn a few extra bucks for the family. Nothing like murder or dealing drugs. If you want to know if guys like Brooks, Dellucci, even Coolidge, let some small crap slide for cash—they did. Hell, I even did some dumb stuff for extra dough, but nobody got hurt. Done."

"Cops on the take—ain't right. What if Brooks is still on a mob, gangster, or cartel payroll? I'm supposed to ignore it?"

"Aw, Jack, he ain't. Times changed. Get real."

"You think so? Seems people haven't changed much."

"Fine, dig. You'll uncover secrets. But be ready for consequences. Could spark a firestorm, maybe even within the entire police force."

"Noted. Following orders, nothing more."

"Why not leave it be? Tons of what-ifs."

Jack's eyes narrowed. "Like?"

"Oh, just thinking." Gary swirled the rest of his beer before draining it.

Jack's expression darkened. What was he hiding or implying, and who was he protecting? "I'm listening."

"Alright. What if stuff comes out, cases get tossed, the city sued, innocent people hurt, reputations ruined, tons of cash needed?"

"Yeah, I get it, Gary."

"You don't care though?"

"Oh, I care."

"But you gotta do the ethical thing, right?"

Jack turned it back on him. "You saying you'd look the other way, Yardley?"

A huffed laugh. "Don't know, Jack. Would have to consider consequences."

Yardley pulled out his wallet. Jack stopped him. "This one's on me."

"Thanks. Hope it works out without biting you. Me? I'd rather not get dragged through the porta-potty dumpsite, if you get my drift."

"Gary," Jack said, standing, "I'll try to keep the spotlight off you."

They walked outside under the dim neon lights of Quinn's.

"Word of advice?"

"Sure."

"Watch out for backlash. Could come your way digging into bygone years."

"I'm always watching. Safe travels on the ocean, Yardley."

"Roger that. See ya when I see ya."

YARDLEY WATCHED JACK AMBLE to his truck, wondering about his determination. Jack West. He'd been a cop years before this young fella reached Homicide. Homicide vets like Scarzzo, DeMitt, and Crane—all buddies of Frank Windom.

Gary sat in his car, hands on the wheel, staring into the darkness. Back then, he'd been an innocent kid, alone in Houston. You had to watch yourself because no one else would.

Jack West. Truth and justice? Or finger-pointing with revenge in mind? Past deeds couldn't be undone. Black or white. But Gary knew better. Sometimes black and white blurred into gray, dark or faint. Blurry lines caused problems. Straddling the fence meant risking your neck—or having someone break it for you. Plant your feet on one side, and you had to pick it. Some cops chose the wrong side.

JACK, HANDS IN POCKETS, head bent, walked to his truck. Would digging cause a tsunami the department couldn't recover from? How many years had officers been tangled in cover-ups, bribes, and payoffs? Officers once dedicated to law and order now hid behind uniforms and gold shields. Crooks—Wygant, Dellucci, Webb, Nichols—caught in the mess? Would he destroy people like Whitmire,

Jones, even Yardley? Who was Sam Coolidge? The man quit; no explanation. Jack's workload was heavy. Roni needed to be practical and let Luck help with Brooks.

———

DAWSON, PATIENT BUT TIRED, sat in his dark gray Nissan in a shadowed part of the lot, with a perfect view of the pub entrance. He could glimpse Jack and his dinner companion when they left. Photos would be useless if the guy wasn't in the facial recognition database; if so, he'd need the license plate.

Forty minutes passed. Jack exited with another man. They talked, shook hands, walked away separately. Dawson tracked the unknown male to his pickup. He braked for another car, giving Dawson time to get the plate.

Dawson reversed, shifted, and headed home. Tomorrow, when Jack was away from the squad room, he'd run facial recognition on the man. He hoped for a name, maybe other connections. Meanwhile, he turned to sports talk radio to take his mind off Jack while driving.

17

He hit send to transfer the photo to his computer, yawning. Dawson had trouble sleeping. He'd admit his anger outweighed his concern. Jack was an excellent cop and could handle most situations. But keeping secrets? Nope, not this time.

He entered his password. Next, he retrieved the picture from his email, saved it, and reopened it in the facial recognition program. After waiting for several minutes, nothing appeared.

"Well, crap." He lowered his voice, tapping his pencil. He then accessed DMV records using the plate number. Personal use, prohibited. Only this was for Jack. He'd worry about consequences later.

A green 2015 Nissan sedan and a prehistoric 1986 red Dodge Ram registered to Gary Yardley of Galveston, Texas. The old truck still running astonished him. He printed the name and his Galveston address down. Luck was seconds from opening the background checks program when Jace Severson's entrance startled him into closing it.

"Man, Luck, it's the butt crack of dawn."

"Getting a head start on the day." Dawson faked closing a file and said, "Fixin' to put on coffee. Want a cup?"

"Yeah, thanks."

Jace Severson's muscle-bound arms were encased in a crisp light blue button-up shirt. A tie dangled around his neck, not yet on or knotted, and a navy-colored sports coat was draped over his free arm while his other hand held his leather briefcase. His longish hair was slicked back and pulled in a tight ponytail held by a clear rubber band.

On his feet, Dawson asked, "Why are you here early, Jace, and dressed up?"

"We're meeting with the DA to present our very circumstantial case; and we, more appropriately, Xi, decided it'd be best to dress for success."

"Circumstantial?"

Jace dropped the briefcase next to his chair, hung the coat on the back, and plopped in his seat. "We can't find the murder weapon. We have no prints or DNA; but hey, otherwise we got the pissant and one eyewitness. Know how far that gets us, right? If they don't bring a case against him, the shitbag's gonna walk and get away with killing two older women after pistol whipping them, all for a measly two hundred dollars."

"No cameras caught this?"

"One camera, but the angle didn't catch a face, and the alleyway was dark. The witness is an old homeless fellow. He'll take a beating on the witness stand. The gun's unaccounted for; betcha a million the asshat dumped it in the bayou, but the slugs were found and ballistics matched them to the revolver used in another crime—and it's unregistered. Xi and I figured someone stole it, but the owner never reported a theft. This is a huge cluster. This man's a turd bastard. He'll be back out there doing it again. Pisses the hell outta me."

"Yeah, me too."

"Well, this buttface has a record. Juvie, sealed, and two assaults, one with a deadly weapon. Did a nickel. Got out in two for excellent behavior. This always amazes me; they are model prisoners and as soon as they're uncaged, act like uncivilized thugs. Know what I think?"

Dawson had a puzzled expression when he said, "That I should make a fresh pot of coffee?"

"I wanna know what you think, Jace." Xi Chang's voice sounded out from the back.

Jace increased his volume. "Don't have to tell you, 11, we're of the same mind, but I'll say it again for Lucky's benefit. I think we should build an island prison on Snake Island; let all of them bastards try to escape, and nature can devour them."

Xi strolled by, placing his jacket on the chair, and directed his gaze towards Jace. "Last month, you suggested we should buy the Galapagos Islands to do this."

"Snakes would be better guards, especially the golden viper."

"Snakes, uh-uh, no way in hell." His voice bounced off the ceiling, and his boots tread without sound on the grayish Berber carpet, seconds behind Xi Chang.

"Heya, Jack."

"Jace, Xi, you boys look spiffy. Y'all got a date with the DA?"

"Uh-huh, Luck can tell ya all about it. We gotta go meet with Roni first. Let's get our ducks in a row, Xi, and start the coffee Lucky was promising me."

Chang grabbed his soft-sided leather case. "Right behind you, 7. See you fellas."

Jack said *adios*, booted his laptop awake, and waited.

"Want coffee?"

"Yeah, Luck, are you buying this time?"

"Ha ha ha. Be back in second. Gonna make an extra pot. I've seen Jace's coffee mug, the doofus dumps half a pot into one mug."

Jack typed in his password. "Make it strong."

"You bet." Lucky left, frustrated. His plan to dig into this Gary Yardley had to be postponed.

THEY'D WORKED ALL MORNING, not many words exchanged. Jack never minded not hearing Luck's incessant chatter. He did wonder if Dawson was okay, though. It wasn't like his partner not to be a chattering monkey.

Jack stood, stretching his full frame. "How about I make a run for a couple of Antone's', and coffee—Starbucks—my treat?"

Dawson stated without looking, "Make mine a Columbian, venti. Get me two subs, no chips—have a bag of Fritos stashed in the breakroom. I'll fetch 'em."

"Perfect, see ya in twenty." Jack darted out and, once Dawson knew he was gone, he opened the program they employed for background checks. He keyed in Yardley's name, street address, and date of birth, and included the guy's driver license number. Dawson crossed his fingers once he punched Enter. Not having his Social Security number wasn't a big deal; he wasn't hiring him. If the guy had other addresses, or aliases, an SSN trace would be helpful.

His computer began searching, and he started tapping his foot. Jack wouldn't walk in on him, but if someone else did, such as Captain Justice, she might grill him. Heaven forbid Skip Webb or Earl Nichols were walking behind him because they'd be nosy. Both his feet were tapping, as the program was slow to populate. He glanced behind him. As he looked back at the screen, he wondered if this fella even existed because nothing was populating. He was about to quit when a page blinked and the message: *Your report is ready* popped up. Dawson hit transfer, downloading the information into a printable PDF, then delivered it to a private file on his desktop and signed out of the program. After this, he opened the file, selected Print, and made copies for his eyes only. He made sure not to leave it on his computer screen, in case anyone came snooping.

A smirk flitted across his mug when he got to the printer. Same printer on the fritz. Or so Jack said. What an out-and-out lie. Maybe Jack had a viable reason. Maybe not. He just knew Jack was hiding something. He carried the printout to his cubical and read.

Gary James Yardley retired from Houston PD twenty years ago, almost to the date. Once upon a time, he'd been an HPD patrol officer with several accommodations. Excellent credit rating. No bankruptcies, no liens, his license to carry up-to-date, and he held a PI license.

"Hmm," Lucky spoke under his breath, "maybe he works in the private sector." He glanced at his birth year again. Yardley would turn sixty-five this year, retired when he was forty—twenty-four years ago. Guy wasn't too ancient, but he'd been kinda young to retire, though he'd put in his twenty. Dawson understood some folks were susceptible to burnout, and this might have been Yardley's case. He read on.

An incident report revealed someone shot Yardley in the knee in 1995. Dawson's eyes widened as he read. *In an incident unrelated to a case, Officer Brody Brooks' firearm discharged inside the station locker room, shooting Patrol Officer Gary Yardley in the patella. As Patrol Office Brooks unstrapped his gun, removing it from his holster, it discharged; ricocheting, the bullet bounced off a metal locker, catching Officer Yardley in the left kneecap. This accidental shooting prompted an internal investigation. After interviews with fellow officers present, the internal investigation report stated there was no horseplay and no heated words; it was a bizarre incident no one could've foreseen. Patrol Officer Brody Dean Brooks' firearm was sent in for a thorough inspection. Conclusion: the pistol's safety malfunctioned, causing a hairpin trigger when grasped just right. Office Yardley, taken to Hermann Hospital, underwent surgery to repair his shattered kneecap and soft tissue damage.*

Dawson read on. *Yardley spent several weeks in the hospital and months in physical therapy. Officer Yardley would no longer be fit for street patrol because of his injury and he opted out of disability, staying on in the capacity of desk work.* A side note stated Yardley was lucky he hadn't lost his leg.

Brooks shot his partner in the knee, and they cleared the bastard? Dawson scoffed. Brooks. The guy was still dangerous. Hairpin trigger, my fat Aunt Bee. Only thing he considered hairpin trigger these days was the man's actions and words. Luck leaned his head back, looking at the ceiling, wondering if Yardley knew Frank Windom, and if this was why Jack contacted him. Nah, Frank had been dead for almost eighteen years. He exhaled, sticking the report on Yardley in a folder, dropping it in his bottom drawer, shoving it to the far rear, and sliding the drawer closed just as the door screeched and the sounds of feet plodded toward him.

"Subs and hot coffee." Jack set them on Lucky's desk. "Where're the Fritos?"

"Um, forgot, I'll get 'em."

"No problem, I'll start without ya." Jack watched his goofy partner mosey to the door, heading to the breakroom, his head hanging with no zip to his step. Lucky wasn't acting himself the past couple of days. His partner was in a funk. Jack was sure Dawson sensed a secret, and that his droopy partner felt left outta the loop.

Jack spent this time to call Lamont Jones.

The phone rang in his ear several times and he was just ready to disconnect when a fellow answered, winded, saying, "Hello."

"Jones?"

"Yeah, yeah, hold on, let me catch my breath a minute."

"Sure." Jack sat, waiting on his end, and he listened as the man chugged water.

"Sorry, you caught me on the treadmill, finishing up my run."

"You Lamont Jones?"

"Yeah, who are you?"

"Detective Jack West, Houston Homicide, and to ease your mind, just need to talk."

Jones' eyes puckered. "About?"

"Was wondering if we could meet somewhere, talk in person?"

Lamont, being the suspicious type, was all, "You could be lying."

Jack puffed into the mouthpiece. "Brody Brooks. You were his TO, right?"

"Yeah, so?"

"Frank Windom, you knew him too?"

"Again I say, 'So?'."

"I was his partner in Homicide for two before he bought it with a heart attack. Now, do you believe I am who I say I am?"

The phone pressed to the older man's ear. "You wanna meet?"

"Yep, Quinn's pub, ever been there?"

"Nope, never been. Text me the address. When?"

"Tomorrow night, eightish. If I can't make it, I'll call." Jack hung up, texted the info.

On the other side of town, Lamont took a towel and wiped off his sweaty neck and his cell phone. Why did an active detective wanna talk with him?

18

BACK FROM THE FACILITIES, Dawson began his search through a list of residents in the neighborhood who'd been robbed, and all the outside vendors each homeowner used—from catering companies to exterminators—trying to make any connections.

Jack's fingers drummed atop the heap of papers, a muffled thud only he heard. Hands on the rim of the desk, he pushed away and stood.

"Hey, I'm going to Five. Get the inside scoop on the other robberies those guys have been working, see if they have a theory we haven't thought of, then drive to the hole-in-the-wall burger joint, grab us greasy cheeseburgers and garlic fries, my treat."

Luck's eyes shifted to his cell propped in a business card holder. Three twenty-eight.

"Cool. And buy Otis Spunkmeyer cookies—oatmeal raisin, uh, and sugar."

"Sure." A grin flickered across Jack's face. Whenever food was in the mix—free food to boot—Dawson Luck was amicable. One day that might change, but for now, Jack rolled with the flow, grabbed his keys and phone, took his pistol out of his desk compartment, secured it, and headed to the stairwell.

———

THE DOOR ON THE side swung open. Jack's fake ostrich-skin boots emitted an inaudible cushioned noise as he stepped inside the noisy Robbery unit. Everyone was there, working, taking calls, or yakking.

A light tap on her shoulder made Penny jerk around in a flash, ready to wallop him.

"Hey hey—what the heck, Penny? Why are you jumpy?"

"Oh, it's you, Jack. I thought it was—well, never mind. Guys have been effing playing jokes on me. What are you doing here?"

Jack pointed to an empty chair.

"Sure, have a seat. I'm not busy, just resting my laurels." She smirked.

"Holy cow, what's stuck in your craw? I came to talk with y'all about the case. Heck, I ain't here to gossip—uh, unless you've got any juicy tidbits you can share." His forehead arched up and down.

"Maybe I do, maybe I don't."

"Care to explain?"

"Means we should talk, but not now. What about the case?"

"Get prints and camera activity?"

"We've got nada, not one usable print. Camera footage wasn't worth a damn. With these two missing..." She held her hands palms up with a shrug.

"Can you think of any similarities? Or why it is your perps never pinch large electronics—laptops, stereos, nothing?"

"No, none."

Craig Gilly walked up and took his seat across from Penny, giving Jack a look.

"Hey, you here slumming again, or buying us dinner tonight?"

Jack stuck out his hand. "Nah, just getting info on your cases, which could help with our murder."

"Right now, we've asked our CIs to keep ears to the ground for anyone looking to sell or fence higher-ticketed items." Gilly rifled through notes while Penny and Jack brainstormed.

A booming voice cut through the air, its owner unseen, but Jack recognized that bellow anywhere: Brooks.

"What the hell? West, what're you doing here again? Don't you ever work in your department? Should I ring your captain and file a complaint?"

Jack's middle finger shot up as he stood with his back to Brooks, eyeballs rolling. Penny fought back a giggle at the sight.

He turned, face devoid of expression. "No, sir, unnecessary. I am here on official police business. It concerns the robbery your detectives and I are working on. Do you mind butting out? We're trying to work."

Brooks' face reddened as he lifted his fat belly, hiked his chest, and gritted his teeth.

"West, you are an insubordinate detective—"

Jack butted in. "Why thank you, Commander. That's the first time you've inserted the words 'detective' and 'West' in the same sentence. Excellent progress. As for everything else, call Captain Justice if you wish, but she told her detectives to play nice with all departments," he paused, "even yours."

He rounded to Gilly and Penny. "If you find any connections, call me. Or next time, walk upstairs, where everyone is welcomed with open arms—unlike your department." His eyes shot over to Brooks with a steely glare. "Commander."

Jack spun on a dime and strolled to the rear stairs. He was looking forward to meeting the guy who had been Brody's field training officer. Maybe Lamont could tell him what made Brooks ... Brooks. The fat SOB.

PENNY STOPPED IN THE stairwell of the fourth floor, pulled out her cell, punched the number, and waited.

On the other end, a voice sounded. "Sparks."

"It's Penny. Got a minute?"

"Sure, uh, give me a minute." Eight seconds later, she was back.

"What's happening, girl?" Katherine grabbed a cup, poured the last dregs of coffee from the pot, and sat in the breakroom, facing the exit. One sip and she pushed the cup away. She detested burned coffee.

"I think Jack is watching Brooks."

"What makes you think so?"

"Because it's peculiar how he keeps coming to Five so often these days."

"You told him anything?"

"Sparky," she exhaled, reverting to the other woman's nickname, "I wouldn't, not without talking to you first." There was a pause. She spoke again. "This situation is tricky for Jack, and it's best if he stays out of it."

"If he's watching Brooks, he's involved." Katherine frowned into the phone.

"Maybe, or he just enjoys coming to Five to aggravate the old goat."

"Penny, whatever you do, watch your back."

"You know I will. Okay, gotta go. Craig's waiting for me."

"Sure, talk later."

Katherine Sparks stuffed her mobile device in her front pocket. She detested Brooks, same as Penny did. He never mixed well with his women officers; he was a chauvinistic creep. Unauthorized videotaping, lord. She felt her stomach lurch. This was her private Watergate. The only other person who knew her secret was Penny Salato.

She rested with her back to the door, hands flat on the countertop, eyes closed, until she heard the breakroom door creak open.

Lieutenant Wilson Deeks stepped in. "Hiya, Sparks. We have any fresh coffee? Need a jolt."

Katherine blew out a long breath and turned, putting a smile on her face. "About to make a fresh pot if you wanna stick around."

"Yeah, I need the jolt." Lieutenant Deeks leaned against the counter, watching her go about making coffee. She hadn't looked like she was ready to put on a pot. She looked distressed, but he didn't pry.

After pouring water into the Mister Coffee and hitting Brew, she smiled and decided they needed small talk to fill the awkward silence.

"Hey, LT. You gonna strut your stuff again one day and rock the streets with your ruby red lips and high heels?"

"I don't know, Sparks. I am one hella woman when I'm in drag—I put the rest of you gals to shame—it's sorta embarrassing."

What a way to start a conversation, but it worked. They gabbed about how his undercover sting had gone when he was the decoy, laughing while waiting for the coffee to brew.

19

LAMONT JONES, A SLENDER Black male, six-foot-three, boasting muscle mass men his age only dreamed of, leaned against the bar, sipping a Seven and Seven. When he saw Jack, he lifted his hand and waved.

"You Lamont Jones?"

"Yep, and you're West." He proffered a hand.

Jack reciprocated. "How'd you recognize me?"

"After our phone conversation, I looked into you."

Jack eyeballed him. Well-dressed, marked posture, muscular forearms and large hands. Tall—about two inches taller than Jack—and he was no slouch at six-foot-one. Jones carried a no-nonsense look even at his age, which Jack guessed was mid-to-late-sixties. He gave the distinct impression he'd have no problem kicking your ass and asking questions later.

"You still working—I mean, in the private sector?"

"Contract work. It's why I stay in shape." He lifted his glass, drained it, tapped the bar, asked for another, and looked at Jack. "What's your poison? I'm buying."

"Dark Guinness and Jägermeister. How about I spring for a double order of wings and fries. Okay with you?"

"Sure. Grab a stool, or you prefer a table?"

Jack scanned the restaurant. "Over there, okay?" He inclined his head. "Want to see who comes and goes."

Jones nodded. "I get you. Corner table works for me."

Seated, order placed, Jack remained silent. Lamont wasn't inquisitive. Since Jones didn't bombard him with questions, Jack wondered if he had any clue why they were meeting.

Lamont sipped his cocktail; his eyes roamed the pub. "Quinn's. Never knew it was here. Gotta remember this joint."

"You married, Lamont?"

"Used to be. Two wives, both passed."

Jack's lips curled upward. "Married to them one at a time?"

"Lordy, yes. Two of them at once might've killed me. Both were headstrong because I liked my ladies independent—because of my line of work. Never wanted a hanger-on-er, if you get my drift. You got a girl, West?"

"Used to." His tone held a lilt of sadness.

"I heard the story, man. Sorry." Lamont raised his glass. "To your girl. May she rest in peace." He paused, bowed his head, then knocked back the rest of his booze, looking at Jack. "Word travels in our world. Heard about the punch you gave Brooks, too."

Jack's gaze stayed on his glass mug, head bobbing, mind whirling. This chatter of people knowing about his altercation with Brooks was news. Was there a policeman's gossip pipeline?

"How does it travel?"

"I'm on the committee for the Fallen Officers' Orphans and Widows Fund and chair another committee for disabled officers." Lamont signaled to the bartender for another round. Once fresh beverages arrived and the empty baskets of wings and fries were removed, he placed his muscled forearms against the tabletop, leaning in. "What do you want to know? Ain't like you and I are old friends catching up." His eyes bored into Jack's, expression stanch.

"Brody Brooks. You were his FTO?"

Lamont leaned back, took a sip of his Seven and Seven, and set his glass down. His expression transformed. "I was. So why are you asking about Brooks?"

Jack stared at this formidable person for what seemed like eons before he spoke. "Just working on something for my captain. Don't know why, just following orders."

"What's Brooks' current position?"

"Robbery Commander."

Lamont's lips turned downward as he nodded. "I'll be damned. He rose in the ranks."

"You're surprised?"

Jones snickered. "An unpredictable rookie, blatant hatred for those higher than him who gave orders. He believed himself invincible, tough, and was arrogant. Sometimes I think he thought he was untouchable—I never could figure out why."

"Oh," Jack said, sipping his beer, letting Lamont guide the conversation.

"Inexperienced with delusions of grandeur, and he didn't like me. But in the beginning, most of my trainees didn't, and I didn't give a rat's ass. My job is to keep 'em alive and make cops outta 'em. Like with the six boots before him, I was gonna be tough, wanted him to turn out respectable, know the ropes, use his head. Understand?"

"I had a dude named Carl Dupree as my FTO. Fifteen years of experience, not only smart, but wise. Yep, there's a distinction."

"Yeah, there is. Dupree? Killed in an auto accident, wasn't he?"

"Seven years ago, eleven months after retirement. Damn shame."

Jones nodded. "Never got to enjoy his retirement. Listen, Jack, what do you want to know about Brooks?"

"Whatever you can tell me, I guess."

"Look, for six months I had the guy in my car as a boot. Felt like a lifetime. Brooks was belligerent, noncompliant, a show-off. I didn't trust him to have my back, even as his FTO."

The crease between Jack's eyes deepened. "Why not give him rips, get him suspended, teach him a lesson if necessary? I don't get it."

Lamont leaned back, glass in hand, eyes downcast. A heavy sigh. "You never dug into him, even before punching him?"

"Never considered it necessary. He arrived as our new captain and hated me from the start. Still don't know why." He didn't mention his conversation with Joan Whitmire.

"Let me give you some history. Know your enemy."

"I'm all ears." Jack sat back.

"Brody had two sisters, fifteen and twenty years older. His arrival shocked his parents. The oldest, Cora, married Judge Michaels when Brooks was one. He was seventeen years older than her. Five years later, Jane Brooks married a cop, Harry Evans—and became related to the mayor by marriage."

"Sounds like a freaking soap opera."

"Oh wait, it gets better. Cora had an affair, got pregnant. Michaels forced her to give the child up for adoption, though not legally."

"Sad business for the baby."

"Her husband didn't want kids. Cora needed to be near the baby, so the kid was raised nearby. Somehow she had pull, but her husband never knew."

"Lord, soap opera is right. Any of these people still around?"

Jones pulled a face. "Sisters dead, parents dead. Cora's husband, the Honorable Judge Michaels, is in a nursing home. Harry Evans died in a car accident a year after Jane died from respiratory issues."

"Brooks ever meet his illegitimate uncle?"

"They were neighbors as kids, but whether they knew the real story is a mystery."

"You know a lot about Brooks. How's that?"

"Look, kid, he was my boot. I dug into his background further than the academy does. I needed to know the type of person I was dealing with. I did this with every rookie. Some people are willing to spill gossip." A laugh eluded him.

"These people from the old neighborhood—think they'll talk to me?"

"Nah, the ones who would gossip are dead or senile."

"So, what happened to Cora's baby?"

"Don't know who the kid went to live with. Only that's not the end of the story. Brooks had an adopted brother."

Jack smirked. "Now you're gonna tell me his adopted brother was his oldest sister's kid, right?"

"That would've been a spectacular twist, but nope. You ever meet Ethan Wygant?"

"If you mean Lieutenant Wygant, in Evidence, nah, never met him."

"He's Brooks' older cousin. The boys grew up together. Ethan's mother was Brooks' dad's sister."

"In the same neighborhood?"

"Same house. Ethan's parents died in a car accident. Brooks was two to three. Ethan, six. Lois Brooks, Edith Brooks' sister, and her husband Norman Wygant, stipulated in their wills that Edith and Butch would raise Ethan. So Ethan and Brody consider themselves brothers."

"Seems reasonable at such young ages. I never dealt much with Wygant, though."

Jones drained his watered-down mixture, raised his hand to the barkeep. "Coffee, black." He regarded Jack, who nodded, motioning for two.

"I don't have a schedule to keep, and it's pushing ten. You got time?"

"Heck, Lamont, cops sleep when we can. Sometimes a power nap in the common room, or kick back at our desk after forty-eight hours of no sleep."

The bartender appeared. "Two coffees and, uh, Jack?"

"Yeah, Teddy?"

"Quinn said food and coffee's on the house. Pay for the booze and we're square."

"Mighty nice. Tell Grady we appreciate it."

"Absolutely." He smiled, flipped the bill over, and left.

Lamont snatched the tab and withdrew fifty bucks. "Hey, why don't we split it? If you pay the same, the bartender gets a nice tip."

Jack concurred, putting his money and the tab under his empty beer mug. Lamont slipped his fifty underneath.

"Are you familiar with Carmine Berutti?"

"Everyone in Houston, I'd imagine."

"Italian Mafia, Costa Nostra. Not like the early days. Only still active. Brody and Ethan grew up in the original neighborhood. Friendly with the Beruttis, Castellanos, and De Lucas. Only now, all family names have changed, except Berutti's. Believe they are still active, under the radar."

"How's this concern Brooks? He's a cop, not a mafia assassin." Jack's expression twisted in confusion.

"You're right, he's not a hitman, but don't mean he didn't get his hands dirty. Got no proof, Jack, but he is, or has been, involved in shady dealings. I haven't worked with him in over a decade. Maybe he's flying straight now. You talked to Yardley and Whitmire?"

"Yeah."

"Sal Dellucci?"

"Not yet. Can you enlighten me?"

Lamont's bushy eyebrows V'd on his nose. "Did you know Dellucci is Carmine Berutti's love child?"

"No one's mentioned it."

"Yeah, he didn't know either, until Carmine's wife, Lenora, passed. Sal was almost thirty. Mother never told him, but the rotten apple didn't fall far from the evil tree. Only I think the kid knew."

Jack scooted closer. "What makes you think so?"

"Kid got away with stuff. Trouble came knocking. Carmine Berutti bought him out, kept it off-the-record. Swiping things, breaking into places, running illegal bets, strong-arming, and worse when he got older. Story goes, Sal didn't know his dad, but I think he did, and used the Berutti name. Mom's a Dellucci, hence last name. But just by looking at him, you knew he was Carmine's boy.

Lenora knew, never said a word. Stayed with Carmine, probably for money and lifestyle."

"Or," Jack said, "she felt trapped, or scared. Berutti's still a big name in Houston."

"A definite possibility. Well, the story goes," Lamont continued, "Carmine loved Sal's mom, but being Catholic, he'd never leave his wife. Mistress wanted her son safe, enrolled in police academy to straighten him up. Only Sal already had a police record."

"If he had a rap sheet, how'd he get in?"

"Money, Jack, knowing the right people. Records got expunged. Carmine made it happen. They put a shield on a guy who had no right to wear one. If you poke around, be cautious."

"How well did you know Frank Windom?"

"Enough to know he was one helluva cop, somewhat grumpy, but takes every kind. Frank was serious, lived and breathed the badge. Pretty bummed he passed," Jones said sincerely.

"Yeah, Frank didn't take care of himself. Died too young."

Lamont leaned back. "You and he ride together long?"

"Two years. Retirement wouldn't have suited Frank. He'd have been like you, working private if he wasn't pissing bosses off." Jack's countenance softened with fondness.

"I remember him and Brooks riding together. Frank hated him. I asked why once, but Frank was closemouthed. Said I should ask Brooks if I wanted to know."

"Did you?"

"Never did. They hit us with a ton of cases which never got assigned—coded 'Lack of Personnel' and suspended. By the time the department recovered, Brooks was riding with Whitmire—and you heard that lasted a minute."

"Yeah, puts me right back to Dellucci."

"What about Sam Coolidge?"

"One hard dude to locate."

"Not many of the original crew around. Hope you don't find him dead."

"Me too. Lots of years have passed. Listen, I gotta scoot."

"Me too." Jones stuck out his hand.

Jack grasped it. "Thanks for meeting me."

"Don't think I was much help."

"Oh, you know, every little piece adds up. Maybe I'll start seeing a big picture. And I'll keep at it until I do."

"Drive safe, Jack. Be cautious, too, hear me?"

"Will do, and thanks."

Jack headed to his vehicle. It was just about eleven, and his mind whirled on the drive home to Deer Park. He had to locate Dellucci and Coolidge. His snooping into Brody Brooks' police family was delicate. Political ties? Damn. He had to exercise caution so he didn't arouse suspicion or raise red flags. Impossible.

20

BLURRY-EYED THE NEXT MORNING, Jack yawned, then for a second time with two giant body shudders.

"Late night, Jack?"

"Uh, yeah, stopped in at Quinn's for a bite to eat, stayed till eleven." He was tired of lying. At least this was a half-truth.

"Eating and drinking alone, pard, not healthy, but won't preach, not today."

"Good, 'cuz we've got no time for Dawson Luck sermons. Let's work."

"Fine by me." Dawson's words were clipped.

Without another word, he dug into the list of vendors he'd matched to each homeowner who'd been a victim of robbery over the past nine months. Their biggest concern was still locating the owners of the last apparent robbery. The only news they'd received from CSU the week before was the blood had not been human, but canine. So where was the dog? Had it died?

JACK BROKE THE SILENCE. "I have a theory."

Dawson shifted the seat back, stretching his legs out. "Fire away."

"I think Robbery needs to check into the electric gate company and its workers. There's a pattern they've yet to explore."

"The fence company, Jack? Are you serious?"

"Hey, you asked. I answered. Look, with the stuff being pinched, you believe someone is climbing over fences with their haul?"

Dawson gave it a second. "Nah, don't imagine so, unless they stuffed the booty all in a backpack—the antique flatware, expensive jewelry, cash, and the like. Unique items they said were gone, paintings, and any bulky objects worth value might've been tough to haul over a fence. You think it's why they didn't steal larger-ticket items?"

Jack shrugged. "I pulled up the current cases Robbery is investigating in that area and started with the first case. Each neighbor who learned of the first robbery had new electric gates installed; and each house with a new gate got burglarized days or weeks later. That's the common denominator."

Lucky's eyes crinkled. "How does this make sense? The gate just allowed them extra security, didn't it?"

"My parents had an electric gate when we lived in Piney Points. I remember we had trouble with the gate not functioning right and it drove my mother bonkers. She contacted the company to complain. They sent a technician out the next day, and when my mom watched him drive up from the front window, she ran around back to meet him at the gate and asked him if he needed her to use her key to open the gate, and he told her no. He had a master key and unlocked the gate by hand."

"Okay, and?"

"He unlocked it with a key he carried around, a master key. It upset my mom because he could come inside with ease. She telephoned the corporate office and asked about it."

"What'd they say?" By this time, Dawson had crossed his arms and was staring at Jack.

"They vetted their employees, and the company was bonded, and she had nothing to worry about."

"Did anything ever happen at their house to cause her or your dad concern?"

"No, but it was well over twenty-odd years ago, and times have changed." He hesitated, slanting a look at him. "So have people, pard."

"I can't argue with you. World's moving downhill fast. You gonna share this theory with Penny?"

"It's only a theory."

Dawson's fingers drummed his desk in thought. "It's a workable theory, and it could pan out perfect; otherwise, the bastards could continue to get away with ripping people off."

"Okay, I'll share with Penny and Craig. Let them take a run at it."

Dawson provided him an over-the-head wave, frowning as he did.

Jack could call up and chat on the phone. There was no need to go downstairs.

He sighed. Maybe Jack enjoyed going to Robbery to bug the piss outta Brooks, and assuming this was true, Lucky wished him well, happy trails. He loathed

Brooks just as much, but after this case was closed, he was gonna start getting nosy, badger his partner if he had to.

West had a hidden agenda.

He aimed to be included.

———

JACK THRUST HIS HEAD inside Robbery for a quick look-see. No Brody Brooks lurking around. Perfect.

His boots made a soft thud, which went unnoticed among the detectives' phone conversations, typing, and paper shuffling.

Craig Gilly felt an unexpected tap on his shoulder and swiveled in surprise. "What the hell, Jack, you trying to give me a heart attack?" He inhaled, letting it out in a puff of exaggerated fear.

Jack drew an empty chair over. "Sorry, Craig. What's up?"

Craig's shoulders dropped a fraction, and he lowered his voice. "Brooks is what's up. Seems our department's closures are too low and he's on our ass."

"I have a theory if you're interested."

"Terrific, 'cuz we got nada, Jack, and could use something."

As Jack talked, Gilly stroked his clean-shaven chin, his head nodding, the wheels in his head turning.

"Gotta say your theory gives us something to check out since we're drawing a blank. Marlo telephoned to tell us the blood found is part of the German shepherd family. Now we're back to no murder, we hope. We still can't track down the owners. We've got confirmation the Jessups own a German shepherd named Molly. There's been another robbery, but this time there's video from a neighbor's surveillance camera. The footage is dark; we're not too hopeful, but tech's working their magic."

Jack frowned. "Another break-in?"

"Yeah, there was a DB involved this time."

"What's the scoop?"

"Wife alone; hubby on a deep-sea fishing expedition in Alaska. She was supposed to visit her daughter and grandsons in Minnesota, but was feeling flu-ish and stayed home. Her oldest daughter is an occupational therapist and lives in

Beaumont. When her little sister phoned her and told her Dad was gone and Mom was sick, she drove in when no one answered the phone. She arrived around sevenish this morning. Found her mom in the kitchen, blunt force trauma to the head."

Jack's eyes narrowed. "No signs of a forced entry?"

"None, and they ransacked the place. The daughter's distraught. She can't identify what's missing, aside from the obvious items." Craig exhaled. "If she hadn't felt ill, she'd still be alive; burglarized, but alive."

"Who's investigating from our squad?"

Craig's lip curled in repulsion. "Skip Webb."

"His girlfriend Earl Nichols sniffing his tail?"

"Not this time. Cooper Norris has gotta tolerate the asshat."

A snarky laugh sputtered from Jack. "Yeah, best if you and Pens solve your burglary first, 'cuz it'll solve his murder, too."

"Hey there, Jack, thinking about joining our department?" Penny stepped around Craig's desk.

"Hiya, Penny. Nah, I like Homicide, but uh, Craig here can fill you in on a theory I offered him."

Jack inclined his head when he heard huffing and saw the ample gut of Brooks rounding the corner.

His tall frame hunkered as he pushed the chair back. He slipped off, keeping his head ducked low. "Oops, gotta scat, sneak out before fat man sees me. Update me later."

Still crouched, attempting to stay out of sight, Jack dashed to the side door, and just as it slammed, a loud voice proclaimed, "What the hell?! Was West in here again? Gawd almighty, I'm gonna..."

Brooks' voice faded as Jack sprinted up a floor, took a quick turn in the hall, and entered six, bolted to his station, sat, and snatched up a file, pretending to read.

"Jack, what in the blazes—" Dawson began, but the back door swung open, banging against the wall, no time to make its usual warning squeak.

Heavy footfalls thudded toward Jack, and Brody leaned over him, his chubby face beet red, breathing hard. "West! You need'ta stay away from my department. Stop bothering my detectives. Understand me?"

A female voice bellowed from the back. "Commander Brooks!" If there'd been a tile floor, Captain Veronica Justice's high heels tromping toward them would've jarred their senses. In less than a minute, she'd reached the other side of the squad room, her expression twisted in fury.

"What do you mean coming up here, yelling at my detective?"

She crossed her arms; her long, burgundy-painted nails tapped against a rigid plastic organizer she held.

Red-faced, Brooks struggled to catch his breath.

"Keep ... your...people...off my...floor." His breathing was labored. "Don't they have cases they're working? If not, find them an unsolved. I guarantee you have plenty to choose from."

"Brooks," she began, noting everyone's eyes were on her.

She needed to stay composed to keep her authority. "I can run my crew. Do not tell me what to do. It was me. I sent Jack. You could have thought to ask, but no, you barge in and start yelling at my guys. Do I treat you and your team this way?"

Brooks moved his lips to speak, but she kept coming at him.

"No, I do not. This would be the ideal moment for you to apologize for disrupting our squad, and to Jack for screaming at him." Her eyes glared, her lips pressed together as she pumped the toe of one shoe, waiting.

Brooks' blank expression morphed into that of the man who hated life, detested the world, and despised Jack West. He hitched his pants up, as much as his rotund middle allowed, staring at her with a hard coldness reserved for the people who'd crossed him; and there had been plenty. One of the two expressions he could pull off without a hitch. Smiling or jovial, not so much.

His eyes cut over to Jack who was seated, his long, lanky legs stretched out, his arms folded, a slight leer working to keep a smile from leaping onto his face.

"It'll be an icy day in hell when I apologize to you or him."

"Fine. Leave. Oh, and take the elevator, 'cuz I'd hate for you to overexert yourself any further."

She inclined her head to the exit; her tone filled with indignation. "Now." Unfurling her arms, her rigid stare struck like lightning, and Brooks flinched.

Brooks stretched himself up, snorting. "Stay out of my department, unless I invite you." He paused as he surveyed the room. "All of ya!"

His eyes turned to Skip Webb, standing to his right, and Jack watched a small upward nod of Brooks' head and Webb's insignificant nod. Those two were birds of a feather. Better put: they were puppet and puppeteer.

The room back to normal, Justice finished up her short meeting with Detectives Cooper Norris and Tate Minton and strolled over to where Jack and Lucky were discussing a plan of action.

She looked at Jack. "My office."

"Yes, ma'am," he said, his eyes locked on hers. She broke the stare, looking at Dawson.

"You too, Detective Luck," she said, walking away with a confident yet pissed off stride.

"Now we're in trouble—thanks, Jack," Dawson huffed.

"I doubt we are in trouble. Me, maybe—you, I doubt it."

"What, I'm not good enough to be in trouble?"

Jack emitted a tiny chuckle. "Dawson, you oddball. First, you act pissy because she doesn't summon you and now you're scared you're in trouble."

His head craned to see Jack. "Earlier, did Roni or Yao give you a rip?"

Jack rose and stepped around his desk to glance at Luck. "No, and you won't get one either."

Detective Dawson Luck stood and nudged his chair in, grumbling under his breath. "Better not get an effing rip. Never had one before. Not gonna start now."

IN THE ELEVATOR, BROOKS' fat finger jabbed the button to the top—the number to Oz.

The floor housing the Chief of Police, his assistant, the executive assistant chiefs, the Chief of Detectives, Internal Affairs, all the top dogs.

He was a damned commander.

The commander of Robbery, yet so far down the totem pole he didn't deserve to breathe the same air as those so lucky to be on the top floor, in the Land of Oz, as everyone dubbed it. You had to travel that yellow brick road to be a person of value and integrity; or so he'd heard. Integrity—his ass.

Every living being had some sort of deviant inner self; no one was that pure, nor perfect.

The elevator rattled, stopping to pick up two travelers, then three floors later depositing them on the ninth floor. It stopped again to let on three females: a civilian secretary and two officers. A lanyard dangled on one's badge, and the other clipped it to her belt. Both were plainclothes.

Each woman nodded to him. Brooks eyed the women. His disdain grew, especially after his most recent dust-up with Veronica Justice, whom he despised.

The doors swooshed open, and all three departed. Brooks punched the button, this time with more vigor.

Jack West popped into his thoughts.

He wondered when the proverbial shoe was gonna drop right on his head. Frank had been the kid's partner. Brody knew Frank possessed a lot more information than he'd disclosed in the past.

Too many years.

Shitload of water under the bridge.

Loads of people involved and stuff got covered up. Out of the people still around, who would, with their one last breath, need to confess their sins before meeting their maker?

The elevator bumped, halted, and the doors slid open to his destination.

Getting summoned up to the Assistant Chief's office didn't concern him. Brooks hiked up his trousers, squaring his shoulders, brushed his hand over his bald head, exhaled, and knocked on the closed door, awaiting admittance.

They'd been pals a long time, much to Brody's regret.

The Assistant Chief's voice harsh, "Brooks. Shut the door and sit."

After situating himself in the chair across from the executive, walnut-grain desk, he waited for Chief Croce.

"Brody, we've got a problem that's spiraling out of control, and I'm relying on you—as always—to handle it."

"I understand, but—"

The Chief's raised hand silenced Brooks. "I don't believe you do. That book is not to be found. Start squeezing people."

"How should I accomplish that, Tony?"

Tony Croce pushed his chair back and tugged open the center drawer. He laid the pistol on the desk and exhaled.

Brooks' eyes widened. He didn't have to ask; he knew.

"Fuck me, Tony, where'd that come from?"

"The Assistant Chief of Police can go wherever he wishes, whenever he chooses, and take whatever he needs, and no one questions him."

"Yeah, but, Tony, you can't avoid cameras." Brooks' stare fixated on the pistol.

"Wanna bet?" The Assistant COP removed a soft cloth from the same drawer and wiped his prints off.

"Get it done; however you need to."

He forcefully slid the gun to the desk's edge.

BRODY TOOK THE STAIRS, his steps slow.

The handgun felt like a bag of rocks in his jacket's inner pocket, weighing him down. He stopped three floors down, gasping for air; he needed an elevator, or he'd have a heart attack.

He dashed into the men's room on the 18th floor.

Empty. Good.

He splashed his face with water, then braced his hands against the cool, white, porcelain sink, and lifted his head to see his reflection.

Overweight, bald, red-faced, and in way too deep.

His precarious situation was about to implode. He felt an urge to get the gun, go back, and shoot Assistant Chief of Police Tony Croce in the face. Tony Croce—Antonio Crocetti—another Italian bastard he had to deal with.

The door pushed open. A civilian staff member traipsed in to use the facilities. Brooks jerked an acknowledgement grabbed a hand towel, dried his hands, and left with the gun poking into his flabby ribs.

21

"CLOSE THE DOOR," RONI directed.

Dawson complied, taking the empty seat next to Jack.

"Jack, what the devil did you do? Why'd Brooks come up here screaming?"

"Went to chat with Salato and Gillespie, to tell them about my theory regarding the robberies."

"That's it?" She slanted her eyes at him.

"Yeah, I swear. I wasn't up there to annoy him. I was trying to leave before he caught me, and the fat bastard—oops, sorry—Brooks saw me, so I hoofed it back."

Veronica Justice sat back, a teeny smirk playing on her glossed lips. With a flicker in her dark pupils, her face lit up as her white teeth shone against her mocha-chocolate skin. She just sat, staring and smiling.

Jack cleared his throat. "Uh, Cap?"

"Just savoring the moment."

Lucky's caterpillar tufts dipped and danced across his prominent forehead. "Ma'am?"

"Brooks' disruption gave me an odd moment of victory."

A chuckle sounded deep in Jack's chest before emanating as a full, measured laugh. Out of the corner of his eye, he witnessed Dawson frown and shrug.

Jack turned to see him. "You don't get it, do you, Luck?"

"Guess not. Somebody wanna enlighten me?" His arms crossed; his scowl deepened.

"Brooks cannot stand me. He hates any woman in a management position, or in any position of power, which is what he considers my position. He's a chauvinistic ass. It's the first time since I've been your captain that I've stood up to that narrow-minded asshat—and in front of a third of my crew."

She raised her palm to keep them from speaking. "He despises you, Jack, have no clue why, but he does." She sat back and rested her weight against her chair.

"Dawson, in order of Brooks' hate, you come in second to Jack. It's because you guys are partners, so I'd be careful of what you say or do around the fat jerkoff."

Roni grinned at Jack.

"Yes, ma'am. Understood."

"Good. Now. Dawson." Her gaze cut to Jack, then back to him. "I want to tell you what I have Jack involved in. You can refuse to join, but what I say stays between the three of us and is not to leave my office—no ifs, ands, or buts. Understood?"

Without hesitation, Dawson Luck said, "I'm in."

She rested her elbows on the arms of her seat, her head tilted. "Without hearing what it is?"

"Yes, ma'am. I trust Jack with my life, have for several years now, and if he's in, you bet your ass I'm gonna back him up."

Captain Veronica Justice regarded Jack. "You're fortunate to have Dawson as a partner, as he is you." Her gaze moved to Dawson. "Detective Luck, your partner has been urging me to involve you, so you won't be working alone. The deal is, I'm concerned if you would or not."

"Concerned if I would or not what?" Dawson squinted in confusion.

"Cross a blue line."

"I'll bite. What blue line you mean?"

"Digging into a fellow officer," Jack clarified.

"As in Internal Affairs?"

Veronica Justice's gaze grew thoughtful before she spoke. "At their request, not mine."

They got Luck up to speed.

"Now, help tie up your investigation with the robbery and turn it over to the DA's Office—and do it in a hurry. I've learned the husband and wife from the first theft-slash-missing persons case you're assisting Robbery with are friends of the former mayor, who's gotten word you can't locate them."

"And why does this matter?"

"Well, Jack, it shouldn't, but the rumor is our former mayor may take a run for governor, and these people—Gilbert and Jennifer Jessup—are huge backers."

"So, our two AWOL rich people are involved in politics?"

Roni's shoulders twitched. "I suppose. Why does it matter?"

"If they fled the country, our former mayor is SOL."

"Do you think they just vanished?" Roni considered this narrative a plot for a horrible novel.

"Both workplaces say they'd each taken an extended leave of absence—no word on when either of them was returning."

She exhaled, nodding. "And no return calls from either of their children?"

Dawson Luck rejoined, "No. Both daughters are traveling abroad. No way to contact them, and no one has their itineraries—except maybe their parents. Which puts us back at square one."

Roni laughed harshly. "Rich people. They do whatever they want whenever they want, with no concern for others. Man, they even think they're above the law, don't they?"

Dawson couldn't help himself. "Law enforcement officers too."

A solemn ambiance shrouded her office at the thought that cops could be criminals, getting away with who knew what.

"Yep. Crossing the blue line blurred by greed, power, or fear. Jack said it best the other day, Cap."

"Oh? What did you say, Jack?" She turned to him.

"Dunno. What'd I say, Dawson?"

"You said fellas like that were nothing but faded blue bloods, with zero integrity or real policing skills, and debatable moral fibers."

Veronica Justice's lips pinched. Her gaze traveled from Luck to West. "Sums it up, I'd say, Jack."

———————

IN THE OUTER HALL, Jack turned to Luck. "Let's not discuss this here. Too many ears."

"I'd say it wouldn't even be wise to talk in any place where other officers hang out—like Lone Star, Quinn's, or uh—" Dawson flicked his fingers in a mock snapping motion. "What's that new place called?"

"Cuffs."

"Kinda a goober name, ain't it?"

Jack stifled a laugh. "I gotta name for a club."

Dawson gripped the knob, turning his head. "You gonna open one in your twilight years?"

"Maybe. Gonna call it Shoots and Ladders. A club for cops and firemen. Only you spell it S-H-O-O-T-S, not like the kids' game."

"Funny, Jack. Why not call it the Holster and Hose?"

He opened the door; the squeak sounded and everyone turned to look.

"Nah, we're both dummies. We got no clue how to run a bar, only how to drink in one. Let's get to work."

AT EIGHT THE NEXT morning, Jack stopped at the cage and was signing the clipboard when the sergeant in charge showed up from the rear.

He was a portly fellow, clean-shaven, a frown pasted to his face. No cap, revealing a noggin balding in the center, creating the appearance of a beach with islands on either side. Teenage acne scars showed on his shiny forehead, and his orbicular nose was spattered with unsightly blackheads, giving him an old-man appearance. Overgrown gray nose hairs fluttered as he breathed. The buttons of his uniform were strained by his enormous belly, and Jack could see his white T-shirt peeking through the gaps.

His voice was gruff. "What'd ya need?"

"Here for video copies," Jack said, peering at his name tag. "Sergeant Wygant."

Wygant snatched the clipboard, glanced down, then back up at him. "You West?"

"Yeah."

"Why you need these? You ain't Robbery, are ya?"

Jack had written the case numbers of the videos taken by the videographer of the last three burglaries.

"My partner and I are assisting, and we'd like to look at the past crime scenes. See if we notice anything different." Jack assumed Wygant knew all about him; Brooks would have spilled the story in a heartbeat.

Wygant gave Jack a dirty look, his mouth turned down at the corners. "Got your badge? Need to document I seen it."

Jack unclipped it from his belt, palming it. He laid it with a thud on the counter, lifted his hand, and said, "Here—by all means, don't wanna go against department regs."

Fat fingers snatched the badge. He looked at it, then glanced at the clipboard, then at Jack. "Wait here." All said, none-too-friendly.

The sergeant turned, hiking his trousers over his belly, and went to track down the items requested. Jack sneered. Overweight, just like Brooks. Enormous bellies ran in the family, he figured. This wasn't a secret—he'd belted Brooks in the snout, and he was positive Sergeant Ethan Wygant got an earful of lies from the bulbous-nosed Brooks.

"This is the first time meeting Wygant," he noted. "Odd—I've had no interactions with him before, and I've retrieved evidence many times in my career."

"Here." Wygant's stare was sharp. "Get this logged back in. Would hate to see you get a rip cuz of mishandling or losing evidence. That clear?"

"Understood." Jack reached out, and Wygant drew the disc cases back, provoking a pucker of annoyance on Jack's face.

"One more thing."

"Yes, Sergeant?"

"Stay out of the crosshairs of what ain't your business."

"Meaning what?" Jack's frown deepened.

"I got friends, and they've seen you."

Jack's jaw clenched. Was Wygant threatening him?

"I'm not following you—sir," he said, mimicking respect.

"Keep your nose outta stuff you need to let lie, alls I'm saying." Wygant left, leaving a stupefied Jack standing there.

⸻

DAWSON WAITED IN THE monitor room, pacing , when Jack arrived tape recording in hand.

"You get lost, Jack? Crud, dude, Evidence ain't far away. You've been gone over twenty minutes."

"Had an unplanned chat."

"With?" Dawson queued the video player.

"Ethan Wygant," Jack said, giving him the rundown on the conversation. Dawson's hairy forehead moved like ocean waves.

"Sounds like a threat to me, too."

"Yep. Gives me the distinct impression someone's shadowing me."

"Who?"

"One of Brooks' boys. Only I would've guessed none of them were that good. I'm only gonna say we need to watch our sixes."

Lucky agreed.

Nothing on the videos gave them any inkling of a lead. The place wasn't tossed and ransacked like a normal burglary. This puzzled them, especially Jack. His brain worked funny, and he had another thought which kept popping into his head, but he kept it to himself—it seemed a tad odd, even ludicrous.

———

JACK'S DESK PHONE RANG.

"West, Homicide. Hi, Gilly, what's up?"

Jack's head bobbed, interjecting uh-huhs and ahs, his face contorting into several expressions while he listened. Reclining, he fiddled with his pens, jotted a note or two, and said, "I'm glad to hear it. Thanks for the update. Oh, and we watched the three other recordings, but nothing new, sorry. I'm gonna return them later."

"You tried, best you can do. Right? Okay, gotta go. Penny's motioning to me; Brooks wants us. Oh boy." Craig whistled into the phone.

"Better you than me. Have fun." Jack clicked off. "That was Craig."

"Yep, I heard ya. What's he have for us?" Luck scooted to the side of his desk.

"The Jessups checked in with their housekeeper."

"'Bout damned time. Where've they been?"

"In the freaking Caymans, settling up accounts, of all the damned things."

"In person? Shit, they could do it via the internet. Did they say why?"

Jack's eyes rolled a bit. "They have property there, and in St. Kitts and Antigua. They needed to decide on who takes what, or if they sell, so they visited all three properties. One daughter contacted Craig, worried. Told him she and her sister had no idea their parents' marriage had gone down the toilet like it had. All they'd known was they weren't happy but had been seeing a marriage therapist."

"At least we found out where they've been. Jesus, how irresponsible can some adults be?" Dawson expressed his aggravation.

"You wanna hear about the dog?"

Dawson leaned back with a huff, rocking his seat with the toe of his foot. "What happened to the pooch?"

"Milly, the German shepherd, got a thick crafting wire and sticky tape wrapped around her paw kinda tight. The wife didn't realize it when she let the dog out. The wire entangled on the scrolled design leg of a patio chair. The pooch yanked it, biting into her flesh, and she yelped and kept pulling, which upturned the chair."

Luck shook his head. "Which was what shattered the glass topper she cut her foot on, right?"

"Spot on. Her leg and her paw. Poor mutt got twelve stitches in total. They left Molly at the vet since their vet boards dogs. Afterward, they jetted off to get their cash and to negotiate the sale of their island properties."

"Well, hallelujah. We've solved the missing persons mysteries—and before lunch too," Lucky's sarcasm leaked out. "I'll return them, Jack. Give you a break from Wygant."

"Thanks, Dawson, appreciate it. And get a return receipt and give it to me. Wanna keep my proof in case the dickweed wants to make a fuss about it later."

"Got yer six, pard."

22

"I'M DRAINED, LUCK," JACK said, sitting in Captain Justice's office, waiting for her.

"Me too. I'm ready to put this one behind us."

"Can you believe it?" Jack glanced over.

"What?" Dawson stretched his legs out, leaned back, and closed his eyes.

"It's been almost two weeks, and we're done; Webb's case is closed too."

"My body feels it. Looking forward to a full night's sleep. And to spending time with my wife."

Roni Justice stepped in, clicking the door in place, and walked to her desk. She sat with a huff, a glower on her pretty face.

"You alright, Cap?" Jack's tone roused Dawson, and he straightened, yawning.

"No. Brooks is on my tail about their investigation not being any of your business."

A puzzled expression crossed Jack's face. "What do you mean?"

"They closed the case, found the culprits, and in the report Detectives Salato and Gilly wrote up, gave you the credit for their lead."

Dawson looked from Roni to Jack. "Your theory ... it was right?" A smile flitted across his tired face.

Jack gave a minuscule shrug. "Guess so."

"When they started an investigation into the gate company, things added up. Two of their employees falsified employment records, and no one knows how, but they beat the background checks. One employee got arrested four years ago for burglary, but his records got sealed because he was sixteen and it was a first offense. The other guy had a list of petty thefts. The corporation is checking into how they missed this. They got egg on their face, though."

"Can't believe I'm in hot water for helping them solve a case," Jack grumbled.

"Brooks'll get over it. Just you giving them the idea to investigate the business rankled him," Roni said.

"They used a master key to open the fence, and what'd they do, pick the locks on the rear entry?" Dawson asked.

"They didn't have to because of the security gate. It gave them false reassurance, and some of them didn't lock the back doors. The houses they robbed had no separate alarms, and even though some homes had signs in the yard touting different alarm companies, all they had were signs—not accounts. They did their homework."

"Guess they got them for robbery and now homicide, too. The new victim—a lady, right?" Dawson adjusted his posture.

"Yeah. Ending up with the dead woman messed up their flow for sure. In a rush to get the hell out, one of 'em left his prints on the rear door. Robbery matched them to his record, and he sung like a bluebird, giving his associate up."

"You'd think Brooks would be happy to have the investigation closed. It's a win for Robbery."

"Ya'd think so. When it got to the Chief of Ds, your name was on the report, and the praise shifted. Brooks thinks you did this to make him look like a jackass."

Jack leaned to one side of his chair, his weight resting on his left arm as he contemplated his next words. "Should I go smooth it over, have them take my name off the paperwork?"

"No. It's done. Let it be. Brooks needs to just grow a pair of balls, and whatever it is he has against you, he needs to get over it, let it go, or bring it out in the open and deal with it. Now." She rubbed her hands together, her eyes traveling from Dawson to Jack. The smile dropped from her face. "Let's talk about your special assignment, shall we?"

THEY SAT AT A rear table at Antone's, and Lucky ate his sub with vigor. Jack munched on chips. The place was not crowded, but it could change as soon as the construction and road workers ended their day. Some days you craved an Antone's, some days a James Coney, or just an old-fashioned greasy hamburger with fries—or tots covered in cheese. Fast food: any type of detective's friend, and enemy—the food to live by and die by.

"We should try to be healthier, eat better, ya think?" Jack asked, taking a mouthful of his Antone's Super Original, enjoying the flavor of the chow-chow and added meats and cheeses. He figured his current diet was clogging his arteries. Frank Windom's face flashed in his mind. He didn't want to one day die of a heart attack from poor eating habits and lack of exercise. Man, he needed a life coach—or some major lifestyle changes. Brody Brooks popped into his thoughts as he took another hefty bite of the sub. Oh man, after this, he needed to eat chicken—not fried, but roasted or baked—and salads, fruits, and veggies.

"Jack, why are you making a face? Your sandwich taste bad?" Dawson took a bite and chewed, popping in a handful of chips to add a crunch to his sandwich.

Jack finished chewing, swallowed, and shared his thoughts about Frank and Brooks not taking care of themselves.

"Aw, come on, Jack. We'll start hitting the gym at the station, start jogging. I hate giving up Antone's."

"Dawson, you're a garbage disposal. You eat everything, and I wonder how you don't weigh three hundred pounds."

"It's the famous Luck metabolism." He went back to the original subject. "I cannot believe you convinced me to work with Wygant. Matter of fact, I can't believe Roni agreed to it."

"Better you, Dawson, than me. I'll wager he's heard all about me and hates me just as much as Brooks does."

"As your partner, he ain't gonna have much love for me either, Jack."

"Yep. Bet he's gonna hate you, too."

"Jack, how's this gonna work? Wygant won't confide in me if he thinks I'm a mole."

"We're gonna have to have a falling out. He's got to hear about it."

Dawson polished off the small bag of tater chips, wadded up the empty wrappers, and laid it all on the tray. "Means us sneaking around to communicate. We can't get caught being buddy-buddy. If I'm in evidence, who's gonna be your partner?"

Jack settled back, his stomach full. "I gotta be a free agent, and if Roni agrees, I can pick cases I can walk away from if need be."

"Might mean you got to work with Webb or Nichols, even Golan."

"Could be I can get one of them talking. Who knows?"

"Or get yourself killed, Jack. Don't like the idea."

"The thought of being whacked doesn't thrill me either, dork."

"No, I mean—" Dawson scowled when Jack laughed.

"Yeppers, and you worry too much. I can handle myself. I'll be cautious. There's more to this. Don't think it is just about Brooks hating my guts. I will say though, after all the dust settles, guess he'll have a valid reason to dislike me."

"Yep. Be nice to find out what's going on in his fat head. Jack, it didn't start with you. This began long ago. Who knows who it involves?"

"Yeah, and?"

"Remember what you said about the faded blues—guys who stopped caring about the job? What if you find out how deep it goes, and it brings this city to its knees? It might hurt the department, even some decent people."

"We can't brush this off, Dawson. I realize we aren't gonna win any popularity contests, but damn it, I took an oath to protect the people of Houston. Let me take it one step further. The oath is to serve and protect everyone, no matter what town I lay my head to sleep in. I'm a cop, and I uphold the law, trying to make the world a safer place. I haven't lost my urge to do the right thing, and I hope I never will. Chief Yao told me something back after I punched Brooks in the snout and turned in my badge."

"Yeah, what'd he say?"

"Said I bled blue, and always would."

"Jack, you do. You're the job, and the job is you."

"Okay, Dawson, we're gonna do this then. And if there are consequences, we handle it best we can. Deal?"

A serious expression crossed Dawson's face. He clasped Jack's hand. "Brothers in blue, Jack."

"Always, partner," Jack said, his voice a low rumble, pledging loyalty.

23

HOUSTON. CRIME.

An always ongoing, bustling hornet's nest. Some days the police wished crooks took a break—or a holiday. Thieves, rapists, murderers—none of them punched a time clock. Why not back off for a week? Just relax?

Jack deduced it was because some were crimes of opportunity and others crimes of passion, happening when situations turned heated. Nope. In certain places, crime was an inescapable reality.

What an amusement park carousel the station was: once Homicide completed a case, it was Robbery's turn; after them, Auto Theft, then Vice picked up another ride. A never-ending, ferocious circle keeping day and night shift commanders weary and officers juiced up on coffee—or any other pick-me-up that pumped caffeine straight into their bloodstream.

For weeks now, Lucky had worked in the evidence department while Jack flip-flopped working cases with Jace Severson and Cooper Norris. Three weeks ago, Xi Chang flew to China for a vacation. He returned late in the week, and Jace was off to California for two weeks. Chang's return made Jack happy, as it reduced his chances of being paired with one of three clowns: Webb, Nichols, or Golan.

Penny Salato's efforts to organize a meeting between Katherine and Jack had been thwarted by Commander Brooks, who kept sending her into the field. This annoyed Craig Gilly too. It seemed their tubby commander was trying to create a divide between him and Penny.

"What the devil is going on, Pens?"

Craig Gilly held his cell phone against his ear, using his chin to balance a stack of files while carrying them to the situation room to work at one of the eight-foot tables.

Penny stood outside at the garage entrance, waiting for Alex to pick her up. Her slim shoulders twitched, and the frown on her face deepened.

"Hell if I know, Gill. Brooks has me riding with Dunwell on some stakeout, which I think is bogus. I've only got a sec to chat. Can we meet for a beer tonight?"

"No can do. Brooks has me moving crates from storage after my tour tonight. Said it was non-negotiable and I'd pick up OT. Can't pass up the extra dough."

"Yeah, he's giving me OT, too. And Gill, gossip down the pipeline is we've had significant budget cuts. How's he getting this cleared?"

"Penny, this is Brooks we're talking about. Could be he's stealing the cash to give us, or he's misappropriating funds somehow. Hell, who knows?"

"Gotta split. I see Dunwell's car coming. Talk to you later." Penny clicked off and pocketed her phone just as the car came to a stop.

"Hop in."

Penny shut the door and buckled up. "Where we off to?"

"Got a pawnshop we're gonna sit on."

"They robbed or what?"

"Got word they're taking stolen goods. We're gonna watch, see who comes and goes for the next coupla days, check out how many repeat customers they have, and take their pretty pictures. Camera's on the back seat—grab it and you can play paparazzo while I take notes on the automobiles and people."

Penny leaned over and grabbed the camera case. She noticed a couple of bags on the floorboard and two large thermoses. She set the camera bag in her lap.

"You've brought food and hot coffee. Is this an all-nighter?"

A sigh left his lips just before he said, "Yeah. And I'm guessing Brooks didn't mention that?"

"No, the fat—uh, no he didn't." She huffed.

Alex laughed. "It's okay, and you're right. He's a fat bastard."

While Alex circled the area, looking for a spot to park, Penny texted Gill: *On a stakeout all night, maybe longer. Going dark until later. Pens.*

Next, she shot a message to Katherine Sparks: *We need to talk. Brooks. On a stakeout with Dunwell, call you later.*

Katherine Sparks' phone pinged. She checked, scowling, but delivered a thumbs-up emoji and stuck her phone in her jeans pocket.

THE PROJECT JACK WAS doing was boring, but it wouldn't last forever. Captain Justice had him working with the cold case unit, sorting files and cleaning up murder books that had gotten mixed up, broken open, scattered, and then misfiled—or moved to an off-site storehouse in boxes with solved cases.

The work was tedious, but not useless. It allowed time for his other project: Sal Dellucci.

Hunting down this retired cop was a puzzle. Jack had information on his whereabouts, but he was nowhere to be found. His address was a PO Box only, and his number unlisted. The file remarks had a basic *"need to know"* statement—meaning if you needed to locate him, you were authorized to do so; otherwise, buzz off.

He'd called Lamont Jones and Joan Whitmire to ask if they knew how to find him. Both stated they couldn't stand the guy when they worked together and had zero desire to keep in contact with a man they felt wasn't a decent human and not worthy of wearing a badge. Gary Yardley was out of pocket, so no help.

Dellucci's vanishing act had Jack asking himself several things.

One: was he in hiding? If so, who was he hiding from?

Two: was he dead, and no one realized or cared?

Three: had he gone down a Mafia rabbit hole? With the last name Dellucci and his family connections—could that be possible?

Lamont Jones said Sal was Carmine Berutti's illegitimate child. A member of the old Italian Mafia, during the height of Mafia movement.

Sure, there was still Mob activity and mentality. Gangs were not the gentlemen of the Mafia. He'd learned there was a code of conduct, even in the underworld.

Carmine Berutti. Perhaps he should start there, because sometimes working backwards brought you to the finish line. Brody Brooks and Ethan Wygant grew up in the same neighborhood, which meant they already knew Sal Dellucci—besides being on the force with him.

Jack replaced the pages he'd been organizing in the three-ring binder, his brows knitting in thought. If Frank were still alive, he'd hear the scoop on Dellucci and Brooks.

An idea came to him: see if he could locate detectives Frank had served with in the past. It didn't take long to find several of the names he'd given to Yvette in HR. It yielded him nothing.

Jim Crane, known as Jimbo, passed ten years back from cancer, followed by Detective Joseph Scarzzo, AKA Scars, three years afterward from a stroke. Another guy, new on the team, Sam Coolidge, Frank never spoke about. And Harold DeMitt.

Mitty was still kicking, and Jack knew Frank Windom trusted him. Coolidge he was having trouble locating. DeMitt it was, so Jack punched in the number.

"Hello?"

"Harold DeMitt?"

"No, this is Paul DeMitt, Harold's son."

"Oh. Is your father available?"

"Who's this?"

"Jack West. I'm, uh—was a friend of Frank Windom. He and your dad were part of the police department, back in the day."

"Ah. I remember Frank. Dad called him Frankenstein."

"Same guy. Paul, is your dad there?"

"What's this about?"

Jack let out a sigh. "About yesteryear, I guess you could say."

"You a cop?"

Jack's soft laugh blew into the phone. "Uh-huh, Homicide. Frank was my first partner."

"I see. Well, Detective West, I'd let you talk to him, but they gave him pain medication and a sleeping pill, and he's out. Can I take a message?"

"You're at the hospital?"

"Yeah. Pop had surgery four days ago, and when he's awake, he's not a happy camper."

"Surgery? Sorry, hope he has a speedy recovery." Jack didn't pry.

"Diabetes. Got ulcers on his foot, and they worsened. He had to have his right leg amputated below the knee."

"Damn."

"Be nice if you visited him though, take his mind off this setback. Sit and talk about cops of yesteryear. You game?"

This was an unexpected invitation, and if Harold DeMitt didn't refuse to see him, this was fate.

24

Memorial Hermann Southwest Hospital.

Jack disliked hospitals.

The odors were distinct: sickness, death, and disinfectants, all filling his nostrils as his boots clicked against the white-and-gray tiles in the open pavilion. Visitors scattered, going to elevators, the information desk, the gift shop, or grabbing coffee at Starbucks. Nurses, doctors, office staff, and janitors passed each other, rushing to their destinations.

Paul had given him the room number, so Jack moseyed to the elevators.

The doors opened, and he stepped back as a nurse pushed a wheelchair with a patient carrying a large vase of flowers and three helium-filled balloons in her lap. Three other non-hospital visitors exited, and Jack stepped in, pushing four. The doors slipped shut, and the elevator hummed, jerking to a stop on the second floor to admit two orderlies and a nurse.

"What floor?"

"Six, please."

"Eight for me."

"Push five for me, will you?"

Jack punched the corresponding floor numbers. The elevator whirred once more, stopping at four to let him off. Everyone mumbled, *Have a nice day,* as the doors whooshed closed, airlifting its occupants to other floors.

The nurse's station buzzed with activity: alarms sounded, the intercom echoed responses to patient requests, and phones rang.

"May I help you, sir?" a frazzled-looking desk attendant asked.

"Room four-twenty-one?" Jack inquired.

Her head turned. "That hallway. Go left. Next-to-last door on the right."

"Thank you, ma'am."

"You're welcome. It'll thrill Mr. DeMitt to have company." She shifted her focus to a ringing phone.

Jack followed the hallway, finding 421. He rapped his knuckles on the door, pulled the handle, and heard a voice call out, "Come in."

The patient squinted, trying to place Jack.

"Harold, how are you?"

"I'm short—" he coughed, sputtering a chuckle. "Half a leg that is. But better than the alternative, I suppose."

"Mind if I sit?" Jack's gaze shifted to a chair, wondering why Paul hadn't mentioned he was coming.

"Grab a chair, pull 'er up closer, so I can hear ya better."

Jack slid a chair over and sat. Harold used the bed remote, sat up, and pulled the sheet higher. Jack stared at the older man, ignoring the missing limb. Losing a body part was hard to fathom, but the idea of losing a leg? Terrifying.

"Okay, young fella. You have me at a disadvantage. Who are you?"

"Your son didn't mention I phoned?"

"Guess he forgot. Paul's plate is full with twins coming and now me."

"I'm Jack, Jack West. Frank Windom's old partner."

Lost in thought, Harold bobbed his head and asked, "Hotshot Jack, you him?"

"I guess so, if Frank called me that." Jack offered his hand. Harold's grip surprised him.

"Might 'a lost my leg, but I ain't a weakling. Once I knew my leg had to go, I started working out my arms."

"Tough situation." Jack's expression filled with sympathy.

"Better than being in a satin-lined box, with nickels on my eyes."

"When do you go home?"

"Four or five days, but not home—off to rehab to get fitted with a prosthetic and learn how to walk again. Lord willing."

"You'll do it. Look how strong your arms and hands are. Don't quit."

"My kinfolk say the same thing. They're all very supportive. I wished I'd taken proper care of myself, though. Jack, take care of your body. You only got the one."

"Been thinking about it. Time to hit the gym and ditch the crap I've been eating."

"Jack," DeMitt said, "you didn't hear I was in the hospital, so I'm betting you've been looking for me, and can even tell ya why, too."

"You reckon?" Jack's curiosity piqued.

"Yep. Brody Brooks. Right?"

"How'd you know?"

"Oh, back right after you came to the table. They put me on a desk when it was RHD—uh, Robbery Homicide Division. My damned diabetes was causing me issues, and I had to stick out the last few riding a chair. I knew this day would come, though."

Stunned, Jack said, "You did?"

Harold gave a slight nod. "Yep. Been what, twenty years since Frank passed?"

"Twenty-two."

"Poor Frank. Jack, I think retirement would've done him in if he hadn't had the heart attack first."

"Me too. I half expected him to try the private sector, work in security, or become a PI. How'd you know I'd contact you about Brooks?"

"So, Frank never mentioned his suspicions concerning Brooks?"

"No, not a word. Wanna fill me in?"

"Scarzzo dead, Frank's dead, Jimbo's dead, haven't heard about Coolidge. He was an odd one, though."

"Who's Coolidge? Frank never mentioned him."

"They transferred Sam to run evidence lockup six months before your promotion. None of us cared; we were kinda glad. Sam acted like his shit didn't stink and he was above the rest of us."

"We still got men like that."

"Shoot, Jack, we had plenty of guys we couldn't stand like Brooks, Dellucci, and Moretti."

"Raymond Moretti? Was he friends with Brooks?" Jack only met Moretti once. He would move heaven and earth to change that night. With an invisible shudder, he shook himself out of the memory.

"He was. You know the guy?"

"Recognize the name. Met him once."

Harold's straight-laced expression caused Jack some discomfort.

"He made my brother's death notification. Rather not discuss that, though."

"Yep, I understand. Old wounds. Now I'm the last one left from the original group. Look, Jack, none of our group was on the take, but—" Harold reached for his water, took a sip, his face contorting in slight pain.

Concerned, Jack asked, "You need a nurse?"

"Nah, it'll pass. Give me a second."

Once the pain subsided, Harold exhaled. "Gotta try to stay off the painkillers. Don't wanna get hooked."

Sweat beaded his upper lip. Jack got up, found a washcloth from the basin area, wet it, and handed it to DeMitt.

"Thanks."

Jack only nodded, resuming his seat.

"Me, Scars, Jimbo, and Frank—we were top-notch cops, always trying to make ethical choices, but couldn't control the others. You talk to anybody else about Brooks?"

"Yeah. Yardley, Lamont Jones, and Joan Whitmire. Can't find Sam. I got pretty much nothing except what I already know, which is Brooks is a real bastard and presumed to be a corrupt cop."

"Ha! Ain't anything presumed about it. He's evil to the bone; has been from day one. Him and his pals. People know stuff, Jack, and lots of folks are already dead who were involved—"

Jack raised a hand. "Wait. You saying this might involve murder?"

DeMitt shrugged. "Could be. It started even before Brooks. That newbie flatfoot got caught up in something he couldn't escape."

"Give me a starting point, Mitty."

"Find Sal Dellucci."

"I've looked, Harold. He's vanished or could be dead, and nobody cares." Jack exhaled, reclining in the guest chair.

"No one disappeared him, Jack. He ain't Jimmy Hoffa."

Jack laughed. "Alright, Mitty, how do I find the turd?"

"Start with his pop, Carmine Berutti. Oh, and you should also search for the girl who was Berutti's mistress—Sal's momma."

"Sure-sure. Search the Yellow Pages. Check under *Mistress of Carmine Berutti*? Is that how she's listed?" Jack's brows dipped in frustration.

"Jack West, you're a friggin' detective. Frank would be rolling in his grave knowing he didn't teach you better!" Mitty's frown was real. His words made Jack feel an inch tall.

"Smitty. He still at the off-site storage?"

"No—retired several years back. Why?"

"There's another starting point. Contact him."

"Smitty?"

"Jack, that old geezer knew everyone, and I'm betting he kept a few secrets, too."

"Smitty did?"

"You ever have a reason to venture to the off-site storage for the department?"

"Sure. Why?"

"Was a mess, wasn't it?"

"Yeah. So?"

"C'mon, Jack. You ever wonder why it was such a disastrous nightmare and why Smitty didn't care?"

"Smitty was only one person. Shit like that happens when moving a large amount of cargo. Stuff gets mishandled and misplaced in a large warehouse, I suppose," Jack rejoined.

"One man, my ass. He could've got them to hire temps, approve OT, put the place in order. Did you ask who spearheaded the move?"

"Ah, come on, Mitty. No, I had no reason."

"Well, now you do, don'tcha?"

"You gonna tell me it was Smitty or Brooks?"

"Nah. It was a higher-up, a joint effort, but you can bet Brooks played a part in the move all the same. Smitty went along for the ride. Then we were all dealing with missing evidence, our cases getting tossed out, and the likes. Get what I'm saying?"

"Someone paid them to alter stuff, misplace, or destroy evidence?"

Mitty jabbed the button to lower his upper body, tiring out. "That sums it up, Jack. With the mess created, they sent guys in, tried to get it organized, but we heard they paid fellas to do shoddy work, or contaminate evidence. And it didn't stop there. This chaos led to cases being dismissed or ignored."

"They were getting paid? By who?"

"Who do you think, Jack? Crooks. Shot callers like Berutti, anyone wanting to keep themselves or their hired thugs outta prison. Shoot, even judiciary members got paid off. What about the dishonorable Judge Wolff?"

"So, you're implying there's still ongoing corruption within the police department, just as there was during your time?"

"Yeah. I also believe Smitty took bribes to turn a blind eye once they moved him to the warehouse full time." DeMitt became pensive. "Jack, my kiddos, wife, and illness kept me on track. Otherwise, I might have gone down the same dark path too."

"Frank? You gonna tell me he took part?"

"Nah. He was a cop's cop—never a guy truer to the badge. That was Frank. Hell, he bled blue, and I'd bet my retirement check he shit blue, too."

Jack chuckled. What a coincidence; Davis Yao accused him of bleeding blue, too. He said, "Seems I've got a mess to dig through to get my answers."

"Frank always said you were a go-getter, a bright star on a dark night, and you'd do justice for Houstonians."

"He did, did he?" A small smile flitted across Jack's face. Frank. He missed the old noir cop.

"He did." Mitty opened his eyes, staring at Jack. "Frank said one day you'd be asking about Brooks, and he hoped he was alive when you did."

A frown creased Jack's forehead. "Why?"

"I can't say, 'cause Frank never told me anything except Brooks was gonna hate your guts, just like he hated his. Frank Windom wasn't a boat rocker. Only he knew Brooks was hiding something—him, Moretti, Coolidge, and Dellucci."

"How far back do you think this goes?"

"Been going on forever. But when Brooks and Sal first hit the streets together, that's the time I know. That'd be over twenty-eight years or longer, I imagine," he uttered. "We were young and dumb, but some of them like Brooks, Dellucci, Moretti, and Coolidge were dumber knuckleheads. Eager to make the dough, or make friends in high places," he paused, "or in the gutter, where immoral people with money lived."

"You saying this was about money and power? 'Cause Brooks doesn't seem to have either. I mean, the guy's headed for thirty. Why would he wanna stay on at HPD?"

"Kid, sometimes folks got your ass in a vice, no matter if you want to or not. You're stuck, with no way out. Or you live with the illusion that you are in control."

"Illusions sound about right," Jack voiced.

Harold closed his eyes, breathing out, relaxing his upper body. "Feeling kinda tired."

Jack couldn't badger him; he needed his rest. After pushing the chair back to the wall, he stood next to Mitty's bed and pulled a business card from his shirt pocket, laying it on the nightstand.

"I'm gonna let you rest. Here's my card."

Mitty's eyes closed. "Sure. Appreciate you coming to visit."

"Yeah. Guess next time we can talk sports, or cars, and I can leave off with the Spanish Inquisition. Sound like a plan?"

Mitty coughed, and a coughing fit ensued. Jack propped him upright with pillows, so he didn't choke.

"Here, sip," Jack instructed, offering a cup of water with a straw.

Harold sipped, and his face returned to its pallor.

"Gotta rest now."

"Yeah. I appreciate you talking with me. You'll do fine with the physical therapy and the prostheses. Got no doubts."

Jack waved, letting the door to 421 close silently as he made his way to the elevators.

Smitty.

Time for a closer look. Maybe give the old fart a call.

25

Jack carried the file copy to his desk. *HPD ex-employee Pete Smitherson, aka Smitty.* He chucked it into the deeper bottom drawer with the others. If anyone were snooping, it would appear he'd started a personal collection of HR files. He locked the drawer and shoved the keys into his pocket. He'd read it later.

Right now, he had a meetup—which included lunch.

———————

At a table in the far back corner of a Texas Roadhouse off FM 1960, twenty-two miles from the station, they sat facing the entrance so they could see who wandered in. They ordered drinks.

Jack looked over the lunch menu. "Haven't been here in a while."

"Me either. Would've liked to go to Lonestar Sausage & BBQ, but lots of the fellas eat there, and we need privacy." Luck took a sip of water.

The petite brunette set two iced teas and a basket of hot rolls and cornbread on the table. "You fellas ready to order?"

After a half slab of ribs and two country-fried chicken plates were ordered, the server left. Lucky immediately went after the hot rolls while Jack broke off a piece of cornbread.

"Here I am trying to eat healthier. You're a cruddy influence, Dawson."

"No, I ain't, Jack. You ordered chicken, not beef, and got salad instead of a tater."

"Yeah, okay. You're right." Jack chewed. "How's it going with Wygant?"

"Slow. The guy's breathing down my neck. His eyes never leave me. You'd think he didn't trust me." Dawson gave Jack a look. "What's going on with you? Any news?"

Luck smashed butter on another roll and nibbled as Jack filled him in on his talks with Whitmire, Yardley, and Jones.

After that, Dawson confessed that he'd followed Jack to Quinn's to spy—but not about his deeper digging into Yardley.

At first, Jack was furious. Then impressed. He let the anger dissolve. Dawson cared what happened to him and was watching his six. No better partner, he figured.

"Penny told me Katherine wants to talk to me," Jack said, eating the last piece of cornbread.

"Sparky? In Vice? Why?"

"Because—" Jack stopped when the waitstaff arrived, placing hot plates on the table.

"Need anything else?" the brunette asked, looking at Jack.

"Nah. Looks delicious. Thanks."

Once she was gone, they ate in silence until Jack spoke again.

"I think Katherine wants to talk about when she worked with Brooks in Robbery."

"You gonna tell her what Roni has us doing?" Lucky's bushy brows caved in.

"Nuh-uh. Not before getting Roni's approval—especially since IA is involved. She'd have us—me—busted to foot patrol in a heartbeat."

Lucky nodded, taking a rib. He chomped, swallowed, wiped his mouth and hands.

"I'm hoping neither of us gets busted down, or fired, Jack. Or ... hurt." He avoided saying *dead*, but it lingered between them. "What about this Coolidge fella? Ever get a line on him?" Dawson drained his iced tea.

"Nope. The guy's elusive, like Dellucci. Only a PO Box. Got a number, but he hasn't returned my calls." Jack laid his fork and knife across the plate and covered them with his napkin.

"I'll see what I can find," Lucky said, "but I gotta be careful. Don't wanna raise any red flags with Wygant."

"I'll meet with Roni this afternoon. See what's up. Catch you up later. Just us three and the IA director know about this so-called investigation, and we've gotta keep some things hushed."

"I hear you loud and clear."

Jack decided he'd investigate Harold DeMitt's information before involving Luck further. Since Dawson worked with Wygant, there was no need to put him in an unpleasant position until there was reason. Jack knew it was flawed logic—but it's how he justified holding back.

His real concern was how deep this went and who would surface—and whether they'd surface face-down in Buffalo Bayou.

———

TWO LONG-ASS WEEKS OF going through old HR files, calling numbers that either no longer belonged to the original owner, or hearing the horrid, deafening message that the number you've reached was no longer in service. Jack's frustration climbed to a new high.

"Jack?"

"What!"

"Wow, man, you're in a foul mood. You okay?"

"Sorry, Xi. Just frustrated. Wassup?"

"Anything I can do?" Chang shifted to get a better view of Jack.

"Nah, but thanks for asking. What'd you need?"

"Got a minute to quiz me on the sergeant's exam?"

Jack strolled to Xi's desk and stuck out his hand. "Yeah. Those the questions?"

Xi giggled. "Yes, and no. They keep you on your toes, mixing up the wording."

"Sure. Pull up Luck's chair. We'll give it a go."

"How's Dawson liking it in Evidence?" Chang kept a straight face, but Jack knew he was dying to know why Roni transferred Lucky to the cage.

"He's getting the hang of it, I suppose. But we aren't talking much these days," Jack fibbed.

"You two have a falling out?"

Jack didn't want to lie to Chang or Jace. They were as much his partners as Luck, and he trusted both with his life—but circumstances justified a small fib.

"Can we save this for another time?"

"Sure, Jack." Chang leaned closer, lowering his voice. "I've got your six. Luck's too. So does Jace."

"Yeah, I know—"

The door squeaked. Webb and Golan strutted in. Jack immediately buried himself in an exam question, giving Chang a wink and a slight nod.

"Hey Chang," Webb called, "you think you'll be a hotshot if you make sergeant?"

"Zip it, Webb. And if I do, I'll be one step over your sorry ass. Why don't you file something—or better yet, clear a case? Don't you have a dozen unsolved?"

Golan walked up next. "Just like West, ain'tcha, Chang? All hoity-toity."

"Nah," Chang said calmly. "I ain't as good a cop as Jack—but I'm working on it."

Jack's eyes narrowed. "Xi, you're heads above most, an outstanding cop."

"Oh yeah," Skip Webb sneered, "you two stroking each other now?"

"You morons should give it a shot," Chang fired back.

Golan made a vulgar motion. Webb gurgled like a twelve-year-old boy.

Jack stood, towering over them. His face hardened, and both men instinctively stepped back.

"You're pathetic, Golan. You too, Webb. Neither of you would recognize good policing if it slapped you in the face. Now go find a fat commander's ass to kiss—or better yet, blow him. That oughta move you up the ranks."

"Watch what you say, West," Webb hissed. "There are other ears around here—some of them don't like you either."

Jack leaned in. Webb retreated another half step.

"Get to work, Webb. You too, Golan."

The female voice snapped behind them. Veronica Justice stood there, hands planted on her hips, glaring.

"Yes, ma'am," Webb and Golan muttered, retreating to their cubicles.

Jack handed the exam sheet back to Chang. "Maybe I can help you later, Xi?"

"Sure. Or Jace can when he's back. No worries, Jack." Chang nodded at Justice. "Boss."

"Detective Chang, you'll ace the exam. No doubt in my mind." Roni smiled, then turned. "Jack. My office."

Once inside, she closed the door.

"Alright. What was all that crap about?"

"Are you interested, or just asking for the sake of asking?"

"No. I can guess. Webb and Golan being their obnoxious selves." She exhaled. "Forget about them. We've got other fish to fry."

She leaned against her desk. "I got a call. A man says you've been trying to reach a member of his family. Says you've been pestering people."

Jack shrugged. "Who says I'm pestering?"

"Gino Berutti. Says you're looking for his half-brother, Sal Dellucci."

Jack straightened. "Did he say where I can reach him?"

Roni blew air through her nose. "No. He said for you to back off."

"Do you want me to back off?"

Her head dipped slightly, eyes never leaving his. "Oh, hell no. I want you to press harder—but be smart about it."

"Alright. They're worried. That's progress."

She sighed heavily.

"What, Cap?"

"If they know, Brooks knows."

Jack thought it over. "He can't come at me without showing his hand, though."

Roni smiled—briefly—then frowned. "No. But that doesn't mean he won't find another way. Watch your step."

26

THE SQUAD AREA WAS peaceful. Jack scanned the room. Webb, Golan, and Chang were gone. At the rear, Austin Reed sat with his head bent, reading, while Cooper Norris typed at his keyboard. No phones ringing. No mass chaos. It was a pleasant change—short-lived, but nice.

His gaze swept over his desktop, landing on a folded message taped to his stapler.

Yvette in HR called at 4:20, said it's important — Almost Sergeant Chang

A smiley-face emoji followed.

He snickered and dialed Yvette's extension.

"Human Resources, Yvette."

"This is Jack. You called?"

"Yes, sir, I did. I have files for you. Can you come down here?"

A frown creased his face. "Did I ask for files? I don't recall—"

"Detective," she cut him off, "somebody left them for me to give to you."

"Who was it?"

He couldn't see her shrug, but he knew she did.

"Yvette—who was it?"

"Can you just come down here, please?"

She wasn't her usual flirtatious, bubbly self. That concerned him.

"Be right there." He hung up.

Something had her spooked—or someone had her spooked.

Yvette stood on the opposite side of the counter and motioned for him to follow, leading him into a conference suite. Once the door hardware clicked shut, a deep sigh left her curvy upper body, and she began lifting the hem of her long tunic.

One of Jack's eyebrows rose. He stopped her hand with his palm.

"What on earth are you doing?"

"Delivering a package." She smirked, brushing his hand away as she extracted a manila envelope. "Got told not to tell anyone about these."

She handed it to him, one fist planted on her hip, one toe tapping the carpet. Her eyebrows arched, lips pulled into a half sneer. "What did you get me into?"

The confusion on his face was genuine. "Can't say—'cause I don't know."

He pulled out a chair and sat at the conference table. She followed.

Jack opened the clasp and slid the papers out.

Page one: a brief list that looked like case information.

Next page: a list of evidence box numbers.

Pages three and four: a printout of HPD employees—names, ranks, hire, retirement, dismissal dates. Phone numbers. Addresses.

Jack examined them. A dozen names of officers who'd served in different HPD divisions.

At first glance, none were familiar—then one caught his eye.

Moretti.

Officer Ray Moretti.

"Detective West," Yvette said softly, "you look like you saw a ghost."

Eyes glued to the page, Jack pointed. "This was the officer who told us about my brother's shooting."

Her face softened. "That was a long time ago, right?"

"Almost twenty-three years."

"He still with the department?"

"Moretti? No. Retired." Jack slid the papers back into the envelope.

"Why do you think somebody wants you to have this?" she asked. "It's not like a letter—just old names and case numbers."

"Who gave it to you?"

"Can't say. A man called—told me to check my bottom drawer. Sticky note said to call you to pick 'em up." She hesitated. "Found this too."

Yvette pulled a folded note from her front pocket, her face creased with worry. Jack read it.

Stop giving information to Detective West.

"Am I in danger?" she asked.

"I don't think so. Someone's trying to scare you."

She huffed. "Well, it's working."

Jack stood. She did too.

"Yvette, keep this to yourself. Take my number. Call me if you need me, alright?"

She frowned. "I will. I sure enough will."

Jack took the stairs. In the seclusion of the stairwell, he opened the envelope again.

That name jumped out at him—Raymond Moretti.

Back at his desk, he mulled over why anyone would threaten Yvette. It troubled him, but at least the hallway and lobby cameras monitored who came and went.

What relevance did this data have?

Over two dozen case numbers. A list of evidence box numbers. He could research the cases—try to locate the books and boxes in that cluttered warehouse, if they still existed.

His attention returned to the employee list. Jack ran his finger down the names.

Moers, Alan. Vice. Gang Unit.

Hired 1949. Retired 1972.

Deceased 1982.

He realized—this was a list of last names beginning with *M*. Men and women he'd never heard of.

Except one.

The flatfoot who'd delivered Cole's death notification.

Moretti, Raymond. Patrol.

Hired 1974. Retired 1998.

Residence: Chicago, Illinois.

He leaned back, page in hand.

Moretti was why he had this list.

Moretti retired four years after Cole's shooting.

Jack's brows knit as he tried to connect the dots into something meaningful—but what?

A sudden shroud of sadness settled over him.

Cole's death should've been an ancient memory after twenty-three years, but some days it still tugged at his heart.

Today was one of those days.

He closed his eyes, inhaled, then exhaled, letting the heaviness lift. His pencil eraser bounced against the stack of folders on his desk—thump, thump, thump.

Ray Moretti.

The name pulled at him only because this was the man who broke the news.

Jack never spoke to him. He'd stood behind his parents on the front steps, then collapsed to his knees—hands reaching for his mother, face buried against the backs of her legs, sobbing.

Time spun backward.

MAY 1994. SCHOOL ENDED. Summer began. In August, Cole would head to LSU on a football scholarship.

Big brother had an arm—an exceptional quarterback. His dream was to go pro.

Jack whined, "Come on, bro. Lemme go with you."

"Nope. Tonight's just the fellas from the team. We're blowing off steam, and I can't promise how rowdy it'll get. I don't wanna worry about you. Got me?"

"Aw, come on. Don't treat me like a baby. Dang!"

"Jackson West, stop whining. You just turned fourteen—you're not a baby. But there'll be older kids there, and I don't want you mixed up in that." Cole ruffled Jack's hair. "How about tomorrow we hit the gym, grab breakfast burritos, then ask old man Magnus if we can take his boat out?"

"Okay. Fine." Jack punched his arm. "But not his dumb rowboat. His speedboat."

"Ow, you creep." Cole fake-wrestled him, pulling him into a hug—never knowing it would be the last time.

At the far end of Richmond Avenue, the road was unfinished. A place kids partied, drank, and did other forbidden things.

Cole's dream of becoming a superstar shattered—turning into a haunting nightmare.

"JACK—WHAT'S UP, MAN?"

The deep voice snapped him back to the present. He gathered the papers quickly, shoved them into a folder, and stacked another file on top.

"Hey, Reed. Where's Cooper?"

"Parking the company jalopy. We're playing a waiting game right now." Reed flopped into his chair, feet propped on the corner of his desk.

"Waiting on what?" Jack asked. "DNA? Ballistics? Autopsy? A suspect?"

"Pappy. Him and the boys are chasing down two suspects."

"If anyone can run 'em down, it's Pappert and his goons."

"Yep. Pretty terrific. They got commendations for that hostage situation."

"Yeah. Luck and I missed the ceremony—court that day. DePaul and Tenney are remarkable cops."

"Yep," Cooper said from behind Jack, tipping his chair back before letting go.

"Coop, you ass." Jack righted himself as the chair wobbled.

"Sorry. Easy target." Cooper grinned. "Reed, let's grab a bite. I'm starving. Pappy'll text when they find those pieces of shit. Jack—you coming?"

"Nah. I'll grab something later. Got paperwork." He nodded. "Thanks, though."

Almost alone.

Jack glanced down the line. Nick Becker, Alan Landers, and Moshe Rybak stood at Nick's desk, sipping coffee. Moshe nodded to Jack, who returned it.

Good men. Solid cops. Family guys. Long-timers. HPD had a levelheaded detective squad—except Webb and Nichols.

Too bad they'd hooked Golan. The man had turned into a zombie, following them blindly.

Jack took a deep breath and let it out.

He spread the pages again, staring at the case numbers. "Alright," he muttered, "these aren't gonna talk to you, you dork."

He slid a wooden ruler under the first number and typed it into the system. *Not Found.*

Each one bounced back the same.

He leaned forward, elbows on the desk, brow furrowed.

Bogus numbers? Or so old they predated the electronic system?

Before digitization, they used logbooks.

Now where the hell would those be collecting dust?

Another mystery.

He dialed Smitty.

Voicemail.

"Crud." Jack sighed. "Hey, Smitty—Jack West. Need to talk. Call me."

Smitty was the one person who might know—assuming he wasn't out sailing the deep blue, fishing his ass off.

None of the employee names caught Jack's attention on a second pass.

Only Ray Moretti.

Was it just the memory?

He set that page aside and picked up the list of box numbers.

Cross-referencing them against station storage and the off-site warehouse turned up nothing.

Nothing at all.

Annoyance flared.

Why sneak these into HR if they meant nothing?

Why threaten Yvette afterward?

Two people had been in her office that day. No official reason. In and out.

Jack filed the papers away and locked them in his bottom drawer.

Time to visit Russ Hardy.

27

THE STAIRWELL DOOR OPENED. Jack entered a semi-lit hallway. Knee deep in frustration, he hadn't realized it was this late; it was eight minutes after ten and the only lights on at this hour were the night service lights. At the far end of the hall, he saw the custodian's cart, sans the janitor or her staff. They were there, though, moving from office to office, getting trash and dusting, and he could hear the roar of a vacuum.

He'd passed many nights chatting with the janitorial staff. They were a nice group of various ages and backgrounds, mostly young, some of whom were even college students. Each one he'd learned had to pass a background check and undergo drug screening from time to time. Maria Sanchez Smith, whom they called their fearless leader, hired each employee, and they'd laugh when they'd say, *and her grumpy old husband.* Lorenzo and Maria Smith owned the company—L & M Janitorial Services. They'd won the bid for the contract on the Edward A. Thomas Building owned by the City of Houston.

Jack treaded down the hallway, trying not to sound like a bull moose tromping on the worn indoor-outdoor, brown-swirled carpet squares. It was ugly, but sufficient for the heavy traffic. Who were they trying to impress? Lawyers and criminals? Without the hustle and bustle, a single man walking these hallways was like a train ripping through the silence.

Russ Hardy would be at the desk by the elevator doors. He'd be working the night shift intake, fielding calls from separate command posts, sending out call-outs for night commanders—odd jobs and paperwork. In addition, he monitored cameras for the entire building, the underground parking facility, and the streets surrounding the twenty-eight-story building. His duties also included archiving surveillance footage.

Russ sat, his head down, his glasses perched at the tip of his nose, writing in a record book. Jack *tap-tap-tapped* on the glass to alert him he had a visitor.

His head rose as he peered up and over the monitors stretched over the long, curved countertop/desk area. "Hiya, pal, what are you doing here at this hour? You work nights or just goofing off?"

"Oh, just got my head buried in some stuff, didn't realize how the hours had flown by. How are you these days—er, uh, I mean nights?"

Russ snickered. "Can't complain. No one would give a rat's ass if I did. Okay, Jack, you aren't one for just dropping in just to say hello. You need something?"

Jack spurted a laugh. He'd need to be more sociable. Drop in and say hi more often. "Yeah, was wondering if I could take a peek at this morning's surveillance tapes?"

"Yep, just finished them up to nine this evening. You looking for someone, Jack?"

"Not sure. Wanna observe who came and went today."

Sergeant Hardy knew when not to keep probing. Jack was working on something, and it wasn't anything he wanted to discuss. Aware of Jack's respectable character, he unlocked the side door, letting him in.

At the monitors, the sergeant set him up with the day's recordings and showed him how to maneuver through each and how to switch camera views: floors, hallways, and the lobby.

"Have at it, Jack. You need anything just holler." Russ took a stack of files, the logbook, and his mechanical pencil, moving his chair aside and switching to a small wooden desk at the back to carry on with his work.

Jack observed the monitors, fast-forwarding and rewinding different time frames, seeing folks coming and going; the entire building was busy during the day, and he, being stuck in his defined world of murder, just now realized this. Each floor of the twenty-eight story building was a mini beehive.

He rolled it back to eight a.m. in the lobby and settled in. No telling when this person walked through the front doors; could have been any time. Just because someone gave her a message to deliver the files to him didn't mean she did it right away; Yvette had work to do and wasn't his personal secretary. Boy, he'd love a private secretary—nah, never mind, he had Lucky. He pinched his lips to hold in his chuckle.

In-out, in-out—faces, faces, and more faces. He was up to the noon hour and getting no hits whatsoever. Jack leaned back, watching as it played. Afterward, he changed his view to the camera at the elevator near the thirteenth floor where the Human Resources offices were located. Someone familiar with the building likely used the stairs.

"Heya, Russ. Is there a view of the thirteenth floor hallway and back stairwell? Russ's frown creased his forehead as he turned his chair to look at Jack. "Don't know. Never viewed them."

"And you ain't curious why I want to, are you?" Jack's brows raised.

Russ's semi-balding head shook. "Nope, ain't my business. Figured you've got your reasons." Out of his chair, he stood behind Jack and punched several buttons, then smiled. "Well, damn. I didn't realize we had cameras on that end."

Jack said, "My bet is each hallway has a camera. Wonder how many times we got guys flipping fellas off when they've gotten pissed?"

They had a laugh over what they might catch on film in the hallways of departments like Vice, Robbery, and Homicide—and the management floors of the department chiefs and the COP.

"Well dang, I'm gonna have to go back to see what fun I've missed by not watching these dumb videos." Russ sat, grinning.

"Yeah, I'll bring the popcorn next time. Deal?" Jack rejoined.

"Sounds good. Okay, back to my reports." Russ Hardy resumed working, and Jack concentrated on the hallway of the thirteenth floor.

Forty-five minutes in, when he was ready to quit, the stairwell door at the farthest point of the HR hallway opened.

The time stamp said it was 1:10.

A slender man entered, carrying a folder. He was five foot ten, around 165 pounds, in his late sixties, and wearing an old, dirty, light beige ball cap that was frayed at the edges of the bill.

The cap he'd pulled low, the ragged bill covering his eyes, and he never looked up. He touted a bushy salt-and-pepper beard that covered the lower part of what Jack could catch of his face.

His Levis were baggy, and he wore grayish tennis shoes and a pale blue pullover long-sleeved shirt.

From what Jack could tell, his hair, longish and unkempt, matched his beard. The man ambled slowly, with a pronounced limp on his left side. Taking deliberate steps, one foot in front of the other, his right hand came up to the wall, and he steadied himself.

Once he reached the door to HR, he strolled in, then came out two minutes later without the folder. Back in the hall, he watched the old fella ambling, his eyes on his feet, his gait strained.

He never raised his head, but Jack glimpsed his right hand when he again steadied himself. His fingers were thin and bony and his fingernails looked dirty. Jack's gut said this fella didn't belong in the building.

"Russ, you recognize this dude?"

Hardy looked over his shoulder at the frozen frame. "Can't see his face, and his frame don't look familiar. He somebody I should know?"

"Nah, just wondering." Jack clicked a picture of the man on his phone and resumed looking at the lobby recordings, searching for a man dressed the same.

Nothing.

No person fitting that description walked in or out of the front lobby doors.

This man came up the back stairs from the parking garage within the building, which meant he had to have an access pass.

Could he be a cop, or an ex-cop?

Jack exhaled, running his hand over his face and across the top of his head.

"You okay over there?" Russ was polite to ask.

"Just tired. Okay if I watch a little longer?"

"Take all the time you need, Jack. You ain't bothering me at all, and it's sorta nice to have company, even if we ain't jabbering."

"Appreciate it, Russ." Jack went back to the camera on the thirteenth floor and looked again. It was clear this man was behind the files in Yvette's desk drawer and the call asking him to retrieve them. His next task was locating the individual warning her to stop giving him information.

28

Reclined, he watched regular workers go in and out of the Human Resources office. It wasn't a revolving door, but several non-HR personnel passed through as well. Lenora—Yvette's boss—and other women moved in and out, along with staff housed at the other end of the hall in the employee file room or the administration office for the civilian crew. The seamless operation of the elevator doors allowed individuals to access and exit the floor with ease.

By midmorning, as noted by the timestamps, Jack spotted three uniformed officers—one female and two male—fresh-faced and all smiles. Newbie recruits, he figured, probably getting HR paperwork started for insurance or direct deposit. Who knew?

Around noon, the corridor grew busier as people came and went for lunch. Some brown-bagged it, heading to the breakroom, while others made a beeline for the elevators to escape the building for an hour.

When he caught a foot sticking through the back stairwell exit, his eyes crinkled as he leaned forward. An older gentleman entered—uniformed patrol. Jack didn't recognize him, but that wasn't unusual. HPD had over five thousand cops and thousands of civilians. He knew many of the old-timers by their weathered faces, and this guy looked like a long-timer.

Once the man reached the center of the hallway, Jack paused the recording.

"Hey, Russ, you recognize this person?"

"Lemme see." Russ wheeled his chair behind Jack's, peering over his shoulder. "Yup. That's Corey Carver."

"He's on street patrol? Looks kinda old." Jack studied Carver's face.

Russ leaned back. "I'd say he's about ten years older than you, Jack."

"Huh. He looks too old to be patrolling. Man's outta shape. I mean, I'm no youngster either—I sure as shit don't want to run down some kid. Might pass out." Jack laughed.

"Nah. He ain't on the streets anymore. He took over Smitty's position at the off-site warehouse."

"You know him?"

"Not personally. He was in Gus Freeman's unit. Gus said the guy was just working for a paycheck—being a cop wasn't a career to him. Gus didn't care for the guy and was damn glad to get him outta the unit. Freeman must've written Carver up a dozen times. Frankly, I'm surprised he didn't get tossed off the force."

"What kind of rips?"

"Same old stuff. Excessive force, late for duty, insubordination, conduct unbecoming. You know—usual crap."

"How'd he keep his job?"

Russ eyed him. "You investigating him, Jack?"

"Not at all. Just curious why he's still on the force if he's such a rotten egg. Never met him—hope I don't." Jack half-lied.

Russ scratched his chin, eyes dropping to the floor before he answered. "Carver wasn't the first pick to replace Smitty. Brass had a list of ten qualified candidates—guys who would've straightened the place up. Smitherson ran it for seven years, but he already had one foot out the door. Guess the old geezer did the best he could with no help. You ever there when Smitty was?"

"Five years back, when Luck and I worked the Troy Wolff case. Place was a mess. I remember how pissed Dawson was about the disorganization."

"You been back since?"

"Haven't had a need." Jack thought of the list locked in his desk.

"The place is a FEMA disaster now—worse than five years ago. Stuff's gone missing or permanently misplaced. Boxes ruined from flooding in a back corner. Roof leak, too."

"I take it Carver's over there fixing things?"

Russ barked a laugh. "You shitting me? Him? Nope. The turd's a fuckup. Plenty of folks wanted that job and got passed over. They were mad as hell."

"Stan Grable picked Carver? With that record?"

"Looks that way. Word is Carver had someone pulling strings to get the transfer."

Jack grimaced. "Who could pull strings like that?"

Russ met his look. "You know who Carver's related to?"

"Guess not."

"His old man is Sal Dellucci. Corey took his grandmother's maiden name—Carver."

"Same Dellucci who worked HPD?"

"Same one."

Jack leaned back. "You heard the scoop?"

"Only gossip. Heard Sal's mom was his high school sweetheart. They never married, though she wanted to. Ever hear Sal was Carmine Berutti's illegitimate son?"

"Bits and pieces."

"Sal didn't find out until he was almost thirty—after Berutti's wife died. Old man never admitted it before that. And if Sal didn't know, you can bet Corey had no idea who his granddaddy was. Never met Berutti myself, but everyone says he was one mean sumbitch—and Carver's a chip off the block."

"How does that tie into the warehouse?"

"Gossip says certain folks needed it staying a mess. Can't prove it, but I think Carver's getting paid to keep stuff missing. Hell, maybe Smitty was paid, too. When detectives try to find old files or evidence, they get stonewalled. Appeals? Cold cases? SOL."

"Lawyers must be losing their minds."

"Yeah. And the building's bursting. But that's supposed to change."

"What's happening?"

"New warehouse—state-of-the-art. Climate control. Cameras everywhere."

Jack nodded. "Houston humidity kills evidence. Guess brass'll approve OT for the move."

"Nope. Professional movers. Then the Chief's hand-picking a new Evidence Department to inventory everything. Big job—but it'll get done right."

"When?"

"Plans are still forming. Budget's the hang-up."

"Figures. They letting Wygant run it?"

Russ snorted. "Wygant? He's ancient. Should've retired years ago."

"Yeah," Jack said. "Some folks can't quit. Or won't."

"Can't quit," Russ replied. "Appeals are coming. Parole hearings. Folks are gonna need evidence."

"Didn't they microfiche old files?"

"Started, but never finished. Physical evidence is the real loss. You can't DNA-test paper. Brass still can't figure how it got this bad. Feels intentional."

"Thanks for the ID." Jack nodded toward the screen.

"Anytime. You staying?"

"Nah. I'm done for the night. Mind if I come back?"

"Just give me dates."

"Appreciate it."

Jack studied Carver's face once more, stopped the recording, and headed out.

In the lobby, he glanced at the obvious cameras—the elevators, the atrium, the front doors. Nothing new.

Up on six, he paused in the corridor and finally noticed it: fake wall plugs near the ceiling, hiding a camera.

A whole department of detectives—and nobody noticed.

He shook his head, amused, and headed home.

29

Nine-thirty a.m., only a handful of guys in the office. The rest were wearing out their shoe leather walking the streets. Dawson took a day off. Jack was on his own.

He booted his system up, yawned, and waited. He'd been up half the night researching the list of case numbers and evidence boxes and had come up empty-handed. The numbering scheme was off, like someone was playing a game with him, challenging him to crack the code. Perhaps these weren't case numbers at all, if no such numbers existed.

Another possibility crossed his mind: they originated from a period prior to modern technology and were later digitized from microfiche or archived in a location where they'd gotten misplaced or lost. He'd tried to make sense of it, but all he had was a square peg that didn't fit into any round hole.

No word from Smitty, either, and no handle on Dellucci. But he'd come up with a plan and needed the boss's help.

If this was a conspiracy—and in his head this thought ran rampant—then anyone catching him riffling through old files and physical evidence was gonna ask why. Especially when there were more current cold cases he should be reinvestigating.

He was gonna need a plausible excuse to be rummaging through old crime scene boxes. The place being a natural disaster meant it could be a futile mission. And with existing security cameras, how would he navigate without restrictions?

Would Roni let him go in after hours and turn off the video recorders? It couldn't hurt to ask once Roni returned from her administrative meeting.

The door squeaked open, alerting Jack.

"Hiya, Jack." Jace passed behind him. "Xi here?"

"In the breakroom, making coffee."

"Good, we're on the move."

"Where ya headed?" Jack asked, half interested.

Jace U-turned. "Couple of teenage boys looking to fish this morning reported a body near the Sheldon Reservoir about an hour ago."

"Man, hope the gators didn't get busy on the body."

"Me too, and I hope they stay outta the way. Hate to shoot one, but I will if they crawl up." Jace shuddered. "See ya."

"Later, Severson, tell Xi howdy."

Jace waved and was out the door.

Jack didn't envy them. It was gonna be a long, sweltering day outside going over a crime scene. And, hell, who were they gonna interrogate? The gators?

Not a fan himself of reptiles—gators, snakes, lizards. Give him a dog—man's best friend. A warm-blooded, furry animal to snuggle with. Who on earth would wanna cuddle a cold-blooded snake?

His head went one way, and he laughed to himself. Brooks was like a snake, an ugly python with bouncy jowls in a reddish face and a forked tongue. Well, this got him back on track: how to dodge the cameras and snoop in the warehouse. He couldn't wait to discuss his plan with Roni.

A FROWN CREASED HER face. "Uh, no, Jack, we can't shut off the feed. We've got to keep the 24-hour monitoring active. Try keeping what you're looking at out of view. Who's gonna know, anyway? Place is disorganized as hell."

"They'll know if we swipe our key cards."

"Excellent point. Then you're gonna hafta break in."

"Done. Hey, Hardy told me a new facility is in the making."

"Yeah, after approval of a budget. You know how it is, HPD has zero cash in the kitty. Scuttlebutt is about a bond."

"A new state-of-the-art storage lockup has my vote."

"Mine too."

Eyes on his lap, Jack rubbed his chin. Should he mention the files and list Yvette gave him? He opted against it. But if he began riffling in the old warehouse, it might arouse suspicions.

"Anything else, Jack?"

"Yeah, how about this comes as a direct order from you and you write me up a bogus list? You sign off on it, make it look official?"

"Any reasons?"

"Yeah, deniability. Then I can inform whoever asks to ask you, and you can tell them it's above their pay grade."

"Roger that. Be in your inbox."

───────

HE WAS BACK AT his desk for three minutes when his phone jangled. "West."

"Hey, Jack."

In the background, he heard people yakking and order numbers being hollered out, along with the sounds of pots and pans clanking.

"Penny, where are you?"

"A new Japanese place. Toshi's. We're on a stakeout—don't ask, cuz I don't have time."

"Okay, g' bye." He paused, holding back his laughter.

"Screw you, Jack. I need a favor."

"What?"

"Write this address down."

"Whose address is this?"

"Katherine Sparks."

"Why do I need it?"

"You have her cell?"

"Yeah. Again, why?"

"Text her a time you can meet her. Look, I gotta go. Alex is coming."

"Sure, Pen, I'll—" The line went dead. She'd hung up, leaving Jack sitting with his mouth open.

───────

ALEX SAUNTERED UP, YAWNING, hot cup of Japanese coffee in hand. "Who're you on the phone with?"

Her anger surged. "You think everything I do is your business? Cuz it ain't. Now move, I wanna order food." Penny brushed past him and headed to the front counter.

Alex followed, his voice low. "No, what you do ain't any of my business, just asking. Why you gotta be a hothead?"

"Look, forget it, just tired. We've been at it for eighteen hours." She yawned. He'd bombarded her with question after question. It was getting on her last exhausted nerve.

"I'm the new guy," he'd said. "You've been here awhile and know the inside scoop."

"Ask them questions, cuz I ain't your pipeline for gossip."

"Tough cookie," he smirked, taking a bag of noodle chips to eat.

JACK TEXTED—SPARKS. SEVENISH TONIGHT. That work?

Katherine replied: Perfect.

Why did Katherine Sparks wanna talk? They hadn't crossed paths in months. He saw her, but only in brief passing.

He recalled that two years had passed since their last real interaction—he'd requested Vice's help on a serial. Right before his sting operation, they all met at Rodeo Goat for lunch: Homicide, Robbery, and Vice.

What'd she tell him? After we wrap up the case, Jack, we need to talk.

Afterward, with all the crap that happened—Gretchen's murder, his quitting, the triple murder, his working with the DEA—the days slipped into years, and they'd never talked.

Had it been important, she would have sought him out, so he gave it no more thought, dedicating the rest of his afternoon helping Reed and Moshe Rybak on a cold case, pursuing leads and contacting people. And not having much luck, either, since most of the players in the investigation were dead or incarcerated.

Some days, in Homicide, clues were like tossing water balloons at a brick wall on a sizzling summer day—everything dried up quick.

30

"NICE PLACE, SPARKS." JACK glanced around her condo. "Homey, yet spacious."

"It's a perfect spot—neighbors are low key. It's convenient for the gym and work. Want a drink?"

"Coffee, straight up, black."

Drink in hand, Jack sat in a wingback chair. Katherine paced.

"Look, Jack, I trust you. I mean—can I trust you?"

"What kinda double talk is this? Of course you can. Why?"

"Brooks."

His radar went up. "Okay. Talk."

Katherine sat on the couch across from him, placed her cup on the end table, and looked at him.

"I worked for the man eight years, and when I got the chance to leave Robbery and join Vice, I jumped like I was on fire. You know, I liked Robbery, and most would say I took a downward slide to Vice. People think the pecking order is flatfoot, Vice, Robbery, up to the ultimate gig of Homicide. No offense, Jack, but I never aspired to be a homicide dick."

"None taken. But where're you going with this?"

"I like Vice—more than I figured I would. Rick and I are well-matched, and it's why I don't want to leave. Just saying. He's a solid partner, and I trust him. Only, he's not who I want on board with what I'm doing."

Jack blew out a sigh. Did she ever get to the point?

"I'm all ears, Kat. What's up? Why's Brooks on your mind? You got a thing for the guy?"

"Piss on you, Jack. No, I don't. Jesus! I've been following him, but not for that effing reason, you asshole," Katherine Sparks spat out. Her and that fat son of a bitch? Jack must be out of his mind.

"I'm just kidding, so jeezers, unwad your bloomers. Tell me—what's the deal?"

"Right at five years ago, I caught Brooks in our pre-evidence lockup."

"What'd he say when he saw you?"

Katherine Sparks cleared her throat. "Um ... he didn't see me. I was, uh, hiding."

Jack's brows knitted together. "I'm gonna ask, so you might as well tell me why you were in hiding."

A pink blush spread over her face. "I, um, wasn't alone. And um—because of our current state of undress—I couldn't just pop out and announce, 'Here I am!' And before you say anything, no, I'm not gonna spill who else was there. That's old news."

"Alright, I get it. Private is private. But it would've been funny if Brooks had caught you in such a state while you were catching him at who knows what he was doing. Ya know—sorta double blackmail."

"Anyway," she said, peeved. "The person I was with didn't see who it was and ducked behind the shelving. I peeked out to see who'd come in. I never told my companion it was Brooks—just said someone came in for a box. One thing I knew was Brooks had no reason to be getting evidence out of our secured storage room, because he wasn't working a case. After he left, me and—um—well, we hotfooted it out. But I went back later to see what he was digging through."

"Which was what?"

"A new case about a truck hijacking."

Jack crossed one leg over the other. "What physical data did you have?"

"I checked the manifest later. A pair of work gloves was missing, and a second set of keys to the truck."

"You say anything to anyone?"

"You're kidding, right? I wasn't supposed to be there, and I was half naked." She blushed.

"Okay. Then what?"

"Any items that came in afterward and got locked into pre-evidence, I tried tracking. Houston is full of robberies, and sometimes the physical evidence is slight. So, I cross-referenced with the case logs, then made a note of everything transferred to main lockup."

"Anything come of that?"

"No. But that doesn't justify tampering with evidence. The caseload was huge, and I had no idea which boxes he was pilfering in."

"Did it hinder any case?"

"I wish I could say for sure. All I'm sure of is it didn't affect any of my investigations. But later, I found out it wasn't just Robbery."

"How, pray tell, did that happen? You get caught with your bloomers around your ankles again?"

"Hilarious, wiseass. No. Late one night I was moving pre-evidence to the main lockup. I was sitting on a stack of boxes, double-checking contents in the back, when he came in. I heard him tell the guard officer not to worry about what he was doing and to keep his nose out of his business. He spouted he was a senior officer and told him to keep his trap shut."

"Well, he is a senior official. He say anything to you?"

"Nah. I hid again. Look, I hate the guy. He's a misogynistic pig and makes me nervous."

"Why do I need to know this?"

"I'm getting to that, Jack. After that day, I wondered why the heck he was in both pre- and post-evidence rooms so often. My caseload was heavy, and I couldn't watch him like a hawk. But I needed to keep tabs. Here's what you cannot say a word about, Jack—and you gotta keep this to yourself, or it could cost me my job." Sparky's face scrunched up, the elevens between her brows puckered.

"On my word, Katherine," he said, using her given name, "I won't tell a soul."

She inhaled, gazing at the ceiling, thinking. Jack waited as the minutes ticked by.

"I installed a nanny cam in post-evidence lockup."

Jack leaned back, expelling air. "Sparks ... wow. Is it still there?"

"No. Took it down three weeks ago."

"You saved the recordings?"

She eyed him. "Yeah. Why?"

"Give them to me and back off. Let me handle things from here, okay?"

"Leave it to you? What am I—chopped dog meat? Is it because I'm a girl?" She folded her arms over her chest, taking on a hostile attitude.

"Don't get your panties in a bunch, and no—it ain't cuz you're a girl." He cast a lengthy glance at her. "Someone has tasked me to dig into things. And no, I cannot tell you more—not until I get the go-ahead. Where are they?"

Katherine relaxed her tense muscles. "On a flash drive."

"Here, at your house?"

"Oh, shit no. Got 'em hidden in a safe place, though."

"Anyone else know about the nanny cam?"

"Penny does. She's sworn to secrecy—I had to tell someone. Listen, Jack, I'll let you take the lead on this, but only for one reason."

"What's that?"

"Because you coldcocked that son of a bitch Brooks. I'm sorry if it dredges up memories, Jack, but it's true. You're a hero for all of us who've had to deal with the fat man. Plus, everyone was glad you shot that murdering rapist piece of shit, Cyrus Shelton."

Jack didn't speak for a second.

Then he said, "I don't wanna be a hero. But since we're sharing secrets, it felt phenomenal hitting the SOB—watching his fat ass go down. Since we are sharing secrets ... about that night you hid—"

She waggled her finger. "Uh-uh. Ain't gonna be a secret we share." She paused. "Unless one day you guess and I tell ya who it was. You know—like the story, Rumpelstiltskin."

Well, now. Another mystery for Jack, but not a damned clue to start with!

31

Four-thirty in the morning, the station's security lights around the perimeter of the squad room the only lights on. Oddly, he was alone, so no need for lots of lights. He needed to meet with Dawson and find out who put those files in Yvette's desk. The unknown older gent was his strongest guess, because Jack was positive it'd been Corey Carver who'd left Yvette the warning.

He texted Luck.

Jack: We need to talk. Breakfast. Waffle House over off I-45, you know the one.

Luck: Why are you up so damn early?

Jack: Get your butt up, be there, one hour.

Luck: Fine.

Jack smiled. Dawson wasn't a morning person.

Lucky slid into the booth. "Too damned early, Jack."

"This is a safe place to chat; no ears. How's it going?"

"Ethan Wygant makes me wanna hurl."

Jack, sympathetic to Luck's situation, said, "I feel for ya, bud."

"It's like jumping in and out of hell and you can't tell which fire will get hotter first and burn your ass. Man, Wygant or shitty Skip, both suck, but at least with Skip I had seniority."

Jack snorted a laugh. "So true."

"You fellas gonna order, or gab?" The older waitress huffed, her pen held aloft next to an order pad, her stare blank.

"Oh, uh, sure. I'll have the All-Star Special with an extra waffle. Jack?"

"Two eggs, scrambled, wheat toast, and hash browns. We need some fresh coffee, too." Jack held up his stained mug. "This is yesterday's."

With a huff, she turned, calling out the order in Waffle House speak as she headed to make a new pot.

"An extra waffle? Dawson, you'll get fat."

"If I were going to get fat, it would've already happened."

The waitress sauntered over with fresh-brewed coffee and their food. They dug in while it was hot, savoring the food and the silence for a minute before Jack decided it was best to eat and talk.

In between bites, he filled Dawson in on the papers and Yvette's cryptic warning, leaving out his meetup with Katherine Sparks.

Chewing a hefty chunk of maple syrup-covered waffle, Dawson's fuzzy unibrow dipped to the center of his face, and his eyes softened. "Sorry that dredges up unhappy memories, Jack. You think Moretti is part of this?"

"I don't see how any of these pieces fit together, not yet anyway. What's Wygant got you working on?"

"I'm the flunky. He's got me rechecking anything checked out, typing up reports, using a damned label maker 'cuz there was a shitload of evidence bagged with handwritten labels, and cataloguing all this crap."

"Who was working with Wygant before you got 'assigned'?" Jack said, using air quotes.

"Six months ago, the doofus was bossing around rookies. End-of-probation boots and, before them, some other guys getting extra hours. Didn't last long when brass cut down on OT."

"So he has you doing busy work, huh?"

"The job needs doing. Remember way back we worked the Mason/Cutter case and Smitty said the place was a mess? He'd been right."

"I remember."

"It's the same chaos here onsite. How anyone finds anything is a mystery."

"I saw Katherine Sparks last night." Jack decided it was best to keep Dawson in the loop.

Lucky wiped the syrup off his mouth, laid his fork down. "Oh? You two go on a date?"

"No, you dip. We discussed Brooks."

He adopted a focused expression, leaning forward, his forearms on the table. "Okay, you have my attention."

"First, I didn't explain to her what Roni and Idiots and Assholes asked us—" He had to pause while Lucky snickered.

"Sorry, Jack. Idiots and Assholes. Greatness. Go on."

"My unexpected visit to five has Penny thinking I'm watching Brooks, so she called Katherine to blab."

"Well, no duh, Sherlock. Penny's a detective. What'd Sparky say?"

No love connection for Jack. Dawson needed to help the guy find a girl; after all this, he'd ask Viv if she had a friend. He'd keep this thought to himself for now.

The waitress laid the ticket down and looked at Jack. Her tone harsh: "No one mentioned separate checks. Split it at the register." She huffed off.

Jack picked up the tab and said, "Wow, what a sweetheart." He viewed the receipt. "I'll get this. You buy next time."

"Should expense it, Jack. Now back to Sparky's story. There's a nanny cam in the cage? Holy shit. Thank heavens I don't parade around doing stupid stuff. She say where it is?"

"Yep."

"Okay, you prick, where is it?" Dawson's face screwed up in frustration.

Jack hemmed and hawed around, messing with him.

"She took it down and has a copy of the recordings in a safe place. Since Katherine's involved, I wanna run this by Roni. Suggest adding another pair of eyes."

"More people involved means they could slip up, say something they shouldn't. You consider that?"

"The difference is I trust Katherine like I do Xi and Jace. It ain't like we're telling Webb, Nichols, or Golan."

"I wouldn't tell those penis-punchers what my shoe size is, even if they were buying me shoes."

"Dawson, with your big-ass feet, no one can find shoes for you."

"Beside the point. Look, anything else you wanna tell me?" He noted the time. "I gotta get to work. Wygant's a jerk. He'll give me a rip for being late."

"Nah, I needta go too. Need to catch Roni up. You head out while I pay the tab. We can talk later."

"Thanks for breakfast, Jack."

"No prob, bud. See ya."

Jack stood in line for the cashier, thinking about his next move. Which was ... what?

He counted them down.

Talk to Roni about Sparks.

Run facial rec on the man he'd captured in the hall by Yvette's office and pray.

Look for old case files in a warehouse perceived to be a natural disaster.

Try locating the case logs and decipher the case numbers, if possible.

Add ten more hours to his day.

"Your ticket. Sir, your ticket." Her behavior was agitated, her hand out, her frown hard. "Cash or card?"

Deep in thought, he hadn't heard her. "Sorry, miss." He handed her a twenty and a ten. She made change, shoving it at him. "Next." Her glare remained fixed on him.

Jack left the change on the table. He didn't get angry, but he didn't have to come back to this Waffle House, either.

This was Texas.

Besides, waitresses were a dime a dozen.

She'd not last long with her attitude.

As he pulled onto the feeder road of I-45, he groaned.

Traffic wasn't as free-flowing as it had been at three a.m., and he hoped Dawson got to Travis Street on time.

Jack didn't want him to land in hot water with Lieutenant Wygant. It made him no never mind if the man's Jockey shorts bunched up his crack, but he didn't want Dawson to receive a rip.

32

Parked, Jack reached over and unlocked his glove box. He retrieved his Glock, grabbed his phone and keys, hopped out, and locked the doors.

The sound of his boots echoed on the pavement as he passed all different modes of transportation, not recognizing who owned what, but wondering as he passed each one.

Who was driving the Chevy Nova, the Jeep Cherokee, or the 1985 VW Beetle classic, baby blue (first time he'd seen this vehicle; nice ride)?

Lots of trucks. Ford, Ram, GMC, Chevrolet, a few Nissans, and several mini-vans. He smiled, thinking about football, baseball, and soccer moms who worked at HPD.

He felt melancholy when he thought about family and children, his thoughts spiraling backward to Gretchen Benson. That gal would've made a fabulous mom, and this saddened him. Some sick bastard had cut her life too short.

Unease washed over him as he grasped the doorknob of the sixth floor. Once seated at his desk, he scanned the room. Cooper, Reed, Rybak, and Potter were present—but the usual boisterous chatter was absent. So when his phone jangled, he jumped half a foot.

"West."

"Jack, my office."

His stomach tightened at her tone. "On my way."

He tapped on her door and entered.

Jace and Xi sat, faces somber, and Jack got worried. Had Luck been in an accident?

"Shut the door and sit." Roni's tone was also somber.

"I'm sitting. Now, I ain't gonna ask twice. Is Dawson alright?"

A tiny puff of air escaped Roni's glossed lips. "He's fine. This is something else." She gestured to Xi.

"Jack, you heard we received a call about a body over at the Sheldon Reservoir yesterday."

"I did. What's up?"

"We found two DB's," Jace interjected.

"Two?" Jack looked at Jace. "Who?"

Xi Chang answered, "Sal Dellucci and Pete Smitherson."

It took a minute before he found his voice. "How and how long?"

"Bodies been there for a few days. Fortunate for us, there was no gator activity. Sal took one shot, execution style."

"Smitty?" Jace spoke. "Looks like he killed himself."

Again, Jack's brain processed. Smitty, suicidal? Nope, couldn't be right. The old man planned it for ten years: retirement, a sleeper boat, and fishing.

"Wait. Jace, you said, 'looks like'. What'dya mean?" Jack couldn't accept that Smitty killed Sal and turned his pistol on himself. He knew the guy. At least, he assumed he did.

"Mack and Benny are all over this." Jace said with sympathy because he knew Jack was fond of Smitty.

"Jack." Roni grabbed his attention. "They found this hidden in Smitty's jacket."

She handed him a clear protective bag with a four by six photo. Permanent creases marred the photo where it'd stayed folded for some time, and the colors were faded. Jack stared at it as a deep furrow rutted between his eyes, trying to identify the faces.

"I didn't recognize them either until I turned it over," Roni stated.

Jack flipped it over. The ink faded. Sal, Brody, me, and Sal's kid—Galveston fishing trip. He noted the date: summer 1988.

All he could say was, "Wow. Brooks was skinny once. Who'da thunk it?" He handed it back. "They went on a fishing trip, so?"

She exhaled. "Jack."

"No, Roni. I just can't wrap my mind around this. Just cuz Smitty's in this picture with Brooks and Dellucci don't mean shit. The guy loved to fish. You guys find a weapon?" He looked at Xi first, then Jace.

"Yeah, we sent it to ballistics."

Jack raked his fingers through his hair. "I can't believe Smitty would kill anyone, including himself. He loved life and wouldn't've hurt a flea."

Roni stood. "This is top priority." Her eyes rested on Chang and Severson. "I want reports in my office yesterday. Your fellow officers know two cops are dead, but not who. The press hasn't gotten wind either, so let's keep it under wraps. Jace, inform CSU, tell 'em to keep a lid on this one."

Xi sat forward. "What about family notifications?"

Roni's eyes scanned her desktop. "Yeah, we gotta make the notifications. Being who it is, Xi, we can't sit on it. We don't know what's what. Tell them about the deaths, but don't give any details."

"It ain't suicide." Jack raked his hand across his face in absolute frustration.

Roni gave him a side-glance before continuing. "Tell them it's top priority, and we intend to keep them informed, but don't mention suicide. Let them believe whatever they wish for now."

"It is suicide until it isn't. Got it?"

"Yes, ma'am." His gut felt sick.

"Jace, you take the lead on the notifications; Xi, you watch reactions. Get back to me."

Xi and Jace stood to leave. So did Jack, but Roni stopped him. "Jack, a word. Xi, close the door."

The room fell silent as Jack struggled to process this news. Roni broke the silence. "Something's off with all this crap."

He'd been studying the swirling browns in the flat carpet in her office. Some spots were brighter while others had faded. He recalled Yao had the desk facing a different wall when he was in the office, before Brooks took over, two years before Roni's arrival. Jolted out of his reflections about desk placement, he spoke. "I'm listening."

"I received a call from Gino Berutti. He told me you needed to stop looking for Sal. Why would he do that?"

A shrug lifted and dropped Jack's shoulders. "Don't know."

"You think Sal was hiding."

A harsh laugh escaped Jack. "From Smitty? That old fart wouldn't have been able to whoop Sal Dellucci in a thumb-fighting contest."

"Maybe."

"No. There is no maybe. Smitty never told anyone he was using a cane. Arthritis set in, and he was having trouble getting around. Because he wasn't up to the job, the warehouse ended up a mess."

Her posture shifted. "News to me. Everyone thought he was a tired, ancient cop waiting to retire. Not a lot he could've done alone anyway; the place was too big of a mess for one old man."

"Thing is, I always worried about him being on a sailboat alone, using a damned cane. Smitty told me he had a friend who was gonna retire about the same time and they were going in together on the boat and—" Jack stopped. He reached for the picture of yesteryear.

"Roni?"

"What?"

"There's a name missing on here."

She took the plastic bag, reading the names, counting them. Next, she studied the faces. "No, same number of names as faces."

"Who's taking the picture, then?"

"Huh, smart question, Jack. Who *is* taking the picture?" She eyeballed the faded photo.

"Can you get me a copy? Front and back?"

"On it."

"Did they find Smitty's cane at the reservoir?"

"I'll ask. Anything else?"

"Yeah." Jack began Katherine Sparks' story—but the captain's hands shot up, waving in the air.

"Stop. Gonna pretend I didn't hear what you just said. I don't wanna know what she did without proper authority. I'd like to have plausible deniability. Understand?"

"Fine. Because Carver works the old warehouse, gonna need a reason to be there digging. Can you send a bogus order to locate unsolved case evidence?"

"You'll have it when I send you a copy of the photo."

"What about Xi and Jace? I don't want them to think I'm stepping on them."

Her eyes grew thoughtful. "Let them work the case. I've got your six."

In the corridor, Jack sent Lucky a text.

Jack's mission: to take a list of random box numbers and case numbers and head over to snoop around. Russ Hardy's statement lingered in his thoughts. Once they started transporting stuff to a new, more efficient warehouse, they were going to be inventorying and cataloging all the evidence before relocating it. If certain pieces of cogent evidence were missing from their boxes, what would happen then?

Who would they hold accountable?

It would be an investigation to end all investigations.

The breach would require an internal investigation, with IA reviewing all personnel back to the day they were born. They would leave no stone unturned.

Given her knowledge, would Detective Sparks risk her job to guide IA towards the truth? Jack had to consider: if it were him, would he? Yeah, he'd take a chance, but he could only answer for himself, not Katherine.

Jack sat in his truck, looking at the entrance of the crumbling warehouse.

Smitty's face popped into his head. Could he have been on the take? He found this hard to believe. How well did he know Smitty?

He guessed it didn't matter because the guy was dead.

And Brody Brooks. How did he fit in?

33

OFFICER CARVER SAT AT the desk, feet propped up, a cell phone stuck to his ear and a frown plastered on his face.

"So what? It's not my problem."

The person on the other end said, "That old guy must've stashed it there. Find it, numbskull!"

Carver, rolling his eyes with a hateful expression, clenched out, "Fine! But who cares? If it stays lost,—good for us."

The unknown person on the other end clutched the handset so hard his knuckles turned white as his jaw tightened and popped. "If someone finds it, you boob, then what? We can't destroy it if we can't find it, you numbskull. Am I gonna hafta come over there and kick your ass—or make a phone call?"

Carver leaned forward, stiffening, his voice tight. "Alright, I'll—" He saw a car pull in. "Gotta go, someone's here." Disconnecting, he sat up, trying to appear busy, his gaze fixed on his task. Holding up a finger, he said, "Be with you in a minute."

Jack peered at the man's bent head. "No hurry." He cast a suspicious glance at the paperwork Carver was working on. His brows furrowed. Looked like a ruse to him, but he said nothing and waited. He kinda felt sorry for the guy. In a brief time, he was gonna discover that his father was dead.

Carver glanced up. "Can I help you?"

"Yeah, I need some old boxes."

"Name."

"West."

"Got a requisition?"

"No, call my superior." Jack's stare was intense.

Carver's lips curled in a sneer, and he huffed. "What box are you looking for?"

Jack handed him numbers relating to real cases, only not ones he wanted. "Can you get to them right away?"

Carver looked over the numbers, knowing nothing was where it should be. "You need 'em now, or want me to call you after I've located them?"

"Per my captain, need them now," Jack lied.

A hefty lament exited Carver's lips. "Gonna hafta buzz you in and you'll have to search yourself. I can't leave the desk since there's no one else here."

"They didn't have all this before."

"All what?"

"The cage. Smitty ran the unit several years ago. You remember Smitty?"

Carver's face was stony. "Nope, never met the old geezer." He slipped a clipboard through the opening. "Sign in, name and badge number so I can buzz you in."

Jack complied, and waited, his thoughts on one dead Pete Smitherson, aka Smitty, and an old photo. Carver was only a kid back then. He was lying. He knew Pete.

"How long you think you'll be?"

Jack's eyes bored into Carver's. "Depends on how organized this place is. Here's the list. What do you think?"

Carver studied random names and case numbers. "Long list. You'll be here for weeks searching. The place is a disaster. Hell, I'm just one man."

"Yeah, so I see." Jack turned and disappeared into the warehouse. Carver stared at the closed door. He didn't like it. Why was Jack West, in truth, here?

In the back, Jack groaned.

He and Dawson got fortunate to find the boxes they'd needed for the Mason/Wolff case. Lord, six years had blown by.

He stood, his hands on his hips, eyeing the mess. His boots clunked on the concrete floor as he made his way to the back.

He guessed older cases were in the back. Jack slipped off his jacket, hanging it on the edge of a shelf, and began the tedious job of searching for an unmarked box with case logbooks.

INSIDE THE FRONT OFFICE cage, Corey frowned. He wondered if he should call Brody, tell him Detective West was snooping around. The phone rang, shaking him out of his thoughts.

"Evidence Warehouse, Carver."

He listened, his hand gripping the receiver.

"Get there as soon as I can." He hit the power source, ending the call, and dialed another number.

"Central Evidence, Luck."

"Lieutenant Wygant."

"Who's calling?"

"Carver."

"One minute."

After relaying the message, Dawson Luck lifted the receiver, pressing down the bar, giving it to the count of five before letting it up to listen in.

"Ethan, something's happened. Send someone to cover me."

Without asking what, Wygant said, "Lock up and take off."

"I can't. Someone's here."

"Who?"

"Jack West."

"What's he doing there?" Wygant asked, agitated.

"Captain Justice sent him with a list. How should I know? But I hafta go, right now."

"Can't you wait?"

"No, I got a call. Don't ask me anything else."

Ethan reined in his retort. "Let me find someone to cover and don't you dare leave until someone gets there, you hear me?"

"Fine, but hurry." Carver hung up. His face squished in concern.

Why was Gino calling him? Uncle Gino, yeah right. He no more acknowledged him as his nephew than he did Sal as a half-brother.

Corey hated that family for not giving his father a birthright, not letting him become a legitimate Berutti and join the family business.

Nope. He and pop were stuck being cops—poor, law-abiding cops.

Ha! Cops for the Beruttis' benefit.

Gino sounded distressed. Had dear old Grandpa Carmine died?

This would be fantastic news if Grandpa Carmine left a will with his name in it.

ETHAN WYGANT DIALED ANOTHER number, hating to have to ask a favor from any woman. "Captain Justice, Wygant in Evidence. I need a favor. I'm short staffed today and if Webb ain't on a case, can you send him to cover Carver at off-site? Oh, so Nichols ain't free either—how about Leon Golan? Excellent, appreciate it."

Dawson disconnected after Wygant did. Carver had an emergency and needed to leave. It happens.

Lucky rubbed his chin. He requested Webb or Nichols; only they were working a case, so his third choice was Leon Golan. All three were minions of Brody Brooks.

Why not ask for a patrol officer to cover for a short time? This issue was weird, and he figured Jack needed a heads-up Golan was on his way.

From the adjacent office, Wygant jerked out his cell, opened his contacts list, hit call, and, when the other party connected, said, "Berutti called Carver, shit's fixing to hit the fan." He disconnected.

COBWEBS COVERED MOST BOXES. Jack ventured to the back section, spot-checking box numbers, hoping for a miracle. He figured the boxes he searched for, being older, should be shabby, so his eyes scanned the shelves, in particular the top shelves, and toward the back. Boxes were crammed haphazardly on the shelves, the labels hidden so you couldn't tell what was what—the boxes all looked the same, their contents unknown.

It was hot, although the warehouse had overhead fans and an aftermarket AC system. His hands sweated inside the latex gloves. He wiped the perspiration on his upper lip with his wrist and sighed. His cell rang. Dawson Luck's name popped up.

"Hey, Dawson, what's up?"

"Jack, Wygant has Golan on his way over there to relieve Carver."

"Why?"

"Maybe Carver heard about Sal. It's all I can think of. I listened in on the call. Carver sounded stressed, but didn't tell Wygant anything, except you were there. Wygant was quick to say he was sending someone over to cover."

"I see. Thanks for the heads up." He disconnected. Golan would say something to Webb, and of course, they'd tattle to Brooks. It didn't matter, though. If Wygant knew, Brooks would, too.

So far, it'd been a bust. He'd have to come after hours, bring someone with him. Dawson or Katherine.

Better disappear before Golan showed up.

Jack wiped sweat off his lip and shoved the list into his pocket. He was grabbing his sports coat off the back rack when someone called his name.

"Hey, West? You back there?"

Golan. Damn.

He got here fast.

"Yeah, back here."

Leon strode in like he was on a mission. "West."

"Where's Carver?"

The other man glowered. "Had an emergency, I was told, and I'm covering. What you looking for? I thought you got taken off the cold case?"

"Captain Justice wanted me find stuff she needs."

Leon's eyes narrowed. "She ain't working a case. Why she want these?"

Jack drew himself up to his full, six-foot-one frame, his eyes boring into Leon's, who was a foot shorter. "She's the boss—or have you forgotten who the boss is? If she wants something, I don't ask, I just do."

"Well, hooray for you. Bring them if you find any and let me log them out." Leon left in a huff.

He guaranteed Leon Golan would watch the warehouse monitors, so he kept his back toward any camera. As he moved from shelf to shelf, he put on an act of frustration—tapping his boot or pencil against the metal frames, scanning the area and the bogus list, not seeming to locate what he searched for. He gave it about an hour, folded the list, shoved it into his back pocket, and returned to the front office.

"Didn't find it, did ya?" Golan sat, his feet propped up on the counter, smirking.

"No, you're right. Place looks like an F-4 tornado hit it and hasn't stopped. Similar to five years ago. Smitty was still on the job then. You meet Smitty, Leon?"

Without pause, he replied, "Nope, never dealt with the old geezer."

Jack's lips turned down and his brow wrinkled. "Thought for sure you met him. Didn't Brooks have you, Skip, and Nichols work that old cold case together?"

"What case are you yammering about?"

"The robbery at the diamond exchange."

"Shit, that case is ancient. Waste of time, if you ask me. I didn't work it; Webb and Nichols did. You wanna know, ask one of them."

"So," Jack said, slipping off his gloves. "You never came over here?"

"West, is there something you need? Cuz I damn well ain't one of your buddies, and you can stop with the effing third degree."

"Lord, Leon, you're a pisser! I hope Roni never partners us."

Jack turned to go, and Golan said, "Be your lucky day, asswipe, maybe you'd learn how to be a real cop."

Jack sneered.

'Real cop,' indeed.

34

Corey knocked, popping his head into the doorway. "You called for me?"

"Come in," the patriarch commanded. He frowned, pointing. "Close the door. Sit."

His grandfather, Carmine Berutti—a larger-than-life presence—made him feel inferior as he sat.

Neither spoke.

The traditional grandfather clock ticked behind the old man's impressive desk.

A place where men sat, getting orders to whack other men or told which trucks were gonna get hijacked. The boss communicated info like which thug had the goods, where to sell them, and prices.

Same place this powerful man sat instructing his capos on union business, and where and when the next shipment of cocaine would arrive. A place where soldiers or associates got orders. A piece of furniture where plans to exchange money or to buy favors from politicians or cops were discussed.

This is where his old man played a role.

A cop on the take.

"Corey." Carmine's voice rumbled in his chest. "Have you heard?"

A puzzled look crossed Corey's face. "About what, sir?" Although he hated his grandfather, he showed him respect.

"Someone killed my boy."

Uncle Gino called him. He wasn't dead. A beat of silence. Corey's face crumpled, his voice breaking. "My—my—someone killed my dad?"

"This is not the time to show weakness. Smitty got whacked, too."

Corey's brows dipped as his gut wrenched. His stare was hard. "What happened?"

"Answers later. After they log the gun into evidence, get it, and bring it to me."

"Why?"

Carmine hit the top of the desk and bellowed, "Do as you're told! Don't question me, you insignificant bastard."

"Just like my papa. The other bastard. Right, Grandpa?" Corey's scowl contorted his face into an ugly expression. "I'm sick of this. Get somebody else to do your dirty work—or did you already? Was it you? Did you pay someone to whack my old man? Betcha it cost a pretty penny. That right, Gramps?" His eyes bored into the elderly man's, his hatred erupting.

Carmine leaned into his desk, his dark black eyes snapping in anger. "You little prick, you've been nothing but trouble for our people." As Carmine leaned back, the side door swung open.

Corey looked over; his face fell.

Gino Berutti strode into the room, Brody Brooks trailing close behind, followed by Gary Yardley, who said, "Carver, you do what the boss says or I'll make your life a living hell."

JACK'S TRUCK LURCHED FORWARD as he pulled out of the parking lot, the tires crunching on the gravel. Via Bluetooth, he called Luck.

Dawson's voice was low. "Let me call you back in two." He hung up without waiting for a reply.

Jack had driven down the road a few miles when the Bluetooth in his truck bleeped and Luck's name came up on the ID.

"Luck."

"Yeah, sorry. Wygant walked up. Didn't want him to hear me. What's up?"

"It's the same mess as last time. I'm heading back. Text me before you leave. Got a plan I wanna run by ya."

"Will do. Okay, honey, I'll see ya at home."

Jack hung up with a laugh. Ethan Wygant was within earshot, so Dawson pretended he was talking to his wife, Vivian. Smart fish.

As THEY SAT IN the large, paneled study, Corey Carver's heartbeat increased. He was positive one of them killed his dad and Smitty. His dad, dead—it wasn't something he could fathom.

His father was a cop, but as Corey aged, he knew the expensive lifestyle they lived wasn't on a police officer's wages.

As a happy youngster, he'd never questioned where things came from.

Luxury box seats at the Astrodome; seats on the fifty-yard line, so close you could almost touch the players. The men his father associated were, or had friends who were, friends with famous athletes, and he remembered instances where a prominent football or baseball player would ruffle his hair and shake his hand.

The name-brand shoes and clothes; high-quality food, nice restaurants. And his mom seemed happy.

With age, he embraced these gifts as an unseen benefit for putting your life on the line as a police officer and never questioned his father's actions.

Corey recalled his dad telling his mom he was working overtime. Extra shifts at night. Turns out, it had nothing to do with police work. It had been Berutti family work. Moonlighting for the Mafia. Terrific work if it didn't get you whacked or land you on death row.

One day it stopped.

Dear dad sat him down when he was sixteen because rumors had begun and the kid was asking questions.

Sal Dellucci explained how things were—and that, if he liked his lifestyle, he'd keep mum.

Corey idolized his old man. He swore he only did minor illegal things, but as a cop, well, best if no one knew, so he could keep his job with the force.

He trusted his father and kept his mouth shut as Sal sank deeper into the family business, dragging Corey in with him when he turned twenty-three. That was the night everything shifted. Afterward, his father ordered him into the police academy, insisting it was for his own good. Sal was forty-two then, no spring chicken. Corey felt bound by duty—but never by choice—to step into the shadows of a world he'd never wanted.

"CARVER, YOU KNOW THE drill." Gary Yardley's deep voice brought him into the present.

"What drill?"

Brooks frowned at him. "Don't act like an idiot, son."

"Brody." His eyes burned into the fat man's. "No, I ain't gonna fucking call you Commander. You don't got that title in this room, hear me?" Corey Carver grew brave, even though it felt as if, at any moment, his stomach contents were gonna be all over Grandpa's ugly, six-thousand-dollar Persian rug. "I don't know what fucking drill you're talking about."

His face drew up in anger, and the aged gent took his cane from where he'd propped it and stood, stepping around his magnificent desk. With his aging and weakened limbs, Carmine Berutti was not as strong as he used to be. None of that mattered, though. These men were his arms and legs, and Corey knew it, and if the old man took his walking cane and pointed it and said shoot, he'd be dead with a bullet between his eyes without getting to blink.

"Gino, help me to the car. Corey, you too."

"No. I'm not taking off with you, not knowing where we're going. Might be heading to my unexpected death." Carver's heart pounded.

Carmine sighed. "I am too old and too tired for this." He gazed at the boy who was his illegitimate grandson and his face aged forty more years. "Right now, we're going to the funeral home to make the arrangements for when they release his body from the morgue." Carmine regarded Brooks. "Get your people to help facilitate his release ASAP."

Brody nodded. "I'll do my best."

Gary Yardley opened the door for Old Man Berutti. "What do you need from me, Carmine?"

Carmine stopped to stare at him, his face puckered in thought, then said, "Inform our contact at the Chronicle that this is not about family rivalries. Find out from your inside contacts if the Department is going to begin an inquisition into the cases Sal worked. Move paperwork around and make sure they think Smitty is the doer."

Yardley nodded his understanding and glanced at Brooks. "You think Webb can help?"

"Yeah, he will. I got him by the balls."

Carmine planted his cane and turned his head back. "People are gonna start digging and we need to keep that from happening." He looked at Corey. "Lots of sins in our family we want to stay buried, ain't that right, boy?"

Carver's eyes smoldered. He nodded without speaking.

Not once did he ask to be rescued that night.

Now, these years later, his participation in "family business" would cost him the rest of his life—or be his death sentence.

35

It was nearing ten o'clock when they pulled into the unmonitored parking space beside the building. Jack cut the engine. "You still wanna go through with this?"

"Will you stop it? I can handle myself—lipstick or gun. Shit!"

"Hey, just asking so you won't blame me for losing your job."

"You dork. We'll both be unemployed. Besides, I know how to break into buildings. Man, I learned from crooks back in Robbery. Get the ladder out; let's cover the camera."

Jack took the roof ladder from his truck, and they moved in at an angle, ducking beneath the camera. He propped it against the wall under the device, and Katherine climbed up, placing a brown lunch sack over the monitoring apparatus and securing it with tape.

As she climbed down, he whispered, "When we get inside, the other closed-circuit television is three feet in, so we gotta duck low."

"Yeah, Jack, I've been in here before. You forget who I am or what?"

"Kinda bitchy, aren't ya?"

The feisty redhead rolled her eyes. "Just let me break in, will ya?"

With a single sweeping motion, he signaled for her to lead the way.

"Oh, and don't let me forget my ladder."

Katherine bent her head as she concentrated on the lock, snickering. "Why? Is your name and address written on it in Sharpie?"

"No, but I didn't wipe it, and my prints are all over it."

"Point taken," she said as the click of the lock sounded. "Gotta hurry and disarm the system. Come on, duck down, tall man." She rushed in, bent low, and made it to the alarm box in three seconds flat. She opened it and punched in the code.

"Good to go. Now, let me disable the inside monitors. Give me a second." She walked to the front desk, flipped some buttons, and voila—no more eyes watching.

Jack smiled, shaking his head. "Who gave you the alarm code, missy?"

Her laugh rang out. "I broke into Brooks' desk, got it from his list."

"Remind me not to let you near my valuables. You'd make a decent thief."

"Jack, you're a cop. You have nothing of value other than your piece. Oh, and maybe some secrets." She winked as she passed him. "Come on, they're down. Russ Hardy can monitor these whenever he wants—he controls the mainframe."

"No worries. I talked to him and asked a favor."

"Oh?" She turned, hands on hips. "He owes you a favor?"

"Nope, but I trust him. Asked him to ignore these cameras tonight."

"Yeah, and he said?" She gloved up, eyeing countless boxes.

"'What cameras?'" Jack gloved up and sneezed.

"Gesundheit," Katherine responded.

"Thanks. You brought the list?"

"Yep, and you're right—these aren't legit case numbers, not the way they're written. I had to think back on the old numbering system."

"Old numbering system?"

"My dad was a former LAPD officer. They had an intricate fifteen-digit numbering structure, and it got me thinking."

"Your pop was LAPD? Wow, learning new stuff about you, Sparky—this and your romp in pre-evidence, and who the other party was." His grin was lecherous.

"Still not telling ya. Dad died five years ago—liver failure."

"Sorry, Sparks."

"Thanks. Now, back to these numbers. In LA, the numbers meant a retention year, location—like Metro, Transit, or Sheriff's Department—and patrol section. There were three digits denoting type of crime, like 011 for murder. The problem is, I don't know how HPD did it back then."

"Me neither."

"Well, if we look at it like an LAPD case number, it'd mean this was a case from like 1978-79. What kind of case, though, who knows?"

A thought struck him as they stared at the numerals. "What if we truncate the digit sequencing? In the middle?" He underlined the middle numbers.

Katherine eyed it. "This is ancient history."

"Yeah," Jack replied, "I was born in '80."

She grinned. "Old as dirt, aren't we?"

"Are files kept this long?"

"Don't know. Never asked." Her flashlight guided her as she dashed to the back of the warehouse.

His light followed her, his face contorted. "Where're you headed?"

"Back, a few decades. Come on."

AT THE FARTHEST POINT in the rear of the drafty storeroom, the concrete floor was dirty, and dead insects, as well as live ones, scurried behind storage containers or across the floor. Dust lay several inches thick. Cardboard cartons covered with spiderwebs, dead roaches, crickets, and rat droppings were stacked box on box, their weight causing lids to split at the corners.

Plastic totes of varied sizes sat askew on racks; their hardened lids cracked under the stress of stacked totes. Not a well-traveled area of the over fifteen-thousand-square-foot repository. They'd started filling center aisles every five feet, moving ancient records farther back for newer physical data.

A new facility with tech advancements could have regulated temperature and organization—a pressing need for Houston. Lord knew how much evidence—DNA and other physical proof—was no longer viable, not having survived the test of time. Not all property was vacuum-packed or sealed for proper preservation.

With a gloved hand, Jack wiped away grime to read the label at the end. "Kinda faded ... looks like 1999."

She examined it. "Yeah, '99, and there's a name. Horace Hicks, and a file number underneath. That's how the files got listed. Let's search for 1979. The next five digits must be a case number."

"Maybe. Twenty years is a lot of cases." He exhaled, scanning the rows of shelves. "If we each take a side, we'll make better time."

Forty-five minutes later, he heard her call out in a low undertone, "Over here, Jack."

He located her four rows away, perched on a ladder.

"I found the first box of 1979."

"Correct case number?"

"No. But we have a starting place. Wait." She climbed down, wiped dirt off her gloves, and pointed. "Nineteen seventy-eight ended there. Nineteen seventy-nine starts here. If the cartons stayed in any kind of order, depending on caseloads, this box"—she looked at the middle numbers on the list—"should be two or three rows over."

"One way to find out," he said. "Lead the way, Sparky."

After two tries, they found the right case number, grabbing the box. Angelo Conti. Murder victim from 1979, stamped Unsolved.

"Ever heard of this fella, Jack?"

"No, but look."

"At what?"

"The tape. It's newer."

Her head bobbed. "Yep, someone opened it and resealed it, not too long ago."

Jack snapped a photo of the info label. "Let's stash this one and search for the others."

An hour later, they'd found two more: Ed Gresham, 1996, and Lloyd Olsen, 1998, both stamped Unsolved and resealed.

"Jack, it's one-thirty. We gotta scat. I have early roll call."

"Yeah, and I—" He halted, a finger on his lips, signaling her to turn off her light. "We've got company."

"Well shit, now what?"

Jack motioned. "Come on, duck down."

At the end of the row, he turned left, heading to the farthest corner, behind a stack of aged wooden pallets.

"Uh, Jack, we've cornered ourselves." Worry clenched her stomach.

"Stay here." He pulled his handgun, chambering a round. "If things go bonkers, call for backup."

"You can't go out there. What if—"

He cut her off. "Stop acting like a girl and arguing."

Oh lord, the look she gave him could have melted Iron Man. Katherine removed her piece from her hip holster, chambering a round. "I've got your six.

Plus, Rick and Penny are on speed dial—they'll have the wrath of hell down here in a heartbeat."

His face hardened.

"Fine. Follow me."

36

JACK, AT THE END of the aisle, gave a "watch me" signal before moving past the first shelf. Ducking low, he paused at the end, then motioned for her to follow.

With enough space for two adults to stand side-by-side between the rows, he whispered, "There's an exit in the back that opens from the inside. We're gonna sneak up, get eyes on our company, then scram. Clear?"

She tucked her revolver into the back of her jeans, covering it with her shirttail, and pulled out her iPhone.

"Whatcha doing now?"

"Kodak moment. Keep your fat head out of the way."

He swallowed a laugh. "Fine. I'll go left; you go right. Be careful."

Jack reached the end of the shelving and took a quick look.

"CAN'T BELIEVE THE DILDO forgot to set the alarm. Gonna hafta ask Leon about this mess-up. Hey! Watch where you're walking, would ya? You're stepping on the back of my shoes, moron."

"My bad," the other man said. "You know where to look?"

"No, I don't. Zip it, will ya?"

"What's stuck up your butt? Nobody's here but us. Stop acting like a dame."

He turned; his heavy frame knocked against a metal post. Four double-stacked rows over, Jack thrust his face out enough to get a rear view. Brooks! He'd recognize that wide rear and bald cranium anywhere. With stealth, Jack retreated, concealing himself behind a box-filled shelf.

The other man's voice was unfamiliar.

"We got too much at stake, that's what's up my big fat butt," Brooks said. His tone hardened. "Quit yapping and look for the damn book, or you'll be next—with a bullet to the brain."

With care, Jack began backing up, then his foot hit another. His heart stopped; he held his breath.

"Jack." Katherine's voice was low, almost a whisper. "It's me."

He turned deliberately, lowering his piece. "You scared the dickens outta me." His eyes met hers. She nodded, mouthing the name Brooks and pointing behind him.

Jack backtracked to the right, but paused midway, placing a finger to his lips. Footsteps sounded—time to run. He grabbed her hand and hurried to the farthest end of the row, ducking behind the sixth shelf. With their backs to the shelves fifty yards away, they held their breath.

"You hear that?"

"Just rats. This place is full of 'em. Let's move. We gotta find that book." Brody exhaled.

"Got any idea where to look?"

"All I know is it's in a box from years ago, but the dildo moved it." Brooks' agitation rose.

"I can't believe about Smitty and Sal, can you, Brody?"

"Got what was coming to 'em. So will you if you don't zip it! Stop gabbing and help me. Jesus, you talk too much!"

Jack and Katherine exchanged glances. Had Brooks just implied someone murdered Smitty and Sal?

"Yeah, yeah, fine, you fat bastard."

Brody turned on a dime, facing the short but burly man. "Look-it, greaseball. I might be a fat bastard, but it ain't my ass we're looking out for, so shut your pie hole."

"Oh yeah? Huh, I gotta beg to differ with ya, Brooks. It's yours too—not to mention a few others'. Shit. This went downhill so fast. And Smitty? Why him?"

Brooks turned back, tugging his pants over his sagging middle. "I don't give that type of orders, numbskull. I do what I'm told, and God forbid I don't."

Jack listened, Katherine's slow breathing on his neck, her fingers gripping his arm with every word. His breath hitched. Time to skedaddle. With his head angled around his right shoulder, he whispered, "We need to make a break for the rear exit."

Katherine stepped back, the corner of her shirt catching a long screw on the steel bracket. She yelped, then bolted; he followed closely.

"Who the hell's here?" Brooks' feet shuffled fast for an overweight man, and he screamed again, "State your name! I got a gun, and I will shoot!"

He stared at Sam. "What are you waiting for, nimrod? Run, motherfucker! Catch 'em!"

Sam Coolidge sprinted, but his slick-soled shoes produced no traction on concrete. He slid into a rack, overturning a shorter standalone shelf. Boxes spilled, tape breaking, evidence sliding under racks and onto the footpath. He stumbled over a lid and a large sack filled with clothes from a crime scene, along with other evidence bags.

Brooks panted behind him, red-faced from exertion. When the back door slammed against the wall, the warehouse rattled.

Instead of heading straight to his pickup, Jack sprinted to the front entrance.

"Jack, we can climb the fence and hop over; it's faster," Katherine said, pulling at his arm.

"Gotta get the ladder. Also, you handled that camera barehanded! Hurry!"

Her eyes widened, sprinting ahead. Jack grabbed the ladder, steadying her as she reached it. She yanked off the sack and tape, cramming it in her pocket, then slid down.

"I'll carry the ladder. Take my keys. I'm right behind you." Jack pitched her his keys.

Katherine ran, climbed the chain-link fence, unlocked the pickup, started it, and did a U-turn to be next to the palisade. Jack hurled the ladder; the metal clanged thunderously. He hauled himself over, grabbing the strands of barbed wire, avoiding injury.

Just as his door slammed, Katherine took off, the momentum pulling him flat to the seat. He grabbed the seatbelt and buckled in.

"Alright, Speed Racer. When you reach the end of the street, turn right. Then slow the hell down. AND," he eyeballed her, "where were you hiding those roughneck work gloves?"

"Jack, you didn't think my boobs were that big, did you?" She winked, turning right.

SAM SAW THE TAILLIGHTS of the truck but not the plate number—the night made it impossible. Brooks panted, almost running him down.

"You get a look at 'em? Or the plate number?" he wheezed.

"No, and stop shoving me, you fat pig. It's too dark. I got old eyes, same as you." He brushed past and went inside, Brooks following, securing the exit.

"Why would anyone be nosing around?"

Brooks sighed. "I told ya West was here snooping today. Gotta be him, I'm sure."

"How would he know what to look for?" Sam scratched his chin and hocked a loogie.

"Wipe that up, you idiot. He knows because Frank Windom told the kid everything."

"Frank's dead. The kid never said or did anything. Too late now, ain't it?"

Brooks shook his head. "You think we can't go down for this crap? The evidence we've tampered with over the years? And the crap from one night a kid gets shot, and we gotta cover it up?"

"He doesn't know. No way he can, and more to the point, we've covered our tracks."

Brooks jabbed Sam in the chest. "Yep, but one person kept a diary of everything since '74, and he's dead. Shit! We gotta find that fucking book."

"Get your pudgy paw off me," Sam snapped. "Smitty was old, but he wasn't dumb. No one but Frank suspected, and if he had proof, he'd have turned, brother in blue or not. We'd be wearing orange jumpsuits, living in an eight-by-eight cell."

Brody snarled, "And I ain't going to prison now, either. They'd fuck us ten ways to Sunday in jail."

"Or the old man will have someone cut us up and use us for fish bait down in the Gulf," Sam bit back.

37

"You're kidding! Brooks was sneaking around in the warehouse?" Dawson couldn't contain his surprise. His voice carried.

"Shush," Jack signaled. "Yeah. Didn't recognize the other voice, and I heard him say Brooks. Katherine snapped a photo with her cell, but it was too dark."

"What was he hunting for?"

Jack updated him on the book and about Smitty and Sal.

Dawson fidgeted. "Holy mother, he knows about those two and ain't saying anything?"

"Yep, only we can't say a word since we were never there."

"Gawd almighty, Jack, this means Brooks could be involved in a conspiracy to cover up a murder."

"Uh-huh, with what proof?"

Dawson's face crumpled. Jack was right. "Okay, what else?"

Jack pulled out his cell. "I took snaps of the labels for each box we found. Let's check into these investigations. We can use the unoccupied office on nine. I'll bring my laptop. Brooks knows I was at the warehouse yesterday, and we can't risk him showing up on six. What's Wygant gonna say about you not showing up for work?"

Dawson shrugged. "I left him a note. Told him to contact Captain Justice about my absence. I'm betting she can handle him as well as she did with Brooks."

Jack nodded, tucking his laptop under his arm. "Let's get outta here."

THEY SHUT THE DOOR and locked it. Jack booted up his computer and began typing in the ancient case numbers: Angelo Conti, 1979 homicide, unsolved; Ed Gresham, 1996; and Lloyd Olsen, 1998.

"Alright, Jack. One unsolved and two dismissed without prejudice—but not closed."

"Only suspect was Paulie Baglio—they cleared him. No statute of limitations on murder, so we need to figure out what happened. Problem is the cases are old. Lots of players might be dead, missing, or in jail. Crap shoot." Jack leaned back, tilting the worn office chair. "Only the boxes had new tape, meaning someone was looking at physical evidence. So, what were they after?"

Dawson frowned. "How about connecting dots with these victims? Whoever gave Yvette this list had a reason to group them together."

"We need the murder books too, not just physical evidence."

Dawson exhaled sharply. "Jack, no way we can just walk in and grab stuff without a requisition or explanation."

"Easy-peasy. We'll get Roni to type up an official retrieval order saying we are reviewing these cases. You go talk to Roni while I chat with Katherine, okay?"

"Sure. I want to get on this ASAP so I can stop reporting to lard-ass Wygant and come back to Homicide."

———

"WHAT A RUSH, JACK. I thought we were dead meat." Sparky put her booted feet up on the metal desk.

"Glad they didn't catch us, but we know who was there—Brooks. Did you recognize the other voice?"

Her red tresses shook as she bit her bottom lip in thought. "Wish Brooks had used his name. Oh, too bad we disabled the—oh shit, Jack, we didn't reset the feed. Crap."

Jack let out a short, sputtered laugh. "No worries, Sparky. Thought about it after I got home. I shot Russ Hardy a text, asked for a quick remote reset. No questions."

"You're certain he won't ask questions?"

"Nah, Russ is cool. Look, I need those nanny cam files. How fast can you get them to me?"

Katherine slid off her desk, opening the bottom drawer. She dug to the back and pulled out a box, making Jack laugh when she handed it to him.

"Tampons, Sparks? Have I given you the impression I'm ready to start?" He arched his brows.

"Best place to hide anything you don't want some dude snooping. No guy will bother a box of a gal's pull strings."

Jack glanced around, then held out his hand. "Dump it into my palm. Don't wanna be that one guy with a box of tampons in his back pocket."

She dumped the contents. A USB drive fell out, along with four tampons. He palmed the drive, letting the sticks roll onto the floor.

Katherine laughed, bending to retrieve them and shoving them back into the box.

"Anyone snooping would think it's just tampons. Let's talk about what's recorded."

"I already know what you're gonna say."

The spunky redhead crossed her arms, leaning back. "Oh?"

"Not admissible in court. No orders given to place the device, nor was it approved. But my plan is to see what files he was digging into if I can. Then figure out why."

"You need me to dig into anything?"

"Nah, might be better if you stay out of it. Otherwise, you'll have to explain why you were hiding in pre-evidence." One brow sprang up with his lecherous grin.

"Yeah, best for me to stay out of it. No proof I was ever there, except for what you hold in your hand."

"Promise to keep your secret." Jack lifted his hand in oath. "Gotta run—Dawson gets impatient when I take too long. Say hey to Rick."

"Sure. Oh, keep those eyes in the back of your skull open, Jack, 'cause Brooks knows people from all departments."

"Will do, Sparky, will do. Adios."

In the stairwell, Jack looked at the thumb drive, hoping it would lead somewhere. But he wouldn't review it here. He'd wait until home. He hoped to catch up with 7-11 first.

———

"Jack. About time."

"I wasn't gone that long. What's up?"

Lucky lowered his tone. "First, you get what you needed?"

"Yeah."

"What's on it?"

"Didn't look. Gonna take it home."

Lucky's face darkened. He was about to let loose when Jack shook his head. "Before your noodle explodes, wanna grab KFC, have a beer, eat, and watch together?"

Dawson was surprised. Jack never invited him over.

"Well?" Jack prodded.

"Yeah, sure. I'll buy the sides. Taters, gravy, fried okra okay?"

"Perfect. You hear from 7-11?"

"I texted Jace. They're headed back from the morgue. Be here in ten."

"I'll text Xi to meet us in that vacant office on nine." Jack's stomach tightened. He was sure 7-11 had more info on their case, and his gut said Smitty did not off himself. He prayed he was right.

38

ALL FOUR FOUND RAGGED, worn-out office chairs in the vacant office.

"You guys look beat."

"Thanks, Jack, love you too, brother."

"Sorry, Jace. I know this has y'all worn to a frazzle."

Xi let out a long sigh. "That ain't the half of it. The Berutti family is breathing down our necks to get it out to the press that an ex-cop executed Carmine's son, then ate his gun."

Lucky's brows dipped. "Isn't that the story, Xi?"

"No, Dawson, we don't think it is."

"Xi's right. It's still undetermined."

"Come on, Jace. You can't give us that bullcrap. What's Mack saying? Bennie? Who's doing the autopsies?"

Jace gave Jack a look. "Alright. Bennie's performing Smitty's autopsy. You wanna hear what he said?"

"Nah, I want you to sing and dance, you moron. Shit."

"Don't be mean, Jack. You know Jace has two left feet."

West smirked. "Xi, you're a funny guy. Let's hear it."

"Right. The stippling on Smitty's temple suggests someone pressed a revolver against it, hard, but it's still not proof he killed himself."

"When they say a cop eats his gun, it means just that. In the mouth. Can't miss. Instant death."

Dawson edged his battered, dusty chair closer to the banged-up, dented metal desks, propping up his elbow.

"Same as I thought, but let me continue," Jace said. "Gunshot residue was on his hand and all over his shirt, but it still doesn't prove he killed himself. Might mean he shot Sal, though. Shit, maybe he just fired off a round. Hell, who knows?"

"And Mack's doing Sal, that it?" Jack glanced at Xi, who nodded.

"Bullet in the back of the skull, pants torn at the knees, ligature marks on his wrists. Mack said likely from tight cuffs. He had a black eye, bloodied nose and lip, and a fractured right cheekbone."

Jack jumped up. "God dammit. Ain't no way Smitty could've inflicted that damage. Pete Smitherson had arthritis and couldn't beat the likes of Dellucci."

"Whoa, man, settle down, wouldja? No one here thinks Smitty did it, just telling you what the autopsy reports say so far."

"Sorry, Xi." Jack eyed his colleagues, who stared at him, mouths agape.

"We all liked Smitty. He seemed decent. No, he wasn't the murderous-suicidal type, but that doesn't mean he was pure as the driven snow either." Jace leaned back, eyes darting to Xi's, who exchanged a knowing look with him.

"Alright, fellas, what aren't you telling us?"

Xi cleared his throat. "Jack, we started checking Smitty's financials. What we've found isn't the type of cash flow a retired cop should have." He held up a hand. "We're still investigating, and yes, I'll keep you updated."

"Another thing—I wanna point out. Sal had a fractured left cheekbone, right?"

"So?" Xi, Jace, and Dawson said in chorus.

"Did Smitty have bruises on his knuckles?"

"Mack didn't say."

"Well, no matter. Pete was right-handed. Make certain she documents his right middle finger. It got chopped off at the first joint in a childhood bicycle accident. If he hit Sal in the left cheek with a right-handed uppercut, he couldn't make a tight fist anymore."

"He could've got him at gunpoint, cuffed him, and used a rock, Jack."

"Won't believe it was Smitty, Dawson, not without proof, Xi." Jack scooted his chair closer to Xi, who sat with a murder book unopened on the desk.

"You got photos of the scene?"

"Jack," Jace began, but Jack cut him off.

"Oh, my lord, you guys. I'm a homicide detective. I've seen gruesome stuff."

A memory of Gretchen Benson's murder flashed through Chang's mind. He pushed the binder over. "Here. It's all we have for now. Other things are still processing."

The first pages showed the area. Next, he moved on to victim one, Sal Dellucci, face planted downward, hands and arms at odd angles. Close-ups of his wrists displayed ligature marks.

"Looks like someone cuffed Sal, then uncuffed him after shooting him. Why would Smitty care if Sal was uncuffed—especially if he was about to eat his gun?" He looked at the others, who all shook their heads.

He moved on to the next few photos—Dellucci from different angles. When he turned the page to the first image of Pete Smitherson—he gasped.

"Jack?" Xi's eyes crinkled with concern.

"You okay?" Dawson asked.

"Yeah, it's—well, it's Smitty. You know how it is when it's someone you know in this condition. I'm fine." He closed the book, wanting to talk to Dawson alone.

"You mind if I dig through the binder again, let y'all continue your investigation?"

Xi gathered the book. "Sure, anytime. If we aren't available, ask Roni. She'll have access to our reports. Her or us, only. Okay?"

"Still keeping this all under wraps?" Dawson stood, pushing his seat out.

"We were, but after informing the families, even if we asked them not to talk, everyone's talking. Tiny details are what we keep close to the vest."

"Oh?" Jack arched a brow.

"Once Roni gives us the green light. Not until then, Jack." Xi's tone was firm.

"Sure, we understand." Jack didn't press.

All four were standing. Jack's hand on the doorknob, he glanced back. "Thanks, guys. Appreciate your trust."

"Goes both ways, Jack. Come on, 7. We've got people to interview."

With a nod, they watched 7-11 leave through the elevator. Once the doors closed, Lucky looked at Jack.

"Alrighty, partner. What gives? What did you notice in the photo that I didn't?"

"What time is it?"

"Almost six. Why?"

"We need to see if we can locate Russ Hardy."

"Jack, you gonna tell me what's going on?"

"Nope, I'm gonna show you. Come on."

39

THEY WENT TO THE electronics room next to Sergeant Hardy's office. Jack found the disk and scanned to the part where he remembered seeing the older man. He hit pause as the thin gray man froze mid-stride; foot suspended in the air.

Lucky's jaw dropped. He pointed. "Jack, that's Smitty. Same clothes as the victim in the photograph—same beard, hair, pants, scruffy hiking boots. I'll be damned."

"I didn't recognize him at first with the longer hair and beard; hadn't seen him in six years. Wait." Jack hit play, let the man enter, waited for him to exit, then paused the recording again. He enlarged the frame to show skinny, long fingers with dirty nails on old fisherman's hands.

"Okay, pard, what's missing?"

Dawson frowned. "Uh-huh, part of his middle finger is missing. It's Smitty. Why was he in Yvette's office?"

Jack updated him on the case files and Moretti, the officer who did his brother's death notification all those years ago.

A mix of emotions crossed Dawson's face. "Jack, you think it could connect to your—"

"No, just saying it's how I know Moretti."

"You reckon Smitty's trying to give you a clue or warning?"

"I don't know. I cannot wrap my brain around Smitty hanging out with Brooks or being on the take."

"Smitty and Brooks hung out? When, like the original days?" Dawson looked confused.

"I didn't show you the snapshot found in Smitty's pocket?"

"No. Where is it?"

"Locked in my desk. Let's take this back to Russ. Ask him if he can burn a copy."

"Won't he ask why?"

"Not if I tell him it's for an ongoing case. He's cool. Don't mention this to Roni or 7-11—not yet."

———

DAWSON STARED AT THE photo. "So, what, Jack? Smitty was buddies with Brooks and Dellucci. They went fishing. I don't find it suspicious."

Jack studied the picture. "Cops who liked to fish, sure. But two of them are dead—not by natural causes. Brooks, our third guy—Dawson. We know he's dirty. At least I do. Then Sal's kid, Corey Carver. From what I've learned, he's a mediocre cop."

Lucky squinted. "You got a magnifying glass?"

"No. Why?"

"I wanna look at the background better."

Jack examined it. "At what?"

"The parking lot. There." Dawson pointed.

"A truck?"

"Yeah, got a hunch. Let's ask tech to enhance it."

Jack shrugged. "Alright, you explain."

"Yep, but I don't wanna speak out of turn until I'm certain. Let's go."

———

"NEED TO ENLARGE AND sharpen this snapshot—pay special attention to the lot." Dawson handed it to tech.

"I'll work on it in the morning."

"What about now?" Dawson pressed.

"I'm off the clock and need approval for overtime."

"Tomorrow's fine. How long?" Jack interrupted.

"Seven a.m., an hour or two. If urgent, I can ask Art—"

"No, we'll come back. Thanks. Come on, Detective Luck, we've got fried chicken to buy."

———

DAWSON PARKED AT JACK'S townhouse, grabbed the KFC, and locked the doors.

"You have a nice yard, West."

"Yeah, my neighbor Carl helps. Small yard, small backyard, works fine."

Inside, Dawson nodded approval. Lived-in, clean, homey touches like framed landscapes, a vase with flowers, a candy dish with chocolate crumbs, a few books stacked, an old-fashioned coat rack.

"You keep a tidy home, West. Nice cookie jar, adds pizzazz." He set the KFC on the counter. "Paper plates?"

"That cupboard, middle shelf. I'll get the beer."

They ate, chatting casually, appreciating a simple moment.

"You let Viv know you were here?"

"Yeah. She needed to go grocery shopping. Let's dump the trash and clean up. Can't wait to see what Brooks is up to. The camera caught everyone who walked into the room."

"Yeah, no telling who we'll see doing what." Jack thought about Sparky and her unknown lover, wondering if other people might be on the nanny cam. He might have to rename it the "kiss cam" or "rated X" cam.

———

"HARD TO READ THE label on the box." Dawson craned his neck.

"Yeah. Too small on a laptop."

"Hook it up to your flat screen? USB port?"

"You asking me technical questions? I might not know."

"I'll YouTube it. Wider view might help." Dawson had it up in seconds, Jack scratching his head.

TV on, Jack plugged in the thumb drive. Luck reminded him multiple times not to turn it off.

"Alright, Dawson, I heard you. Here, hold the remote. Jesus."

"Why sixty-inch flat screen?"

"Gretchen and I loved oldies—better on the big screen, even black and whites."

"I apologize, Jack, didn't mean to touch a painful subject."

"S'okay, fond memories. Open the video—fingers crossed."

They watched, pausing. Brooks' fat head or rump blocked some views. A few words on labels were visible, but not the whole label.

"Pause it."

Dawson, holding the remote, did so.

"You get something?"

"No, but wait." Jack used his phone to take snapshots each time the man moved. Maybe they could match areas with photos.

Frames didn't always show Brooks. Other officers rotated through evidence duty; Brooks' cousin, Lt. Ethan Wygant, also spent time there. Jack captured pictures of him, too. Fast-forwarding, they ran through the video twice, then Lucky unplugged the drive and turned off Jack's TV.

"Not much to work with."

"Katherine linked her cell to the feed; she should have recorded what he did." Jack lofted his beer. "Here's hoping she wrote it down."

"Too late to text her?"

"Better in person. No digital footprint."

"Smart move, Jack."

Dawson left Jack's house twenty minutes later, never mentioning his visit with Dave Finston. His hope was tech could work with the photo he left. If he was right, Jack would be stunned.

40

XI CHANG TURNED WHEN the door hinges squealed. "Hey, Jack. Where's Lucky? You two make up yet?"

"Nope, he's still pissed, said something about talking to Roni on his way out." A harmless lie. Jack took a seat at his desk. "You guy's coming or going?"

"Going. You wanna come with?"

"Where're you going?"

"We got the warrant for Sal's apartment. Still waiting for the one for Smitty's place and his boat."

"You haven't searched their places?" This surprised Jack.

Jace pushed his chair back and spun around. "Both places are under tight lock and key, since they're retired cops. Heck, IA is champing at the bit, too. The legal system is making us wait on some bureaucratic bullshit."

"Red tape? You gotta be kidding. Don't they realize this stalls the case?"

"Jack, Jack, Jack. We all know how slow the legal system is, and if you push, they shove back harder, 'cause they like having muscles over us cops," Xi voiced.

"Yep, I get it." Then Jack asked, "You guys got any clue why Idiots and A-holes is involved?"

"Because Sal and Smitty were cops. Can't think of any other reasons, can you, 11?"

"Nope, I mean there wasn't any investigation on either guy that I heard about. What about you, Jack?" Xi returned.

Jack shrugged, a nonchalant gesture masking the whirlwind of scenarios playing out in his head. One of the deceased officers being Sal Dellucci made the situation intriguing. He wasn't about to expound just yet, so he asked, "What are the addresses, and where's Smitty's boat docked?"

Xi opened his notebook. "Sal lives—lived, sorry—on Fulton Street, a place called the Station Apartments. Smitty had an apartment off Wallisville Road. Thorntree Apartments."

Jack had Google Maps up. "About fourteen miles apart. Plus, traffic sucks no matter what time of day it is. The marina. Where is it?"

"Seabrook Marina and Shipyard, in Seabrook, Texas. Here's the address." Xi reeled it off.

"It closes at five, and the warrants aren't back either," Jace remarked.

Xi's cell chirped. "Chang, Homicide. Yeah, we are. Oh? You got names? Tell me—no, email me your findings later." Chang listened, his face devoid of emotions. "You're positive? Right. Yep, and keep this to yourself. We'll update our skipper. Sure thing, and thanks, Olivia." Xi clicked off, sat back, and let loose a mammoth sigh. Disbelief and concern etched his brow.

Jack broke the silence. "Brasher from ballistics?"

"Yep, you know her? Nice gal."

"Cut to the chase, Xi. What'd she say?" Jack's tone hinted at impatience.

"The bullet in Sal was a .45 caliber. The second bullet a .38 that Mack found in Smitty."

"Two guns?" Jace let swear words fly. "Fantastic. Now we gotta look for a second pistol."

"CSU went over that entire area, Jace, plus, an extra two hundred yards," Xi reminded him.

"Well, 11, Sheldon's Reservoir ain't like a backyard, so it means dragging the basin and involving the game warden since the place has known gator activity." Jace shuddered.

"Best they can do would be drag the area near where they found the bodies. Not much else can be done." Xi continued the discussion on dragging the lake, but not about the ballistic findings.

Jack's eyes tapered in question. "And what else, Xi? From your end of the conversation, I'd say something else is going on, so just spit it out." With crossed arms, he waited.

"Ballistics matched them with three separate murders. Sal's slug matches bullets from two cases. Both unsolved."

Jack's internal radar twitched. "And the other slug outta Smitty?"

"It matches another case, also unsolved."

"Damn it, Xi. Stop hem-hawing. It's like pulling teeth with you." Jack's aggravation level rose. "Who were the damned victims?"

Xi looked at Jace, then at Jack. "The slug outta Sal matched one in '99 that killed Angelo Conti and another fella, Ed Gresham, in '96. Only the .45 is the gun that's missing. At one time, Jack, that gun was in evidence lockup."

"Inside job—you think Smitty? And these other two cases were seventeen years apart and are still cold. Now, that's unusual. So, who's the third victim, Xi, the one that matches the slug outta Smitty?"

"It doesn't matter. What matters is you might be right about Smitty not eating his gun, Jack. Let's work with this."

"Is there a reason you're not telling me, Xi? Do I need to call Olivia Brasher myself?" On his feet, Jack yanked up his phone, causing Xi Chang to say with abruptness, "It's an unsolved case from '94, your brother's shooting."

The room spun a little. West felt sick to his stomach. His feet cemented to the spot where he stood, even though his body wavered. With a thud, Jack dropped onto the chair like a fifty-pound sack of wet dirt. His face paled as he tucked his chin into his chest. He inhaled and let it out bit by bit, trying to slow his heart rate down. He stared at Xi, then in a quavering tone said, "This has to be checked and double-checked. We've gotta—"

Xi cut him off. "They checked, and double-checked. That's what Olivia said. Jack, you need to step back from this, hear me?"

Jack was on his feet. His anger grew. "The fuck I will!"

Jace put his hand on Jack's arm. "Sit down, pal. Let's talk about this, okay?"

He shot Jace a stern glance. "Ain't no talking about it. I'm not backing off. I'm on this case, and if you ask Roni to shut me out, you can forget my loyalties. You two can hang out with Webb and Nichols because you won't be hanging with me."

"Damn, Jack, that's cold." Jace looked at Xi. "Look, 11, the man owns a personal copy of the murder book. He's the expert on that case."

Yes, this slug matching a gun to his brother's case disturbed him, and had this information surfaced years ago he would have been a bull in a china shop; only, today, he behaved composed. *Do it by the book,* a voice screamed inside his head, because getting all worked up will not help. When he was alone, he'd attempt to connect the pieces of the puzzle, which now concerned his dead brother.

"Tell you guys what." Jack took his seat. "There's a lot more to this. Let me get you up to speed. After I do, then we'll go talk to Roni." Jack might leave out a few details, but as it was, he was gonna go out on a limb with his captain and involve 7-11 without her authorization. There was an adage he loved, and it fit this scenario to a T: better to ask for forgiveness than for permission.

7-11 SAT, SLACK-JAWED, WHILE Jack explained enough to keep them captivated, but did not reveal everything.

"You're telling us IA asked Roni to ask you to snoop into Brooks?"

"So it would seem, Xi. Look, they didn't give her a reason, or maybe she's holding back, I don't know."

"You've already talked to his original FTO and two partners?" Xi was still trying to process everything Jack said.

"Yep. Got squat, though. Brooks was an asshole then, too. Not much changed."

"Gotta say, I'd hate the guy if his carelessness parked me behind a desk. You say this Yardley dude seemed okay with it?" Jace intoned.

Jack shrugged. "Yardley held no grudge against Brooks, so the story goes."

Xi's long fingers splayed on the top of the desk, and a soft, padded sound ensued as he rolled them in a rhythmic manner. "What if Yardley wanted on a desk? How old was he when this incident happened, and did he mention what job he did on a desk, Jack?"

Jack's eyebrows dipped in thought. "No, he didn't. The report would say his age. What you thinking, Chang?"

"Maybe Yardley wanted a desk. It would've given him the opportunity to see and hear more. Hear all orders, intake reports pass from desk to desk; overhear phone calls. Nobody thinks too much about privacy 'cause it's the job—everyone knows the job. Some blob gets behind on paperwork, shoves it into a pile. Anyone can rifle through the inboxes. Then things get left on a back burner. Shuffled around, you know the drill. Back then, it was physical paperwork—not the computer programs like today.

"You reckon this Yardley fella was fudging paperwork, 11? For what purpose?"

"Jack, those names on the ballistics reports are also on the list Yvette gave you."

"And?"

"Let's dig into those cases. They gotta mean something."

Jack kept the fact that he and Katherine Sparks found the case files to himself, and glanced at the clock. "It's getting late. You still wanna head to Sal's apartment, dig around?"

Xi sighed, hoping Jack didn't go rogue on this. "Nah, traffic's gonna be a bear. Jace, how about you meet me at Sal's in the morning? We don't have the warrants for Smitty's yet, either."

"Aren't you concerned Sal's family might toss the place?"

"Jack, if they wanted to, they'd already have done it. We've had patrol surveilling both places, though."

"Excellent point. What about the marina?"

Jace yawned. "They got a rent-a-cop on 24/7. We've informed them too."

Xi stood and pushed his chair in. "We're gonna call it a night."

"Yep, it's been a long day and we need to get divers in the morning to drag Sheldon," Jace said, surprised they were calling it a night.

Jack stood, stretching out his legs. "I'll catch up with y'all tomorrow. Before I leave, gonna go see Roni."

They parted ways, and Jack headed to Roni's office, bracing himself for a reprimand.

JACE SEVERSON'S CELL VIBRATED. A text from Xi: *Meet me at my car.*

He sent a thumbs-up emoji and went.

"Get in, I'm driving."

Jace complied. "I thought we're calling it a night."

"Nah, I just said that. Wanted Jack to believe we were."

"You wanna leave him out? He's gonna get pissed."

"He'll get over it. I know Jack. Let's go to Sal's."

Jace buckled up, stretching his motorcycle-booted feet out. "By the way, why didn't we just tell Jack IA asked us to look into Sal's police record?"

Xi blinkered to make a left near the end of Joseph Street. "I'm betting when he spills to Roni that he told us some things—and I'm gonna wager it wasn't everything—she'll tell him about our orders. It'll serve him right too. He held back. I'll tell him we were just returning the favor."

"Xi Chang, you can be an ass, ya know."

"Just practicing my sergeant's skills." A small laugh escaped Xi's lips.

41

DAVE FINSTON GAVE THE old snapshot a makeover. After adjusting the brightness and contrast, he did the best he could to sharpen all blurry areas. Next, he enlarged the area Dawson had pointed out and started the process over again, bringing out a decent shot of the background parking lot. He then enhanced the fronts of the vehicles facing the lot so that they might see license plates clearer, which he guessed was what they were searching for. Kids' work, and his initiative impressed Dawson Luck.

"I hope this is to your satisfaction, Detective." Dave bounced back and forth on his heels, beaming.

"This is outstanding," Dawson praised him.

Finston beamed. "Thanks, glad I could help."

"Say hey to Art." Photo in hand, Detective Luck headed back to six.

"SPARKY HERE?"

"Breakroom. And hi, Jack."

"Sorry, Rick, in a rush. Don't mean to be unsociable. Can we chat some other time?"

Rick waved him off with a chuckle. "Sure, go find Katherine."

Man. He was gonna have to be a bit more friendly, or they'd nickname him Detective Antisocial.

He pulled the door open and poked his head in. "Sparky, you alone?"

"Yep. Want coffee?"

"Sure."

She poured. "Did you guys notice anything on the thumb drive?"

A grimace creased Jack's face. "Not box labels. His fat bald head was always in the way."

"Yeah, I tried to identify what boxes he'd tampered with, but he was good at re-taping. I made notes of certain boxes, but didn't check them, 'cause untaping and retaping is a bitch. I'll text you a copy of my list, but don't expect it'll do much good." She leaned back against the kitchen counter, sipping her brew. "Now what, Jack? What about the boxes we found?"

"Gonna hafta waltz in and take them, I guess."

A glint reached her eyes. "You, waltz—nope, can't see that. But knowing you, you'll think of a way."

"Yep, knowing me. Hey, thanks for the crappy coffee, gotta scram."

ON THE NINTH FLOOR, in the unoccupied room, Dawson handed Jack a magnifying glass.

"What am I looking for? Or at?" Jack scanned the photo with the magnifier.

"There," Dawson pointed, "the plate number of the truck."

"So?"

"Here's the registration. Notice anything?"

"Belongs to Gary Yardley, so?"

"Now we can link Yardley, Dellucci, Brooks, and Smitty. And by default, Corey Carver by being Sal's kid."

Jack rubbed his jaw in thought. "Not sure it adds up to anything."

"Tells us who took the Polaroid. It had to be Yardley. And Jack, if they were fishing buddies, it means they were close. Enemies don't fish together."

"To be honest, Yardley's comments about the past didn't sit well with me. How guys did what they had to do to get by. Made me feel like he straddled the fence, both feet touching the ground, if you get my drift."

"If he was on the take, what can we do about it?" Luck's elbows came up, and he rested his face in his palms, staring down at the old photo.

"Funny, he said if I kept digging, I might start something, causing cases to get reinvestigated, and people could sue the department for wrongful imprisonment. I swear, the way he said things sounded like 1940s movie dialogue."

"Like what?" Dawson leaned away from the table.

Jack said, "Stuff like cops turning a blind eye to certain crimes to make a coupla extra bucks. I don't think murder or drugs, but hell, who knows at this stage?"

Luck's concern was real. "You figure we should let it lie?"

Jack leaned back, his sigh heavy. "Ain't my call. Gonna let Roni decide, and even then, she's gonna refer it back to Elijah Vance."

"You know as well as me that if it's up to Internal Affairs, they'll move forward, no matter the consequences."

A text dinged. He showed Luck Katherine's list.

"A list don't help us," Dawson said. "We go snooping and that's gonna stir up Wygant's nose hairs. Any suggestions?"

"Not without involving someone else." Jack looked up at white ceiling tiles no longer made of asbestos but of mineral fiber. A few were stained with water, others cracked, and he stared at one light brown spot, lost in thought. His eyes on Katherine's notes, he sat forward. "It's gonna fall on you, Luck."

"Aw, shit, you want me to go back and work with Wygant?"

"It's the only way. I can't do it."

"Jack, don't you think it will make people more suspicious of you? I just got back to six."

A long exhale left Jack's lungs. "You and me will get into it in front of everyone and you go talk to Roni. Explain what we have, have her send a memo to Yao. Say you need a break from me and from Homicide; ask her to put together a bogus transfer stating you're unhappy or whatever. I'll find 7-11, get an update on their case."

"Should I explain all of it, or some of it to her?"

"Keep this new stuff on Gary Yardley to yourself. Let's see what else we dig up. Then we'll tell her."

A huge puff of air exited Dawson Luck's enormous nose. "Man, I'll be glad when this is over. I hate working in that freaking cage."

Jack didn't voice his concern to Dawson, but if Sal and Smitty, both ex-cops, were dead, who might be next? A prickling sensation crawled up his spine; his cop intuition told him somebody was cleaning house.

HE WASN'T GONNA GET into it with Jace and Xi, but calling it a night? Nope, he didn't think so, but he let it go and sent Lucky a text.

Jack: You still here?

Dawson: Yeah. Walking out of Roni's office. Where're you?

Jack: In the garage next to your car. Come on, you're driving.

Dawson: Be there in two.

Buckled up, engine rumbling, Dawson asked, "Where to?"

"Seabrook Marina and Shipyard." Jack set his phone on the console. "I've mapped it."

Lucky drove toward the exit. "What's there?"

"Smitty's boat."

"Is there more to this story?"

"Yeah, a helluva lot more."

It was a forty-minute drive or more with traffic, and a spellbound Dawson Luck listened.

"Given everything that's happened, you believe it connects to your brother's case?"

"Nah. Cole wasn't famous, or mobbed up, so it doesn't make a lick of sense."

"Dairy Queen or Jack in the Box?"

With a scowl and a sigh, Jack said, "Jack in the Box is fine. Damn. Forgot you're a bottomless pit who never misses breakfast, lunch, or dinner, with the triple in-between snacks."

"Just for your catty remark, I'm not buying your dinner." Dawson slowed, taking the exit to NASA Road One, and hit the light to turn right.

Jack swapped seats with Dawson after ordering food and took the wheel, allowing his partner space and time to eat, especially since all he'd ordered was an iced tea.

"You sure you aren't a little hungry?" Dawson stuffed his empty wrappers into the sack as he finished his meal.

"Get a bite later, too keyed up to eat. There." Jack pointed at the sign. "Seabrook Marina, five miles up."

"How you gonna get into Smitty's slip?" Dawson slurped the last of his Dr. Pepper. "We don't have paperwork, or do we?"

"Nah. I have my universal pass." Jack tapped the badge on his belt.

After they brandished badges and informed him they were with Homicide, the night security officer fiddled with his large array of keys, stuttering, flustered.

"No one called ahead, thought someone was gonna call ahead if you guys were coming. I ain't supposed to let you pass if I don't got no permission, understand?"

Jack glanced at his name tag. "Ned Dickson, we understand your hesitance to let us pass. Hell, you're just doing your job."

"Um, yeah."

"So, you work every night?" Jack took a relaxed stance with the older fella.

"Nah, part-time, here every other week, and one weekend of the month."

"Anyone tell you what's going on? Why the police security is here?"

"Nope, nobody said why. Suppose it's a need-to-know thing, and I'm guessing I ain't got clearance."

"I'll be damned." Jack scratched his head. "It'd be helpful if you understood why security matters and why it's crucial to keep things safe," Jack played the old guy.

"Jack, I think we should bring him into the loop on what's happening. Beneficial for us to have eyes inside." Dawson got into the act.

"Oh, well, sure, yeah, I'd like to help the police. Be an honor, yes sir, it would." The old guy's head bobbed.

Jack pressed his lips with a nod. "Perfect. So, Officer Dickson, you acquainted with Pete Smitherson?"

The middle-aged man with a bit of pudge around his belly lifted his service cap to scratch his head. "Call me Ned. Yeah, Smitty and I gabbed about deep-sea fishing. Went out a time or two, to fish and drink beer. Is he in some kinda trouble?"

"Not exactly, Ned. Someone murdered him."

Dickson's mouth opened and closed like a fish. A funny analogy, given the circumstances. "Murdered? Smitty? Who'd want him dead?"

"It's what we're trying to find out. I take it no one's questioned you yet?"

The man pulled up to his five-foot-ten height, pushing his chest out a bit, hiking up his gray uniform pants over his stomach. "You looking for my alibi, is that it? I didn't kill the old man, I swear."

"I'm sure you're not involved. We need to look around, though." Jack widened his eyes at the older gent. "Are we gonna have to go through the hassle of getting a warrant, or will you let us take a quick look-see, you know, an officer-to-officer courtesy?"

His lips set firmly. "You bet, officer-to-officer, I can do that. Smitty's slip is number 138. Wait here. I'll get you a slip map, and you can use the golf cart."

Ned turned, went into the guard shack, and came back with a map marked with a red Sharpie, denoting Smitty's jetty, and the keys to a cart.

"Use the one at the end of this walkway. Gotta keep mine handy, you know, in case."

Jack thanked him, shook his hand, and promised to check in with him on their way out.

——————

"Jack, you played that old guy. Shame on you," Luck said as he hopped into the golf cart, letting Jack drive.

"Yep, and it worked," Jack said, taking the curve of the road to the end, following the directions on the map Ned marked.

The safety lights and the piling lights illuminated the area, and they boarded the docked vessel. Jack pointed. "Perfect name for Smitty's boat." Painted on the side: *The Artful Codger.*

"Smells wet and fishy."

A laugh burst out before he could stop it. "It's a damned boat, Luck. It's supposed to smell fishy."

Dawson pulled gloves out of his back pocket. "Yeah, I know, you ass, but fishier than norm. Wonder if there's a catch somewhere he hadn't got off the boat." He stepped, conscious of where his foot landed, determined not to crush any fish guts.

Jack squatted, moving his gloved hand through a pile of ropes sitting near several tackle boxes. "One thing someone might be looking for, I reckon,, though."

Dawson used his mini flashlight to look under a short bench after nudging a half-filled five-gallon bucket with his foot. "What's that?"

"A gun or a suicide note, or something proving Smitty was dirty."

"Jack, whatcha gonna do if you find out he was?"

"Deal with it, I suppose. Man, bro. If any of you—you, Jace, or Xi—were dirty. Don't think I could come to terms with that." Jack's tone conveyed his sincerity.

"No worries there, only ones in the entire Homicide Department you need to be concerned with are Webb, Nichols, and Golan. I'm gonna stay topside, you go below. Let's get this search done. I needta get away from this godforsaken smell."

42

BELOW, IN THE CABIN of the Wellcraft vessel, Jack noted clothes, personal hygiene paraphernalia, and shoes. There were books on fishing, outdoors magazines, a deck of cards, and a crossword puzzle book. A single old man on a fishing vessel. Was that all Smitty had? Dishes piled in a small dish drainer—a plate, bowl, and two cups, along with metal flatware.

He pulled open a small cabinet door. Canned goods, boxed food, crackers, and dry cereal. Next to the microwave sat an open package of generic microwavable popcorn and a TV Guide. Who got the TV Guide anymore?

Jack sifted through a narrow closet.

Work shirts. Navy blue and dark gray quick-dry cargo pants. T-shirts, long-sleeved cotton button-downs; three checked, blue-and-white flannel shirts and a heavy-duty yellow rain slicker with matching coveralls.

In his humble opinion, it was all very ordinary. He moved back the clothes to see the bottom and saw rubber boots, deck boots, socks, and skivvies.

Again, all normal stuff an old dude batching it on a fishing boat would have.

Jack perched at the edge of the cushioned seat.

His eyes skimmed the space. Nothing appeared out of place.

Smitty never spoke of family. A question he had was: who would inherit his possessions?

What red tape had kept them from searching this craft?

He had zero family. Smitty owned a boat, his largest property, and had a cop's pension.

What else did he have? Was there a will in place?

He stood facing the bow, looking at the grouping of pads where a person would sleep.

The aqua blue and black stripes were still vibrant. The cushions, made from marine-grade cotton, had very few water spots or stains. Removable cushions formed an inverted V on the sides and a larger one in the center.

A half-shelf on either side—for storing life jackets, blankets, extra pillows, or whatever—was lined with vinyl padding so that when you slept, it did not rock you into a hard surface.

He sat at the end of the padded area, facing the cabin door. They hadn't checked out Smitty's apartment, and he didn't think they'd find much.

This rowboat was the old man's dream. He reckoned it had been six years since Smitty retired. The cabin's messy state prompted him to wonder if a woman in Smitty's life would have changed things.

"Jack?"

"Yeah?"

"Headed down, don't shoot," Dawson joshed.

Jack stayed seated. It depressed him that Smitty's life had come down to this. "You find anything topside?"

"Nope, but there are nooks and crannies everywhere. Tackle boxes, tackle drawers—and the bait tank—revolting. Oh, and I found the extra fishy smell. There's a bucket of dead minnows shoved under a tarp, which I put right back. What about you?"

"Just the remnants of an old man's existence, or so it looks. Heck, he might've been having the time of his life, and we'd never know it."

Dawson opened the narrow door of the food pantry.

He inventoried the shelves: microwaveable mac and cheese, canned chili, soup, crackers, potted meat—and two cans of Spam.

A smile crept up on his face as he plucked a box of dry cereal.

"The old man eats Trix? And Cocoa Puffs, I haven't eaten these—" Dawson frowned, eyes on the back wall of the cupboard.

"Since last week?" Jack kidded.

"Hang on a minute." With his phone light, he examined the rear panel. A small seam appeared cut. "Jack, there's a loose panel." Dawson slid it open, then, with guarded movements, stuck his hand inside until his fingers brushed the handle of a bag.

"Anything?"

"Yeah, wait." Dawson tugged with force, pulling out an army-green canvas sack. They fell silent, gazes fixed on it.

"Well?" Dawson sat on the metal chair next to the table. "Open it, or not—I dunno, Jack. There's a lot of what-ifs."

"Don't know about you, but I want to see what we're up against." Jack lofted the pack, sat it on the end of the padded sleep area, and unzipped the main compartment. A low whistle emerged from his lips.

Dawson rose to his feet and looked in. "What the hell?"

Inside, they found cash—packs of one-hundred-dollar bills—and three unique passports with matching driver's licenses issued out of different states. One official birth certificate for Peter Wendel Smitherson. One nine-millimeter Glock, an older Kimber .45, extra ammo for both, and a gun cleaning kit; each gun's grip wrapped with electrical tape. Four unused, pre-paid burner phones and a plastic box. Folded under it all were two pairs of pants, two T-pullovers, socks, boxers, and a pair of extra tennis shoes.

Jack picked up each item, lining them up on top of the vinyl pads.

Dawson, still gloved, picked up the plastic container and popped it open: several bottles of aspirin, Band-Aids, cut and abrasion ointment, gauze, scissors, and a couple of ACE bandages.

"I'll be—Smitty had a go-bag." Jack reclined, eyeballing the stuff.

"Uh-huh, and I'd venture to say he was a crooked cop, Jack. And this key." Dawson held the key up.

"What about it?"

"It's a lockbox key. Viv's mom had a lockbox, looks very similar."

"Time to leave. Let's put everything back."

"Then what, Jack? Let the others swoop in?"

"Not a chance. We'll get a warrant and come back. Get Vince Stoner or Suzy Wong to go over this boat until they've done all but scrape the barnacles off the hull. I need to talk to Dickson, the security guard. I have a job for him."

Jack climbed out. Dawson followed.

***

"You bet, Detective West. I can keep everyone away and off Mr. Smitherson's craft. I'll talk to the owner and manager and set up a blockade around the end of the jetty. Once I tell them ole Pete's dead, I'm sure they'll be upset and want to do the right thing."

"Pete—he was a longtime customer?"

"Yeah. His docking records go back a ways. This place opened in '39, and old Pete's had a boat here since '72. They don't keep records that far back, but old timers love to reminisce. A few are still around."

"Oh, and Ned, we were never here, got it?"

"Who was never here?"

With a chuckle, Jack gave him his number, shook hands, said thanks, and they were gone.

They stayed silent as Luck drove out of the marina and onto the freeway. The darkness was heavy, or perhaps it was the portentous mood that created the shroud of blackness.

"Finding out Smitty's been docking here since '72 pisses me off." Jack stretched his legs and leaned his head into the headrest, closing his eyes.

Dawson decelerated, turning off Bayport Boulevard onto East NASA Parkway, headed back to Interstate 45 and headquarters. "Pisses you off, why?"

"Smitty talked about buying a boat. Not once did he ever tell me he had a sailboat, rowboat, canoe, or kayak."

"Smitty got mixed up with dangerous people, Jack, and it got him killed, but he's dead and won't face a jury."

Both eyes opened, and he turned to look at Dawson's profile.

"Makes me mad too. I might've liked the old geezer, but if he needed to pay for his sins, he should've had to. If he blew out his own brains, he took the coward's way, and if he got whacked, well, someone afforded him an easy way out." Frustrated, Jack reclosed his eyes.

Dawson looked over his left shoulder to move over a lane. "You ready for another brain buster?"

Eyes still closed, Jack said, "I suppose. What's on your mind?"

"How does all this connect with Brody Brooks or your brother's shooting?"

"Don't know, pard. I'd sure like to find out."

BACK AT SAL'S APARTMENT, Jace's nose crinkled when he opened the fridge. A plate of dried-up ham, dried green grapes in a container, three bottles of Miller High Life, a half bottle of off-brand red wine, and a small tub of butter on the bottom shelf. A package of moldy cheese, opened off-brand bologna, a jar of mayo, and a squeeze bottle of mustard in the door ledge, with three diet sodas underneath. Two frozen pizzas and three Hungry Man TV dinners sat in the tiny freezer with three ice trays. The man was no Galloping Gourmet or Julia Child.

Sal's cupboards echoed. Enough tableware for two.

A coffeepot that had seen better days, stained and unwashed. Sal was not a homebody, not a cook, not a maid, had zero company, and lived like a slob.

"Hey, Chang, not sure what kind of dump you're sifting through, but this guy, O-M-G, what a slob!"

"Yep, gross doesn't cover his bathroom, 7. I swear, I need a shower, but not in this one." Chang's voice raised. "You find anything useful yet?"

"Nope, still looking through this fetid kitchenette."

Chang snickered. "'Fetid,' Jace? Reading the word-of-the-day toilet paper again?"

"I do have an exceptional vocabulary, Xi, so—fuck you."

"Ah, now that's the Jace Severson I know and love. Fuck you back."

Jace grinned as he opened another cabinet door. A roach the size of Kansas ran down the wall, then out of sight. He shuddered.

The bed was unmade.

Dirty clothes piled on an old cane-back chair and in a heap next to it, along with running shoes and work boots.

He lifted the edge of the bedcover and bent to peer under the bed. Boxes. He drew one box out, then another. Flaps folded down in the four-flap fold without tape. Xi lifted one flap. Old T-shirts from HPD. A stack set on the bed. Underneath were old service caps and two pairs of uniform britches. Nothing of interest.

Other boxes contained civilian clothes. Chang bent over, looked under the bed, and didn't see any other containers, but an object stuck up under the box spring caught his eye.

The lining—ripped on one corner but sealed with masking tape, off-white, yellowed. Chang plucked off the tape and used his phone light to see what was stuck under the wood slats.

"Hey, Jace. Step back here?"

Jace pushed the cushion back onto the sofa. "Coming."

Xi was on his knees, light shining under the bed, and Jace joined him. "What we got?"

"Looks like someone stashed a pistol between the slats of the box spring."

Jace lay flat, stuck his gloved hand in and pulled out a .38 caliber handgun, slid back out, and stood. "Looks like it might have been his throwaway." He handled the piece carefully, opening the cylinder to find it loaded. He removed one bullet. "Look at this, 11. Lead semi wad-cutter hollow-points."

"Lemme see the gun." Xi took it from Severson, smelling the muzzle. "Been fired recently too, and is still loaded. Find that odd. Someone reloaded it."

Jace pulled out a paper bag and dropped the pistol in. "Now what?"

Xi said, "Now we get this to ballistics, and push it to the front."

Two dead retired cops. This took top priority.

43

"I'M WORKING UP WARRANTS. One for the boat and for Smitty's apartment." Dawson yawned for the second time.

"Perfect. I'll go chat with Roni. I'm not sure how ticked off she'll be because I clued Xi and Jace in."

"You gonna tell her we were on the boat?"

Jack's right hand massaged the back of his neck. "No. You okay with that?"

"It ain't like we killed anyone. I can live with a little white lie." Dawson smirked a tad. "It ain't like it's the only white lie coming from my lips these days. All this sneaky crap with Wygant and the fellas in Robbery. Only thing I worry about is how easy it is for me to lie these days. I don't like it."

"I hear ya, pard, loud and clear. Don't care for it much, either. I always figured I was nothing but an honest man."

"Jack, we're ethical, even if we sometimes bend the truth."

Shoving his chair back, Jack stood. "I have faith in us and Roni. She's a cop's cop, and I can't see her being anything but pleased that you, me, Xi, and Jace are working together. The four of us make one hell of a team—we have a track record proving it."

CAPTAIN JUSTICE, NODDING, PURSING her lips, crinkling her brow, and widening her eyes at the right times, listened as Jack recounted his conversation with 7-11.

"I know you didn't authorize me to tell them anything, and if I need a rip, I'll deserve it."

"You're right, it wasn't your place, but it does save me unneeded time pulling you four together." Her manicured finger came up, halting his words. "I'm not gonna give you a rip, but in the future, when I assign you a task to be kept confidential, and you need to let others in, you ask for my approval forthwith, understand?"

"Yes, ma'am." Jack let the conversation lag for a second, about to bring up Smitty and the boat, but she spoke first.

"They set the services."

Jack felt less than human right then. He hadn't given one thought to the funerals of either Smitherson or Dellucci.

"Pete's being cremated, no viewing, just an early-morning service at a funeral home in Kemah at nine tomorrow. His last request was that his ashes be dumped over Clear Lake."

"Way out there?" Jack feigned surprise.

"Smitty's vessel is at Seabrook Marina, but Jack, you already knew it was, so don't lie to me." Roni's eyes widened as her brows arched.

"Fine, I did. You said services. When's Sal's?"

"The viewing is day after tomorrow, eleven to one. Funeral is at Our Lady of Mercy Catholic Church at three." Her gaze fixed on him. "Jack, this needs to be done by the book. We leave nothing to chance since they were both cops. Get a warrant for Pete's boat and apartment." She sat, pensive.

"Anything else, ma'am?"

"Contact Harbor Patrol. Have them put someone on the craft, make sure no one goes aboard until after you and Dawson walk it. Call CSU, ask for Suzy Wong. Meet her out there and let her process the boat."

This was like having everything he needed handed to him on a silver platter, and he wondered if there was a catch.

He stood, ready to leave. "That it?"

"Don't forget about Brooks. I've gotta keep Elijah Vance updated."

"Still on our radar, Roni."

"And, Jack."

He turned, his hand on the doorknob, his head angled back to see her.

"Go tell Lucky to fax the paperwork he's already typed up."

"Ma'am?"

"7-11 told you about the boat, Jack, and knowing you, you're itching to get onboard and dig. Figured that's why you came to see me."

A slow smile crept to his face. "Ever thought about going back, Cap?"

"To the streets?"

"Yeah, 'cause you'd excel as a detective."

"Shut my door, West."

BEHIND HER CLOSED DOOR, Roni moaned. Jack's brother's murder—a sore spot in his life and career. How did the recent deaths of two retired Houston police officers connect to the unsolved 1994 Cole West shooting? She couldn't imagine what was going through her gold-shield detective's mind. The tip of her yellow No. 2 pencil tapped at the blank sheet of paper before she began writing.

Brody Brooks. Two retired HPD officers slain. The murder weapons linked to three other killings. Evidence missing or destroyed—this seemed to be a key factor. Roni felt confident Jack and his three skilled colleagues would find the truth. To what extent could the truth's revelation devastate the city?

"FAX WENT THROUGH." DAWSON stapled the fax confirmation to the paperwork.

"You talk to anyone over at the courthouse?" Jack set a Styrofoam cup on his desk.

"I called. Got Mava. Told her to look for 'em. Push 'em through. Asked her who was in chambers today; she said Chase, Banks, and Ritter."

"I like Chase." Jack sipped his lukewarm coffee.

"Me too. Her first name's Greta, same name as my Glock."

Jack typed in his password. "Makes no difference if it's the Honorable Nora Yorke-Carlson or Greta Chase. Either holds any cop, magistrate, or mayor accountable for illegal acts that harm our city's reputation. They are staunch on the law."

The telltale squeak of the door sounded, and heavy footsteps pounded their way.

"Detective Luck." The tone was sharp.

"Lieutenant Wygant." Dawson stood.

"Why are you here—shouldn't you be working the evidence cage?"

"Sorry, Lieutenant. I stopped to retrieve my personal effects. Had to clean out the old one."

"What was in the desk?" Wygant frowned.

"Just some old papers and notes Officer Pete Smitherson left. Guess he forgot about them. Oh, and some paperwork some dude named Corey Carver left."

"Oh, uh..." Ethan Wygant cleared his throat. "Where did you put their junk?"

"Chief Yao has it; wasn't sure if I should trash it or not." Dawson looked down for a split second, and Jack saw him grin.

Wygant got flustered, but regained his composure and said, "Alright then, now grab your personal gear and get your ass to work in my department."

Jack had no idea Dawson could think on his feet that swiftly, and it impressed him.

MAVA'S VOICE CRACKLED OVER the phone, telling Jack the warrants were ready. This gave him the green light to contact CSU and set a meeting time with Suzy Wong at Seabrook Marina.

He texted Dawson and called Suzy Wong, then called the forensic lab to let them know he was on the road.

MACK SAT, GOWNED UP, reading files, when Jack knocked.

"Hey, Jack. Have a seat. Let me finish this."

He sat on the edge of the chair, watching her facial expressions as she read. Whatever she read caused her forehead to wrinkle in dismay or perhaps anger, but he didn't ask. She set the file away from her and grabbed another.

"You wanna go over Smitty's autopsy?"

"Captain Justice call you? She tell you I'm on the case?"

"Yep, and she mentioned Luck was working in Evidence for a short stint. What's up with that?"

His face pulled as he scratched his head, and she closed her eyes in a nod. "I see, can't tell me. I understand. So, Pete Smitherson, age 79, cause of death gun shot— a through-and-through in his right temple. His knees full of arthritis, and his hands, the knuckle joints showing signs of calcified periarthritis. The stippling of the revolver and the indented pattern of the end of the barrel tells me it got pressed extra hard to his temple. You know, Jack, Smitty wouldn't have had to push it too hard to kill himself." She glanced up.

"You mention this to Xi or Jace?"

"Didn't have to. I put it in my notes; that and the missing first joint of his middle finger. If Smitty was right-handed and it was his trigger finger, no way, you know?"

"I do know, and I know Smitty learned to shoot fine without the end of that finger, only that was in his younger years. With his age and the noted arthritis, he wasn't capable."

"Let's also talk about the GSR. Jack, there was GSR on his hands and on his person, his clothing—and before you jump in here, let me finish." Mack gave him a look. He stayed silent.

"If the man fired a gun to kill Dellucci, then himself, of course we expect to find residue—a lot, since Sal got shot at close range. If Smitty didn't shoot Sal, but only himself, then, yep. Same thing. There'd be GSR, but not as much. There wasn't much GSR on Smitty's hand. We have a hypothesis on that."

"I'm still listening, Mack, and would like to hear what you two think."

"Transference. We might conclude Smitty did not kill himself, or Sal, but there is GSR on his hand transferred by whomever put the revolver in Smitty's fist."

"Sounds reasonable. Is that in your report, too?"

"You know we can't write in a theory, only facts. I've sent this information to CSU, though, and have requested they run tests reenacting the shootings in different scenarios."

"Who's leading that team?"

"Loren Taylor. Jack, you in a hurry to leave?"

"No, why?"

"Because your ass is on the edge of the seat and you look ready to bolt." A grin spread across her face. "On a personal note, how are you?" Marlo Makos had seen little of him since he'd left for Mexico, and all this not long after Gretchen's murder. She'd worried about him and for him.

"I'm better, Mack. Yeah, I still miss the hell outta her. But the nice memories keep me going."

For a second, they sat in silent contemplation, the stillness enveloping them, but she sighed, then continued. "Other news regarding Smitty's autopsy."

Jack gave her a look. "More?"

"Yeah. He was dying. He had six months left to live, perhaps as little as three."

"Cancer?"

"Yeah, melanoma."

"Skin cancer?" Jack knew the old geezer was out in the sun a lot if he lived on his boat.

"Yes, it metastasized to his brain. He was most likely having a lot of headaches and lost weight."

That accounted for the bottles of aspirin in his go-bag. Poor Smitty.

Mack picked up another file and continued. "Sal Dellucci. One shot in the head. Someone roughed him up beforehand; proof is on the corpse. I also have to agree with you, Jack. Sal wasn't much older than Smitty, but he'd stayed in shape. He also didn't have the maladies Smitty did." She hesitated, but only for a nanosecond.

Jack, however, didn't miss her hesitation. "What else?"

"Oh, nothing, except I might understand why Smitty shot himself. Anyone with brain cancer can experience personality and mood changes. But his physical strength—Jack, he could've never overpowered Sal. If I were writing this, I'd say Sal killed Smitty first, then shot himself; 'cause this all seems bass-ackwards."

A sudden thought crept to Jack's mind, and he said, "As if someone choreo-graphed it, you mean?"

"Perfect way to say it. Now, all you gotta do is prove it. As soon as the reports Taylor and Stoner are working on cross my desk, I'll let you know."

On his feet, he thanked her and headed to the courthouse, then to haul ass to the marina.

44

WITH HER BAG OF tricks in hand, Suzy stood at the end of the jetty. "Jack, over here."

"Wong, how've you been?"

"Just busy, as usual. Sorry to hear about Smitherson. Heard he was a pal of yours."

"Yeah, not sure if I'd say we were pals."

Suzy frowned. "Gotta say I'm not sure how to feel about Sal Dellucci, after what I've heard. But getting murdered, well, it ain't right no matter what kinda scum you were when you were alive."

Silence ensued. Then she hoisted her gear. "Alright, Detective West. What are we looking for?"

"I suppose proof either Smitty was on the take or wasn't, or perhaps a clue he planned to kill Sal and commit suicide."

JACK WATCHED HER WORK. Not once did he guide her in any direction, yet he was antsy for her to get below.

"I enjoy sushi, but after today I think I'll lay off for a while." With a giggle, she returned the bucket of decaying minnows to its hiding place under the tarp. "So gross."

"Come on, Wong, I am sure you have seen worse stuff than rotting minnows."

"Uh-huh, I have. But I'm not a flesh-eating zombie. Thing is, I do eat Japanese cuisine. Dead bodies I can handle, for odd reasons, but not stinky fish."

"I avoid raw foods; I'll eat some vegetables raw, but my steaks are always well-done."

A wispy laugh escaped as she pulled open the fourth and last drawer of a custom-built storage cabinet. Flat boxes of various fishhooks, line weights, fish lip grippers, and braid scissors, and two used fillet knives. No item is over two inches thick. Still squatting, she moved back a tad and angled her head to see the front cabinet. On her knees, she pulled up on the drawer handle, lifting the wheels off the track to guide the drawer out. Careful not to dump the contents, she set the drawer aside.

"Find something?" He stood behind her, looking over her shoulder.

She looked to see where the drawer had been. "Not sure." With her fist, she rapped on the bottom. Hollow. Suzy slid her fingers across the drawer floor, feeling a slight indent at the end. With the tips of her fingers, she pulled up at an angle, lifting the false bottom to reveal a hidden compartment.

"Jack, shine your phone flashlight in here, will ya? I ain't gonna have my fingers bitten off by a piranha or a gator he's been keeping as a pet." She laughed nervously.

Once she saw what looked like a skinny rope, she reached in, pulling out a beige waterproof canvas kit. Suzy untied the slipknot of the drawstring and extracted a large, clear waterproof bag.

"What do we have here?"

Jack narrowed his eyes. "Looks like official HPD files."

Rubber-banded together were classification folders with top-loading prongs and the seal of the HPD on the top sides. She flipped the bag and under the files, also bound by a thick, stretchy band, appeared to be a journal.

A frown on his face, Jack slipped his gloved hand into the sack, pulled out the journal, removed the rubber band, and opened the book.

"Well?"

"Most of the writing is unreadable. I can only make out the dates." Jack re-bound the book.

"Those are old police files." She nodded to the other articles in the bag.

An outdated departmental seal was on the cover of the top file. He flipped it open. A robbery report from 1970, over fifty years ago. The second file, more of the same. File number three, an assault charge. He frowned. "Makes no sense," he said, not looking for Suzy to remark. He picked up the last file and out slipped another plastic pouch filled with Polaroids. Suzy picked it up. She shook the packet, and they eyed the photographs. Some were stuck together. Instamatic shots and old camera photos.

"You wanna look at them, Jack?" She was on her haunches next to him.

"Better in a more controlled atmosphere. Let's go below."

Jack felt a bit like throwing up; Suzy still hadn't found the other bag, and none of this looked good for Smitty. How wrong was he about him?

SUZY FOUND THE BAG quickly.

"The old man had a go-bag?" She counted the bundles of hundred-dollar bills—there were twenty. "Oh lord, Jack. Wow. This is, what? Right at two hundred thousand?"

He squinted. "Just like mobsters used to say, two-hundred large."

"Man alive. What if his boat had sunk?" She shook her head while documenting the contents, tagging and bagging them. After another twenty minutes of searching, she found nothing more.

As a precautionary measure, Suzy conducted a second sweep. They'd been on the boat for four hours. Satisfied there was nothing more to find, she began readying the finds to be carried back to the lab.

"Sorry it took so long, Jack. This is how I do it. Might even come back later. Just in case."

He patted her shoulder. "You're the most thorough CSU operative Houston has ever had, and one of the brightest. If you do and find anything useful, you'll call me first?"

"You bet."

Police files, images, weapons and ammo, a notebook with unreadable shorthand needing deciphering, and a shitload of cash Jack hoped was traceable. They headed back to HQ.

Hours later.

"No, I'm not happy about this, Roni. These items should be in my hands, our hands, not IA's."

"I agree, Jack, only my hands are tied. When I told Vance about the files, the journal, and the cash, he was all over me like flies on horse shit, said they needed to go through the book and examine the police files since Smitty was a retired cop. He also took all the cash to be examined. Before he came to steal this stuff, I snapped photos of the currency. All the money straps have dates but not the same dates, and certain straps are from 1986. This is all fucked up." Roni appeared more frazzled than he'd ever known her to be.

"How about the photos?"

"Vance took the files, but I got the photographs." She pulled the clear baggie from her top drawer.

"Why did Infernal A-holes let you keep them?"

"They didn't. I didn't tell Elijah I had 'em. Once I said the word police files, he cut me off, telling me his lead guy was on his way over to pick everything up and I had to hand it all over. After that I stopped telling him anything more cuz I got an uneasy feeling."

A long, hard stare passed between them.

"Vance? You're kidding."

She rolled her shoulders back, lolled her head, and closed her eyes. "I don't know what to think. And not giving him those photos—guess I'm gonna be in hot water."

"Suzy photographed them and there's a chain of custody. Let me have them and the chain of custody paperwork. You pretend you never saw them. I'll take the heat. And I'll call Suzy, tell her to dump them off her logs."

"Jack, Suzy won't do it."

"Yes, she will—if I tell her why, then she will. She used to be a flatfoot. The girl was one of us before she was CSU, and IA ain't any cops or former cop's friend. Let me handle it, Roni. I'll tell IA I found them when I did a second sweep on Smitty's boat."

Dawson was right. The white lies were getting too easy.

After contacting Suzy, and her agreeing—he shredded the paperwork and stopped worrying, then went to his emails with the photos Roni sent of the bands of cash. They yielded him little information. Each band was from a small, independent bank, all of which had closed, and one long-defunct credit union. The dates on the bands: 1979, '81, '94, '96. The only year that stuck out was 1994, the year Cole died. Just because something happened in 1994 did not mean it involved his brother's shooting, but damn it, that year was popping up a lot. Stop reading into things, he said to himself. Sitting back, he slumped in thought, picking up the baggie of photos. His phone rang.

"West. Yep, be there in ten." He hung up, shoving the baggy of Polaroids into the bottom drawer of his desk. He grabbed his coat, phone, and keys, then darted out.

XI AND JACE STOOD positioned outside the firing box room in the basement of the Houston Forensic Lab, observing as a technician shot a projectile into a Bullet Recovery Tank, filled with over eight hundred gallons of water. The tank can stop a fifty-caliber projectile. A mesh netting, used to catch shell casings, surrounded the open end of the tank where the tech placed the revolver. Jack stepped up to the small viewing area to watch.

Ballistics Technician Olivia Brasher—five–foot five, reddish-blonde hair, greenish-gray eyes, and all of 118 pounds soaking wet—wore a white lab coat smudged with gunshot residue, one corner of a pocket torn. Her hair was up in a messy bun, messier than normal, as she planted her feet, pulling the trigger in rapid fire, unloading the clip into the tank.

Houston's Forensics Laboratory. Forty-thousand square feet, and three floors, including three thousand square feet of basement space for crime scene processing and for a firing range for other tests necessary to the forensic examination of firearms.

"Jack," Xi said, "Brasher has some news for us."

"She working on our cases now?"

"Nope. Already done. Dead cops are priority. Right now she's testing a semi-auto for a case Cooper and Reed got three weeks ago," Jace stated. "She's a pistol, ain't she?"

Jack looked past Jace at Brasher. "Olivia, or the gun?"

A sheepish, "Olivia," popped out of Jace.

Xi looked at his partner. "Jace, you dog. Why not ask her out then?"

A slight twitch of Jace Severson's shoulders ensued. "Ah, don't wanna mix it up with a co-worker. Never works out, does it, Jack?"

"How the hell should I know? As Dawson tells me, I seem to have a thing for lady bartenders."

A hush fell over Jace and Xi. Jack sighed. "Guys, it's okay. It's been over two years and y'all need to stop wearing kid gloves around me when we talk about women."

Jace cleared his throat. "You're right, Jack. How about you and me go tomcatting then?" His brows arched up and down. "I can be your wingman, or you can be mine."

"Deal. Soon as we get this case cleared, let's do it."

The door opened, and Olivia stepped out. "Fellas, thanks for coming. Let's go to our little meeting room, shall we?"

Everybody grabbed a chair and Brasher took point at the end of the table. "The rounds found were involved in two shootings." Her eyes cut to Jack.

"It's okay, Brasher."

"Jack, some surprise that it involved your brother's shooting, huh?"

"Yeah. What else you got then?" He didn't want any of them to get bogged down in condolences for Cole's killing. He'd been fourteen. It was a lifetime ago.

"The other two, Conti and Gresham. Both killed with the same pistol that killed Sal. Same gun found at the scene of Gresham's murder, and it was in evidence lockup. Be damned nice to know how it got out." She looked at 7-11. "The gun you found at Sal's, we've linked to Smitty and Cole West and—"

Jack cut her off. His eyes landed on Jace's. "You found the .38 at Sal's? When?"

"That same night, Jack. We had a warrant—and before you blow a gasket, just listen. We called Roni and she said keep this under wraps until we knew for sure."

"Xi, you were trying to protect me. I get it. I'm not upset."

"What else, Brasher?" Xi got back to the task at hand.

"Someone filed off both serial numbers. I'll do acid washing, but no guarantees. I'm still digging into old cases, cuz something's been bugging me about these guns."

Jace spoke up, "Like what?"

"Something I skimmed over in a ballistics report from 1979. I'll double check it and get back to you."

"I should let you guys in on some stuff, even though I don't have authorization." Jack stopped short, looking at Olivia.

"Oh, don't mind me. I love all this detective stuff." She beamed.

Jace stood; the other two followed. "Brasher, email me a copy of the reports, and if you figure out what's bugging ya, let me know."

"Aw, you guys are spoilsports. I get it, need to know and I don't need to. Check your email this afternoon. And Jace," her tone teasing, "don't be a stranger."

Jace blushed.

THE HALL DOOR OPENED, and he took the stairs, hoofing it to six. By rigging the side door so it wouldn't lock, he could enter the ballistics labs unnoticed—but he'd have to come back for the gun. All this sneaking around, and he hadn't seen the real money yet; that had better change soon, he thought, his face twisting into a sneer.

45

"YOU GET OTHER PRINTS off the gun, besides Smitty's?" Jack pressed the up button.

The doors swooshed open and Jace entered first. "Come on, Jack, no other prints were gonna be on that gun, not this many years later. Get a grip."

The doors closed and Jack pressed 6. "Okay, tell me about the gun. Serial number? Any way to trace it?"

"Because someone filed off the serial, we're thinking it was a throwaway," Xi divulged.

"Kicker is, if Sal was dead, and so was Smitty, how'd it end up in Sal's apartment?" Jace frowned.

"This proves Smitty wasn't the shooter and didn't off himself. No way he could eat his gun and go hide it at Sal's. Plus, how do we prove it was Smitty's gun, and how on earth did it become the murder weapon in Cole's case?"

"That's the million-dollar question, Jack. 'Cuz I'm sure Sal wasn't hanging out with your brother that night."

The gears in Jack's head spun backward. He'd been fourteen, Cole almost nineteen. Although he was unfamiliar with all his brother's friends, the hangout spot was always swarming with kids, even former students from the preceding years. He hadn't started his freshman year and only knew his brother's football friends.

"Fellas, I didn't know all my brother's friends and, besides that, the end of Richmond was a huge hangout—make out zone, and drag, for half of the high schools in the area. Lots of rivalry, but nothing so serious to justify murder."

"You mean kids from every different type of family?"

"What you thinking, partner?" Jace asked.

"Older guys involved in shady stuff, like gangs or, back then, maybe Mob activities. Who knows, maybe even some dude in law enforcement," Xi thought out loud.

Jack looked at him, then at Jace. "Law enforcement? You're kidding, right?"

"Xi, you saying Cole was a target?"

"No, I'm saying this gun connection makes me think it was a cover-up and maybe a cop was involved."

Jack's face registered confusion and disbelief. "And you reckon his killing connects to Smitty's and Sal's, and all this crap with Brooks and the warehouse?"

"I dunno, Jack. Seems it was the cream that floated to the top of this mess. What I assume is Cole's death was an accident, and someone covered it up."

OPAL KINCAID ADJUSTED HER eyeglasses, looking over and not through them. "Officer Carver, what can I do for you?"

"Can you buzz me in?"

Her flat brown eyes locked onto him. From the moment they met, Opal disliked this kid; in her twenty-six years on the force, she'd encountered many untrustworthy men, and he got added to her list.

"What do you need, Carver?" She set her pen down, moved the clipboard she'd been noting on, and her sizable arms came up to rest on the counter. "You have a requisition?"

Of all people, why her? Why Kincaid the killjoy? "No, I don't, just—oh, hell, never mind. I'll talk to Wygant."

"Get his cell, call him, but I'm still gonna need proper paperwork, regardless." She picked up her pen and went back to work, dismissing him.

It was nine p.m. He stood at the outer doors and punched in a number.

"Yeah, what?"

"Kincaid's working the cage."

With a sneer, Yardley closed his eyes. "Always hated Kincaid, even when she was younger and skinny. Let me call Brooks, even though it won't matter 'cuz him tossing around his weight ain't gonna work with her. Do you know if the gun got logged?"

"No, you jagoff—and I won't know if I can't get inside and I damn well can't just ask." Carver gritted his teeth.

"Hey! Cool your jets. Improvise, ask for help." Yardley's patience was pushed to the limit. Once all his money was there, he was prepared to sail away and never return.

BRASHER'S CO-WORKER ON MATERNITY leave left her a mountain of ballistics to go through, and the last few months had been stressful. Every detective wanted results yesterday. As they handed over the casing, slugs, and firearms, lab techs warned them not to complain about the waiting period, which could be weeks or months. Only certain cases moved to the front of the line: two dead cops was that kind of case.

These long hours were kicking her ass.

Almost eight, and Brasher finished test-firing several weapons. Next was the acid wash testing on 7-11's case. She was focused on the task at hand, but her thoughts kept returning to the handsome Detective Jace Severson.

Upon completion, she emailed Detective Severson's report, then filed the original in a locked file drawer and moved about, locking up the firearms, her mind still on Detective Severson.

Sure, she'd heard he'd been married and divorced three times.

In this line of work, as well as with firemen and lawyers, sometimes marriages were tough to hold together. It had to be the ideal two people.

Maybe Jace never found the right girl. Hell, she'd had her own relationship hiccups.

Her boyfriend of three years ditched her last year out of the blue. The jerk took off and six months afterward sent a telegram announcing he was living in Alaska.

"Goodbye, asswipe," she'd said, tears streaming, finding solace at the bottom of a box of wine, then throwing herself into her work.

Perhaps if she summoned the courage to invite him to dinner, she could learn more about him and decide if a relationship with the handsome biker detective was worth pursuing.

Her mind on her personal life, she regloved and went about cleaning up the acid washing station, ready to call it a day.

It was around nine. With her thoughts preoccupied, she never heard the side door open, nor saw who hit her from behind.

———

"911, WHAT'S YOUR EMERGENCY?"

"Hi, uh, my name's Cynthia Tolkinson. I'm on the janitorial crew at the police department. I just discovered a lady unconscious in the ballistics lab. We need an ambulance."

"Is she breathing, or bleeding?" the operator asked.

"Breathing, yes. She has some blood on the back of her head, but it's not gushing," Cynthia said.

"Is anyone else there? Are you in danger?"

The younger woman looked around. "Nothing seems disturbed. No upturned chairs or anything broken, and nobody else is here," she explained.

"Can you wait with her and stay on the line while I get help?"

"Yes, ma'am, be glad to."

The call for the ambulance went out first, then the call to police dispatch to send a police car to headquarters. It felt weird to call police to come to police headquarters.

The officer took Cynthia's statement while the EMTs revived Brasher with smelling salts and checked her out, then transported her to the ER, where she received seven stitches and found out she had a concussion.

Olivia was livid.

As per police protocol for occupational injury, they admitted her for overnight observation.

Once settled in, she contacted dispatch and requested Detective Jace Severson. What a lousy way to see him again, and in the state she was in. Best now though, she grimaced, because if he saw her at her worst, by golly, he would like her at her best.

"Dispatch, Sergeant Hamilton."

"Sergeant, this is Brasher from ballistics. I gotta reach Detective Jace Severson. It's important. Have him call this number." She reeled off her cell.

"Affirmative. Anything else?"

She pursed her lips in thought, then said, "Yes. Inform him I am calling from the hospital."

"Are you okay, Brasher?"

"Yes, and no. I'm pissed. Someone waylaid me."

"At your home?"

"No, while I was in the lab."

"What the fuck—uh, pardon me—what the hell? You file a report?"

"Yeah, an officer came to the scene, but listen, I need to talk to Severson, and soon. They have me at Ben Taub and are keeping me overnight. Have him get in touch ASAP."

"You got it Brasher, and hey, stay safe and hope you get the bastard."

She ended her call, closed her eyes, and still saw stars dancing behind her eyelids. Indeed, a severe headache was imminent. Olivia kept her eyes closed and sunk her shoulders into the hospital bed to wait.

"You got the gun?"

"Yeah, it's hidden."

Brooks shifted in his seat to see Webb. "Where?"

"Who cares, as long as no one finds it, right?"

A grunt sounded in the back seat to remind them someone else was in the vehicle, and Brooks cut his eyes to the back. "What?"

"Just because he has the gun don't mean shit."

"What the hell are you talking about, E?" Brooks again shifted, this time to see Ethan Wygant face-on.

Ethan's eyes rolled and cut over to Webb in the driver's seat. "Did Brasher test fire it yet?"

"Yeah. I was in the side office, pretending to look at old files, and listened to her telling West and those dildos she had, and ... oh shit." Webb's voice cracked.

"Uh-huh, oh shit is right, you moron. She recorded the ballistics, bagged and tagged them, and she wrote up a physical report. You took the gun, sure, but she's got the other info, and damn it you know she photographed the motherfucker."

Brody Brooks shook his head. He hadn't considered that.

"What about the cameras at the lab? You clear them?" From the rear, Ethan Wygant eyed the back of Skip Webb's neck, his beefy arms folded across his broad chest, a scowl plastered on his face.

"I think so."

"You think? What the fuck! Brody, you said this guy was smart. He's a sub-standard civilian, and a piss-poor cop. Gawd almighty!"

"Hey, Wygant, what the hell—"

Ethan cut the man off. "Shut up, and you address me as Sergeant Wygant, you shithead. Brody, get out, we gotta talk." Ethan jerked the door handle and slid his fat bottom over to get out. Brooks did the same, glowering at Webb as he exited.

"Over here." Ethan walked to the rear of the car.

"E, before you go apeshit, let me handle this."

"Brody, you can't. If he knocked her out, sending her to the hospital, they've already processed the scene. So we can't just walk in and grab any paperwork or files. And there's another problem too."

Brooks inhaled. "What's that?"

"The lab got new security cameras. Hidden cameras are in the hall's upper doorways. Because of potential evidence tampering or loss—the COP made the call weeks ago. Got the memo late today."

Brooks hitched up his trousers, indignant that nobody informed senior officers about these matters. "Why weren't we informed?"

Ethan's face twisted into a sneer. "Because, dear cousin, we aren't part of IA. You need to get that gun, and soon."

"I will, Skip trusts me," Brody said.

They stood without speaking, both staring at the back of Skip Webb's head, and Brooks broke the dark silence. "I ain't gonna make the call; you'd better call Carmine, or Yardley."

A vast exhale left the lips of Ethan Wygant. "After the funerals, I'll let them know. Jesus Christ, if a third cop shows up dead, this is gonna be more than a clusterfuck."

BEN TAUB WAS BUSTLING, as usual, when Jace and Xi arrived. They had moved Brasher to a private room. She sat propped up at a slight angle, her eyes closed, when a tap-tap-tap sounded on her door.

"Come in," she said, and sighed. Her head was throbbing like a bass drum being beaten with a ball bat.

"Olivia, my god, you okay?" Xi was the first to speak when he saw her pained expression.

"Yeah—you should see the other guy," she said with a wince.

"You get hit in the face or the back of the head?" Jace stood over her bed, looking down.

"Back of the noggin. Why?"

"Cuz you got a big purple bruise on the left side of your face, that's why."

Brasher lifted her hand to her cheek. "Hand me my bag, will ya, Xi? It's under the nightstand."

He did, and she extracted a compact to see her face. "Well, damn. I hit the floor pretty hard—guess cement will do that." The concrete impact left her cheek purple and blue.

"Dispatch said you got stitches."

"Yeah, ain't nothing but a scratch. Got seven and a walloping headache, and I'm pissed as hell."

"Any idea who has it out for you?" Xi flipped out his notepad.

"No clue. I'd just bagged up the guns and was cleaning the acid washing station when I got hit from behind."

Jace slid a chair over and sat next to her bed. "Got a feeling someone was after that damned .38."

Olivia smiled. "If someone was, no worries, I emailed you the serial number, photos, and a full report, 7. Aside from y'all, no one is aware of the specifics regarding the gun—even my boss doesn't know. If it's gone, we can investigate its origins with the serial number now."

A slow smile spread across Jace Severson's face, and his eyes crinkled. "You're a pip, Brasher, and a tough broad, one who can take it on the chin and come up fighting."

"She can take a hit on the noodle and get back up, that's for sure," Xi tossed in.

Olivia pushed the button to her bed, sitting more upright, and yanked at the covers that had gotten twisted under her leg. "Well, I hope you find out who the bastard was, 'cuz I owe the son of a bitch a punch in the nose. Oh, shit." She cringed.

"Best not get aggravated until your head stops hurting. Listen, we'll be in touch. And Olivia, you hang in there." Xi closed his notebook.

Her eyes met Jace's. "Check your email, 7. Keep in touch. You have my cell."

"Uh, yeah, I will."

They left her to rest.

In the hall, Xi punched Jace in the arm. "You dog, she likes you, so you'd better call her, ask her out for drinks or dinner, or I'm gonna whoop your ass."

"Not likely," Jace retorted. "I mean about the ass whooping, you dork, but yeah, I'll call her when we've closed our case." Jace Severson grinned from ear to ear as they left Ben Taub.

46

PETE SMITHERSON'S ASHES WERE scattered; Roni attended the service in Kemah, Texas. It drew a small crowd, as no one wanted to stand near the water on a misty morning—a tiny gathering of less than twenty people, including the organist and the personnel of the small funeral home. Smitty had no family, no spouse, and no children.

What a sad life. On her drive back, she wondered about Pete's loyalties and friends in low places.

The following day brought a second funeral. The church filled with men and women dressed in stiff, dark blue uniforms, service caps included.

Corey Carver, in his formal dress blues, Uncle Gino, and Carmine Berutti, clothed in black, sat in the front pew, amongst what family could attend. Four rows of pews filled with known associates of the Berutti family, as well as a few not-so-friendly faces, just paying respects to the old man.

Gary Yardley and Sam Coolidge sat at the far back of the church, hunkered, trying to keep themselves from standing out. Neither man was an active officer of the department, and neither had wanted to dress in full uniform for Sal Dellucci's funeral.

Brooks, Wygant, and Webb sat in the ranks, in full dress blues. Funny, none of them attended Pete Smitherson's service, and she wondered why. Veronica Justice kept cutting her eyes at these three. Something was off—very off.

Her eyes skimmed the crowd. If a rival wanted to take out another family, they could. Only it wasn't like the olden days, where Tommy guns would appear and ammunition would fly. She exhaled, thankful those times were part of the past and not the future.

Jack texted before the service began.

Jack: Got the footage.

Roni: What took so long?

Jack: Someone tampered with the hidden camera last night.

Roni: WTF?

Jack: Finston in tech has it, guy's a miracle worker.

Roni: Jack, music started going silent. Update me later.

She shut down her phone, shoved it in her jacket, and caught Brody Brooks staring a hole through her. Her brows arched in a "what the fuck do you want" look.

No smile, no twitch of a lip, no flare of a nostril. His eyes penetrated hers. He hated her guts and sure as shit would love for her to be on the list of loose ends that needed tying up. He had the men to do it—men who'd love to off a Captain of the HPD. An inner grin filled his eyes.

Roni saw the happy gleam, wondering what the hell he was envisioning, and could only imagine it was a scene with her being blown to bits.

The music changed, and a priest stood in front of the podium. Both averted their angry stares to focus on the vicar and words meant to comfort the living.

———

TODAY'S FUNERAL AND THE attendees such as Brooks and Wygant gave Jack the carte blanche he needed to move around in the off-site warehouse. No Carver, Webb, or Nichols—and no Brooks or Wygant. Perfect.

The file photos Dave got from the incident reports made no sense to him—he needed the binders, which weren't logged anywhere in the system for retrieval. Missing folders, misplaced boxes. This was getting to be common and worrisome. It meant someone was hiding something.

"Stan, how are you?" Jack signed the clipboard the man slid over and gave him the requisition Roni created to get the boxes he and Katherine had squirreled away the night they snuck in.

"Doing alright, Detective, just this cop-killing has a lot of us spooked, ya know?"

"Yeah, we are all anxious."

"You need me to help you locate these boxes? It's a damn mess back there."

"Nah, got an idea where to start. No worries."

"Okay, Detective West, have at it, and watch out for spiders, roaches, and rats." Stan waved him back.

In the warehouse's dankness, where the HPD entombed old evidence, Jack smiled at Stan's warning to watch for spiders, roaches, and rats. His brain translated it: Watch out for Skip "Spider" Webb, dirty cops like Dellucci and Yardley, and big fat rats like Brody Brooks.

His boots stirred up the dust of ancient cases as he walked straight back to the boxes he and Sparks had hidden. Only two boxes, but he needed the detective's binders, too. The murder books held a list of collected items and photos. This was how he would cross-reference. Otherwise, it was all conjecture that the evidence had disappeared.

The last celebration of life Jack attended was no damn celebration. To him, it was about honoring a life well lived, not one taken by a murderer. His girl, Gretchen's, service was not a celebration—it was a tragedy. Now he went to memorial services only if he had to.

———

"You REGRET NOT GOING to the services, Jack?"

"No, Dawson. I'll honor the fallen who were honorable and deserve that respect."

The door squeaked and 7-11 strolled in.

"Got some news about those account numbers, guys." Xi waved papers over his head.

"You ain't gonna believe it either." Jace yanked his chair around to sit next to Dawson's desk.

"At this stage, with all the shit that's happened, ain't a lot I won't believe," Jack said.

Xi Chang sat, laying the pages on the corner of Jack's desk. "These are bank accounts, opened thirty years ago, all closed, and we have no way to trace the money, and none of this is illegal."

"So what's the point?" Dawson scowled.

"Well, we have the account holders' names." Xi flipped a page. "All women. Lenora Berutti, Carmine's wife. Theresa Dellucci, his mistress. And Corey Carver's mom."

"What's Carver's mom's name?"

"Silvia Conti."

Dawson was confused. "His last name is Carver, not Conti, and I'm pretty sure Carver isn't an Italian surname."

With his head doing a bouncy-bounce, Xi said, "Let me sum it all up for y'all. Back in the wiseguy era, when an unwed woman got pregnant while having an affair with a married man, about ninety percent of the time neither the man nor his family acknowledged the child. I wanna emphasize, most of these men were in powerful positions, and even though they might've handed out a few bucks to help support the kid, they did not consider him or her part of the quote, unquote, family. The child born out of wedlock did not receive a family name."

Jace tossed in a quick, "Yeah, and family was everything, right?"

"Back to what I was saying," Xi went on. "Sometimes, the moms borrowed last names from other family members to keep things confidential." Chang took a deep breath.

"It's a jumbled mess of names, so try to keep up. Sal got his mom's maiden—Dellucci. His girl, Corey's mom, was Silvia Conti, but Sal never married her. Her maternal grandma's last name was Carvelli. Silvia Americanized it and changed it to Carver for the kid. Toss in the last name Berutti, and we've got us an Italian salad."

A look crossed Jack's face. Angelo Conti. That name kept coming up. "Hey, didn't an Angelo Conti get murdered in '79, and—"

Jace cut him off, "Yup, the gun used to knock off Sal killed Angelo Conti and another dude, Ed Gresham. Silvia was Angelo's sister and Carver's mom."

"Where's Silvia now?" Dawson spoke up.

"Died when Carver was six. Breast cancer. That's when Sal took full custody. He never denied the kid was his. Only thing was he didn't know he was a Berutti until a few years later when Lenora Berutti passed," Jace said.

"Conti's case never got solved, but now with the bullet match..." Xi didn't finish.

"We need that gun." Jack pushed away from the desk just as his cell dinged with an incoming text. He read the text and looked up. "Come on. Finston has the footage. Let's roll."

THE CEMETERY WAS SOMBER as Carmine watched them lower his son's casket into the ground.

The old man never shed a tear. Sal's half-brother, Gino Berutti, watched, stone-faced, as the copper casket dropped into the dark ground, thinking, *Good riddance to the man.*

A boy who'd become more important to their father than he'd been his entire childhood. That slut of a mother—his father's mistress.

He cut his eyes over to Carver, the bastard grandson, whose face was ashen. Another cop on his father's payroll. The list was shrinking at a rapid speed.

Times were changing. Players not as apt to take part as they'd been in the bygone days. Mob days, gangster mode, had switched to cartel and gang mode; meaner, not so refined or gentlemanly. Killing was killing, but taking out your enemy with a gunshot to the head beat dismemberment and gruesome torture—uncivilized crime.

His father, Carmine, was an old man now, his time ending. Gino had seen the will. His rightful inheritance split with the dead man. His father would need to change the will. Would the old man put Carver into the shoes of his dead father and split the Berutti estate with another bastard? His ire rose as he balled his fists.

The vicar spoke the words, "Ashes to ashes, dust to dust. We lay to rest our brother, Sal Dellucci..." His words droned on.

Carmine tossed in a handful of dirt and faltered. Corey grabbed his arm to steady him, and Gino saw the look of gratitude he gave his illegitimate grandson. It sickened him.

Brooks also watched. Corey was a problem—had been since his youthful, wayward years. Sal doted on his only son, and after Silvia passed, it got worse. Carmine, too, only Carver never knew, not until he made it through the academy and they started him into the family business, albeit in small doses.

The family business: a Mob and cop business. Had been for years. Their early years were lucrative—thanks to bookmaking, prostitution, truck hijacking, and bootlegging—allowing them a lavish lifestyle. Nowadays, it was meaner, more sinister—what with the drug trade and human trafficking—and even more dangerous.

The crowd began dispersing, cops stopping to pay condolences to Carver and ignoring the old man and Gino—men who were not cops, nor respected. Then the next wave of mourners floated by, ignoring Carver because he was a cop, only paying their respects to old man Berutti, the family patriarch, and his son Gino, next in line as head of the Berutti family.

Roni kept her eyes on Brooks and Wygant, who inched their way over to the family but kept it short, and it was then she saw Gary Yardley and another man she couldn't place straight off. She snapped a few photos on her phone, shielded by the passing officers in dress blues offering condolences.

"Officer Carver." Roni extended her hand in politeness. "I am sorry for your loss."

With a sober expression, Corey nodded. Then he let go of her hand like she had the plague when his glance caught his Uncle Gino's.

Veronica Justice acknowledged Carmine and Gino Berutti, but did not speak. Cops and crooks—this was the one time they acted civil to one another.

She walked farther out and turned to watch the rest of the mourners. Clad in formal dress blues, she blended in with the others, giving her an advantage to observe the crowd. Her eyes searched out Brooks again. He stood with Wygant, ex-cop Gary Yardley, the unknown man, and Skip Webb. She could only guess that Yardley and Brooks knew each other from their early patrol days. What a way to catch up.

Then she pondered a minute, wondering where Earl Nichols was, but saw him and Leon Golan walk up to join the entourage of what she considered tarnished cops. Nah, she thought, she liked Jack's description of these types of men better. They were men who used to be true blue, who once upheld and honored the law. Now they were nothing but ghosts, dressed in faded blue.

47

FOR THE UMPTEENTH TIME, Dawson said, "I can't believe it. Can you guys believe it?"

Jace's anger fueled his pacing.

"Sit down, 7." Xi pulled a chair over. "And calm down. He's not gonna get away with it."

Eyes glued to his desk, Jack sat, his boot tapping the floor. Total silence. That a colleague stole evidence and hurt a fellow Houston Police Department member troubled them all.

"He's clueless we're onto him. Besides Finston and Art, it's just us four that know."

A loud *thawaap* echoed as Jace hit the desk. "Jack, we gotta confront the son of a bitch."

"Not yet, we don't. We gotta get some answers and put some shit together that makes sense outta these other cases first."

"Alright, Jace and I are on the Gresham and Conti cases—plus we'll keep looking into those old accounts."

Jack West tightened his jaw in thought. "I'm gonna try to decipher Smitty's notes and dig into the photos Roni kept. You," he eyeballed Dawson, "dig into the boxes that looked tampered with. Find something we can use."

"Jack," Jace's voice was tight, "How long we gonna let that motherfucker get away with stealing the gun and injuring Brasher?"

Jack's eyes went to Jace. "Skip Webb will pay for what he did. We'll make sure."

Jack worried a major blow was about to strike the police department; he wondered how severe the impact would be.

THE HOMICIDE DEPARTMENT GATHERED in the squad room at the behest of their captain.

"Guys, I can't reach Webb. He's been AWOL three days now. Earl," Roni's voice strained, "when was the last time you heard from him?"

"I'm working with Cooper. I'm not Skip's mother."

"Thought you two were close friends?"

"Oh yeah? Well, we ain't!" Nichols popped back. Regretting his attitude, he added, "Sorry, ma'am."

Veronica Justice looked into the sea of faces. "Anybody heard from him in the last few days, or since the funeral?"

Heads shook, murmurs of "no" wafted throughout the room.

Veronica Justice pinched the bridge of her nose. "Jack, will you put out an APB for Detective Webb and send units to do a ten-mile grid search near his home? Take Luck and go to his apartment." She glanced around the room, her eyes landing at the back. "Nichols, you and Norris dig into his computer, look through his calendar, notes, whatever is on his desk. Rybak and Reed, go through his department phone records—"

A hand came up. "Yes, Moshe?"

"How about his personal phone, ma'am—should I trace his steps?"

"Excellent point, Rybak. Gentlemen, even though nobody likes Webb, he *is* one of us, so let's find him."

———

AN APB WENT OUT. Jack and Luck went to his apartment, knocked. Nothing. Jack called his captain. "No one's home. Breach or not?"

"Exigent circumstances. He's a missing cop, breach," she advised.

They drew their guns. Jack kicked the door in, giving them entry and, after clearing the one-bedroom apartment, they holstered their weapons. Skip lived in a sparse bachelor pad. One beat-up pleather couch, a ratty recliner, an end table and scratched coffee table. A bookcase with few books, and a forty-inch flat screen on a black, four-foot folding table.

In the one small bedroom, his bed was unmade, his laundry heaped into a worn wicker basket. The kitchenette/dining room lacked a table or chairs. One lone bar stool sat at the end of the counter. No dirty dishes in the sink, except a coffee cup. His trash was stuffed with takeout cartons. Skip didn't cook. Jack viewed Webb's existence as sad and solitary. He figured Skip, to fit in, had befriended undesirable people without hesitation. Brooks and Wygant, Sal, and even Yardley came to mind. Cops saw it all the time with boys in the hood. Fight or flight, get in the group or kicked out—or worse, carried out on a cadaver stretcher, zipped in a body bag. He hoped Skip was not facing the body bag.

"Wonder how they got their hooks into him." Dawson shut the refrigerator door.

"One thing comes to mind. Money. Skip ain't the sort looking for power." Taking in the entire room, Jack concluded the cash was the only explanation.

Dawson frowned. "Huh, jail ain't much worse than this. I mean, if he's still alive. I don't like this, Jack—my gut says something ain't right."

"Yeah, mine too. Let's see if they got anything on his phone's GPS. Let's roll."

In the car, Luck called the station. "Rybak. Luck. Skip's MIA at his complex. You get anything usable? Right, we'll head that way then." Dawson disconnected. "Moshe gave me an address, over off Montrose. The last place Skip's phone pinged was at a bank."

From Chimney Rock Road, Jack drove to the West Loop South. It wasn't far, yet traffic slowed them. "Want me to contact control, see if a unit is nearby, Jack?"

"No, if his phone is pinging there, he's still there. No sense in spooking him. Call Moshe back, ask him to update us on any changes, tell him traffic's a bitch and we're going in 10-40."

After twenty-nine minutes of weaving in and out of bunched-up traffic, they got to Central Bank on Post Oak Boulevard, hunting for Webb's ride.

"He drives a POS, Jack. A 2009 muddy brown Land Rover. It won't be hard to spot. Someone caved his rear bumper in." Dawson scanned while Jack drove from the front to the back.

Dawson pointed. "Jack, back corner. Webb's Rover. It's empty."

Jack parked four spaces away. "Let's go into the building, get eyes on him."

"Then what? We can't arrest him." Dawson banged his door shut.

"If he sees us, we say we've been looking for him. Department got worried that he no-showed. Tell him it's a welfare check, of sorts."

Dawson's lip curled up in a snarl. "He won't buy it, he's not that stupid, he's gonna rabbit."

"He runs, we chase—that simple. First, we need to get eyes on him, see what's up, but yeah, be ready for anything. Men like Skip, if backed into a corner, will come at you both fists balled up, or trigger finger on the gun," Jack said, unstrapping his weapon.

They'd worried for nothing; Webb was nowhere to be seen.

Dawson pulled a face. "Don't look too favorable."

"Let's check his ride." Jack led the way out of the revolving bank entrance.

The windows were dirty; it was hard to see inside. Jack looked through the windshield.

From his side pocket, Lucky pulled out black crime-scene gloves, handing Jack a pair. "Better to err on the side of caution," he said, offering a bit of folksy wisdom. "This might be a crime scene. We don't know yet."

Jack tugged the gloves on. "I'm hoping not," he said, gripping the door's handle and pulling it open at the protest of rusty hinges. Dawson repeated that action with the passenger door and they peered inside.

Trash: tons of fast-food garbage, old Styrofoam cups, a few empty drink containers from Starbucks and specialty coffees from Quick Trip. Dried, muddy, leafy debris covered the drivers-side floorboard.

"When was the last time we got a hard rain, Luck?"

"Two, maybe three weeks ago, I reckon. Why?"

"Accelerator's covered in dried mud." Jack pulled back to look at the back tires. "Tires too."

"And?" Dawson asked, raising his head after peering beneath the seat on the passenger's side.

His gaze going over the front dash, Jack said, "Perhaps he's driven through mud, maybe like the Sheldon Reservoir?"

Dawson's head came up in a jerk, and he bumped it on the headliner and the edge of the door opening. "Ouch! Hey, you think he ... aw come on, Jack. Sure, Skip's a weasel, but not a killer."

"Damn, Luck, I don't know what to think anymore." He turned his head, glancing at the headrest, and noticed two or three specks of a reddish-brown substance. "Not good, pard."

Dawson opened the rear door and looked up. "What's not?"

"Possible blood. We need CSU out here. Also, have them get samples of this mud and compare it to the dirt at the reservoir. See if Skip's Rover's been out there."

"Then what, Jack? Get an arrest warrant for a detective on our squad?"

"No, we ask Moshe to get a list of the most called numbers on Skip's phone. Go backwards and track who he's talked to."

Jack called the station to fill the captain in while they waited for CSU and Rybak's list.

"HE'S CALLED THREE NUMBERS, multiple times, linked to the names Wygant, Brooks, and Yardley. This is Nichols' number, and he hasn't called the guy in over two weeks." Jack scanned the list Moshe him.

"Kinda odd, ain't it? I mean, by the looks of it, they were tight."

"Goes to show, Lucky. Things are not always what they appear to be. Now this number," Jack pointed out, "he's called..." Jack stopped to count. "...fifteen times in three days, and all calls were under two minutes. No name is associated with the number either."

"Let me see it." Dawson punched *67 and put it on speaker so they could hear. After three rings, a man answered, "Berutti and Son Trucking, Henry Gresham." They exchanged glances and Dawson disconnected the call.

"I know that name. There was a murder victim, Ed Gresham. His case is still an unsolved from '96."

Dawson looked at Jack. "It can't be a coincidence, Jack, can it? Do you think Henry and Ed are relations, and both worked for Berutti? If so, the plot thickens, doesn't it?"

Jack said, the wheels in his head turning, "Lots of names connecting, aren't there?"

"Who else's, Jack?"

"Dead men's like Angelo Conti and Lloyd Olsen, for starters. All men with cases either unresolved or dismissed without prejudice."

Dawson exhaled. "We got a lot of dots we needta connect when we get back to HQ."

48

CRIME SCENE TECHS LOREN Taylor and Vince Stoner arrived an hour thereafter, apologizing.

"Sorry, guys, there was a wreck, you know the drill," Loren huffed, popping on a pair of gloves.

"Yeah, but we're here now. What we got here, fellas?" Stoner eyed the aged brown Land Rover. "Ain't this Detective Webb's ancient ride?"

"Yeah, and this might be blood," Jack pointed out. "Also, could you grab some mud to compare with samples from Sheldon Reservoir?"

That got the CSU tech's attention. "Jack?" Vince eyeballed him. "You don't think..."

Jack cut him off. "Not saying what I think yet."

"Okay, Jack. Not a problem," Loren interjected, looking at his coworker. "Vince, call the Vehicle Examination Building. Get them to tow it over here. Be better if we work inside, with lights—gonna be dark soon. That work for y'all?" He looked from Dawson to Jack.

"Sounds perfect. You guys keep us in the loop; we gotta head back to Travis Street."

KINCAID HAD NO ISSUE with Detectives West or Luck walking into the cage unsupervised and without proper so-called paperwork. Captain Justice called the COD, Davis Yao, who phoned Kincaid with a verbal order to let them pass. After two hours of searching, they located the misfiled, dusty binders. Gresham and Olsen each had two; Angelo Conti, three—however, one was missing.

"Jack, I'm not sure where it is. Maybe it got thrown away, mislabeled, or someone took it."

"Let's work with what we've got. Worry about it later. Nothing we can do."

With the murder books piled on a cart, they rolled them back to the sixth floor and into a conference room.

"That all of 'em?" Roni looked over the binders.

"No. One is missing from the Conti file, but we'll work with what we have for now."

Dawson's voice lowered. "Um, Jack, we need one more case."

"Whose?"

"Cole West."

Jack exhaled, nodding. "Yep, we do, don't we?"

Roni and Dawson exchanged a glance, and she said, "I'll get it, back in a jiff."

"Sorry, bud."

"Hey, Luck, don't be. We could solve my brother's homicide, which is fantastic news. This would be closure for me, and my parents. As old as they're getting, it would ease their pain, even after all these years. How about we call 7-11 in, see if they wanna do some not-so-light reading with us?"

"Sounds like a plan. And, uh, let's order Chinese—I'm starved."

Although the current situation was somewhat dire, that got a laugh out of Jack.

EMPTY TAKEOUT CARTONS LITTERED the table, as well as unopened disposable chopsticks and wadded-up napkins. Binders sat open while Xi, Jace, Jack, and Lucky viewed original crime scene photos and read.

"I can't believe I never paid attention to this."

Dawson looked up. "To what?"

Jack's mouth thinned. "The lead detectives on the Conti and Gresham murders."

Jace had Gresham's, so he flipped back. "Says here James Parrish." He moved his finger down to the next name. "Ah, and Frank Windom."

"Yeah, and Frank was lead on Angelo Conti's case, with another fella, Harold DeMitt." Jack lifted his finger off the page, shaking his head. "Both cases unsolved, and my dead ex-partner was a fireball detective with an internal gut to beat all guts. The man's case closure: ninety-five percent. Evidence went missing, and there were foul-ups on both cases. This seems intentional to me, but we've got no proof."

The room hushed for a moment, then Dawson said, "Guess we need to sort it out and connect some dots. Let's keep digging."

JACK DIDN'T HAVE COLE'S; Xi did. From the corner of his eye, he watched Xi read his brother's murder book, flipping from the incident report and witness statements to the crime scene photos. In Jack's personal copy of his brother's homicide report, he had reproductions of the photos, but had slipped them into a manila envelope and stopped looking at them.

"Jack, stop," Xi said without looking at him.

"Stop what?"

"Watching me."

Jack emitted a tiny, closed-mouth chuckle. "Sorry." He went back to reading Angelo Conti's case file.

Ten p.m. They'd been at it two hours. Jack stood, stretched, and yawned. His cell phone chimed with an incoming text.

Dawson raised his arms over his head, reaching to work out the kinks. "Who was that, Jack?"

"Loren. The tiny droplets were blood, and the mud comparison's gonna take a few days. Loren found prints inside the car belonging to Skip, Earl, and Brooks."

"Ain't odd because these three do lunch together. That'd be normal," Dawson stated.

"That it?" Xi leaned into the table, reaching for a fortune cookie.

"Nope, he found other prints in the back seat."

"Whose are they?" Jace asked.

"Sal Dellucci and Pete Smitherson."

An eternity of silence hung heavy.

"Are we thinking Skip killed Sal and Smitty? I mean I can't stand the guy, but—" Dawson didn't finish his sentence.

"I thought I knew Smitty, and it appears I didn't. Could be Skip wasn't who we thought he was either." Jack approached the whiteboard. With a black marker, he started writing names.

Lines creased Jace's brow. "What I can't figure is how these guys—uh, Gresham, Conti, and Olsen—fit in."

"And Cole, how the heck does his shooting connect to any of this?" Xi said, his hand on the binders as if to guard them or keep them hidden from Jack.

"All brilliant questions with no reasonable answers. So, let's look at each man. Dawson has Olsen's, Jace has Gresham's, Xi, you take Conti's, and we'll put Cole's case aside for now."

Jack finished writing the names in a column and began firing questions as they each gleaned information from the murder books they had. Once finished, they had a mini bio for each man.

Jack stood at the head of the whiteboard. "All were close to the same age and drove trucks for different companies. All had minor arrest records. They lived within ten miles of one another and were married with kids, middle class. I see no red flags yet."

Jace fiddled with an unopened packet of duck sauce. "Could be a coincidence, you know? They might not know each other."

"Do you think we're talking about these particular men by accident?"

"Jack's got a point, 7." Chang stood, working a catch out of his back. "Look, let's keep digging into these guys. Best shot we have right now until someone finds Skip."

"No word on him ain't too promising, fellas." Dawson became hushed when he saw the door opening. Roni walked in, wearing a grim expression.

"Cap?" Dawson stood. "What's up, you find Webb?"

Roni pulled up a chair and sat. "Nope, but another HPD officer is at large now."

"Oh, for Christ's sake!" The duck sauce packet exploded onto the napkin underneath, and Jace muttered an "Oops."

Jack dropped the marker on the whiteboard's trough. "Who now? This is getting ridiculous."

She looked up, eyes boring into Jack's. "Corey Carver."

Jack took a seat across from her. "Isn't Carver on funeral leave?"

"Yeah, and he opted for an extra week, using his PTO."

Dawson asked, "How's he missing then?"

"HR asked me to reach out. He needs to sign some paperwork for his father's pension and other things they need to put in motion sooner than later. I've called everyone. Wygant says he hasn't seen Carver since the funeral."

"Okay, Cap," Xi jumped in, "why's his going dark a concern? I mean, he just buried his old man."

She sighed. "Well, Xi, I've left voicemails and texted, told him it was a matter of importance regarding his father's survivor benefits, and no response."

They were all thoughtful for a second. Then she said, "We need some answers and to find Skip, now Carver too. This is a real mess."

"We're on it, Captain, and, uh, if you hear from Carver, let us know."

"Will do. Fellas." She acknowledged them and left.

"You heard her. Let's get to work. Something has to make sense why I got these men's case numbers from Smitty. Xi, can you dig into some financials for me?"

"Whose?"

"Brooks, Wygant, Yardley, Webb, and Smitty."

He turned to Dawson. "Will you work up warrants for phone records for the same fellas? Add Carver too. Both he and Webb are special circumstances, because they appear to be MIA. Jace, you and I are gonna keep working the books; there has to be something we're missing."

49

"You're a bastard, Wygant." Skip rubbed the back of his head. Ethan had clocked Skip on the head with his gun to get him out of the car. He'd seen Ethan and Brooks storm up to his car, and they looked pissed. One thing he knew was he'd better stay seat-belted, ready to bolt. Ethan had other plans.

"You were panicking, you fool, had to calm you down."

"Gun at your side, yanked out—what choice did I have? Felt like a kidnapping and shit, two against one."

Brody shoved his chair back, the legs scraping the linoleum floor. "You've caused us problems. Even though I pinched the video, they've still seen it and it has you clocking Brasher and taking the gun. How you gonna talk yourself outta that without taking the rest of us down?"

Skip eyeballed Brooks. "No video, then no fucking proof. It's all conjecture, my word against theirs."

"Where's the gun?"

"Tossed it where no one will find it."

"Don't believe you, you little weasel."

"Hell if I care if you do or don't. And no gun, no proof I snatched that gun anyway. Shit, I'm a better liar than you are, 'cause I'm betting you guys have lied to me about the huge payday you've flapped your lips about. Tell ya what: you pay up, I disappear. Easy-peasy."

"The money ain't cash, you imbecile."

Skip sprang up. "I trusted you, Brooks!"

Ethan Wygant watched the tête-à-tête between them and had enough. "Shut it, both of ya. I gotta think."

"E, don't get bossy with me—not now, not after everything I've done."

"We've done, Brody, we. I'm in just as deep. The shit we've done will put us six feet under. We've got one-way tickets to hell. Now shut it and let me think." He eyed Skip, who sat, not realizing he was next.

Wygant's cell chirped. "Yeah?"

"Meet me tonight at the old man's house, ten p.m."

Ethan didn't end the call, pretending to listen, then said, "Roger." Then he pocketed his phone.

Brooks gave him a look. "Well?"

"We'll get you out tonight, Webb."

Webb's voice quavered. "And the money, you bastards? I can't live on my good looks."

"Your share's coming," Brooks said. "You've been a valuable asset."

"Gotta say, being your spy was an ass-whooping. The entire department hating me was no joyride. Everyone but Earl, and that dude makes me wanna puke. Shit, I deserve a medal."

Unamused, Ethan said, "We'll go right out and buy you one."

Webb's eyes narrowed as he stared at Wygant, then Brooks. He felt a sickening twist in his gut.

"Look, I can't hide out forever. Eventually someone is gonna catch up to me. When or if that happens, I won't go down alone. I'll sing like a chorus of canaries. Got me?"

"This ratty trailer park is the best place for you to hang until we figure it out," Wygant said.

They hadn't frisked him, and he had his throwaway strapped to his ankle and an extra clip in his front pocket. But, if they wanted to, they could overpower him. They weren't gonna go that far, right? Uneasy feelings surged within him; then hate and fear seized him, making him frown at Wygant. "I'd rather you not say 'place for me to hang.' Don't like what that implies." He paused. "And another thing, in case you two fat bastards try to pull a fast one: I've left a letter, in a safe place. You know, in case nobody sees me alive again." His voice did not quaver, and his expression hardened.

Brooks found his tongue. "Jesus H. Christ, Webb, we ain't killers!"

Webb looked at him. "Uh-huh, maybe you ain't, but..." His voice trailed off as he turned his stare on Ethan Wygant.

"Quit acting like a puss. Ain't no one gonna whack you. Brody, we gotta go. We've been out of pocket too long, people will wonder." Wygant looked back.

"The cupboard has ramen and soup; the fridge has water. You won't starve. Be back later."

In the car, Wygant huffed. "Gawd almighty, who knew that little shit would grow balls?" He backed the car up, looking around, checking for eyes.

"If he opens his mouth, he'll face serious jail time. Uh, and why did Webb make accusations about murder? Like if nobody sees him again. Shit, Ethan!"

"Quite the chatterbox, aren't we, cousin? Here, use my phone. Text Yardley, tell him to meet us tonight at Carmine's."

"Who was that if it wasn't Yardley?"

"Sam."

Brody grabbed Ethan's phone with a side-glance of concern. The one thing they had never done was lie to one another. His lack of response to his query about murder raised the question: was his older cousin guilty? He sent the text, and Yardley replied.

"What did he say?" Ethan blinkered.

"He'll be there."

"Good. Let's get back to the station."

Brody handed Ethan his phone and said nothing, asked nothing. Back when this all started, murder was the furthest thing from his mind, but now? He wanted no part in it ... but did he have a choice?

YARDLEY READ THE TEXT, then pocketed his phone.

"Wygant and the fellas will be here at ten tonight. Can you get Baglio and Goldman to show up?"

Gino Berutti sat at his father's massive deck, feet propped up, a metal nail file in his hands, digging dirt from under his fingernails. "Sure. We got a job for them, or just in case?"

"They got Webb stashed in a rust bucket in a trailer park on Channelside Street. He's gonna be visiting us tonight, too."

"Look, Gary, not a wise move to have my guys work over a cop. Besides, you piss him off, he'll talk, and you know my boys—they hate cops. They could get a little too enthusiastic in their job, and we end up with another body to dispose of. I mean, don't bother me; what's one more body these days?" Gino's reaction to murder—nonchalant.

"I don't want any part of it, neither does E. We've done so much more this time around than ever before. If you wanna take him out, do it yourself; just leave me out of it." Yardley got off his comfy armchair, scratched his balls, and arched his neck. "I need to see Carmine; he in the solarium?"

"Yeah, and please, don't get him wound up."

Gary Yardley, at the exit of the pristine office, turned. His eyes went to the photos of Carmine and politicians, Carmine and major business owners, Carmine and his son, Gino, and two daughters, Liz and Diana, and wife Lenora. There were none of Carmine with Sal or Corey. His gaze went back to the one with the entire family—Carmine, Lenora, and the three kids.

"Your sisters?"

"What about 'em?"

"You tell them about Sal?"

"No, the old man said he would. Liz is still in Greece and Diana and her husband are still in Istanbul. You know, the old man never wanted our family business to touch the girls, and it hasn't. He wants it kept that way, Gary." Gino scowled.

"Hell, I ain't gonna call 'em, just asking. And you, Gino, you ready to take over, headaches and all?"

Gino Berutti took his feet off the desk, dropping the nail file. He leaned forward, his expression hard. "I want this shit cleaned up so the old man can step down without worry, and I don't care who goes down or gets whacked getting it done."

Gary released the doorknob, resting his back against the adjacent wall. "And you? We all know you hated Sal, and the kid. The old man will change his will, that okay with you too?"

This brought a spark of hostility into Gino's eyes, and he sat straighter. "This is my family, not Carver's, and the old man would never cut me out. All he cares about right now is that Carver don't get killed. Besides, the cops could pin nothing on the old man." Gino stopped and looked at Yardley, his eyes dark. "The gun is one thing, but the book, that'll take us all down."

"All they found was that old fisherman's journal, and his writing's impossible to read."

Gino pushed his chair back and stood. "You'd better hope they don't decipher it. The old man is stepping down, and I'm taking over." His eyes bored into Yardley's. "I know this, though, but I won't be blindly following any instructions and doing shit just 'cause you might advise me. Those days are over."

"Yep," Yardley rejoined. "I get it. Times are changing. Now I wanna go see the old man before I leave. See you at ten."

CARMINE, LOOKING OLDER THAN he had two days ago, sat alone in the solarium. Gary pulled up a cane-back chair next to him. As twilight descended, the room grew dim.

"Want me to switch on the lamp?"

Carmine nodded, his eyes glued to a large print of a 1970s Houston skyline—the heyday of the oil boom. The image was a powerful reminder of the city's oil-fueled prosperity. Silence hung between the two men.

"That old man knew a lot," Carmine said.

"He's dead though."

Carmine turned his head; tired, bloodshot eyes bored into Gary's. "Even the dead can impart wisdom. No one is untouchable when others know the same secrets."

"I understand."

"No, Gary, you don't. Smitty was no fool and possessed knowledge you and others lack. I owe him for my success and freedom, and they cast his ashes into the water without a single mourner. Then the accusations of Smitty killing my son and subsequently committing suicide prevented me from saying my goodbyes." He was enraged, his voice trembling, spittle spraying from his lips.

Gino said not to get the old guy worked up. Shit. Gary's hand touched the old fella's arm. "What do you want me to do, Carmine?"

"Find his book, bring it here, and then leave me be."

"HPD has it; I can't touch it."

"NO! There's another one. It goes back years—more years than you've been alive, you twit. Find that book."

"Just where the hell would it be?" Gary asked, raking a hand through his thinning hair. "I need to be ready to sail in a few days and can't lose that gig, not with things the way they are."

Gary couldn't decide if Carmine's pinched expression was one of irritation or sadness when he said, "All these years, Yardley, you've been on my payroll, and there is still so much you don't have a fucking clue about. You should have stayed closer to Sal and Smitty." Carmine closed his eyes, and the silence engulfed them. He said, "Smitty did not kill Sal, nor himself. What I want to know, Gary, is who gave that order without my consent?"

Yardley looked shocked. His jaw clenched, and his rock-hard stare penetrated the old man's eyes. "It wasn't me, Carmine; I have never, not once, taken those types of liberties with you or the family."

They locked eyes, old man Berutti reading Gary's face. The air was palpable between them; unseen energy crackled as the now-dim room had shadows dancing on the ceiling. Old man Berutti inhaled, letting it out slowly. "I believe you, Gary, and I appreciate your loyalties. There's a snake in the henhouse, and he's slithering beneath us, getting ready to strike."

"Wygant, Brooks—is that who you mean?"

Carmine's head waggled back and forth. "Someone higher up. Find the book, and then get on your ship. And, Gary, might be best if you laid low for a period."

"How long?"

"Forever sounds about right."

50

JACK REVIEWED THE WHITEBOARD after erasing the clutter. Olsen, Gresham's sons, and Conti's nephew were similar in age. He tapped the board, mulling over the boys' place in the story. Except for Henry Gresham's link to Berutti Trucking, there was no apparent connection. He didn't know these guys back then, and Cole never mentioned them.

Lucky's brows V'd inward. "Hey Jack, were you and Cole in the same school district as Olsen, Gresham, and Conti?"

"We lived in the Memorial district. Their old address suggests they went to Heights. The school's name changed in 2016 to Reagan High."

Xi raised his finger. "I know we're not discussing Cole's case, but I got a question."

Jack leaned against the adjacent wall. "Yeah?"

"Kids from a variety of schools got interviewed, as noted in Cole's incident report. Dulles, Memorial, Stratford, and the Heights."

"So, what's your question?"

"Was Richmond Avenue a hangout for all schools?"

"Back then it was. Why?"

Xi grabbed the folder for Cole's case and found what he was looking for. "Report states some kids overheard older boys chatting about coke and a truck losing its cargo. The discussion got heated after one of 'em mentioned one boy had a father who was a cop, leading to speculation about how they financed their lavish lifestyle."

"That place was a hangout for everyone, including gang members—one reason Cole didn't want me going with him. How's this relevant to our case?"

"While the investigating officer considered this statement immaterial to the shooting, my current perspective differs."

A serious expression settled on Jack's face. Chang only offered conjecture backed by solid reasoning.

"Based on what, Chang?"

"The girl who relayed this information named two boys she overheard. Corey Carver and Lucci Conti."

Dead silence—you could've heard a mouse fart three counties away.

"Carver was there?" Dawson exclaimed. "He's never mentioned it to you?"

The news startled Jack, yet the wheels in his head turned.

"Carver and Lucas were at the scene of Cole's shooting; we're investigating Lucas's uncle's murder; add in that Carver's dad, Sal Dellucci—a cop—turns up dead." Jace's head was about to burst.

Jack let out an enormous sigh. "It's all connected, but how? My brother wasn't in a gang, didn't do drugs—he was squeaky clean."

"He have enemies?"

"Nah, Xi, everyone loved him. Cole was the friendliest jock you'd ever come across. Funny, modest—not a saint, but pretty close." A tiny flicker of a smile reached Jack's eyes.

"Girlfriend?" Dawson asked.

"Nah, they ended things when football season kicked off, but stayed friends. Xi, are the witness contact details there?"

"Yeah, but that was over twenty years ago. She might've married, or left Texas—who knows?"

"Xi Chang, we're detectives!" Jack bit back laughter at the horrified look on Chang's face.

"Yeah, 11, you dork," Jace said.

Xi shot Jace a glance and the finger.

Jack went back to the whiteboard and turned to Xi. "Who's this girl?"

"Sandra Burns, alumnus of Heights High School."

Jack underlined her name twice. "Let's look for her first thing tomorrow. How about calling it a night? It's after ten."

ON THE MAKESHIFT PORCH of the rusted-out two-bedroom trailer, Skip eyed the old Buick Regal.

"Where's my Rover?"

"VEB," Brooks responded.

"Why do they have my vehicle, for Christ's sake?"

"You're missing, and they traced it back to the bank."

"Who reported me missing? Oh, my God." Skip sat on the wobbly, 1980s, webbed lawn chair.

Brooks leaned against the trailer. "Seems your captain's been looking for you and you haven't responded to calls or texts. Might be she's worried about your scrawny ass."

He smirked. "Uh-huh, she's worried alright. Worried about me being on video clocking Brasher and swiping the gun. Is that what y'all are worried about too, like where I hid the gun?"

"Nah, we ain't worried about nuttin'." Wygant spat in the dirt, wiped his lip, and gave him a hard stare.

Skip's body tensed at Wygant's dark expression. He knew what the man was capable of. Did Brooks? Ethan Wygant was ruthless. Skip's hands gripped the cracked plastic arm handles of the aged lawn chair when he said, "Only problem you seem to have now is locating that damned book." He let a pregnant pause fill the air before adding, "And the detailed letter I got stashed."

"We can get around your fucking letter, Webb. Everyone knows you're batshit crazy. I mean, you assaulted a member of HPD and stole a gun. But..." Wygant took a step forward, his face contorted in an ugly snarl, his upper body stiff. "If you know where that book is, you'd better talk; otherwise, you're in for a long, painful night."

Skip's gaze remained fixed on Wygant. His eyes narrowed, jaw muscles flexed, and he spoke to Brooks without looking at him.

"This how you roll, Brooks? Torture, then what—kill me after you get what you want to save your ass?"

"Webb, just cooperate. I got no pull here; it'd be in your best interest."

"Wow, Brooks, I had no idea you were the pussy in this mix. I guess Ethan got the balls in the family. I was an idiot for being your lackey. The paltry sums of cash you handed me under the table don't seem worth it now. And I don't understand your hatred of West, either."

A vein pulsed in Wygant's temple. His jaw flexed. "Where's the book, Webb?"

Webb relaxed, leaned back, and shrugged. "I don't know, I really don't. So no matter what ya do to me, I can't tell ya what I don't know. Look, I ain't no hero, and damn sure ain't no martyr, but hey, you can give it your best shot and then kill me. Or..." He paused a beat, "you can arrange for me to leave the country with a substantial amount of cash. I disappear forever, taking my secrets with me."

"Not if there's a letter floating around."

"You get me to a non-extradition country. I tell you where the letter is. Or HPD can get my dead body and the letter, and you two fuckers hang by the balls."

"Get up, we gotta go."

Webb didn't move. "What, we don't got a deal?"

Wygant's eyes registered contempt. "You can ask Gino or Yardley. They're running the show, not me; otherwise, I'd toss your ass to the gators in the Sheldon."

"Like you did Sal and Smitty? How'd that work out for ya?"

A single punch sent him sprawling backward out of his chair; he howled in pain. His nose and lip were bleeding, and the chair had collapsed under him. After wiping the blood from his lip, he sat up and spat. His eyes turned to Brooks, whose mouth was open, catching imaginary flies.

"Fuck, Ethan. What's gotten into you?"

Ethan's silence spoke volumes. Brooks looked from him to where Skip still lay with a half-sneer on his face.

"Seems the truth makes old E here a might testy."

"Zip your fucking lips. Get him on his feet, Brody, and let's get going—Gino hates it when we're late."

"Ethan..." Brooks began, but got cut off.

"We can talk about this later." Ethan's tone was no nonsense; his eyes were hard. Brody felt a sudden chill of fear. Was his cousin guilty of murder?

———

THE BERUTTI HOME WAS a fortress. High steel fences with pointed tips, and a massive, electric-gated entrance. Put a couple goombahs out front with Tommy guns, and you'd have your very own Houston Godfather.

As the Buick approached, the gates opened, then clanked shut.

"Webb, out of the car. Don't be a wiseass—we have guns, and we're not afraid to shoot."

"Got no doubt about that, Wygant."

The front door opened, and Yardley stepped out.

"You're late."

"Traffic. We live in Houston—or you forget?"

"Gino and the old man are waiting." Yardley turned to Sam. "Take Brooks and Webb back. Wygant, you stay. I need a word first."

They sat in silence: Gino, Carmine, Brooks, Sam, and Webb. Brooks got antsy after a few minutes.

"This is horseshit. We meeting or not?"

"I say when we begin, understand?" the elder Berutti said with authority.

Wygant's enormous frame doubled over as the ball bat connected with his flabby middle. Paulie Baglio huffed as he swung again, this time striking Wygant across the center of his back. Wygant dropped face down on the floor.

Gary rested with his back to the only door, arms crossed. He watched as Baglio brought the bat up again, ready to swing.

"You can scream, Ethan. No one will hear you down here. Give him another whack, Paulie."

Ethan barely got to his knees before the bat sent him sprawling. Yardley held up a hand for Paulie to stop.

"Let's hear it again—how did you have that gun when it was supposed to be destroyed?"

Ethan groaned in pain. "Gary, come on, we couldn't destroy the only leverage we had on Sal. You knew him. He was a hothead and loose cannon. It was Tony's idea to keep it." He stood with a wobble, a painful fire in his belly. His back felt broken.

"Who has it now?"

Baglio lifted the bat, and Ethan cringed. "Skip said he tossed it, but didn't say where. I swear to God, I don't know."

Gary knew this to be true since Skip had given him the .38. Ethan wasn't lying.

"Alright, so Tony's an ass. We agree. And Sal, sure, he had a hot temper and would fly off the handle, but killing him? Shit, you bastard, Carmine thought I called a hit on his son." Gary's face was menacing. He gave Paulie a slight nod, and the bat lifted, striking Wygant on the backs of his legs.

"The old man doubted me, Ethan—not cool. You also wanna explain about Smitty?"

Ethan's breathing was labored as he tried rising to his knees. "Everyone ... was after that... fucking book," he respired in pain, "even Carmine. Smitty wouldn't give it up and threatened to ruin us all. I had no choice."

"You didn't know Smitty very well, Ethan. He and Carmine were tight. Have been since they were kids. Smitty would die before giving that old man up."

Ethan snarled. His life was over, and he knew it, so one more smart-ass remark would not make a difference. "I guess he did then, didn't he?"

With a nod from Yardley, Paulie Baglio lifted the bat and, with all his force, gave Ethan Wygant a crushing blow to his skull. Blood spattered from the broken skin, and the large man dropped face-first onto the concrete of the hidden basement, smashing his nose into his skull.

"Call Leo, have him and some goons haul Wygant's body and the bat to the wharfs. And have Jimmy and the boys bleach this place down."

"Another missing cop—how we gonna handle this?" Paulie propped the bat in the corner.

"Not worried about it. Let's go."

51

YARDLEY AND BAGLIO ENTERED the room without Wygant. Brooks frowned. "Where's Ethan?"

"Sent him on an errand," Gary lied, opting to stand near the doorway.

"Don't he need to be here?" Brody looked worried.

"Update him later. Let's get down to business." He eyed Carmine with a minuscule nod, and Carmine's gaze traveled the room, landing on Webb. "You have a letter detailing certain business?"

"Yep, it's my life insurance," Webb intoned.

"And the book?"

Webb shrugged. "Never saw it and got no reason to lie."

"I see. So, if you leave here, are we assured that letter never sees the light of day?"

"Got two demands."

The old man's brows arched. "Being demanding. Hmm, bad for your health."

"Alright," Webb said, his tone smart-alecky. "I got two requests then."

"They are?" Carmine asked, his voice calm, his posture relaxed.

"I get paid what I was told, and I get a way out of the States to a country with no extradition."

The old man motioned for Yardley, who walked to the desk, bent his head, listened, and nodded. Yardley resumed his stance at the door.

"Paulie, have someone take Mr. Webb home." Carmine looked at him. "Wait for instructions."

Brooks watched as Paulie Baglio escorted Webb, wondering if Webb was toast.

Nobody said a word, making Brooks even more uncomfortable. It was he who broke the heavy silence. "When's Ethan expected back?"

Yardley spoke. "Don't expect he'll be back."

A chill traveled up Brody's spine, and he felt sick in his gut. "Gary, you bastard."

"Shut it, Brody, or when Paulie gets back, I'll let him do what he wanted to do to you all those years ago," Gary sneered.

Brody knew Ethan was gone, and if he didn't cooperate, he'd be next. For the first time since his rise in the ranks, Brody Brooks commanded no respect, and he was afraid.

"The man responsible for killing my boy and Smitty has now paid his debt to me." Carmine's eyes traveled the room, landing on Brooks. "Did you know your cousin was capable of cold-blooded murder?"

"It was Ethan?" Brody felt like vomiting. "Why, why would he?"

Gino stepped around the desk and propped his hip on the corner. "Brooks, how'd he get the gun?"

Damn. He'd given the gun to Ethan to stash in any random evidence box after Tony gave it to him. He'd wanted it destroyed, but because they believed it to be destroyed already, he couldn't include it with the guns slated for melting at month's end.

"I—I gave it to him, but could have never known he'd do this, I swear."

"I'm curious, Brody, how'd you get the gun?"

Brody Brooks clenched his jaw. Uncle Tony, that fucking bastard, set him up. "I'm pretty sure you already know the answer to that question."

Carmine addressed Coolidge. "Who's got the gun now?"

"I don't know," Sam responded.

"That damned gun," Gino gritted.

Gino was right—that damned gun. That handgun murdered five people; all people he knew, except for one: Cole West. Frank knew, and he was sure Jack did too—if not before, then certainly now. The book, the damned book. His sins, and those of his colleagues, recorded. Key players: Ethan, Sal, Sam Coolidge, and Yardley. Oh, and yeah, Uncle Anthony—better known as the Assistant Chief of Police, Tony Croce—who, responsible for the destruction of property, failed to liquidate the firearm as instructed in 1978. The shakedowns, payoffs, cover-ups, even murderers set free, all in the name of the Berutti family and the almighty dollar. And Sal, his damn kid; and Corey; and, one night, that kid Cole West, and the cover-up that began the downhill slide into the abyss.

"Sam, take Brooks home," Carmine said.

Brooks stood, more than ready to get the hell outta Berutti's house. "You want me to find and destroy the gun once and for all, that it?"

Carmine's posture straightened, his chin raised, and air blew from his nostrils. "It is too late for that."

THEY SAT ALONE, SIPPING a nightcap in Carmine's office.

Old man Berutti drained his glass and poured another jigger of Dewar's. "Smitty was no fool."

Gino said, "The police reports say he had a go-bag—ready to run."

Carmine's brows rose. "That so?" He sat back, a slight grin on his face. "Like I said, he was no fool. Too bad he didn't get to use the bag and save himself."

Gino poured another half glass of Dewar's and gulped it, letting it sting the back of his throat as he swallowed. "Papa." Gino set his empty glass down, his voice softening. "What about the boy?"

Carmine drained his glass. Under his eyes were dark circles with old-man bags. The whites of his eyes were no longer white, but an aged yellow tinged with redness. He looked tired.

"Your mother, may God rest her soul, was a remarkable woman. I loved her. Sal's mother, Theresa." He let out a gigantic sigh. "May she, too, rest in peace. My passion for her was insatiable. Your mamma looked the other way at my dalliances. When Sal was born, I swore to her I would never put him before you. If your mamma were still alive, she would've embraced her illegitimate grandson and begged for him to be saved. I must allow nature to run its course as it shall."

"Papa, I—" Gino leaned in, but the old fella raised a hand.

"We have vindicated Sal and Smitty's deaths." The old man studied a water stain on his desk as he pondered. "Sal paid for his sins with his life; nothing can change this." Carmine re-capped the Dewar's bottle, pushing his chair back. "If they have the books, they'll figure it out. Everything is there: dates, transactions, names, and specific details." A laugh bubbled from the old mobster. "I saw the book a few times; Pete Smitherson's writing was chicken scratch, but I could read it." Another laugh. "That old fisherman was cunning, though, and ruthless. Did you know that, Gino?"

Brows bent downward, Gino's head shook. "No, I didn't."

"Pete had another book, one that will rip the HPD apart and put our family in chaos. If they have both books, then..." He lifted his hands in a "what can you do?" gesture. "Smitty and Sam," Carmine reverted to Sicilian, "dui òmini cu veri palli comu nu sicilianu, e mancu na guccia di sangu talianu. Two men with real balls like a Sicilian and not a drop of Italian blood. They did my bidding without question, never worrying about the consequences." Again, Carmine became wistful, and Gino waited. "Smitty, the old fool."

"Why is he now an old fool?" Gino was confused.

Carmine leaned back. "Smitty called me months ago, told me he had cancer. We talked about our lives and paths. He was regretful about his wrongdoings, especially now that his time was limited, and he wanted to do good."

"What did he plan to do? Go to the cops? Rat you or our family out?"

"No, son, what he did was done years ago. When he met that detective, that Jack West, he liked the man. Oh, don't get me wrong, he was still loyal to me, even then. After he retired and went out to live on his boat, and got sick, well, my good pal Pete grew a conscience. It was him that gave West the files to look into so the man would get his closure."

Leaning back, arms dangling over the armrest, Gino's brows knitted. "What files?"

"The ones that drew Jack West into the investigation—the details of the gun that shot and killed his brother. Wygant might have killed the old fart trying to get the whereabouts of the second book, and Sal to keep him from starting a war, but all he did was stir up a hornet's nest, and I am afraid we will all get stung."

———

BROOKS RODE SHOTGUN WHILE Sam drove. They were quiet, both clenching their jaws. He didn't trust Sam, but he spoke as they entered the ramp onto US 69, headed downtown.

"Always loyal, no matter how it plays out, that right, Sam?"

"Yeah, Brooks, I do what I'm told, and you, you never learned to do that, did you?"

"Screw you, Sam. I never hurt anyone that wasn't asking for it, and didn't use my badge to bully anyone. Shit, Sam, how many innocent people did you beat to a pulp?"

"No one back then was innocent, and the count's gonna be one more if you don't shut your fat ass up."

"I'm getting tired of this shit. Look, man, I don't wanna do time if this goes south, so let's work something out. If we do that, then on the occasion you need a hand. Hey, I'll still be able to help you out."

"See, that's funny, Brooks, 'cause all these years you've been searching for that book and moving evidence around to keep all of us outta jail. And, more to the point, you were supposed to be destroying that same fucking evidence. And that damned .38. Why wasn't it smelted into liquid metal?"

Brooks watched the road ahead. He hoped this ride was a real lift to his car at the HPD garage, and not to some remote area to take a slug to the head.

"Wasn't my call. It was on the 'to be destroyed' list, and the Assistant COP took the gun. What could I do?"

Sam huffed a laugh. "Why didn't ya ask Tony to do you a solid and make sure they melted the damned thing?" He paused, letting out a vast puff and growl from his chest. "And if you were smarter, West wouldn't be your enemy."

This caused Brooks to seethe. "I doubt that, Sam. He was partners with Windom. Frank always had his eye on us and his ear to the ground."

"Windom would have taken us down if he had concrete evidence, Brooks, and he never did. And nobody is the wiser about what we've done. You let your paranoia ruin you."

Sam stopped on the street beside the HPD parking garage. "Get out."

Out of the car, Brooks leaned in. "Don't wanna be looking over my shoulder. If I see shadows, I will shoot. Are we clear?"

Sam couldn't help but laugh. "Brody, I ain't the one scared of ghosts. Seems you are, and dead Frank Windom is the man who spooked the hell outta you." With that, Sam took off, closing the door as he sped away, leaving Brody Brooks alone on the curb.

52

Six a.m. Their eyes had already burned through Facebook, Twitter, LinkedIn, and Instagram, yet Sandra—or Sandy—Burns remained elusive. No mentions in Houston, no connections to local high schools.

"Hey, we don't know what year she graduated—or if she even graduated," Jace muttered, fingers flying over the keyboard. "I'm digging through the Heights class records. I've got lists of seniors for four years—maybe she was a freshman."

"Or older. Older guys were there. Maybe girls who'd already graduated, too," Lucky added, leaning back with a skeptical squint.

Jack rubbed his chin. "Luck has a point. We can't discriminate by age." He tapped AT&T's number into his phone. "Landline. Do we need a warrant?"

Xi stretched, cracking his knuckles. "If it's an old witness for an unsolved homicide, you won't need authorization, Jack. Just explain the situation to the phone company." He pointed to the empty mugs. "Anyone want fresh coffee? My treat."

The aroma of coffee filled the room, and Xi cradled his mug, staring into it like it held answers. "Still no word on Carver?"

Jack's phone lay beside his elbow. He leaned back, exhaling slowly. "A supervisor from AT&T said she'd call me back. And Carver's still a ghost. If I were him ... hell, I'd go dark, too. That's how I felt after Cole died. Didn't want to talk to anyone, didn't want anyone to see me."

Lucky tapped the table with his fingers. "But ignoring the captain's messages? And she marked them urgent."

Jack's voice softened, haunted. "Cole and Gretch ... their deaths hit me hard. Shook me to the core." His words faltered as the phone rang.

"West," he answered, pen hovering. "Yes, ma'am ... working a cold case, looking into landline history... oh, sure, sure. The number is..." He rattled it off, nodding as he scribbled. "Of course. I'll wait for your call. Perfect." He hung up.

The room buzzed quietly, conversation muted around him. Cole's case could be discussed openly, but Gretchen's murder was a different weight—too personal. They all knew her; the thought of her brought silent reflection. Heads bent back to work.

AN HOUR LATER, THE phone rang again. Jack picked up, pen in hand, eyes scanning the pad. "West. Ready." He jotted notes, thanked the voice on the line, and hung up.

Three sets of eyes tracked him.

"She's now Sandra Burns-Melhoff. That number was hers as a teenager. Her parents had a separate line."

"How does AT&T know this?" Jace's eyebrows shot up.

Jack's grin spread. "Supervisor loves a mystery. Dug deep. Kids got cell numbers, charges were on the main bill until they moved out. Sandra's number never changed—it stayed on the parents' bill until she switched it into her name. Parents went into assisted living; she kept their line. After they passed, number disconnected, last bill sent to her. She's in Conroe now, and her cell matches that address."

Jace leaned back, hands flying up. "My lord, maybe this woman should apply here—or start her own PI business."

Jack tapped the pad. "People love escape rooms, true crime podcasts, mystery games ... nowadays, it's all about puzzles."

"Uh-huh. Minus the dead bodies, blood, and grief-stricken relatives. Sad, isn't it?" Dawson muttered, arms folded.

All eyes swiveled toward him.

"Dawson Luck ... you've got a heart," Jace smirked.

"Yep. And I'd hoped you'd get a brain someday, Scarecrow," he shot back, grinning.

Jack dialed Sandra Burns-Melhoff, fingers crossed she'd pick up. Fourth ring, a click, a voice.

"Yeah, perfect timing," Jack said, shaking his head with a grin. "Yep, 185 is a huge weight loss. Sure. Ask for me at the front desk. See you soon."

"How soon is 'see ya soon'?" Jace asked once Jack disconnected.

"Twenty minutes. She's in town on a girls' shopping trip. Heading out on a two-week vacation afterward."

"She lost 185 pounds? Good for her." Dawson smirked.

Jack's grin widened. "She dropped the Melhof ... along with the deadbeat hubby, who weighed 185."

The room chuckled.

Chang yawned, stretching, and said, "Listen to this. I found a connection between two other victims." He moved to the board. "Olsen and Gresham drove for Hardin's trucking. Trucks got hijacked so much, Hardin sold out. Guess who bought him?"

"Berutti?" Jace suppressed a yawn.

"Negatory. Tino De Luca—a Berutti rival. I'd bet he was hijacking Hardin's trucks. Cargo ranged: spices, liquor, coffee beans, video games, high-end tennis shoes, purses."

Xi flipped open his notepad. "De Luca's trucks got hit several times a month, first and last weeks like clockwork. I correlated shipments; first and last weeks carried spices and coffee."

A light bulb seemed to pop over Dawson's head. "Wait ... drugs?"

Chang grinned. "Could be. Back in '78, GPS was just starting. Drug dogs at customs, but not for local cargo. Smells like spices and coffee could mask anything."

Jace leaned forward. "Any proof?"

"Not concrete. Just hijacking patterns, products, insurance claims. Trucks reappeared days later, wiped clean."

Jack frowned. "Xi, what does this prove?"

"Olsen and Gresham stayed with the company now owned by De Luca. Jack, remember Dawson *67-ed a number Skip called multiple times?"

Lucky straightened. "Yeah. Berutti Trucking. Henry Gresham answered—so I hung up."

Xi smiled. "That used to be De Luca Trucking. Like Hardin, De Luca couldn't handle the hijackings—sold to Berutti. I traced the sale, addresses. Then came a man named Angelo Conti…"

Jace cut in. "Isn't that another unsolved murder?"

Jack grabbed a marker. On the whiteboard, he drew lines connecting five names. "Gresham, Conti, Dellucci, Smitty, Cole. Same .38 pistol. Xi, how does Angelo fit in?"

"Conti worked for De Luca. Son is Lucas; sister is Silvia—Sal Dellucci's wife, mother of Corey Carver. Lucas and Carver are cousins."

Jace exhaled sharply. "Still don't get it."

Xi sank into a chair, eyebrow wiggle aimed at Jace. "Brasher's back. Got serial numbers from the acid wash Webb clocked her with, but circumstances…" He let it hang. "Remember her ballistics report from '79?"

"Vaguely. Followed up?" Jack leaned forward.

"Yep. Gun slated for destruction in late '79. Olivia traced it to '78. Claimed by two people we know—Assistant COP Tony Croce, who sold it to Sal Dellucci in '93."

Silence. Time seemed to freeze.

Jace whispered, "Sal got killed with his own gun?"

"Him, Smitty, Gresham, Conti, Cole. That gun wasn't supposed to exist after Angelo Conti's murder in '79," Xi said.

Dawson scowled, face tight. "So we can link Conti's murder to Croce's gun from before he was Assistant Chief?"

Before they could absorb it, the phone rang. Chang picked it up. "Detective Chang … yeah, someone will come get her." He hung up. "Sandra Burns is downstairs."

Jack grabbed his coat. His phone chirped. "West." He listened, jaw tightening, head nodding subtly. "Thanks. Be there as quick as traffic allows."

"Everything okay, Jack?" Dawson asked.

"Know a LuAnn Collier?"

Three heads shook. Jace asked, "Who is she?"

"Handwriting analysis, forensic document examiner," Xi explained.

"Wants to talk about the book we found on Smitty's boat. Figured something out; wants to see me now."

"Then go, Jack," Jace urged.

"But Ms. Burns just arrived, and I—"

Xi cut him off. "Three of us can handle Ms. Burns. You go see Collier. No sweat."

Jack laughed. "Okay. But don't let her leave till I'm back."

Dawson's unibrow danced. "Divorcee. Check her out?"

"No, Luck. I want info on Cole, that's it. Besides—lordy, I was fourteen back then. Who knows how much older she is?" Jack rolled his eyes. Lucky muttered a muffled, "Sorry."

At the door, Jack said, "You three, even if she's hot—or a MILF as the guys say—don't play matchmaker. I can handle that myself."

Three salutes. As the door swung, Jack stuck his hand back and gave them all the bird, laughing.

53

Jack cranked his truck and eased out of the HPD parking structure. The streets of Houston unfolded before him—Travis Street, Milam, a tangle of one-ways he knew too well. He grinned as he slid under the Gulf Freeway overpass, then onto Webster Street, merging onto 288, already bracing for the crawl of traffic.

His thoughts drifted to the Lone Star Saloon. Memories of Gretchen—the bartender whose laugh still echoed in his mind, the woman he'd loved and lost—made a rare warmth flicker in his chest. Time had softened the sharp edges of that grief, but his heart remained cautious. The guys in the office never missed a chance to needle him. "Hey, my girl knows a girl," or "My wife has a friend who's single." A divorcee witness? That was their first instinct. Jack chuckled, the sound rolling through the cab, shaking off the morning's tension.

He leaned back, letting a full, hearty laugh escape. The radio was next—he fished for something upbeat, classic pop, and braced himself for the start-stop rhythm of 288. Six miles in Houston could stretch to forty-five minutes, but he didn't mind.

Hunger gnawed at him; lunch had been swallowed by the day's chaos. Burger King flashed by, but he didn't pull over. Maybe a vending machine inside? Coffee would do for now.

Traffic had other ideas. By the time he reached the building, half an hour had melted away. Boots clicked over the marble floor, echoing as he approached the information desk.

A petite brunette with a short, sassy haircut looked up, a welcoming smile on her face. Her drawl marked her Texas roots, and Jack returned the grin.

"May I help you, sir?"

"Yes, ma'am. Detective Jack West, here to see LuAnn Collier. Could you let her know I've arrived?"

She tapped the phone, punching in an extension. A moment later: "Ms. Collier will be right down." She glanced up, a shy flutter in her eyes.

"Thanks, I'll wait here."

"Yep—er, uh, yes sir," she stammered, cheeks tinged pink.

THE ELEVATOR DOORS SWOOSHED open, releasing a woman with short, curly blonde hair and tortoiseshell glasses. She scanned the room, landing on Jack.

"Ah, Detective West," she said, stepping forward, arm outstretched. "LuAnn Collier. Will you come with me?"

Jack shook her hand. "Nice to meet you, Ms. Collier." He gave a quick nod to the receptionist and followed.

"Nice to meet you in person," LuAnn said, watching the doors close. "We worked a case together once before."

"You did? Which case?" Jack's mind raced, flipping through mental files.

"The Stegwig case. Rich kid murdered his parents, forged his mother's signature on a trust form. That one."

Jack's head bobbed. "Yep. Punk kid's still on death row. That was you?"

She leaned back on her gray kitten heels, smiling. "Piece of cake. This one though ... the journal. Lord, that handwriting could be alien."

Jack's frown deepened. "You can't decipher it?" He felt a flicker of frustration, the clock ticking, the mystery pressing.

"I didn't say that," she snapped, her tone tight, the elevator's ding punctuating her words. She stepped out, and Jack followed.

"My office is this way." Her expression softened, almost reproachful, making him feel like a novice.

A chair scraped as she gestured. "Pull up. I want to show you." She donned forensic gloves and retrieved the book from a locked drawer.

The table was a small arsenal of tools: lamps of every brightness, magnifiers capable of teasing out the hair on a gnat's eye, UV and infrared lights, jeweler's loupes, video spectral comparators, metric rulers, and devices Jack couldn't name. He sat, resisting the urge to learn them all.

Silence stretched. Jack cleared his throat. "Look, Ms. Collier—"

"LuAnn. Call me LuAnn. Don't apologize. I know your job's tough. I shouldn't have started with negativity. His penmanship stinks, but I've seen worse—pages ruined by fluids or left in decay, not total destruction. Let's start over, shall we?"

A tiny laugh escaped Jack's lips. "Sounds wonderful, LuAnn. So ... what do we have?" He leaned forward, one elbow braced, eyes darting between her and the open book.

She laid the journal on the table, flipping pages and pointing with precision. "Dates are easiest. Numbers are legible. March 15, 1990." Back she flipped. "Six months prior: September 18, 1989."

"Do these dates mean anything?" Jack asked, brow furrowed.

"Not yet. Just how he organized it. Not everyone's date-oriented. This guy, Pete, old-school: date, time, place, deed, dollars." She tapped the page with a metal pointer.

"Five large. Five thousand dollars," Jack murmured.

"Exactly. R for received, P for paid," she explained.

Jack tugged on a second pair of gloves she handed him. Fingers gloved, he traced the notations. Rs, Rs, Rs. Cash flowing, favors paid, shakedowns marked. LuAnn snickered. "Yeah, a first grader writes better. But the story's in the details. Pete was no saint."

Jack's shoulders slumped. "Can't believe I misjudged him."

"All organizations have someone keeping the books. Maybe he didn't do the dirty work, but knew everything," she said, eyes softening.

"Doesn't matter—he saw and did nothing. Guilty in my eyes," Jack said, leaning back.

LuAnn flagged a page, weighing it with a marble paperweight. "See the gutter? Small gap near the binding. Every page, every space gets scrutiny. Around page twenty-five, I noticed a pattern. Mechanical pencil—UNI 9 HB—letters at top, middle, bottom of the gutter. First time, page twenty-five. Then skipped eight to ten pages. Dark lead, smudge-resistant. Looked like doodles at first."

Jack moved closer. F-K-O. Letters at top, middle, bottom. "More?"

"Yes. Went through the book twice. No pattern, just letters." She handed him the sequence: FKOBILBITONOODHOCXEKKRNADEY.

He blinked, then LuAnn rearranged them: **FIND OTHER BOOK AND LOCKBOX KEY.**

Jack's brain sparked. That key in Smitty's go-bag, Lucky said it looked like a bank lockbox key. Someone needed to check Evidence, pronto. He bounced in his seat, energy snapping into action.

"LuAnn, can I get back to you later on the details? Will you transcribe it into a report?"

"Of course, Detective West. You know where the other book is?"

"Maybe. Stuff keeps vanishing lately."

They walked toward the elevators. "Thanks, LuAnn. Big help," Jack said, shaking her hand.

"Anytime. I'll get the readable report to you soon." Doors closed. Jack gave her a thumbs-up.

BACK IN HIS TRUCK, he dialed Dawson—no answer. Crap. Jace next.

"Hiya, Jack, you on your way back with news?"

"Yes, and no. Is Ms. Burns still there?"

"Yeah, Luck's got her in the common room, grabbing coffee."

"Someone needs to get that key from Evidence—the one logged in from Smitty's go-bag. Dawson knows which. Hotfooting back, traffic's a bear. Call me when you get it."

"I'm on it. Drive safe, call you back."

Jack hung up. Wheels turning in his head. The key. The lockbox. Skip's Rover at the bank. Had Webb made off with the gun and the key?

54

THREE MINUTES FROM THE station, Jack's phone rang.

"Find the key?"

"Damn it, no key, and yeah, it's on the chain-of-custody log. Jack, I looked in every box."

"Hold tight, Jace. I'm pulling into the parking garage. Be up in two." Jack clicked off, drove to the closest empty spot, cut the engine, pocketed his phone, and sprang out, hitting Lock on his key fob. He jogged to the entrance, taking the stairs three at a time, lungs burning when he reached the sixth floor. Time to get healthy—diet and exercise—right after this convoluted case got resolved.

Jack bounded into the room. "Hey, fellas, over here," he called, waving them as he grabbed a seat. He quickly recapped what LuAnn Collier had discovered—and the missing key.

Dawson's head bobbed. "Yeah, so whoever got to Skip has the key. That your theory, Jack?"

Jack looked at Xi. "Get a warrant typed up. We need to see if Pete Smitherson had an account at that bank and search the lockbox. If it's empty, at least we can get prints or IDs on anyone who's been in the back vault."

Xi rushed to his desk.

"Anyone hear from Carver or get eyes on Webb?"

"Not a word, Jack," Jace frowned.

"Hey, Jack, we still have Sandra Burns here, too." Lucky inclined his head toward the common room. "Nice lady, and I think you should speak with her."

A pang of melancholy hit Jack. She might've known his brother—maybe they were classmates. He straightened. "Hey, Luck."

"Yeah?"

"That Rover? It was a 2009?"

"I think so. Why?"

"Look it up—see when Rovers got navigation systems."

Dawson slid back in his chair and Googled. "Navigation's available 2001 and up."

"Perfect. Get a warrant to track his Rover—or, since he's missing, we have exigent circumstances. Track it. Check the past month. Jace, get every traffic cam angle into Sheldon Reservoir and Central Bank. I want to see who met up with Skip."

"I'm on it." Jace spun toward his desk and dove into the task.

Jack left to speak with Ms. Burns.

SHE SAT, HEAD BENT over her phone, oblivious to his presence.

"Ms. Burns," he began. She jumped a foot, hand over her heart. "Oh lord, you scared the—uh, well, you scared me."

She exhaled. "Sorry, ma'am. I'm Detective Jack West." He offered a hand, scanning her face for recognition.

Her eyes softened. "Cole's brother?"

He nodded. "Let's walk to the breakroom. I could use a cup of coffee—you?"

"I'd like that." She rose and followed.

AT THE ROUND TABLE where staff sometimes ate lunch, they sipped hot coffee.

"Sorry, our coffee ain't Starbucks, or even Keurig, but it keeps us going."

Sandra shrugged. "Coffee is coffee. Caffeine is what I want, not foamy, creamy flavor—I'm old school. And, if you're wondering, yeah, I went to Memorial, same as you and Cole. I was a junior that year."

"Were you friends with my brother?"

"Not really. Friends in common. I knew who he was because he was a football star. Nice to everyone. Not self-centered like the other jocks. All the girls had a crush, even me." She grinned up at him.

Jack smiled, memories sharp as yesterday. "Yeah, he was a heartbreaker. Mom was the only one who'd tell him that. As his baby brother, my job wasn't stroking his ego—it was being a pain in his butt." He rested his forearms on the table. "Sandra, that night—tell me what you remember."

Her gaze drifted. Horror etched in her expression as she recalled seeing a boy they'd known bleeding from a gunshot wound. A tear fell, and she realized Jack still grieved for his brother.

"You never mentioned guns that night. Any reason?" Jack asked gently.

"Fear." Her brows knitted, a breath huffing out. "They weren't aiming at any-one, or I would've said. From where I stood, I could see lowriders trolling—three cars, crawling. Kids everywhere outside, no one zipping in and out. The cars had guys, affiliated with gangs. I don't know exactly which—Bloods, Texas 288 Boys? Not as hardcore, though."

"I see. You assumed they were firing guns?"

"Detective, I was seventeen, wet behind the ears." She blushed. "First time my parents let me go to the hangout spot. Then that happened. I got questioned by police. Parents freaked the next school year." Her eyes closed, shook her head, then reopened. "As an adult, I've watched crime shows, true crime docs, forensic stories. One made me think of something I never mentioned—years ago. Figured police would've looked into it anyway."

"Looked into what?" Jack leaned in.

"An unintentional killing by a ricocheting bullet. Two boys fired guns that night. I don't know which bullet killed Cole. Did anyone check that?"

Jack's brain whirred. "No. Investigators never considered that theory."

Her lips pulled back, brows arched. "You considering it now?"

Jack nodded, his head bobbing. "Yes, ma'am, I sure am."

After a few more minutes, he thanked her for the candid recounting of the night. He walked her to the elevators.

Before punching down, she turned. "Detective West, I hope you get closure. I can't imagine losing a sibling that way." Without warning, she wrapped him in a bear hug, stepped back, and smiled. She hit the down arrow; the doors dinged. Jack held the door for her, watching her enter.

"You know, Ms. Burns, this isn't over, right?"

"Yeah. I'll be called again. And," she wagged a finger, "I'm leaving on a two-week cruise Sunday, but I'll be back. You have my Conroe address?"

"Yeah. Thanks for coming—I appreciate it." He released the door, watched the elevator zip shut.

He lingered, thinking. Closure for Cole's death? And the odds of solving the other four murders?

Jack returned to the breakroom, making coffee and scavenging for food: an opened bag of Fritos and half a can of bean dip. Cup of fresh joe, Fritos, bean dip—he sat, munching, lost in thought.

A ricocheting, stray bullet. He'd never considered it. Corey Carver and Andy Olsen had guns. Carver had Sal's gun—Olsen? Delucci and Smitty—same gun. Who pulled the trigger and why? The book they still needed likely held the answers.

Lloyd Olsen—Andy's son. Connection? Ed Gresham—his son Henry worked for Berutti Trucking. Angelo Conti—Sal's brother-in-law? Assistant Chief Tony Croce. A cluster to beat all clusters. But put all dots on paper, eventually it made sense. With Houston law enforcement officers implicated, and the journal potentially revealing more—would it rip Houston apart?

55

DAWSON SWIVELED HIS CHAIR to face the famous squeaky door. "Ms. Burns leave?"

"Yeah. Nice lady, and I guess she told you guys what she told me."

"She did, Jack. A stray bullet is a workable theory, but without corroboration from any kids there that night, it's still conjecture, I'm afraid."

"You think so, Xi? Cuz I gotta disagree," Jace returned, brows dipped.

Xi turned to see his partner. "Okay, 7, give it to me." He cut his eyes up at Jack, a slight twinkle in them.

"That gun. That's why I disagree. It belonged to Tony Croce, then he sold it to Sal Dellucci. Easy for Carver to get a gun from his dad's arsenal back then, I'd figure. Don't know why he would be carrying it, or why the Olsen kid had a gun either. What I do know is the slugs they took outta Lloyd Olsen, Angelo Conti, and Cole match that gun, so we know what gun killed them, and we know who owned the gun. Carver had the gun that night if Ms. Burns witnesses him with a gun and saw him shoot it—not aiming, just shooting. It would be a case of involuntary manslaughter if convicted and up to twenty years in lockup. And lord, guys, this was also a cover-up. Because Texas lacks an accessory-after-the-fact statute, everyone involved would be culpable." Jace, his face serious, looked at the others.

"Damn, 7," Xi said, his mouth twitching, "you could've been a lawyer."

"Nope, if I wasn't a cop I'd have been a Hell's Angel, you shit." Jace rolled his eyes.

"Well, Jace, you're right about all of it, and we have a place to start now, except Sal's dead, Carter is missing, and we can't touch the Assistant Chief. Tony Croce no longer owned the gun." This frustrated Jack, but it did not discourage him. "So, Xi, the warrants?"

"Phone records are pending. We need a reason for Brooks, Wygant, and Yardley and don't have one, so that's on hold. None needed for Smitty—he's a murder victim—and since Webb's missing, that's exigent circumstances. I got Art's guys doing some tracking on that and Skip's vehicle."

"Traffic cams, guys—anything?"

"Jack," Dawson said, "lots of traffic footage. I've got CSU helping, and Vince Stoner went back to go over the Rover again, said he'd call after he's done."

"The lockbox warrant?" Jack looked back at Xi.

"Sent it to the courthouse. Only the judge that's there is Ritter, so it's a crap shoot."

"Yeah, Ritter was a buddy of Wolff's—makes me wonder about the fart." Dawson's lips drooped.

"Nah, he ain't like Wolff. Ritter just enjoys beating the pants off Wolff in golf was what I heard. Cuz they played for money, and not chump change, either," Jace intoned.

Roni stuck her head into the squad room. She acknowledged the four, then said, "West, Luck, my office." She went back in and the door shut on its own.

Jace leaned in. "Trouble, you think, Jack?"

"God, I hope it ain't another body." Dawson cringed.

Xi rolled a pencil across papers on his desk. "Nah, she'd call all of us in. She knows we're collaborating on all this crap. Go find out, then come back."

Jack took off, Dawson close behind him.

———

No preamble, no small talk—she jumped in. "Where's the footage of Brasher's assault?"

"Someone was supposed to log it into pre-evidence. Why?" Jack frowned.

Roni was on her feet as she yanked up the phone. "I need a word, now."

Jack gave Lucky an "I don't know" shrug.

A soft knock sounded seconds later and Earl Nichols stuck his head in. "Cap, you wanted me?"

"Come in, close the door." Her tone was harsh.

Earl's hostile glance toward their captain shocked Jack, but he entered, taking a stance between where he and Luck sat, his body language tense.

A complete shift in the captain's tone left West and Luck bewildered. "Pull up a chair, Earl. We have a dilemma."

"Sure, Roni." He repositioned a chair sideways to her desk so he could see all of them.

"The video of Brasher's attack is missing. Who took it to evidence?"

"Golan."

Jack couldn't hold back—he jumped up. "What the hell? Sorry, Captain, but why the—why on earth would you—" He stopped talking to comb a hand through his hair when he saw the intense "shut up" look she was giving him. He sat.

"Earl, was someone watching him?"

This was weird. She was talking nice to Nichols; calling him Earl. Confusion was written all over West's and Luck's faces.

"Yes, I asked Glover to be discreet and follow him to Evidence, and he told me Golan handed it to Wygant in central lockup, not pre-lockup. Afterward, I had someone watch Wygant, and when he left for lunch, I called Kincaid, had her check for the video. It was gone."

Roni sat pensively for a time before addressing Earl Nichols again. "Who was tailing him?"

"Dunwell was yesterday."

"Has he checked in?"

"Yeah, he lost the bastard, though, in traffic, never picked him up again, and Wygant never showed up for his shift. Him or Brooks."

"Have you heard from Webb?"

"Nope, Webb's still MIA."

Jack's and Luck's eyes darted between them like ping-pong balls.

"You think anyone suspects we have the original and they have a bogus copy?" Roni asked.

Earl said, "That I can't say. All I know is they've been hunting for a book Smitty had and can't find it. They're panicked. Webb knows too much. I'm sure he's looking for his payoff so he can scram."

The room went silent. They stared at Earl. Roni stared at them. Earl stared at the captain, then West and Luck. Earl Nichols gave her a blank shrug. The stare-off ended with Jack and Dawson looking at her for answers.

Roni looked over. "Earl?"

He nodded.

What she said next left them stunned. "Jack, Dawson, I'd like for you to meet Internal Affairs Investigator Ernest Nicholson, or as you have known him, Earl Nichols."

A hush fell. You could've heard a pin drop on a sandbar. She let them digest the news. After a momentary pause, she addressed them. "I know this is a total shock—lots of questions, I'm sure, but we'll get to them later. With Webb missing, it's priority to locate him. We think he could be in danger, or already dead."

"Captain, their copy is bogus? Ours is still safe?" Jack looked at her, ignoring Earl.

Ernest spoke up, kind of grinning. "That's correct, Jack. Uh, okay if I call you Jack, since I know you detest me?"

"Wasn't personal, just hate shitty cops—and as a member of IA, you have gained no points," Jack was quick to respond, then said, "Sorry, Nicholson, if you're the sorta cop wearing a white hat, you're gonna have to prove it—and sure, call me Jack, only don't say 'ass' afterward like normal."

Ernest nodded. "Point taken. So, yes, Jack, a copy. Department has the original locked up. No one can get to it. There's other stuff you'll want to look at later, too. We've been building a case against several officers for years, but had no proof until Smitty came up dead."

Dawson's hand came up. "And Alex Dunwell and Glenn Glover, they're IA, too?"

"Alex is, Glenn's just following orders."

Jack's jaw muscle flexed. "Dunwell's cover story—believable, too, and he sells it. Gotta say you have some talented undercovers."

"Yep, we got fortunate: Alex is from Jersey and worked in Infernal Repairs up there. Fifteen years."

Dawson let loose a laugh. "I like it Ernest—Infernal Repairs."

The tension in the room broke.

Jack took the lead. "Look, Earl—ah, Ernest." He flubbed the name. "It's gonna take some time to get used to this. I gotta be honest with you—and to trust you."

Ernest leaned back. "I understand. Look, I know everyone has hated me since day one, but," his shoulders lifted, "that's the job. I'm used to it. Also, if you can't call me Ernest, call me Ernie."

"Yeah, okay, that I can do, Ernie. Now, can you fill us in but, before that, Roni, can we call 7-11 in? Save the time of repeating, and I wanna see the looks on their faces when they meet Ernie." A sly grin played on Jack's five o'clock shadow.

THEY WERE MAD AT first for being duped, then entertained—purely enter-tained. Xi was wordless and Jace flabbergasted—priceless. Both opted to call the former Earl "Ernie."

"Well damn, Ernie, you give up copping—you can take it to the stage. Dude, you can act," Jace said, impressed.

"Nah, don't like big audiences, only like conning cops." He winked, then got serious. "Let me bring you up to speed on the last few years."

Xi's finger went up, stopping him. "Uh, can I ask—just how long has this internal investigation been going on?"

Ernie sighed and said, "Since the day I arrived in Homicide, six years ago."

Xi continued his questions. "No results after six years? Why?" Xi Chang, a seasoned detective, was troubled by the sluggish progress of the investigation into police corruption.

"Lots of reasons stalled the case." Ernie looked at Jack, who frowned, shaking his head.

"Nu-uh, don't blame me. I'd have helped you guys if anyone would have asked."

"Jack, not blaming you, but you busting Brooks in the chops sorta slowed shit down. The man got overconfident. That helped. He hates you, and—"

Jack leaned in, elbows on his knees, and cut in. "About that. He ever say why?"

"Uh-huh, and you ain't gonna like how simple the answer is either."

Jack sat back. "Try me." His mind wandered back to Joan and what she said about Brody hating him.

"He told Webb and I that Frank Windom hated him, and was gunning for him back in the early days. You came along. All shiny and new—a force to reckon with, smart and determined, and most of all, dedicated to the job. Brooks knew Frank watched everything he had his paws on, had done it for years. What he'd figured was Windom had amassed enough circumstantial or real proof he was dealing from the bottom. Frank was no dummy, but he was wrapped up in his job—so much so that he didn't wanna get involved with Brooks' crap. Brooks got an anonymous letter years back, right before Frank kicked the bucket."

Jack frowned. "From who about what?"

"Brooks told us it wasn't signed. It listed some of the crooked dealings Brooks was involved in with them, saying people were watching. A mention of a hotshot cop, and old eyes who saw the truth. It sounded like a lot of garbage to me, only Brooks said it was just what Windom would do to warn him off. At least, that's what he told me and Webb. And Jesus, Brooks hooked Webb by the balls and didn't let go."

Jace asked, "Webb—gambling or drugs?"

"Nah. Just a greedy, cheap son of a bitch. Brooks promised him lots of cash, like he did me, but it hasn't materialized—and before you say anything, I haven't done a damn thing unlawful. All the cases we worked that were effed up, Webb was lead."

Jack's forehead creased. "So he hated me because of my dedication to the job. That's stupid."

"Not exactly. See, Brooks couldn't turn Frank, so he knew you couldn't be turned either. He also knew Frank wasn't a dummy and knew stuff, so he figured Frank told you everything. Brooks was afraid you'd start putting two and two together and come after him. When they moved Brooks to Homicide, it worried the hell outta him. After Frank kicked it, and he eventually moved on to Robbery, he didn't worry as much. You came to Homicide before that, though."

Jack's intent gaze was still focused on Ernie.

"Had to establish myself. With prior knowledge of promotions and personnel changes, that made it helpful. I knew Yao was moving out and Brooks was moving over before it happened."

"Huh, IA people have a crystal ball?" Jace's face wrinkled in disbelief.

"Guess so," Ernie shot back, then shifted his gaze towards Jack. "Brooks' intention was to make it appear there was a valid reason for hating you by treating you with contempt. Frank Windom was a boat-rocker, a loner, and didn't always play well with others. West, your first partner clashed with CSU, the ME, and the DA's Office—both before and after you teamed up. Not known for his finesse, but Frank was a rock-solid detective. He knew Brooks' actions were shady and would've interfered if he'd suspected murder. Back then, though, so much shit was going on. Frank couldn't keep his eyes on his fellow cops while trying to catch criminals.

"Frank's cases getting messed up with missing reports and evidence, or shoddy paperwork—he knew Brooks had his hands in it, but couldn't prove it. Two of the cases that went unsolved that are pertinent to this investigation are Angelo Conti and Ed Gresham. You ever read the reports, Jack?"

"Yeah."

"Frank worked both cases. Things went awry and he was pissed off; you know he got."

"Yeah, worked with him two years. I remember during the Cyrus Shelton case how he was. He was obsessed. Tons of fuckups on that case in the beginning."

"He went to IA on that case, he ever tell you?"

"No, he didn't."

Ernie puckered his lips, then said, "Jack, he went to IA on the Gresham and Conti cases, and several more, about fuckups. Frank was sure they weren't accidental but done on purpose, and Brooks was involved. He told the then IA Director, Greg Frantz, that he had pulled you into the loop, and you were eyes he could count on. Frank died, and things slowed down in the complaint department, but the records were still there."

"And it's just now getting looked back into—You shitting me?" Jack was stunned.

"No, it got overlooked—not on purpose. Other things took precedence. When Vance came aboard, he started a full-scale audit of every record, complaint, and whatnot in the department; cleaning house. This came up, and it's his personal case."

The room went silent as they all pondered the story Ernie spilled to explain Brooks' hatred, and it seemed absurd and very superficial—but then, it was Brooks they were discussing.

Jack snorted in disdain. "Wygant; Webb; Brooks; the ACOP, Tony Croce—guys consumed by greed or a desire for power. Took them down a dark path. Everyone signs up for something."

His gaze landed back on Ernie. "Nice to know you're signed up on our team, Nicholson. So, what's the rest of the story?"

Ernie took the floor, going over the relevant details to date.

56

"What about the second book and the key?" Jack asked after Nicholson had finished twenty minutes later.

Ernie's face was a blank. "Second book and key? What second book and what damned key?"

Jack's phone chirped. He held up a hand. "It's Vince Stoner." Jack listened with a frown, and he looked at his wrist. Seven p.m. The VEB closed at four.

"You sure, Vince?" Jack took a step toward the door. "Okay, can you keep eyes on him? Perfect, then hang tight, man. We're on the way." He disconnected, anger and worry etched on his face. "We gotta go." Jack was in the hallway, the others on his heels.

"Stoner okay, Jack? Do we need Patrol?" Dawson was behind him in the stairwell.

"Just us five for now."

Xi hit the last step, and they darted into the garage. "What happened?"

Jack stopped and turned. "The VEB is closed, but Stoner stayed to finish going over that Land Rover for the second time. Only someone badged their way in. The front door's hydraulics aren't working, and it slammed shut, scaring the crap outta him, so he hid."

As he brought up the tail end, Ernie asked, "Was Skip, wasn't it?"

"Dawson, you drive. My truck is at the far end," Jack said, then faced Ernie. "Yeah, it was. Call me when you're in your car. Got an idea." He turned to 7-11. "Y'all hang back. Park out of sight, with eyes on the front door."

"Yep, can do. Come on, Jace, your jalopy's closer. Let's roll."

Two minutes later, Ernie called Jack, and Jack told him his idea.

"It might work, but you guys need to stay outta sight."

"Roger that. I'll text Vince and update 7-11."

THE PARKING LOT, FOLLOWING staff departure, contained solely vehicles pertinent to an investigation or those authorized for processing, impoundment, or owner reclamation.

Ernie/Earl pulled in and parked near the door. He entered with his badge and quietly shut the front door. His soft-soled shoes padded soundlessly on the flat, worn carpet, and he turned the doorknob, opening the door into the four-car bay area. The room was dimly lit with security lighting, and he saw the beam of a flashlight near the front door to the Land Rover. He didn't want to spook him, so he approached with caution, hoping the dildo didn't shoot him.

Skip bent forward, his head crammed between the split seats, his hand probing, hunting for something. Ernie/Earl saw the gun tucked in the back of Skip's waistband. Okay, good. No need to worry about getting shot.

Ernie vanished as Earl appeared. "Hey slimeball, whatcha doing?"

Webb raised up and hit the roof with a resounding thud. Fortunately for him, they did not make the headliner of marble or he'd have knocked himself out. "You goddamn fool, what are you doing sneaking up like that? Shit, I could've shot your fucking head off." He rubbed his head, then the back of his neck. He'd wrenched it trying to turn to see who'd caught him off guard. Thank God it was just Earl.

"How did you find me?" Webb's face contorted in disbelief.

"Captain said you was missing, and I heard your Rover was here, so I waited, hoping you'd show. What the fuck, Webb?! You wanna tell me what's going on? Man, Brooks and Wygant never showed for their shifts, either." Ernie played it up. After all, he'd been Earl Nichols so long it wasn't hard to fall into that act.

In another room, his eyes just over the frame of an office window, the blinds pulled low, Vince Stoner watched between the skinny slats. Jack texted, saying things weren't what they seemed and to stay put until he gave him the all clear.

Webb exhaled. "I'm looking for a key I dropped, but it ain't here. CSU might've found it and I need that key, Earl." His hand swiped down his face. His eyes were bloodshot, his clothes rumpled, and he appeared desperate.

"You look like shit, man."

"Yeah, been though a bit in the past forty-eight hours."

"Why ain't Brooks helping you? Thought he was our pal."

"Some pal he is. Look, might as well tell ya, Earl, we ain't gonna get no real money. What we're gonna get is a real prison cell, and we gotta get the hell outta here."

"Where's that fat liar, and what about Wygant?"

Skip walked to the other side of the Rover, opened the passenger door, and moved the seat all the way back, sticking his head inside and looking underneath. The beam of his flashlight moved back and forth. His voice was muffled by his chest. "I think they killed Ethan."

Earl's eye sockets tightened. "Hey, what'd you say? You're mumbling."

Skip pulled his body back, lifting his head. "I said," he looked up, "I think they killed Ethan cuz after we got to Berutti's place, those douche bags, Gary Yardley and Paulie Baglio took him somewhere and came back without him."

Ernie played it to the hilt. "What the fuck, Skip—killed him? Jumped up Joseph, next time it could be me or you! Why the fuck they wanna kill Wygant?"

"Earl, you shit. You can't whack the boss's kid and his best friend and not get killed yourself. Now help me find that goddam key, would ya?" Skip all but crawled under the seat with his entire body, looking for a key that Vince Stoner now had in a baggie.

Ernest Nicholson, aka Earl Nichols, pulled his cell phone out of his coat pocket as he unstrapped his holster, withdrawing his pistol. Skip heard him, phone and pistol in hand, say, "Jack, you and Dawson get all that? Oh, and when I get out there, you're gonna spill about the key and the second book. We clear?"

Webb nearly killed himself climbing out, his face mashed in anger. "Earl, you twit, what in the hell are you doing? Are you crazy? You want to go to jail? And stop pointing your damn piece at me." With a sudden lunge, he reached out to grab the gun. Only Ernie was not the slouch Earl had been. With his right foot, he swept Skip's legs out from under him, sending him sprawling.

Webb lay face down. Ernie planted a foot in the center of his back and gritted, "Stay put, you numbskull, and put your hands behind you or I swear, I'll clock you with the butt of my gun just like you did Brasher."

Handcuffs pulled from the back of his waistband, Ernie stooped and clicked one side, then the other, and hauled him up by his arms as the door to the office opened and Vince Stoner stepped out.

"As I live and breathe—I'd never had believed it if I hadn't seen it with my own eyes." Stoner's head waggled in amazement. The side door opened and in stepped West, Luck, and 7-11. None of them looked happy.

Skip's eyes darted around, finally settling on Earl, looking completely bewildered. Jack stepped up to make the introduction.

"Webb, I'd like for you to meet Ernest Nicholson, a UC for Internal Affairs."

His eyes widened, then narrowed. "Undercover for Illicit Asswipes? Really? You? Earl, you're a nimrod."

Ernest arched his brows at Webb, then said, "Ya think? Hey, I'm not the one cuffed with a pistol aimed at him and four veteran homicide detectives and a crazy-smart CSU operative," Ernie glanced at Vince, "ogling me like the criminal he is. Now, zip it, and let me read you your rights—unless you wanna read them to yourself, you piece of shit."

JACK TOOK CHARGE. "XI, you and Jace transport him to HPD and be discreet. Take him to six, tell Roni, and get him locked in an interview room. Wanna talk to Stoner and Ernie, then meet you there, got it?"

They stowed Webb in the back seat of Xi's car, and Jace was his backseat companion. They drove him to HPD, and Jack, Vince, and Ernie watched the red taillights fade out of sight.

"Jack," Vince began, then glanced over at Ernie.

"It's okay, Stoner, Ernie's one of us. Go figure." Jack smirked.

"Well, he's still IA, so..." Stoner giggled; so did Jack, and Ernie did an "oh boy" face. Then Vince got down to business. "I found this key." He handed Jack a plastic evidence bag. "I also find some other prints, one from beneath the rear door handle behind the passenger's seat and another from behind a seat-belt buckle in the third row of seats."

Arms folded, Jack listened as Vince went on. "From all the garbage in the vehicle, I found a used drinking straw wedged in between the seats and some chewing gum stuck to the inside door runner that I'll have processed for DNA. Jack, I found the key stuck in between the seats—you know, the missing-French-fry black hole. Guess that's why it got missed."

"That it, Vince?"

Stoner shook his head and asked Jack and Ernie to follow him to the rear of the vehicle. "No, then there's this." Vince opened the back hatch and lifted the rug and the rear panels that housed the now-missing spare tire. "It was a bitch to get the spare tire since Webb didn't have a tire hoist. If he ever had a flat, he might've had to call AAA for help. Anyway, I borrowed a winch from Jasper at Impound and when I got the tire out, I found this." Stoner pointed to where they sprayed Luminol in the empty spare tire holding.

"Blood?" Jack and Ernie asked in unison.

"Yeah, I think so, but will have to confirm. Found this too." Vince's gaze drifted to a walking cane in an evidence bag laying on a workbench. "Guess Webb didn't notice it when he was rummaging in the vehicle, looking for the key I had with me."

Jack pulled out a pair of black crime-scene gloves from the box on the table and snapped them on. Cautiously, he picked up the cane and looked at Ernie. "This is Smitty's cane." He gave it a once-over, then handed it back to Vince.

Stoner's jaw tightened before he said, "I'll get it processed pronto, Jack—that and the prints and fluids found, be pushing them to the front of the line."

"Appreciate it, Vince, and thanks for calling me, man." Jack clapped him on the shoulder as he passed. "Come on guys, let's go see what Skip has to say."

Dawson walked in step behind him, his face contorted in a snarl. "Asshole Spider Webb. Damn it, can't believe I worked a few cases with that turncoat."

Ernie brought up the rear, pulling the door shut, and said, "Yeah, well, the last six years I've had to endure the man's company, and the shit I could tell ya. He is a gross, greedy fucker, for sure."

Jack, Dawson, Xi, and Jace weren't gonna ask for any details. What they knew about Skip Webb was more than enough to make them wanna puke.

57

Xɪ, Jᴀᴄᴇ, ᴀɴᴅ Rᴏɴɪ sat at the banks of TV monitors. A palpable tension hung in the air on the sixth floor as the three observed Webb's passive demeanor from the monitoring room. Webb, once the investigator, now sat in the suspect's chair, staring at the grungy wall.

Jack slid into the empty chair next to Captain Justice. "He ask for his Union rep yet, or an attorney?"

"Neither, and we have eyes on Brooks. Dunwell spotted him two hours ago, and he's following him."

Dawson stepped into the room. "Jack, who's going in?" He pulled out a chair and sat, his eyes also watching a detached Webb.

"Be best if it's just me, I think. Captain?" His glance switched from the monitors to her profile.

She nodded. "We'll watch from the monitoring room."

Wɪᴛʜ ʜɪs ʜᴇᴀᴅ ʙᴇɴᴛ, Webb moved his eyes up to see Jack. "Guess it's your lucky day, ain't it, West?" His tone was dismal.

"No, I'd say it's your unlucky day. You want your Union rep, or an attorney?"

"I already said I didn't." His head rose, then he leaned it back against the chair, closing his eyes. "No means no."

Jack didn't speak, but watched him and waited.

Skip straightened up, a little pout forming on his lips. He reopened his eyes. "I'll tell you what I *do* want, though."

Jack shifted, draping an arm over the back of his seat, his gaze intent. His tone continued to be nonthreatening. "I'm listening."

A look of "Do you think I'm stupid?" crossed Webb's face. "You mean we're listening, don'tcha?"

The corners of Jack's lip twitched. Skip had him there. "Yep, you're right. Oh, my captain is observing, so you'd better make it good." With a pointed emphasis on the word "my," Jack banished Webb from the elite Homicide squad.

"I wanna cut a deal. I'll give you everything I know, but no jail. Just let me go into hiding where I can die an old man."

"You know how it works, Webb. I can't do that unless you give me something first. After that, we talk. We see if your ass is worth saving and keeping outta jail."

Webb inhaled, and a sour expression curled his thin lips as he cut his eyes down to stare at the worn-out table in thought. The air staled between them—Jack waiting, Skip thinking.

"Your brother's case—it's bothered you for years. What if I can give you and your parents the closure you need? That be enough to make a deal?"

Jack sat up and edged closer, eyes glued to Skip. "If it were my call, yeah, it'd be enough. Only it ain't my call. My brother's case is personal to me, but all the other crap—Smitty, Sal, and Brasher—you see, all those incidents affect the entire department. I'm gonna need more. What else you got?"

Captain Justice smiled as she watched him manipulate Webb with expertise.

"How about the missing evidence to unsolved cases from 1979 and 1996?"

An eyebrow arched as Jack cocked his head to one side. "Conti and Olsen, those two?"

Skip nodded, his lips curving down. "Yep, those two."

Jack stood and pushed his chair back. "Wait here. I'll talk to my captain. She can contact the DA's Office, and if they say deal, then we have a deal."

He turned to leave, then turned back. "Was it worth it, Webb?"

A dejected Webb shook his head. "Lost my badge, my pension, and my life, and never got the payday I was expecting. So, nope. Ironically, cops are more dishonest than criminals. In truth, worse, because we hide behind our shields."

"Why then?" Jack wanted to understand.

"Grew up poor, got tormented as a kid, so I became a bully with a badge. Dangerous." Skip exhaled, and the years of crap settled on his face, aging him twenty-plus years. "Dreamed of being a hero in the beginning."

"Too bad you didn't pick the right friends, Skip."

The door shut, leaving Webb to wallow in his self-inflicted despair.

THEY GAVE ALL THE proper paperwork and info to the DA's Office, the details to be ironed out once they got the go-ahead for the deal. Jack escorted Skip out through the squad room wearing his new Tyvek jumpsuit. Webb kept his eyes downcast, not able to look anyone in the eye as they did an unofficial perp walk to the civilian doors leading out of the Homicide Division. Detectives lined up, eyes narrowed at the man who claimed to be on the right side of the law.

Leon Golan stood at the end by the exit, arms crossed over his chest, his gaze on Jack, not Webb. When Jack passed by, he stopped, and in a low voice said, "Got your Union rep on speed dial, Golan?"

Leon Golan's head whipped around to see who else might have heard. He snarled, "Fuck you, Jack."

Out the door with a grin, knowing he'd rattled Golan's chain, Jack handed Webb over to officers who would transport him to booking two hours later. They got word that the DA took Skip Webb's deal. Two murder cases and one involuntary manslaughter case were gold to them.

The key fit a lockbox where Skip stashed his letter, along with a book—the tell-all of tell-alls for the Berutti, Castellano, and De Luca families. It included every cop, past and present, on the payroll: shakedowns, political favors, bribes, payoffs, and cover-ups. Lost evidence that caused acquittals, leading to more deaths. All for money. If he'd faced the same predicament as Skip, Smitty's meticulous records would've protected him with leverage to cut a deal. In his admiration of Jack West, Smitty had acquired a conscience, torn between loyalty to a boyhood friend, Carmine, and his newfound friendship with Detective Jack West. Just by being himself—an honest cop with a strong moral compass—Jack inspired Pete.

TWO DAYS LATER, THE paperwork was completed and the warrants signed. They had more manhunts planned.

Roni's long, tapered red fingernail tapped at a folder on her desk as she spoke. "Okay, so Xi and Jace are with the warrant squad headed over to bring Gino and Carmine Berutti in."

"What about Brooks, any word?" Jack drained his coffee.

"Dunwell has officers assisting him in rounding up Brooks, and Opal Kincaid is opening an investigation in Evidence on all the crap Skip spilled. God, Jack, how many years and how many cases?" A flat, disgruntled expression filled her eyes.

"Gonna be a helluva tidal wave, and lots of cases being tossed out—or, on the bright side, maybe the right people will get prosecuted. The DA's Office is gonna need to add staff. Us too—over in the warehouse—to sift through, most likely, every box there."

"Yeah, I sent Dawson over to head up that project. He's thorough and organized, and bossy. Guess he gets that from you, right?" A faint grin appeared.

A yawn slipped out of Jack, and her grin vanished. "You need to get some shut-eye."

"Nah, I got a shower and a few hours last night. I'm fine. Any word on Carver yet?"

A grimace wrinkled her forehead. "None, and no signal on his cell phone. It's either off or the battery is dead."

Jack mulled this over, then said, "We got anyone reaching out to Ray Moretti?"

Her lips pursed in a frown. "Elijah Vance is working on that, Jack. He needs to be questioned, and it's, well…" She shrugged. "Vance is doing his job."

He leaned back, resting one ankle over the other, his own face creased, his eyes cast downward.

"Jack, whatcha got on your mind?"

"Wygant. If Skip is telling the truth, he might be dead. So, was thinking about Gary Yardley and his involvement and—"

Roni cut him off. "Me too, Jack. That's why we're looking for him, too, but he's disappeared. We got officers looking for Paulie Baglio and Sam Coolidge too. It's an all-out manhunt in Houston right now and we're shorthanded."

"Yardley—I can tell you where he might be."

"Yeah, where?"

"On a boat to China."

Her eyes widened. "China—how in the hell?"

A burst of air left Jack's lungs. "The man freelances for a cruise line. Not sure which one, because he didn't say, but can't be all of them go to China. He told me back when we first met that his next trip was to China, and if I were a betting man, I'd say he's long gone."

"Bastard. We don't have an extradition treaty with China, and the paperwork process is lengthy, but I'll get someone to check and verify Yardley's whereabouts and see what can be done."

"If you're checking, pull his financials, because I'm thinking he has zero funds here in the US. He's a smart fella, and I'm betting he began moving his accounts the day I met with him to discuss Brooks."

A harsh laugh sputtered out of Roni. "Shit, Jack, we gave them creeps all a heads-up." It aggravated the piss out of her, and he understood, but it wasn't her fault.

"Hey, can't blame yourself, Captain," Jack said.

"Who then, Jack—who can we blame?"

"Much as I hate to say it, I think we need to blame Internal Affairs. I mean, they started this archaeological dig and should've been on top of shit way back in the day."

Her shoulders twitched upwards when she said, "Maybe—or maybe we just blame society. Hell." Her desk phone jangled. "Captain Justice."

He watched her face, a kaleidoscope of emotions playing across it while she listened to the person on the other end of the line. "Thanks for calling. Sure. Will do," she said before hanging up.

Jack squinted at her. "What's up?"

"That was the Port of Houston's Harbor Master. He got a call from the Port of Galveston PD. Pelican Island had a heavy storm blow through last night, and a body washed up underneath the bridge. It's caught on the wooden piers."

"Why they calling us? We have more than enough to deal with. Can't they handle the case?"

"They found the corpse in pretty horrific condition because of the water and marine life, but they did recover an ID. Jack, it's Ethan Wygant."

The shrill ring of Jack's cell broke the room's heavy silence, jolting them.

"West," he answered with the news of Wygant still spinning in his head. "Ned who?" Jack frowned into the phone, then his features softened. "Yeah, sure, Ned, from the marina. How are you?"

"I'm fair to middling but got a problem," Ned said, going into his explanation for the call. Jack straightened up, his posture rigid as he listened, then asked, "Anyone been down there, or looked yet? No? Listen, Ned, make sure you keep people off that boat. You got some caution tape you can use. Tape the area off." Jack waited while Ned responded. "Okay, and hey, thanks for the heads-up. I'll be there as soon as I can."

Jack hung up, eyeing a bewildered Roni, who asked him, "Who's Ned?"

"Security guard over at Seabrook Marina, where Smitty's boat is."

Her gaze narrowed. "What's going on, Jack?"

"Several boat owners who tie up close by reported a foul smell coming from Smitherson's boat."

"Pshaw, Jack, it's a marina, gonna be lots of gross smells." She smirked.

"Yeah, true, but Ned went to investigate, and it's not fish, Roni. He found a body."

She swallowed and knew before she asked who Ned, the marina guard, had found. "This fella Ned, he look for any ID?"

Jack's head bobbed. "Yeah, Ned found a police badge on the floor near the body. It's Cory Carver. Ned said looks like he ate his gun."

58

BRODY BROOKS WAS IN the wind. No sightings of the man. His cell phone was off—no way to trace him. They'd need to stake out his usual haunts. Officers sat on his duplex, but there were no signs of him coming or going.

Moshe Rybak and Cooper Norris traced his financials, locating his bank—but nowadays, who needed a brick-and-mortar building? All you needed was an internet connection; Wi-Fi was free in every coffeehouse and hotel.

If Brooks was holed up in a hotel, it'd be easy to borrow their computers to transfer funds. Every mass-transit location displayed Brooks' photo in case he fled.

The Internal Affairs Division was overloaded with investigations into all officers listed in *The Book*. Listings went out under the categories of Dead, Almost Dead (men who lived in nursing homes or had no family), Inactive Retired, Active Retired, and Current Active Duty.

An inquiry got underway into the whereabouts of each officer implicated in the register of transgressions—men who'd be prosecuted and stripped of their pensions.

Aside from the prevailing chaos, the deaths of two more police officers so soon after Dellucci and Smitherson ignited a firestorm of media attention. Headlines were tearing the department apart, and confidence in the once-prestigious HPD plummeted to an all-time low.

WYGANT AND CARVER'S BODIES were at the morgue. The crime scene for Carver's suspected suicide had been thoroughly worked. CSU found a bloody piece of yellow legal paper with a brief note that said, "I'm sorry—never meant to hurt anyone." It was supposedly signed by Carver and, after being photographed and bagged, was sent to LuAnn Collier for handwriting analysis.

It was impossible to process Lieutenant Wygant's crime scene. They'd dumped his body into the waters off Dike Road, hoping the current would carry it through the Galveston Inlet to the Gulf of America. No one had considered a storm moving the body in a different direction.

Jack walked into the squad room—fresh coffee in hand, bloodshot eyes. Between lack of sleep and hours of combing through records, he was close to burnout as he awaited a call from the morgue. His body thudded into his chair, propping a foot on the corner of the desk, then leaning back with his head closed.

The squeak of the door sounded. He ignored it, keeping his eyes closed, figuring it didn't matter if anyone thought he was slacking off—they could kiss his behind.

Jace rapped his knuckles on West's desk. "We napping, Jack?"

"Are you speaking in the royal verbiage of we, Severson?"

"Uh, I is not napping," Jace mocked, "I is doing important things, like bringing us breakfast burritos."

Jack opened one eye just enough to see the bag of food Jace swung back and forth, then sat up, opened both eyes, and stuck out a hand. "Nourishment. Perfect."

They sat eating the still-warm burritos filled with eggs, potatoes, cheese, and sausage, sipping department coffee and enjoying the solitude—when Jack's phone rang.

"West," he said, chewing and swallowing his last bite. "Yeah? Anything else?" He listened. "Gonna be interested in who's hair it is then. Sure. Oh? Nope, not me, tell Bennie 'to each his own.' 'Bye."

He disconnected, drained his lukewarm coffee, wiped his lips, and wadded up the napkin, then looked at Jace, who continued to eat without worry.

"That was Mack. She found hairs on Carver's shirt collar—his mixed with some others—and she's running DNA. Also found debris under one of his fingernails; she's testing that too."

"That it?" Jace wadded up his empty wrapper and unwrapped a second burrito.

"Nope. The damage to Carver's teeth leads her to believe someone else forced the gun into his mouth. They dug a bit of debris from under his thumbnail—might be skin—but it's being sent for analysis. Mack also found faint marks on his wrists. The restraints were outside his long sleeves, positioned over the cuffs, but tight enough to leave a mark."

"Smitty didn't off himself, and neither did Carver. Now we've got four murdered cops. Shitty business for the HPD. Hey, what'dya mean by telling her to tell Bennie 'to each his own'?"

"Long damn nights and no time to sleep—she said Bennie took a catnap in a cadaver shell after he turned the refrigeration off."

That had them both doing a short spinal shiver and a laugh.

Detectives trickled in over the next hour and a half, and the buzz began: phones ringing, men working new cases, resuming cases they'd gotten new leads on, or possibly reinterviewing witnesses or persons of interest. Veronica Justice's and Davis Yao's plates were full, working with Internal Affairs.

Jack and Dawson worked on finalizing the paperwork for Cole West's case. Their job was to connect the dots that Skip gave them, match stories, and recall anyone alive from that time.

"We have Sandra Burns' signed statement. On top of that, some others told us what they recalled from that night." Dawson hit print and stood.

Jack gritted his teeth. "That damned gun is under lock and key, and I hope it gets melted down like it should have in 1979."

Xi Chang wheeled his chair closer. "What rankles me is Carver didn't pay for his crime, even if it was an accident. I hope they find the guys covering it up—the ones still kicking—just as culpable."

Jack scribbled with a pen to get the ink flowing again, eyes on the blue ink making circles. "Not sure who was active in the cover-up. I suspect Ray Moretti and Yardley were involved, though."

Dawson came back to his desk with his printout. "Heard IA up in Chicago got called, and they're bringing Moretti in for questioning."

"Their IA gonna interview him?" Jace joined the conversation.

"Nah, Roni said since this is more convoluted, Elijah Vance is flying up."

The four sat silent, then Jack let out a hefty exhale. "I called my parents last night, didn't want them getting the wrong scoop."

Xi Chang stood, placing a hand on Jack's shoulder. "Sorry—that had to be tough."

"Not as bad as I'd thought. Relieved to find out the truth, but they still don't have all the details yet. I'm thankful the department's keeping some things close to the vest and out of the media's hands."

A look of disgust leaped to Jace Severson's face. "Yeah, like the info on Tony Croce. Man, I cannot wait for the asshole to get what's coming to him."

"I hope we're all here when Internal Affairs drags that scumbag outta his office, and man, I hope they do a media perp walk," Dawson said.

A gloomy expression filled Jack's eyes. "This scandal casts the Houston Police Department in a negative light, portraying us as crooked monsters. Gonna be a lengthy process to rebuild trust with the community."

Xi sat back down, moving his chair toward his desk. "Then I suggest we work our asses off and raise our closure rate—new or unsolved cases."

Even though they all agreed, doing it might be harder than saying it.

AFTER FOUR, THE SQUAD room was less busy—men out in the field or headed home after a ten-hour shift. He and Dawson worked on reorganizing murder binders for cases listed in Smitty's official journal, and Jack's head and neck ached. His phone rang.

"West. Oh hiya, Dunwell, any news on Brooks?" Jack jumped right in, and Dawson stopped to watch his reactions. "Yeah, sure, and thanks, Alex. Yeah, I will."

Up on his feet, Dawson said, "Hey, how about taking a break? Go get a bite to eat?"

Jack stretched his legs, reaching up to massage his achy neck. "Brooks is still in the wind. Shit, the man can't just vanish."

Without compassion, Dawson intoned, "Maybe the fat bastard is lying in a pool of his own blood."

Jack West's eyes widened. "Jesus, pard, I hope not—be another case to work, and don'tcha think we've got enough? Besides, I need my last fifteen minutes with that fat man."

He closed his eyes, hand still at his neck.

"Sorry, Jack, don't want another murder. You're right. Even though Brooks is a turd, he needs to live long enough to be caged. I hope they find him soon." His fingers tapped the top of the half-partition to get Jack's attention. "Food. Wanna go get a bite or not?"

"I'm tired, Luck. Think I'm gonna head out. I'll grab some chicken or a burger on the way home so I can drop into bed. Be back at seven tomorrow. That work?" He moved his chair back, eyes closed, feeling fifty years older.

"Sounds like a plan. Uh, Jack?"

Eyes reopened, he glanced up. "Yeah, Luck?"

"Everyone signs up for something; I'm glad I got signed up with you, man."

"Thanks, but I'm not hugging you."

Detective Dawson Luck rolled his eyes. "Even in my sincerity, you mock."

Jack rose, outstretched his arms, and said, "Fine, bring it in then."

A derisive chuckle blew out of Dawson Luck's big schnozzle, and he passed on the hug.

ONE STOP AND HE had a burger, fries, and a soft drink. He munched on the fries, then unwrapped the burger as he drove. They did not prosecute deceased people, as the legal proceedings died with them.

Carver, Wygant, Dellucci, and Smitty—guess they were unlucky/lucky sons of bitches. What irked him most was they all got to live a life. Not Cole, though.

Jack's body was tired, but his head was full of things, causing his mind to go into exhausted overdrive. In his younger years, before Cole's shooting, he never considered being a cop—but that night, things changed. His need to find justice for those who could not find it for themselves grew as he did. Righting any wrong became an internal mantra he believed in.

That night, crushed by Cole's sudden, unwarranted death, Jack had thought he'd seen real compassion in Ray Moretti's eyes. Moretti, the cop, concerned and caring, told him and his parents they would do all they could to find out who shot their son, and do their best to seek justice.

Was that all a lie now?

The burger was tasty, yet Jack's appetite was lacking, so he rewrapped it and shoved the half-eaten sandwich into the bag on top of the half-container of fries.

Disposable cup in hand, he slurped through a straw, even the cola tasting flat.

He straightened, looked left, and exited toward home, head nodding. Plan: get his fifteen minutes with Brooks once apprehended, watch IA usher Tony

Croce out and file whatever charges they could muster—another satisfaction. Last—leave Texas for a few weeks.

No matter how much he hated snakes, crocs, gators, or water activities involving squirming, slithering creatures, he would take off for Florida.

59

THE SUN WAS JUST setting as Jack pulled into his driveway, cut the engine, shoved his gun in his waistband, picked up his phone and keys, and grabbed the sack of half-eaten food. He needed to move stuff in his garage so he could park inside—but that could wait a few days. He hit the fob, locking his truck, and headed to the front door, his head down.

Only one other time did someone get the drop on him—it had been Owen McCready, aka Caden Ward. So, when a person shoved up behind him, poking him in the ribs with the muzzle of a gun, it took him by surprise.

"I'm sure you know I got nothing to lose by shooting you, West." Brooks' hot breath was on the back of Jack's already achy neck. With his free hand, Brody reached around Jack and pulled the gun from his waistband, shoving it into the front of his own pants.

Before he could stop himself, Jack smart-mouthed back, "God, Brooks, it's only part of an eaten burger and some fries, but sure, if that's what you want, hey, they're yours." Jack dangled the bag in the air. "Take it and get the fuck off my property."

"I am not in the mood, West. Unlock the door and get inside. Now!"

Jack stiffened. "And you think I'm in the mood, you fat prick?" His key turned the tumblers and the door opened.

Jamming the gun into Jack's ribs, Brooks used his other arm to push Jack inside with force, causing him to stumble over the threshold. He broke his fall by grabbing the small entryway wall. Brooks used the heel of his right foot to shut the door. "Grab a seat, and let's play nice."

Bag of food in hand, Jack plopped down and smarted off again. "Paper plates in the cabinet left of the fridge. Grab us a beer, and we'll finish this burger and fries."

Brody grabbed the bag and flung it into the kitchen. "You don't know when to quit, do you?"

Jack's expression narrowed and darkened, and his neck hairs bristled. "According to my investigation, your happy ass should be rotting in a jail cell."

Brooks exhaled, gun still aimed at Jack's face. He waved it over at the dining room. "Get up, grab me a chair. And I'm warning you, don't be no fucking hero or you'll be a dead one."

Brody stepped back, and Jack went to get a straight-backed chair. He saw the beads of perspiration on Brody's forehead, and the pronounced blush of his cheeks. Jack figured it was Brooks' high blood pressure acting up. The man's weight and health might be Jack's saving grace.

Jack leaned back in the recliner—Brooks facing him in the wooden chair. No one spoke for a minute. Jack had a lot he wanted to say, but this wasn't a party he'd started, so he let Brooks lead.

"Goddamn Frank Windom—the goody-goody asshole. We all figured the man was gonna cross us one day. Stick his flat foot over the blue line."

Here it came. Just like Ernie said. All Brooks' hatred toward him was because of Frank, which made no sense. Jack shifted his weight and crossed one leg over the other, eyes boring into Brooks.

"Frank said zip about you. Sure, he hated your guts, but he never said a fucking word about any shady dealings you might've had your pudgy paws in."

An eye arched up in disbelief. "Liar. I knew Frank. He was a boat-rocker and was gathering evidence against the fellas in my clique. The son of a bitch was jealous."

A laugh popped out of Jack. "Jealous? Frank? Shit, Brooks, Frank was a run-down homicide cop, the sort that got built back in the thirties: a skinny-tie, fedora-wearing, rumpled, noir type. All he cared about was the job—his job, not you guys'. He couldn't care less about you. All he ever told me was to mind my business unless somebody got killed. Murder was my focus."

"Goody-goody Frank didn't care. Shit, then why was he always asking questions and skulking around?"

"Guess you need to have a séance and ask him, 'cause hell if I know."

"It's too late—not for that, but for me."

"Your hatred of me, all it did was fan the fires. You should've let it go. All this wouldn't be happening. You let your pride take this to a place of no return."

"Nope, I could never drop my guard. You're a carbon copy of Frank, a hotshot goody two-shoes. No one thinks you can do any wrong. You got away with socking me in the mouth—who else would've gotten away with that besides you?" A snarl lifted Brody's top lip.

"You know Yardley got out, don't ya?"

"Well, terrific for him. I don't give a rat's ass."

"Whatcha gonna do, Brooks, shoot me and go on the lam? How far do you think you'll get? They plastered your face at every bus station, airport, and cab company. Hell, man, we even informed Uber and Lyft."

"You gave Skip a deal, I heard. I want one too."

"Turn yourself in. Maybe the DA will work with you if you can give them something compelling enough."

His eyes bored into Jack, and the skin around his mouth tightened. "I can give them the Assistant Chief."

Jack shook his head. "They already got stuff on Tony Croce, so no deal."

Brooks took out Jack's gun, emptied the chamber, and released the clip. He pocketed the ammo and handed the unloaded pistol to Jack, who raised a brow. Then he stood, shoving his gun into the front of his pants. "I'll turn myself in and, when I do, I'll get you the evidence you need to solve another murder. But I wanna make a deal."

"Who's murder?"

"Robbery Captain Lawrence Dunne."

Jack was speechless. His brows knitted.

"He got shot during a messed-up bank heist takedown." Jack was well-versed in the story of Dunne's death—two years before Brooks' arrival as Homicide Captain—and Brooks' subsequent advancement to Captain of Robbery. No one would have looked at Brooks if Yao hadn't gotten promoted.

"That's what everyone thinks, but I know what happened. We got a deal or not?"

Jack stood. Brooks hopped up, gun still pointed.

"Keep your cool, Brooks. Tell me, why should I believe you?"

"Tony Croce's real name is Antonio Crocetti. His mother was my older sister—Cora Brooks Michaels. Easy enough to find out the real birth mother when the adoption wasn't closed or legal. My nephew Tony lived in the same neighborhood, and my older sister let it slip one night after too much wine. Heck, we can even do some DNA testing to prove it, if that's what it takes."

Jack let out a sigh. "Why would he murder Dunne?"

"Tony got arrested for aggravated assault when he was sixteen, under the name Antonio Crocetti."

"No way he could've become a cop then."

Brooks laughed harshly. "Jack, when you got friends in high places, you can get away with shit. Haven't you learned that yet? One of his close buddies was Judge Troy Wolff. Wolff made sure his records got buried in the tombs. I have the evidence. Matter of fact, I've been moving the damned evidence around to keep it hidden for years. Tony's been hunting for it. That's how he found the gun. He gave it to me to have it put in the group of firearms to be melted down, only I kept it. That was a huge mistake on my part." He shrugged. "Can't change it now, though."

This was an important question, and Jack watched Brooks' face. "Why'd he kill Dunne?"

"I wanted to move up, so I blackmailed him."

A new and intense dislike for Brooks blossomed within Jack. "You want me to get you a deal with the DA after your admission to blackmailing, which led to murder? Are you a lunatic? They won't go for it."

He wished he could unsay what he'd just said. Jack wanted to lull Brooks into a false sense of security without giving him anything to consider. Shit, he might've messed up.

"Murder outweighs blackmail, West, and I never said for him to murder the guy, just told Tony he'd better work it out or his secrets would be front-page news, pictures and all."

Pictures. That word rolled in Jack's brain. He had forgotten about the baggie of Polaroids he'd shoved into his bottom desk drawer. Brasher's report, then Skip assaulting her—so much crazy stuff went down. He just never got around to those photos.

"Fine. You let me take you in, then we can get our ducks in a row. We can move it straight up the ladder to the COD, have him facilitate everything with the DA's Office and—"

Brooks cut him off by waving the gun at him.

"No. We play it my way or no way. Here."

He handed Jack a prepaid cell from his back pocket. "West, don't be no fucking Boy Scout, just do as I tell you. My number is on the package. Once you get the all-clear and the DA gives me a deal, then you text me. I'll tell you where to fax the deal so I can look it over. If I agree, then I'll turn myself in to you, and I swear to God, if you don't do it my way, Tony Croce will continue up the ladder until he's reached his goal of one day being the stinking mayor of Houston, and any evidence I got gets burned with me on my way to hell."

Jack's jaw tightened as he drew in a breath, then exhaled.

"Fine, Brooks, I'll play by your rules, but if you don't get what you want, I can make one promise to you."

Brooks' small pig eyes glared. "What's that, West?"

"That I will hunt you down and you will pay for all the sins of anyone who will never pay for theirs, including Carver for killing my brother. Oh, and by the way, your shirt..." Jack paused, giving Brooks the disgusted once-over someone gives a cockroach.

Brooks did a quick glance down at his shirt. "What about it?"

"A, what, triple X, chambray, button-down, light-blue, breathable shirt."

"What the fuck is your point?"

"Although light-blue fabric was fashionable in the past, the way it looks on you today evokes a memory of it, and you, once being a deeper, darker blue."

"That's stupid as shit. These shirts were always a faded blue color." Brooks' face wrinkled in confusion.

With a tight jaw, Jack stated, "That dark-blue uniformed officer dedicated to good? That man wasn't you. Both that shirt and you are pathetic, faded blue, and washed-up."

Brooks backed out the door, the gun still on Jack as Jack kept a distance of ten feet, hands in his pockets. Looking beyond the fat man, he searched for Brooks' vehicle.

Jack knew most of his neighbors' cars, but the worn-down, maroon Ford Taurus didn't belong to any of his neighbors.

Crud, he couldn't see the plates; and if Brooks was smart, he'd have removed them. Jack studied the car for telltale marks, dings, and blemishes he could use to describe the vehicle. One tire a little flat, a yellow sticker at the side of the rear bumper, multiple dings on the passenger door—it was all better than nothing.

On the porch, Brooks halted, still facing the doorway, and switched the gun to his left hand.

"Come here, West, and don't make me hafta grab you by the shirt and shake you around."

Jack walked forward and stood facing Brody. The distance between them was the barrel of Brooks' revolver.

Jack's smartass retort popped out before he could stop himself. "If you wanna hug and kiss, I hope like hell you used mouthwash."

In a surprise move, Brody Brooks doubled up his fist, brought it up, and clocked Jack in the jaw, causing his head to snap back and blood to spurt from his busted lip.

"Consider us settled, West."

Pissed off he'd let Brody get his punch in, he rubbed his jaw, then spat blood on Brody's shoes.

"Nah, Brooks, hell, ain't nothing settled. I'm gonna crush your ass."

Jack closed the door with force, ensuring it locked, then took out his phone and watched through the blinds as Brody drove away in the Taurus, confirming his suspicion that the car had no license plates.

First, he called the Deer Park PD, gave them information on the car and Brooks—everyone knew about the APB. He then dialed another number. The person on the other end answered, "Dunwell."

"Alex, Jack. Just had a visit from Brooks."

"What the hell, he get the drop on you? Are you—"

Jack butted in, "Look, I've already called the Deer Park PD. I'm gonna head back to HQ."

Dunwell concluded his first question: "Are you okay?"

Jack touched his jaw, grimacing, then shook his head.

"The fat bastard aimed a gun at me, then he punched me in the kisser. Been dying to do that for four years. My pride's wounded, but after what I've learned tonight, that tap ain't nothing compared to what Brooks is gonna get."

"You got one on him, though."

"I do? What's that?"

"No one saw him punch you, everyone saw you clock him. He's got no proof of payback."

An involuntary laugh sputtered out of Jack as Dunwell ended the call with, "See you at the station, West."

60

In his truck, Jack kept his eyes peeled for a maroon Taurus; not knowing Brooks' whereabouts, he had no idea what travel route he might have taken.

He wasted no time getting to the station, contacting Roni on his cell as he drove.

"He threatened you with a gun—for Christ's sake, the man is insane." Roni's voice was distressed. "Brooks could've shot you, Jack. I mean the guy is a feral cat right now, unpredictable."

"He got his return punch in–thinks he's settled the score between us. Roni, look, with all the crap happening, I forgot to check into something important."

"What are you talking about?"

"That Ziploc baggie of old Polaroids, the ones found on Smitty's boat. I dropped them into a bottom drawer when 7-11 called to go to ballistics. Then, with Brasher's attack and Skip and Carver gone missing, I forgot about 'em."

"Jack, come on," she said. "They're most likely harmless—pictures of his family, friends, and maybe a few goofy events."

He ignored her, knowing his failure; he'd face consequences later if he missed vital information.

"I'm gonna call Dawson. Will you contact 7-11, get them to the station?"

"On it, see you there." She disconnected, then reached out to Xi, keeping it short and simple, then called Jace.

Jack parked, his eyes searching the parking structure for another ambush. He wouldn't put it past Brooks to go after him on his home turf—his turf. Other officers gave him wary glances as he passed, murmuring under their breath. Brody

Brooks was now an interloper, no longer part of the elite team of cops who made up the Houston Police Force.

As an afterthought, Jack pulled his weapon, chambered a round, and left the gun unsnapped as he reholstered. The irony was, he now harbored suspicion toward the men he once trusted.

Inside the building, he breathed, relieved, and jogged up to six, almost colliding with Alex at the breakroom door.

"Sorry, man."

"Coffee?" Alex held up a fresh cup. "No sleep for the past twenty hours. I made it strong."

"Yeah, meet me at my desk." Jack rushed in, grabbed an old, cracked HPD mug, and poured a cup, hotfooting it back to his desk.

"I called the night commander at Deer Park; a patrol unit spotted Brooks near the Sam Houston Tollway. They called it in and radioed a BOLO to the Pasadena PD—if they spot him, they'll let us know, but there's no telling where he headed." Alex, keyed up and frustrated, eyeballed Jack's jaw. "Busted lip, but no bruising yet, I see. You want ice?"

Jack's forefinger and thumb moved his lower jawbone back and forth. "Nah, he clipped me enough to bust a lip, but not any real damage. I'll live. Just pissed off I didn't see it coming—I should have." He sat, bent, and, reaching into the bottom drawer to pull out the baggie of photos, grimaced—more lies were forthcoming.

Alex sat his empty cup on the desk, peering over. "What's that?"

With a silent, internal inhale and a short prayer of Please forgive the lies, Jack said, "After Suzy's initial sweep, I went back to Smitty's boat, found these and brought them back, and was about to dig into the bag, but I got the call from Brasher about the ballistics report and met 7-11 over there. Then Skip's assault on Olivia. He went missing, Carver went missing—you know all the shit that's happened. I forgot about 'em until Brooks made some remark about having certain pictures."

A wide-eyed Alex listened as Jack said all that with one breath, then he sat back, giving him a significant look, and said, "That so?"

"Hey, I'm not Super Cop, and not above making a mistake. Sue me, have Roni give me a rip, do whatever you need to do." He stopped to snag two pairs of crime-scene gloves and popped on a set, handing the others to Alex. "You wanna look or debate my faults?" His brow furrowed in question.

"Let's see what we have—oh, and Jack?"

Jack moved items off his desk to make room, then opened the zipper on the Ziploc. "Yeah?"

"Your findings better be in your report—documented and dated."

"They will be. You have my word," Jack said as he spread the photos over his desktop.

The door opened and Roni stepped in. "Damned wreck off the East Freeway. Betting Dawson got caught up in it too. 7-11 here yet?"

The door swung open and Jace walked in. "Xi's parking, saw Dawson pulling in. The team is amassing."

Jack scooped up the photos, and Alex frowned. "Hey, we're looking at those."

"Alex, I need a word in private with you and Roni. Jace, take the pictures. Go through them with Xi and Luck. See what you can find."

"Sure, Jack," Jace said, putting on a pair of gloves without questions.

***

In the privacy of Roni's office, Jack gave them the rundown of the entire conversation with Brooks.

Alex pulled his cell out and made a call while they watched. "Ernie, Alex. You better get up here, gonna be a lot of shit hitting the fan." Alex's head bobbed as he listened. "Yep, just like we suspected, Dunne's accidental death was no accident. In Roni's office, so is Jack. Uh-huh, we got BOLOs out. They've spotted him a few times. Croce's address—yeah, why?"

Jack's posture became rigid and, once Alex hung up, he said without a beat, "You think Brooks will head to Croce's?"

With a slight lift of his shoulders, Alex rejoined, "Gotta cover all our bases." Alex phoned in a request to the night commander to send a unit over to bring Tony Croce into the station for his safety. "No, I can't tell you why I want him brought in." Dunwell's agitation rose as he listened to the night commander's whining, then cut him off. "If he refuses, cuff the son of a bitch and bring him however you hafta. What?" Alex frowned into the phone. "No, you won't get a rip. I've got you covered." He disconnected, looking up. "Why do people always question straightforward orders?"

It felt like a rhetorical question, so neither Jack nor Roni answered.

***

Ernie Nicholson walked in, phone stuck to his ear, notepad in hand, jotting. "Will do. Yep." He clicked off. "Fellas. Uh, Roni—sorry, not a fella."

"Whatever." She smirked.

"That was Vance. I gave him the rundown and he wants us to let Croce think he is a target, not a suspect—not let him know Brooks spilled his guts to Jack." He looked at Dunwell. "Any other sightings on Brooks?"

"No, we lost him. He's in the wind again, but since Jack has a burner number, we can reach him. You call the DA's Office?"

"Jonell Simone is en route."

Alex looked at Jack. "You know her pretty well, don'tcha, Jack? Worked several high-profile cases, that right?"

"Yeah, Wolff's case—so Croce has never liked me too much. Why?"

Ernie's shoulders shook with pent up laughter. "Jack, not a popular man, are you? Brooks hating you day one, then Croce hating you for sending his buddy, the esteemed Judge Wolff, to the slammer. Skip Webb, and I'm sure Carver, too. These guys can't like you and keep such dark secrets from a man they have a cold one with."

The deep, dark look Jack shot him had Ernie flinching. He raised his hand. "Just saying, Jack, not judging you. In a word, I admire you; I did even when I was pretending to be Earl Nichols and trying to hate your guts, or act like it. Did you ever once wonder why I never worked a case with you?"

That thought had never crossed Jack's mind until now, and he frowned, but let the ball stay in Ernie's court while Alex and Roni watched on.

"I admire your straightforwardness and dedication, but never planned to be in the crosshairs with you. Had a job to do. I didn't want to get to know you as a partner because you are a decent man. You don't know me, West, and I had to make sure you disliked me and thought I was ignorant."

A smile touched Jack's lips. "You were a success. I did hate you and thought you were ignorant. Not much of that has changed, knowing what department you're associated with." Jack glanced over at Alex. "You're falling into that category too, Dunwell. But that aside, let's get these cases tied up with no slipups."

"I agree and hope you can give IA a chance—we aren't here to make cops' lives miserable. Jack, you're a superb cop, and when this is over and done and the dust settles, I wanted to talk to you about moving—"

Captain Veronica Justice broke into Ernie's upcoming proposal when she stood, hands flat on her desk, eyeballing IA officer Ernest Nicholson, and said, "Stop trying to poach my guys, Ernie, now is not the time." She cut her eyes to Jack and winked. "Besides, Jack's a natural-born homicide detective; he'll never leave. Let's go see if our renowned DA has arrived."

***

Jonell's mouth opened and closed as she listened, her pen scratching across her notepad. Once most of the story was out, her gaze landed on Jack. His bloodshot eyes, five o'clock shadow, and, she noted, hair that needed a cut. The room hushed. They locked eyes, and he made the "What?" gesture with his hands.

"Only you, Jack West. Why do complicated issues land on your head?"

His face and shoulders shrugged. "What can I say? My cop life has dealt me a strange hand. Sorta a mixed bag. So what say you, Jonell, what kinda deal are we willing to offer?"

"What say me? I'll tell you what I say. Like the players looking for the big money on Deal or No Deal, I say, 'No deal.' All the—excuse me—fucking cases we'll need to sift through and possibly overturn because of this shit—excuse me again—will make my life and my office's life a living nightmare, and we're gonna be looking like a bunch of monkeys fucking a football. The city is gonna crucify us." Her eyes went to Ernie and Alex. "Your department, too. The city will ask why Internal Affairs wasn't on the ball. This is gonna be a huge shitstorm."

Phones buzzed across the room, staff whispered frantically, and stacks of files teetered on desks. Jonell slammed her pen down, her chair scraping against the floor, and the room felt like it was on the brink of chaos.

Jack felt for her, knowing the workload this caused, and the crappy karma the boys in blue and city officials would face. "Jonell."

She looked up, letting air flow out her nose. "What?"

"Six years ago, we survived the Judge Wolff debacle, and after we got the media involved, using them to put a positive spin of cleaning up the court system, and HPD made a top-notch showing with the community, we got past that ordeal. We can't sweep this under the rug—too much has happened with four dead cops, and at least four more murders unsolved. How about we get what needs to be done—done, and, afterward, work with both the Chronicle and Sun, start a campaign called Cleanup Our System? Offer transparency in all departments; gain Houstonians trust again."

Four sets of eyes were on Jack, mouths were agape, and no one dared speak.

Alex raised his brows. "Jesus, Jack, you running for office?"

Jonell's eyes narrowed. "My lord, Jack, all I said was, 'No deal.' Our office has been through much more. We survived. We don't needta start no flipping campaign. We need to find Brody Brooks, along with his abominable uncle, Tony Croce."

There was a light knock on the door. Xi Chang poked his head in. "Hey, uh, Jack, wanted to tell you we went through every picture from that baggie."

Jonell and Ernie said in unison, "What pictures in what baggie?"

Jack's eyes darted to Roni before he gave them the same explanation he'd given to Alex. Not once did his words falter, nor sound unconvincing. Then he looked back at Chang. "Anything we can use?"

Chang's lips curved downward. "Nah. Nothing implicating them. It does connect certain people, though. There are pictures of different guys drinking on Smitty's boat, on the water fishing, at the station, at bars, and at home gatherings. Two homes stand out, though."

Alex was the first to ask, "Oh yeah, who's?"

All eyes were on Chang when he replied. "Carmine Berutti and Assistant Chief Croce."

Mouths dropped, eyes widened, and hands instinctively went to chests or mouths. The air thickened with disbelief, and no one dared speak for a long, tense beat.

61

EVERY SAYING YOU COULD conjure got said. The shit hit the fan; all hell broke loose; it went sideways and the motherfucking wheels fell off. The media had a day with descriptive words—chaos, destruction, violence, accusatory—and the witch hunt began, with threats to burn officials at the stake.

Brooks, apprehended at a mom-and-pop shop with Wi-Fi after Jack texted him a bogus deal drafted by the cunning Jonell Simone, nearly had to be shot with a tranquilizer to calm down. No one ever noted the fight in him before; however, when threatened, Brody Brooks came out swinging—missing most of the time and out of breath once they had him pinned down. It surprised Jack the old guy fought back so hard.

Entertainment or not, when Croce faced his nephew, Brooks, it reminded Jack of the old game Rock 'Em Sock 'Em Robots—both men screaming and attempting to punch the other. Best of all was the perp walk through the station.

The COP allowed the media to attend to see the shamed and arrested, now ex-Assistant Chief, who the media informed the public was born with the birth name Antonio Crocetti, son of Judge Michaels and Cora Brooks Michaels. That singular revelation began the digging into the retired, rest-home-living judge and the deceased Cora Brooks.

Amidst the bedlam, Jack had overheard a junior reporter make the comment that the story about Judge Michaels, his wife, and their son Tony Croce would make a fantastic made-for-TV movie.

He closed his eyes, hoping it would never happen—sensationalizing the dirt bag, making him famous for the wrong reasons.

What Houston did not need was constant reminders of how their leaders, who were there to protect the people and the city, used their power and hid behind their badges for monetary gains and to climb the ladder of so-called success.

Croce had aspired of being higher up the political food chain: mayor, governor, and more. He would use ill-gotten gains to reach the top rung of the ladder and would step on anyone who got in his way. Stepped on or have removed—that was where his relationship with Carmine Berutti was useful.

Back in the days when he was known as Antonio Crocetti—one of the goom-bahs in the old neighborhood—he'd started off as a runner, gained favor with certain members of the Berutti family, and earned their protection.

As they probed into the life of Antonio Crocetti/Tony Croce, the skeletons began flying out of the closet, so to speak. Even the Honorable Judge Michaels had bones rattling about that were seeing the light of day as the media dug deep to unearth information.

The arrest of a higher official such as the Assistant Chief made enormous waves in the system.

Now the men above that rank were being probed, and none too happy about this turn of events. Under the microscope, the moment for openness and honesty was upon them. Decent moral men had nothing to fear.

There were so many satisfying moments in the department; one of Jack's favorites had been when Brooks learned Earl Nichols was undercover IA officer Ernest Nicholson.

This news nearly caused Brooks to rupture an aneurysm.

He bucked in the chair, rattling his cuffs, acting the part of a caged wild man, cursing and screaming so hard that spittle flew from his lips. Ernie left the room, shocked and shaken at the outburst.

"Nicholson," Vance said, "You want me to issue you a protective detail until this is over?"

"No, sir."

"Well, since we aren't sure of who Brooks or Croce are pals with in the jail system, you'd better be watching your back." The IA Director glanced around the room. "I suggest all of us watch our sixes."

RAY MORETTI'S STATEMENT WAS still not public knowledge. Jack read it while alone at his desk.

Officer Moretti's orders had been to give a death notification blaming it on a random drive by, and to say an investigation would be forthcoming.

Layton Conch, the city's medical examiner, had the body and would call them when it was ready to release to the funeral home.

Back then, Jack hadn't known who Layton Conch was, but he knew the man's rep now. He'd been the medical examiner on a cold case involving a woman who had faked her own death and worked with cops whose names appeared in Smitty's journal.

Conch concealed the fact that the firearm used in Cole's murder had been on a list of supposedly destroyed weapons.

Paid to cover it up, Conch fudged a few details.

Moretti suspected impropriety, but his subordinate position limited his influence. Besides that, Moretti admitted to being paid for keeping his mouth shut.

The Police Department was in a state of disarray for several weeks.

Rush—put a rush on this, a rush on that, move it to the front of the line. The labs, the morgue, and the DA's Office got a pounding.

Internal Affairs hired outside contractors to inventory and manage the off-site evidence storage facility. The personnel consisted of retired officers and detectives scattered throughout Harris and Brazoria Counties; men and women whom IA, and the District Attorney's Office, deeply vetted.

XI ANSWERED A RINGING phone, then looked up from a pile of papers he was sorting through. "Jack, Bennie—line three."

Jack grabbed up the handset. "Yeah, Ben?"

"The DNA results came back on the skin debris found under Corey Carver's thumbnail. They found a match. Jack, it's Gary Yardley."

"Gonna take some paperwork to get that bastard home," he said into the phone. "Yeah, thanks, Ben, later." He dropped the handset into the cradle.

Dawson laced his fingers, stretching his arms in the air. "Bennie have news?"

"Yardley did Carver, DNA confirms it. Betting he dumped the gun somewhere in the Pacific."

"Jack, want me to go back to China, visit my sister, and I can bring the son of a bitch back?" Xi said.

"You'd have to do that on your own—the extradition's not sanctioned."

Jace said, "So the bastard's gonna get away with it?"

Jack cracked his neck, then said, "We've got options. I looked into this and last night I called Jonell with some questions. What I learned was, if someone flees to a non-extradition country and we have evidence to prosecute without the defendant, we can still hold a trial."

"What the fuck does that do if he ain't here to get sentenced?"

"Well, Jace, then we got a conviction in absentia. The evidence, his photo, along with the proper paperwork, go to the DOJ to hand off to the State Department. Then they begin the extradition request via diplomatic channels. Lots of paperwork, red tape, and translating, but even if it takes a few years, worth it."

"I hope they sentence the man to the needle and at least someone gets the justice they deserve—not whacked by another piece of shit. The dirtbags cleaned house for us, ticks me the hell off." Jace rocked his chair back, scowling.

"One positive thing I can say: they saved the city dough with no trials," Xi said in an upbeat tone.

Jack's eyes wandered the squad room. Men worked, heads down, phones stuck to ears, fingers tapping keyboards, pens scratching notes, moving files on top of other files, searching for papers they needed.

He knew Captain Justice was in her office, also working herself to the bone. All of them quality detectives, men who served this city with its best interests at heart.

No more Brooks, Wygants, Webbs, or Golans in the office. He was certain of that.

Ernie and Alex—what a damned shock that had been. However, it put two more men in the "good guys" column.

Men and women who wore the white hats—yep, only in Texas.

Detectives wore casual clothing; sports coats and dress suits were sometimes necessary.

Patrol cops wore the blue uniforms these days. The clothing didn't change these officers' desire to get justice.

Men like Xi Chang, Cooper Norris, Moshe Rybak, Dawson Luck, Jace Severson, and, especially, Jack West would forever be a deep, dark blue, as blue as their blood, never fading.

Epilouge

NINE A.M. THE SUN was shining, and there was a light breeze. Parked, Jack cut the engine and sat, staring out the windshield at the grassy area inside the wrought-iron fencing that surrounded Magnolia Cemetery. It had been a while since his last visit.

After opening the door, he reached in to grab the bouquet of wildflowers, his hat, and sunglasses. With his hat and shades on, he locked the truck and took the steps to Cole's headstone—footsteps he could walk with his eyes closed.

His heart pounded with the news he was about to share with his big brother.

Despite the bizarre reasons for Cole's death, they would have the closure and peace they deserved.

He swallowed hard as he approached, his mouth a little dry. He stood in front of the variegated black-and-gray marble tombstone, took off his hat, and looked to his left, where the headstone said Russell Edward Washburn.

"Russell, I see your family's been here. Beautiful daylilies they got for you." He looked to his right. "Della, my sweet lady, they fixed your broken vase—so your people are still watching over you."

Jack's eyes moved to the middle stone: Cole Arron West. Flowers unwrapped, he placed them into the attached vase and arranged them to look pretty. Then he took a seat on the concrete bench and, as always, bowed his head for a quick prayer before looking back up.

"I did it, big brother."

He paused and began again.

"No, we did it. We closed your case."

Jack sat there for an hour, recounting everything pertinent to his dead brother, knowing somewhere above, Cole could hear him and be proud.

Once he'd finished the story about Brooks, Wygant, Carver, and the lot, he sat back and inhaled, closing his eyes.

He felt spent—but happy. He reopened his eyes, a grin spreading across his face. It was as if he could almost see Russell and Della on either side of Cole, who stood smiling at him.

They clapped Cole on the back, happy that he, too, would now rest in peace as they did.

Jack briefed Cole on Sophia, his last case, how he was coping with the death of Gretchen Benson—moving on with his life as best he could, one day at a time.

"Everyone thinks I need to advance and take the sergeant's exam, but, you know, big brother, paperwork and a desk—not my style. I enjoy being in the thick of it. I don't consider paperwork the same as using my brain to solve the puzzles a murder case brings to the table."

He listened to the serene silence.

The wind blew; a bird chirped in the distance; the smell of freshly mowed grass wafted in the light breeze.

Jack smiled a smile of contentment for the first time in years, sitting in the cemetery.

Cole was free now—free to move on and not wonder why he'd died. There was no reason they had shot him. No one hated him, no one was after him; he had done nothing to deserve this.

"Cole, they say the good die young. Brother, you were the best. Best son, brother, and friend. I still miss you, always will."

He glanced at his watch, standing to leave.

"Hey big brother, don't think I won't be back. We still need to do a shot of whisky or tequila together, and I wanna keep you updated on my life. Oh, and after I visit Mom and Dad, I'll update you on our retired and happy parents."

With a salute, he redonned his cowboy hat and shades and walked back to his truck with a lighter heart.

Inside the old Ram truck, he seat-belted in and started the engine, putting it in reverse.

Airline tickets sat atop the duffle in the passenger's seat.

Next stop: Florida to see Mom and Dad.

The End

Author's Note

Word-of-mouth is crucial for any author to succeed. If you enjoyed Gracie and AJ- The Messy Middle please leave a review online—anywhere you are able. Even if it's just a sentence or two; it would make all the difference and would be very much appreciated.

Thanks,

Deanna

Deannakingwriting.com

Acknowledgements

Thank you to my beta reader- Sharon Jaeger. Her input to me is invaluable.

About the Author

Faded Blue – A Jack West Novel is the fifth novel in Ms. King's Jack West Series.
She lives with her husband Travis; a wild Yorkie and chilled Poodle in Texas.